Praise for The Metaphor Maker

AN INTRIGUING ADVENTURE OF THE SPIRIT . . .

I picked up *The Metaphor Maker* on Friday afternoon and couldn't put it down until Saturday afternoon.

I was transported back to the Sixties, to a time of hope and adventure—I smelled the sea air of Southern California beaches, walked the streets of Laguna Beach, felt the excitement of the Berkeley anti-war movement, heard Beach Boys melodies, and experienced the idealism of the 1968 presidential election.

The Metaphor Maker is a spiritual adventure. It is "spiritual but not religious," easily accessible to seekers of all faiths or no faith at all. It's an adventure of self-discovery, of finding your identity in the quest for the soul. The journey is spiritual at heart, inviting us to let go of outworn images of the Holy, so that healthy and creative images of the Holy may emerge.

This is a perfect "book club" book. I've just finished reading it with my family and best friend. Even my 92-year-old mother-in-law found it enlightening and engaging. It provoked many interesting conversations in our household.

This book joins theology, relationships, self-discovery, and a descriptive walk through Southern California.

Bruce Epperly, Ph.D.
Progressive Theologian, Spiritual Guide, and author of
Holy Adventure: 41 Days of Audacious Living

Praise for *The Metaphor Maker*

A PRISM WHICH GIVES US A SPECTRUM OF HOPE . . .

Praise and puffery can be produced with ease by a reviewer. Admiration for the elegant literary style and most certainly praise for tackling a pivotal time in America are owed to Patricia Adams Farmer. But something else happened to me while reading *The Metaphor Maker*—a re-awakening of emotions I thought were deeply buried. Let me explain.

Madeline Prescott struggled during the '60s, a time while I was a physician in the Central Intelligence Agency stationed in Athens, Greece. The horrors faced by Madeline---the assassinations, an immoral war in Vietnam and the warping of democracy in our country—were doubly magnified for me simply because I did not have the support that Madeline had during this upheaval—no discussion groups or politically sympathetic friends.

The Metaphor Maker re-awakened in me the deep despair of those times. Had Patricia Adams Farmer's book been with me then, the climb out of the abyss would have been easier. Madeline's strength and persistence in seeking answers to what seemed unanswerable problems is more than an inspiration to those of us who can't seem to relax and let the world go by. Her book is the perfect metaphor: a prism which gives us a spectrum of hope.

Patrick Clement, MD
Physician in the Central Intelligence Agency, 1965-1970
Political Activist who proudly stood with Martin Luther King, Jr. in August, 1963, and attempted, with Norman Mailer and others, to levitate the Pentagon

The
Metaphor Maker

Also by Patricia Adams Farmer

(Non-Fiction)
Embracing a Beautiful God

The
Metaphor Maker

A Novel by

Patricia Adams Farmer

Martha & Bob,

Blessing & Peace,

R Farmer

Estrella de Mar Publications

For Ron

and

for all the empowering women in my life —
especially my sisters,
Lexy and Cheryl

The
Metaphor Maker

~ Part One ~

Driftwood

Chapter One

Madeline Prescott stretched out atop rumpled sheets, squishing the feather pillow just so to avoid a brassy slice of sun cutting through a gap in the curtains. She wore an oversized UC Berkeley tee, washed so many times it clung to her like rose petals. The touch of it against her skin—an extension of her own skin, really—comforted her, grounded her, caressed her like a lover, like a new layer of herself forged with passion and effort and necessity, away from Orange County. Away from this childhood bedroom with its gingham curtains and dust-ruffled bed. Away from her parents. And *them*.

Soon they would be coming.

Since hearing of her parents' plans to open their home to these people—and would she help with the coffee?—Madeline had sworn inwardly at this insult added to injury. The awkward New Year's Day soirée would consist primarily of Pastor Bob and the heaven-bent flock from the New Hope Baptist Church.

Church had always irked her. Mainly because of Pastor Bob. Combed over strands of oily hair languishing against a pink scalp did nothing for her spirituality, not to mention his Thou-Shalt-Not sermons highlighting the evils of rock-n-roll. And what about those agonizing altar calls for sinners to come forward and be saved? Week after week the same sinners came forward to be saved again and again, like free root beer refills at the A&W.

Under siege, that's how she felt. Like in high school. Once

she reached eleventh grade and refused to attend church in full-frontal defiance of Pastor Bob's shiny pink head (that glowed like a halo under the pulpit lights), she was added to The List—the Wednesday night prayer list—along with people who were in jail or mental hospitals. She imagined the supplications for her salvation must have accelerated in the fall of 1963. That's when she left God-fearing Orange County for the secular temptations of UC Berkeley and the devil's cunning web of drugs, sex, and rock-and-roll—a trinity of evils, one down from Communism itself. The flock's prayers must have gone into overdrive during her fame as an anti-war protester.

And now, here it was, 1968, and nothing much had changed. *Except everything.*

Madeline opened her eyes and, with the slightest turn of head, caught her wayward reflection in the beveled mirror attached to her childhood vanity, a painted white monstrosity laden with old bottles of *Chantilly* perfume and stale pink body lotion. Her expression was something between a scowl and a pout—the look of a spoiled child rather than a twenty-three-year-old grad student. She did not relish the sight. Never did she judge herself as beautiful, but now, with this disgruntled face, she wasn't even pretty. Her only saving grace at times like these—or just about any time, for that matter—was her hair. She had *hair*. Flamboyant hair. Head-turning hair. Hair that evoked envy and awe and smiles and ice-breaking conversations with strangers. *Is that your natural color? What beautiful curls you have! Hey, groovy hair. Dig that hair!* Now it lay about her pale face—oblivious to grief—coiled, curly, happy and shining with an unapologetic wildness, the whole red heat of it.

Fresh tears surged. *Oh, for God's sake! Get hold of yourself!* Perhaps she just needed the shock of it to linger awhile longer, so she could get used to the idea that her brother would not—would never—be coming home.

The news of Sean's death in Vietnam came on Christmas

Eve, around noon, in the god-awful sunshine. Normally she reveled in the sunshine of Southern California and longed for the cheerful warmth of it during perpetually cloudy, chilly days in Berkeley. But now this warm, golden Southland gift had turned on her, indifferent to her loss, glaring like a flashlight in the face. *Garish*, that was the word: *the garish sun*, a phrase from somewhere . . . .

She wiped her eyes with the back of her hand and remembered. Bobby Kennedy said it back in 1964 at the Democratic National Convention. She had, through watery nineteen-year-old eyes, watched the still mourning RFK on the downstairs dorm television as he accepted the unrelenting ovation on behalf of his own dead brother, John Fitzgerald Kennedy. It was something he quoted. *What was it?* Something from Shakespeare, but she could only remember the last two lines—

> *That all the world will be in love with night*
> *And pay no worship to the garish sun.*

Ben would remember the whole thing—of course he would—with that photo of the "Brothers Kennedy" sitting on his desk right next to Carl Jung. Who could resist talking about JFK, the assassination, the lost possibilities hovering over everything like a huge, invisible sigh? And the war. Of course, the war. After Sean had enlisted, Ben would always begin each counseling session with, "How's your brother? Heard from Sean?" They talked endlessly about Sean, the war, and her parents' disgust at her anti-war activities.

Ben Schwartz would want to know.

He could also help her with these constant replays in her head. Every time she closed her eyes she saw the Messengers of Death lodged behind her eyelids. She closed her eyes now, testing it, and there they were: The polished officers from Camp Pendleton wore crisp dress uniforms and well-buffed shoes. They stood gravely silhouetted in the morning light, white hats in hand. Very proper. They stood right there at the door of her childhood home, a door decorated with evergreen and plastic holly berries gushing Christmas cheer.

It all happened with their eyes; no words had to be spoken, no telegram handed over, even though they must have had one (didn't they always bring telegrams?). But the moment she opened the screen door and glanced from their shiny shoes to their eyes—sympathetic eyes that locked onto hers—there was nothing but a sensation of something within her falling, plunging headlong into an abyss, into a place without light or air or definition. Only a mantra of desperate denial: *No! No! No!*

"Maddy, who's at the door?" her mother had called cheerily from the kitchen.

Madeline stood dumbly, gasping for air. Kate Prescott left her oven, filled with perfectly cut-out Christmas cookies, to see what was wrong. Madeline wanted to yell, *No! Mother! No!* But all she could do was run to find her emergency inhaler.

When Madeline returned, lungs relieved, she saw her mother—a hand covering her mouth—backing away from the door as if that would somehow stop things from going forward. One officer stood mute, holding the screen door. The other one spoke in low, measured, respectful tones. Kate Prescott, with her lacquered blonde flip and flour-blotched face and apron bearing the face of Jolly Old Saint Nick, stared back with bright terror—even as their shadows in the doorway spread over her like a protective wing, shielding her from the sun's direct glare.

Finally the two marines stepped inside, the screen door closing behind them—first with a creak, then a thud. The taller one grasped Kate's shoulders in a compassionate gesture; she collapsed like a rag doll.

Madeline blinked hard to dislodge the memory, swung her legs over the side of the bed, and searched for her macramé purse. It sat on the floor like a miniature bean bag chair, bloated with a hodgepodge of necessities she had brought from the apartment in Berkeley. She rifled around until she found her pack of Pall Mall and Zippo lighter. She had planned to give up smoking for her New Year's resolution because it didn't exactly mix well with her asthma. But self-improvement schemes seemed rather self-indulgent in the wake of bigger issues like war and death and the surviving of them.

She lit up with relief, and a split-second feeling of optimism zapped through her like an electric current. She pulled back the gingham curtains and peeked out. Southern California was most beautiful in winter, she thought, so green and fertile—paradise, really—while the rest of the world turned brown and dull. She studied the orange tree in the center of the backyard, its iridescent leaves framing the fat, ripening fruit. Despite her rebellion at being raised in the ultra conservative center of the world—the very hub of the military-industrial complex—she had to admit that Orange County had its moments.

Her eyes moved to the wooden swing hanging from a branch of the live oak: its sad, warped seat silent and still, as if waiting for something. *Someone.* She could picture her hyper-active little brother careening through the air, Superman cape flapping in the breeze as he leaped from the swing and somersaulted onto the grass, ending on his feet with puffed out chest and arms akimbo like George Reeves himself.

He always was a Super Hero kind of brother (even if he did look more like Jimmy Olsen than Clark Kent).

Now he was gone. But where? Heaven? Oblivion? And she was left to remember him, here in her old room filled with pastel promises of all-shall-be-well.

Enough. *Enough.* She needed to say something, to protest these plans for today. After all, didn't she specialize in protest? She should not have to deal with people right now, especially "godly" ones. She stubbed out her cigarette in the peanut butter jar lid on the nightstand, grabbed her robe, and headed downstairs to the kitchen.

* * *

"I want to grieve in peace! Do they have to come . . . today?"

Kate Prescott looked up at her daughter, her ultra-plucked eyebrows rising like half-moons. Sunlight through the kitchen window illuminated her lined forehead and the coffee stain on her quilted bathrobe. She braced her hand on the counter and settled a look on her eldest child as if she'd threatened to burn the flag.

"Maddy, they're coming to give comfort, not for a party. We need comfort, don't we?" Her voice tilted upward with each word, threatening utter discomposure.

"Of course we do. It's just that I'm not comfortable with the church people." Madeline started to reach for her mother, but Kate turned away to attend to the coffee percolator. "I mean, they were close to Sean, but never to me," Madeline pressed, not meaning to speak his name. They had not yet uttered his name. Not Madeline. Not her parents. Only Jilli, her little sister, had dared to breach the taboo: *What happened to Sean? Is Sean in heaven?* Jilli, at thirteen, had not yet learned the visceral anguish of naming the freshly deceased.

Kate appeared strangely unaffected by the sound of her dead son's name. She looked suddenly strong, resolute, even dignified, despite her tootsie-roll flip askew in several places.

"I need this, Maddy. I just do. And so does your father. *Please—*"

Madeline stared at her with an unexpected rush of tenderness, slightly tinged with shame. She leaned her head on her mother's shoulder, as if she were six years old, taking in the aroma of coffee and toast and day-old Aqua Net hair spray.

* * *

Shortly after noon the doorbell rang. Madeline, dressed in her familiar blue sweater and brown corduroys, headed downstairs to face the inevitable. She paused on the stairs, catching sight of the Christmas tree, neglected and languishing in the corner of the living room. The needle-strewn presents cried out to be opened, or at least stored away until the family could bear their unwrapping.

One by one, long faces converged upon the Prescott home. Sympathetic, yes, but with an edge. Madeline thought she could see it in their eyes—that *look*—reminding her that she was "the wayward one." Her soul was the one in peril, not Sean's. He was the "Onward Christian Soldier" who marched off to war.

And for what?

A tightly controlled ball of sadness broke open inside her. She grabbed onto the back of the sofa to brace herself.

As the flock huddled around Kate Prescott—she was, after all, the Gold Star mother—Madeline imagined Sean's way with them. He charmed them, all of them. He was a likeable kid with coppery hair and slightly protruding front teeth (not enough for braces, but just enough to keep him looking like the eternal kid). She remembered his face all lit up with patriotic pride the day he left Camp Pendleton for Vietnam. She could still see his freckled face and squinty eyes as he waved good-bye in the same unforgiving sunshine that brought his death messenger.

Then his face vanished from her mind and the auburn haired Mrs. Mahaney came into view.

"Maddy—dear Maddy," said the woman with open arms. Mrs. Mahaney was one of the exceptions to Madeline's church allergy. She was one of the sweet ones, a widow from some-where in the South with a lovely unaffected drawl. Unlike the others, Mrs. Mahaney never treated her like a lost soul, but as a teenager "on her way to adventure," which were the very words she had written inside Madeline's high school graduation card. Now her Southern accent and graceful carriage tempered Madeline's resistance to the group of mourners.

Over Mrs. Mahaney's shoulder she gazed at her father with his close-cropped curly red hair and forced smile. The 8x10 photograph of Sean in his marine regalia loomed behind him on the mantel. Not standing to greet the guests, John Prescott sat unmoved, gripping the arms of his easy chair so tightly you'd think he was riding the Matterhorn bobsled at Disneyland. Her father had hardly spoken since the tragic news and offered only robotic expressions of affection. But then, it had been a long time since there had been any meaningful father-daughter connection—that is, outside of raised voices and door slamming.

Mr. and Mrs. Gregory entered the living room together with the Brugeman sisters. Each of the four, in turn, offered their condolences. Madeline watched her father reluctantly heave himself up to face the inevitable. The Gregorys were solid and reliable in their way, but ultra zealous in their beliefs, showing visible disgust at the mention of The Catholics or The Mormons (both equally damned), joined in everlasting agony by The Liberals, The Communists, and The Beatles.

The Brugeman sisters, Marge and Mable, were identical twins who were, pound for pound, identically fat. They had never been married but cried ostentatiously at weddings. With identical gray-blue bubbles of hair, the Brugeman twins rarely smiled. Perhaps they had bad teeth; one could never know due to their ever-sorrowful, cross-bearing expressions. Just as the Brugeman sisters had seemingly remained the same—given a few identically added pounds—so were her feelings toward them.

Madeline sat with Mrs. Mahaney on the rose colored sofa, wincing at the sound of crinkling plastic beneath them. She hated the way her mother kept the sofa covered, as if the 1950s were still in full bloom. *For God's sake, what was she saving the sofa for, anyway? A visit from the President?*

"And how are your history studies coming along?" asked Mrs. Mahaney.

The question stung. "Didn't Mom tell you? I graduated last year." She wanted to say, *I graduated with honors and my parents don't give a damn.*

"Oh, of course," Mrs. Mahaney said with a wave of apology.

"I remember now. Yes, Kate said you graduated magna cum laude."

Madeline felt a rush of shame. Of course her parents were proud of her. Embarrassed because of her anti-war protests, yes. Mortified by her part in the Free Speech Movement, of course. But still, they were proud. Weren't they?

Then she caught sight of Jilli sidling up to her mother and finally disappearing into the dizzy flock of New Hope Baptist comforters. Madeline wanted to yell, *Jilli, save yourself!* Jilli was the reason Madeline had to be strong. But tears threatened to break loose at the sight of her little blonde sister with her Twiggy hair style and stick legs. She reminded Madeline of a baby bird, waif like and unsullied by the world—not yet jaded like her older sister. She wore flowered peddle pushers with a mis-matched tunic of yet another variety of flower.

The doorbell rang again. With her mother busy in the kitchen, she excused herself from Mrs. Mahaney's comforting presence to greet the latest arrival.

There he stood: worn black leather Bible in hand, pious solemnity hovering about his mouth.

"Pastor Bob," she said with labored politeness.

"Maddy," he said, looking professionally sympathetic, eyebrows knit together. "I was sorry to hear about your brother."

She could tell that he was uncomfortable, especially since they had a bumpy history. On her visits home from Berkeley, she seized every opportunity to vex Pastor Bob with questions about his sermons. After one Sunday morning service, she had asked why he didn't preach on themes of peace and justice and concern for the poor, like Martin Luther King, Jr. Dr. King was a Baptist, too, wasn't he? Pastor Bob had answered, "To each his own, Maddy, to each his own," and turned to shake hands with less curious parishioners.

She felt a touch of pity for the "to-each-his-own" preacher, now only a few oily strands away from full-blown baldness. He

looked a bit shop-worn, too, and heavier around the middle. He
did have clear—and, one might argue, sincere—blue eyes under
his permanently furrowed brow, but this was offset by sagging
jowls: not a pretty sight, but not altogether repugnant. He was
familiar, and that was something anyway.

"Come in. Can I take your jacket?" Madeline hoped such
labored formality would stave off any attempts at awkward,
hypocritical hugs.

He removed his dark jacket with difficulty, switching his
Bible from hand to hand, as if handing it to an apostate even for
a moment would be sacrilegious. He wore his usual thin, black
tie, complete with the "God Bless America" tie tack shaped like
the American flag.

God *help* America, she sighed silently.

Pastor Bob stood waiting for her to hang his jacket in the
coat closet, arms folded across his Bible, holding it close to his
chest like a bullet-proof shield protecting vital organs. She returned to him, not knowing what to say next.

"Maddy," he said to her stiffly, "We can't always understand the ways of God."

Here it is again, she thought (instructing her eyes not to roll),
the same old spiel, infecting the air like a bad case of halitosis.
She had expected it, yes, but she wasn't prepared for it. *We
cannot question the will of God*, the pious pastor would always say,
no matter what: a car crash, a broken leg, the death of a child,
the sinking of the Titanic. It always provoked her, his stale
platitudes, his way of putting it all off on God. Why was it
always God's fault? Did God pull the trigger that killed Sean?
She was just about to ask him this when he soldiered on—

"But of course, God's will is always for the best." He spoke
with a mouth forming iron-clad sureties, but with eyes that seem
shaky, vulnerable, lacking conviction. *Did he really believe what he
was saying?*

Pastor Bob could turn anyone against God. He had a knack

for it, like someone who can play the piano or fix car engines. He was just gifted in that way. But did she, Madeline Prescott, believe in God? She didn't know. She held fast to her agnosticism, a stance that some called intellectually lazy, but not so for her. She wanted to take her time, to really *think* about The Big Questions, to wrestle with them, talk about them. Argue them. But with whom?

She had tried to talk about larger issues with Mike since they were, after all, a couple—and didn't couples talk about everything? But he wasn't interested in discussing anything except political theory, and only political theory that related directly to his dissertation on the Cuban Revolution.

But didn't Socrates say that "the unexamined life is not worth living"? Then, by God, she would examine it. All of it. What is Truth? Beauty? Love? Goodness? Was this not the Socratic Quest?

Quest. The very word elevated her. She had embraced the idea of the quest for meaning when she signed up for the graduate philosophy seminar "Existentialism from Heidegger to Sartre." She loved the arguments, the counter-arguments, the syllogisms.

But all her former enthusiasms were now swallowed up in the black hole that was her heart. Still, her quest would go on, for it drove her: this yearning to get above things, below things, to the heart of things. And now, in the face of death-up-close, her quest seemed to take on a capital Q, as if she needed it more than wanted it. As if the Quest had taken hold of her, turned her upside down. Shaken her. All in hopes that a few answers might drop out of her pockets. It scared her—it did. But what was the option, really? To be like . . . her parents?

And now, in front of her stood a slack-jowled, pot-bellied incarnation of the Anti-Quest, one who knew truth to be simple and literal and hermetically sealed, like those foil pouches of dehydrated food the Apollo astronauts took with them into space. For Pastor Bob, she guessed, the whole idea of a quest beyond pat answers would be a sinful lack of faith. But for Madeline Prescott, philosopher-in-training, the whole idea of sealing up truths—starving them of air and water and light—was itself a crime.

She wanted to say all of this to Pastor Bob, but escape seemed more practical. "Well, we can talk about it later," she finally said to his waiting eyes. "I really need to help Mom with the coffee."

Pastor Bob's eyes belied a hint of relief. He patted her shoulder and set his pastoral sights on her father.

In the kitchen she removed foil wrap from the food brought by the guests and pinched off a mouthful of the Brugeman sisters' airy angel food cake.

The ring of the wall phone next to her head made her jump. She grabbed the receiver on the second ring, swallowing cake while trying to squeak out a hello. It was, as she had hoped, Mike. Calling collect.

Collect? Why should her parents pay for his call? "Yes—I'll accept the charges."

"Happy New Year, Red!" Mike's voice sounded cheery and light and wholly inappropriate for the circumstances. But still, she was relieved to hear his voice.

Her live-in boyfriend was tall and angular with a jaw that seemed to jut out in defiance of bourgeois hegemony. He—a product of bourgeois hegemony—wore vintage round glasses, earning him the nickname "Trotsky." The endearment "Red" was Mike's doing. She had warned him early on that she was no longer going by Maddy, as it was not as sophisticated sounding as *Madeline*—but Red? She tolerated it, but it also got on her nerves, as if she were nothing but a nameless, faceless, soulless mop of hair. If there were ever a time to call her by her *real* name it was now, when she needed more support and intimacy than he had ever given her.

While Mike groaned on about his dissertation problems and the politics of the university, she tore off large chunks of angel food cake and mindlessly stuffed them into her mouth. Finally, her voice broke through—

"Mike, I need you. I mean, I *really* need you."

"I'm here," he said in a flat tone, lacking the warmth she craved.

"No, you're *not* here. You're *there*. That's the problem."

At that moment, one of the Brugeman sisters, Marge (or was it Mable?) entered the kitchen and started arranging the tray of coffee cups. The woman stopped short when she saw her angel food cake half-eaten and the remaining portion squashed into a deformed remnant of its former glory. Madeline shrugged apologetically and stretched the long cord around the corner, not waiting for what would surely be another you're-not-going-to-heaven look.

"Hey, I'll be down as soon as I can," she heard Mike say.

"How soon?"

"Really soon."

"Define soon."

"I just have to meet with Professor Aiken today, but Friday, for sure. Promise." He paused to clear his throat. "And, uh, when is the . . . you know, the actual funeral?"

"The *actual* funeral? As opposed to the *fake* funeral?"

"Oh, you know what I mean, Red. I'm not good at expressing myself when it comes to . . . this sort of thing."

"Well 'this sort of thing' is my life now. I don't know about the funeral, when it will be," she said, picturing a flag-draped coffin in transit from somewhere, "but it doesn't matter. I just need you to be here. Right now. Mom and Dad have their church friends, but I'm alone here." She hated the pathetic neediness in her voice, but she was, in fact, quite needy at the moment. With good reason.

"I'll be there, Red," assured Mike, still too chirpy.

"And don't call me that when you come down. I have a name, you know." Her tone exposed mounting irritation. Was this her grief talking? Or was it simply that the brilliant campus radical, Mike Riley, was, in fact, an emotional Cretan?

Something wasn't right with Mike. Something more than miles separated them. She could feel it.

Chapter Two

The next afternoon, Madeline sat nursing a Pall Mall at the kitchen table, taking stock of the room that had nurtured her through eighteen years. Even with the new touches, a portable TV and a modern avocado green refrigerator, the place still vibrated with the past, odd slices of memory: the smell of Jiffy Pop (Jilli clapping at the growing aluminum bubble); Kate washing dishes to the sounds of Frank Sinatra on the radio; Sean sitting on the kitchen counter, Coke bottle in hand, the heels of his tennis shoes hammering against the oak cabinets below. His nervous habit had — much to her mother's consternation — battered the wood. She stared now at the lower cabinets and reached out to feel the dented places.

The drop-leaf table where she sat used to host weekend games of *Parcheesi* and *Monopoly*. Now it was piled high with foil-wrapped breads and cakes. Sean, with his ravenous appetite for sweets, would love all this.

If it weren't for his dying.

As the sun began its descent into a stark desert chill, she shivered like she used to at her grandparents' beach cottage at Crystal Cove. She used to love running from the chilly surf into the brightly colored beach towel held wide by Grandma Daisy, who would wrap her up like an Indian princess.

She stood to flip on the light switch before the gloom got the best of her. *When in God's name would Mike call?* She flicked ashes into the sink and reached for the phone, but stopped. She didn't want to sound as needy as she had the day before. But then, she had never been with Mike under these circumstances. *New territory.* It worried her, what it would be like when Mike arrived for the funeral. Would he make her coffee? Dry her tears? Hold her hand? Make an effort with her parents? She was sure her mother would double her up with Jilli while Mike took her room, in spite of the fact that she and Mike had been living together for six months.

She heard the creak of the stairs and quickly stubbed out her cigarette in the sink, running water until the ashes disappeared down the drain. She turned to see her little sister, bleary-eyed and disheveled, having napped much of the afternoon.

"I'm starving," said Jilli. "Where's Mom?"

"Hi, sleepyhead. Mom and Dad are at the church—" She stopped herself from saying, *to make arrangements for our brother's memorial service.* "But there're stacks of food in the fridge." Madeline opened the angular avocado marvel. "Look, we've got enough sandwiches and Jell-O salads and tuna casseroles to feed an army."

Jilli sniffed and scrunched up her nose. "If Mom finds out you've been smoking in the house, you'll be—"

"I know. I *know*," Madeline said, adding a conspiratorial wink. "You won't tell, will you?"

"Not if you feed me," said Jilli with a mischievous smile. She leaned against the kitchen door frame, one foot pressed up against the opposite side. "What's Mike like?" she asked out of nowhere.

"Mike?" Madeline paused. "Well, he's tall. And intelligent, but not terribly humble about it." She pulled out a plate of snowy white triangular sandwiches and set them on the table.

"So, how did you guys meet? At the school cafeteria or something?"

Madeline stifled a chuckle. "Close. We were both involved in the Vietnam Day Committee on campus, and I was in charge of the coffee. Mike kept coming back for refills."

"Neat," said Jilli. "Is he cute?"

"So many questions! Here, sit down and eat."

"Well, is he?" Jilli grabbed a sandwich as she sat down. "Cute, I mean."

"Of course. Would your sister go out with someone who looks like the Hunchback of Notre Dame?"

Jilli giggled, the first care-free sputter in the house since the bombshell.

"But there's more to a man than his looks, Kiddo," Madeline added with a sudden air of elder-sister authority. "In fact, you have to watch out for *really* good looking men. I mean, they tend to be jerks. At least that's my observation."

Jilli sipped the Fresca Madeline had opened for her. There was only the sound of the fizz until Jilli finally said, blushing, "And you *live* with him?"

Madeline bit into her egg salad triangle and smiled into round eyes.

"We do share an apartment. At the moment, anyway. To save money."

"Is that the only reason?"

Madeline stalled for time, reaching for a napkin to wipe her mouth. *Living in sin was hard to explain.* "I'm also helping him with his dissertation." She paused, sandwich mid-air, and added in an acerbic tone, "Mostly in the form of *typing* it."

Jilli's eyes glowed with intense interest, but her mouth puckered nervously. Madeline noted the conflicted expression and touched her sister's arm.

"Look, Jilli, I'm not as wild as Mom thinks. Mike is very special to me."

"Does that mean you're not coming back home, then? Mom said that's why you got a history degree, to come back here and teach history at the high school."

"Well, it takes more than a history degree," Madeline said.

"You have to get a teaching certificate, too, which means education classes and student teaching and—"

"Then what are you doing up there in Berkeley? Why aren't you getting that certificate thing?"

"I just need some time off, that's all," Madeline said gently. "Time to think about which way I want to go. I have to be really sure whether I want to teach or do something else. So I'm taking a break—you know, like graduates do. Some of the lucky ones even backpack through Europe."

She suddenly wondered why she hadn't seriously considered it. She could be snapping pictures of all the palaces of Europe, homes to kings and queens: those deliciously paranoid Machiavellian types (with the possible exception of Frederick the Great), who clung to their omnipotence—their brutal, childish control over others—even to the point of self-destruction. A sorry lot, most of them; still, their houses and gardens were great. But Mike would never go. He only wanted to get to Cuba, and since Che Guevara's murder, that's all he talked about. It was a stretch to imagine him touring Hampton Court.

"Anyway," she continued, wiping crumbs from her hands, "that's what happens after four years of having your nose in a book. You have to clear your head before you join the rat race. As for me, I'm serving coffee at a *really* groovy coffee house and taking a graduate course in philosophy."

"What's phil . . . osophy? We don't study that in school here."

"Well, it literally means 'the love of wisdom,' and I suppose that's where I am right now, just looking for . . . well . . . wisdom."

Jilli went back to her sandwich, glassy eyed, probably not so much satisfied with the answer as simply bored with it. Madeline wanted to tell Jilli about Socrates, the strange little man who made people think—and drank hemlock for it. But her little sister would not understand, not at thirteen.

Madeline's friends at Berkeley understood. After all, Berkeley was where philosophy mattered. In the classroom, it mattered. On Sproul Plaza, it mattered. At Cody's Books on Telegraph Avenue, it mattered. *Ideas mattered.* And the endless critiques of the Establishment—infused with heady ideas of the way things *should* be—went down best with coffee and cigarettes and the guitar strums of half-stoned folk singers. She was not ready to give all that up for a classroom of hormone-crazed teenagers. Not just yet. And despite her desire to be closer to her little sister, Berkeley was her home. She took another sandwich from the plate and bit into it. Yes, she mused, wiping the mayonnaise from the corners of her mouth, she was quite secure in her Berkeley identity. Despite this sudden storm of grief, she was tethered to shore by a very strong rope. *Of course she was.*

"I have a sort of boyfriend," Jilli said with sudden energy.

"A *sort of* boyfriend?" Madeline asked, bemused. How she wished for more time with this tiny bird-legged child—a child who needed a big sister.

"Well, yeah. Sort of. Tim Littleton. He's in my grade. He's pretty neat." She paused to blow across the top of her Fresca bottle, making a low whooshing sound like the Santa Ana winds. "Except that he likes the Beach Boys better than the Monkees. I told him you like The Beatles and Joan Baez and that you went to UC Berkeley. He said that his parents told him you were on the news with the protesters." Jilli inclined her head. "Is that why Mom and Dad were so mad at you?"

"Yeah, I embarrassed them, but I didn't plan on it. It just happened. I got caught on camera by Channel 4 News during a protest at the recruiting center in Oakland."

"Was the protest in color?" asked Jilli. "On color TV, I mean."

Madeline nodded. "It's just my luck to be a redhead at the dawn of color television." And it was also just her luck to have scandalized the family of John Prescott, a managing engineer at Rockwell Aerospace and Defense, a partner in the military-industrial complex that supported LBJ's war.

* * *

At 9:00 p.m. the phone rang. Madeline was just out of the bath, feeling refreshed and warm and wholly comforted by the steamy soak. With Calgon suds still clinging, she wrapped herself in a fluffy, sweet-smelling, oversized bath towel (another forgotten amenity on the home front).

"Maddy, pick up the phone!" Kate Prescott yelled from the bottom of the stairs.

Just like the old days. Madeline padded down the hall to her room and grabbed the receiver of the white princess phone.

After accepting more charges from yet another collect call— *was he really that broke?*—she flopped down on the bed, holding her towel snug to her body. "Hey, I thought you'd never call. I've almost gone through an entire pack of Pall Malls."

Mike didn't respond immediately. "Well . . . things have been happening here. Lotta stuff to work out."

"You mean about the dissertation? How did your professor like the changes?"

"Not exactly. He liked the changes, by the way. Thanks for all your help on retyping those. And for everything. I'll never forget all you did."

Never forget? Like, good-bye-let's-write at the end of summer camp?

"What's up, Mike? You sound strange." She sat up, letting go of her tight grip on the towel as a million goose bumps rose with a million anxieties.

"It's just . . . it's just that I can't come down to Orange County." He cleared his throat as if trying to muster his confidence. "I'm not coming down."

"What?"

He sighed. "I just don't think I can deal with it right now."

The short-lived firmness in his voice was now replaced with a near whine, something Madeline despised in anyone, especially in one who was supposed to be her rock at the moment.

"Deal with it? You can't *deal* with it?" She felt her cheeks redden and her temper rise. "That's such a cop-out. For God's sake, Mike, I just expected a little support after I've typed your dissertation and run down library books for your stupid footnotes and been your basic Girl Friday. Not to mention, your lover. I mean, don't you think I deserve a little support in return? *God!*"

Mike sighed again. "You know I have to keep focused before the dissertation defense. Be reasonable. A trip would throw me off right now, not to mention all the stress of your family. And the funeral."

Madeline's jaw dropped. There was the slightest pause in which she tried to take in the blatant self-absorption of this man she had lived with, made love to—believed in, for God's sake.

"And exactly how would this stress—"

"Sarah says so, too."

"S-Sarah?" Madeline sat up straight and grasped her towel tighter, for she was cold, shaking. "What's Sarah got to do with anything?"

Silence on the other end.

"Damn you, Mike!"

"Red . . . I . . . it's not—"

"Don't *ever* call me 'Red' again. Do you even remember my *real* name? Huh? I have a name, you know."

"Calm down . . . *Madeline*—"

She slammed down the receiver and sat motionless, half expecting him to call right back. But the room held silent. Madeline knew Mike's lack of long-term commitment had been a sore point in their relationship, and that eventually they would have to deal with it. But not now. *Not now!* Was he . . . was he actually sleeping with her former roommate?

She got up, threw on her UC Berkeley tee, and pilfered through her macramé purse. *Where was the damned Zippo lighter?*

An hour later the pretty white princess phone, which used to be her lifeline to silly teenage gossip, now rang with sinister adult overtones. She caught it on the first ring lest her parents answer on the extension. It was a person-to-person call from Sarah Warren.

"Hi, Madeline. *So-o-o* sorry to hear about your brother."

"Thanks, Sarah," Madeline said cautiously, pulling out the third cigarette within an hour.

"Some of us want to send flowers . . . that is, when you know about the arrangements."

"Well, that's . . . nice. But is that why you called? To offer condolences?"

"What do you mean?" Sarah sounded defensive.

"I mean, what's going on? I get the distinct impression that you had some influence on Mike's staying in Berkeley."

Madeline waited. And willed herself to breathe.

"Oh, it's just that . . ." Sarah said haltingly, "Mike and I have been spending some time together, just trying to figure things out, you know. He's freaked out about his dissertation defense and all. And he's trying to get his adjunct teaching job extended, and you know the political science department—it's so *political*." She laughed nervously.

"Yeah, I'm sure it equals the death of a loved one."

"Oh, no. No! I didn't mean that at all." But there was more exasperation than regret in her tone.

"Sarah, just tell me this. Are you sleeping with Mike? Is that what this is about?"

Now a heavier silence settled in: a thick, muddy silence, like the quicksand in "B" movies at the drive-in theater.

She took a long drag on her Pall Mall, as if it were her last one before the muddy swamp took her hand, cigarette and all, into the proverbial pit of no return. This must be a bad joke. Or a bad dream. Anything but reality. She'd had too much reality in the space of a week. Too much. *Too much!*

She heard Sarah trying to form a sentence, but stumbling. Madeline listened for a few moments, then pushed down the button, breaking the connection. She placed the receiver gently in its cradle, as nonchalantly as putting an empty pop bottle in its carton.

Chapter Three

Eve van Gelder stood, tray in hand, at the Henry James table, one of two window tables offering a view to Main Beach. From where she stood she could see sail boats dotted about in the distance; closer in, expensive, showy cars whizzed past on Pacific Coast Highway. The table where she stood was occupied by two women who followed the tea tray with expectant eyes. She tilted the pot and poured the steamy Ceylon tea into a china cup, finishing with a practiced flourish to the wrist. The antique egg-white porcelain with tiny pink roses seemed to blossom into life—a literal full-fill-ment of its purpose in life. Just receiving, with quiet repose. This idea had never occurred to her before, not in all the years she had poured tea. Odd, she thought, how the mind works when one reaches middle age.

"Are you from England?" asked the older of the two women seated at the table. "You sound British, but there's something else I'm picking up. German?" The woman had walnut colored hair that had surely been teased to within an inch of its life, smoothed down, and sealed with hair lacquer. The high-haired lady sat with her daughter, a quiet, pretty young woman with bright tangerine lipstick.

"I'm Dutch," Eve said as she filled the second cup. "But I fell in love, you see. First with the English language —and then with an Englishman. The Englishman is out of the picture now, but the rest of it stuck."

"So, Van Gelder . . ." She tapped one long, frosted nail on

the name *Van Gelder's Tea and Books* in a news clipping under the table top glass. "That must be your maiden name, then?"

"That's right," Eve nodded, setting the teapot gently on the glass table top.

"But that's so brave of you . . . at your age," the woman said through the steamy fragrance, cup mid-air. "Not many women take back their maiden names after—"

"Oh, it was my daughter's idea, really," Eve said smiling, trying not to show irritation. "But I rather like it."

Eve rather *disliked* the high-haired lady's choice of words, *at your age*. She still had trouble thinking of herself at fifty-two, as if the years of hop scotching across Europe and finally landing in Southern California had not aged her at all. Of course it had. But not the divorce itself; it had, in fact, liberated her, given her the freedom to fulfill her dream. *If only her aching feet would get on board.*

"You make drinking tea into an art form," the younger woman said, as if trying to make up for her mother's tactlessness.

Eve smiled at the compliment and turned to the tray sitting on the table behind her to retrieve a plate of warmed scones. The presentation of the round floury scones—accented by lavish dollops of cream and jam on the side—was met with murmurs of delight and appreciation.

"I don't think I've ever had tea like this outside of England," said the high-haired lady with (upon closer inspection) false eyelashes.

"Oh, you've been to London, then?" Eve said with interest.

"Once. My husband's business trip. We went to Claridge's and had afternoon tea. It. Was. Exquisite." The woman punctuated every word with a click of her nails against the glass.

"Well, this isn't exactly Claridge's, is it?" Eve said with a chuckle. "Just a bookshop that offers a bit of English refreshment on the side."

"But," the woman said, "it's the only English shop we have in Laguna. Tea. Scones. Biscuits. The real thing. People like myself, who have traveled abroad, do appreciate such distinction."

The daughter, with her tangerine smile, added sweetly, "You're obviously a great success. The shop, I mean."

Eve nodded a genuine smile and left the women to their tea. She began re-shelving books left on another table, pondering her "success." For most people in America, she mused, a bookshop without coffee was an odd duck of a place. It was a coffee-mad world, was it not? But wasn't California open to the unusual? She wanted her shop to be different, to be a restorative—a refuge of sorts—for a society exhausted with bad news, war, and discontent. Tea could calm one, help one think, restore one's frazzled soul. Coffee just drove one faster into the fray. Yes, she resolved, what the world needed was a good calming down with a good cup of tea. At least Walter Cronkite's news reports suggested that the world needed calming. Her adopted county —the whole world for that matter—seemed to be in some tormented adolescent phase: moody, irrational, given to extremes. If a cup of tea and a good book could soften the hard edges of it all, she would indeed consider herself a success.

She opened the worn hardback book abandoned on the William Blake table. *First Love* by Louis Untermeyer, she read on the title page. She smiled to herself. Mr. Larsen probably left the volume on the table when he was in for his afternoon tea. Eiler Larsen, the Greeter of Laguna, loved his poetry and would, in fact, be so absorbed in a poem that his long beard would often sink into his tea without his knowledge.

She adjusted some falling volumes in the section her son had named "California Writers." Still thinking of the comment about her *British* shop, she sighed over the fact that she had meant to highlight British authors, but as she glanced to the four shelves of classic English novels, she noticed they had stayed exactly the same size since the shop opened almost two years ago. The "California Writers" section, to the contrary, with authors such as Steinbeck, Hammett, and Bradbury, had expanded to include an entire bookcase and threatened to spill over to another. At least English mysteries sold out as soon as they hit the shelves; and what was a British tea and book shop without Agatha Christie? Dorothy Sayers? And that new critically-acclaimed mystery writer, P. D. James? All disappearing as fast as her scones.

She glanced back at the woman with the elaborate coiffure. It must reach four or five inches above her head, Eve estimated. Perhaps (she smiled to herself) Mr. Cronkite's *hair-raising* news reports might indeed be the cause of all this high hair. But of course she should be gentler in her judgments, especially when it came to hair. Her own dark hair—a simple French roll with more than a few strands of gray twining through—would probably win no fashion awards. But, she rallied, it was practical.

Eve finished with the books and began gathering the insides of a newspaper left strewn about on the Jane Austen table. Folding the *L.A. Times*, the Arts and Leisure section fell out. She picked it up and gazed at a photo of a young man sporting long sideburns and a dark turtleneck. He faced the camera with arms folded (thoroughly satisfied with himself, no doubt), positioned next to a painting. The canvass looked like someone had dumped jam all over it: blueberry, boysenberry, and a dash of strawberry. *And they call this art?* At least the *plein air* landscape artists of Laguna Beach believed in form and beauty, not just making some nihilistic statement with whatever paints happen to be lying about. She wondered what Mr. Steiner would say about abstract art. She would save the paper and ask him his thoughts on the matter.

But was she just looking for things to ask him? Mr. Steiner of the prestigious Steiner Gallery, just around the corner, played too much in her mind as of late. *Be careful.*

She tossed the paper.

In the kitchen, her assistant, Karen, stood over the sink cleaning the china with baking soda and water to remove the tea stains. Eve grabbed a sponge and the teapot next in line for the scrub down and sidled up to her employee.

"Karen, don't you think all civilized society is in some kind of cataclysmic change?"

"What?" said the young brunette, who had seemed distracted all afternoon. "Oh, yeah, I suppose so. But the world does need changing, Eve."

"Yes, it does. You're right," she said, sponging off the tea-darkened spout of the otherwise white teapot. "But that's no reason to consign the entire past to the rubbish heap, as if grandmother's silver-framed pictures and intricate needlework were to be tossed out along with her condescending views of 'the help.' I mean to say," pressed Eve, for she felt passionate on this point, "there's no real character left these days, not with all the *avant-garde* art and the sterile modern décors stripped of any vestige of the past. It's as if grandmother never existed at all—"

"Eve," interrupted Karen, "I need to talk to you about something, if you don't mind." Eve set down the teapot and turned to give her employee her full attention, for the young woman looked pale.

"Yes, dear, what is it?"

Just then the bell above the front door jangled, signaling a new customer. Eve put down her tea towel and offered her employee an apologetic look. "Hang on, Karen."

She started to leave and then turned back. "Better check on the ladies at the Henry James table. They'll be needing refills about now. And please get Mr. Steiner's teacup ready. He likes the Lenox, you know, the cup with the silver rim." Eve gestured toward the teapot, cup, and saucer that she held back for Mr. Steiner who, for the past few weeks, had made a habit of stopping in each day after work. Eve took some pride in her ability to match teacups with customers. Laguna was filled with artists and bohemians, so she often mismatched the cups and saucers for those "hip" customers. Cardigan-sweatered gray-haired women appreciated the traditional chintz and roses. But men like Mr. Steiner preferred simple and elegant.

Eve emerged from behind the wall separating the kitchen from the main room. She expected—and hoped?—to see Mr. Steiner, as he had not missed an after-work tea for almost three weeks now. But instead, she was surprised to see her son. He must have come directly from work, dressed as he was in a dark suit and tie, looking every bit the professional accountant.

"Hi, Mum," he said with an energetic smile.

"Alex, what are you doing here? It's not Sunday." On Sundays, Alex would not only balance the shop's financial books but bring in armloads of actual books—mostly used—with him. He loved to peruse bookstores all over Orange County and managed shrewd deals. And, as of late, he had managed a few "hot of the press" books as well.

"I've got something to show you that couldn't wait until Sunday."

"Show me?" Eve lifted a brow. "Sit, I'll bring you some tea."

"I can't stay. Got someone waiting in the car."

"Someone? That pretty brunette from last month? What was her name?"

Alex rolled his eyes. "No. Just a co-worker from Hughes. We're going for cocktails at the Hotel Laguna, if you must know."

"Right. Well, sit for a minute anyway, and let's see what you have," she said, pulling out a chair.

Alex placed a package wrapped in plain brown paper on the George Orwell table, the second of two window tables, and sat down across from his mother.

"A real find, this," Alex said, eyes glowing.

When Alex was animated, as he was now, his beauty became

almost unbearable. *Too good looking for his own good, this son of mine.* It worried her, for too much beauty, she knew, could be as hazardous as too much wealth. He could so easily fall prey to his father's lifestyle, the film crowd gathered around the kidney-shaped pool with their martinis and their perfect teeth. But still, when she looked at him she felt pride. This was her son, her beautiful son. And, aside from his revolving door of girlfriends (she hardly bothered to learn their names anymore), he stood on solid ground, preferring books and numbers to glittering Hollywood parties.

"So, what is this great find that couldn't wait?"

Alex slid the package toward her. "Go ahead, open it."

Eve pulled away the string and unwrapped the crisp paper. Inside was a book, a beautifully bound volume. "Ah, *Tortilla Flat.*"

"First edition Steinbeck," Alex said with pride.

"Mint condition, I have to say," she said, turning the book over in her hands.

"He wrote *The Grapes of Wrath*, you know."

"Of course, I know. But I'm not familiar with this particular title."

"He wrote *Tortilla Flat* while living in Laguna. Right here in Laguna Beach. Can you believe it?"

"I had no idea." Eve shook her head in amazement. "This must have cost a fortune. Where did you find it?"

"Can't give away all my trade secrets, but I have to say I got a really great deal. And it's from my own pocket, a gift to the shop. I thought we might put it on display, not to sell of course, unless—"

Alex stopped and frowned as he looked down at his feet. "Mum, the cat is in the shop again. You've got to keep him up-stairs in the flat. If the health inspector were to walk in right now, you'd be fined. Do you want that?"

Eve looked down at her beloved gray tabby, Earl Grey,

plopped on Alex's shoe. The cat looked up at her with the same baleful look that had moved her to pluck him up from the Laguna animal shelter.

"Alex, if I had wanted him to stay alone upstairs all day, I would not have put cat flaps in the doors." Her son had been against the cat flaps, but she and Earl Grey had outnumbered him.

"But, Mum," he said *sotto voce*, "the customers." Alex glanced at the two women at the Henry James table.

"The customers love Earl," she said in a normal tone. "He adds character to the place. Not one customer has complained. Not one."

Eve and her son continued to exchange words over Earl Grey's presence until the shop bell jangled and the cat-in-question trotted off toward the cat-flap-in-question.

In walked the owner of Steiner Gallery.

Eve's heart skipped a beat at the sight of Mr. Steiner, an unwanted effect the man had on her. She smiled and moved to greet him. "Hello, Mr. Steiner. I want you to meet my son, Alex—Alex Moore. He's usually here only on Sundays. Alex, this is Mr. Steiner, of the Steiner Gallery."

Alex stood to greet the older man with a handshake. What was it, Eve wondered, about this Mr. Steiner that made her so uneasy? She studied him as he engaged her son in small talk. He was not particularly handsome, and certainly not beautiful like her son, not at all. But attractive, nonetheless. His thick gray hair and wrinkles belied his age, probably ten years older than she. He had huge, dark, intelligent eyes and an oddly sensual space between his front teeth, a tiny imperfection that gave him, well, character. (It also vaguely reminded her of Omar Sharif.)

Mr. Steiner was attired, as always, in a crisp white shirt and a handsomely-made suit. He wore a gold watch and shiny Italian shoes and—

A slim gold wedding band.

But the ring was not a problem, she told herself more than once. In fact, it was a relief. She was only interested in casual friendship, light conversation, something to look forward to at the end of the day. Of course that was all it was to her. Decidedly so. Eve believed women—especially housewives and mothers—needed a place to get away, to read and discuss significant issues with other women. And men. Of course, men. Why not? Men and women could be friends, after all. Equality was all the rage these days, and wasn't 1968 the U.N. "Year of Human Rights"? Mustn't that extend to women, too? So, she reasoned, men and women could be friends, *should* be friends. It was a new age, this.

"You say you work at Hughes Aircraft?" Mr. Steiner asked Alex. "Is that Hughes as in Howard Hughes?"

"One and the same, but I've not seen even a hint of the man. He's a regular recluse from what I hear. How about you? Your accent—New York?"

"Very good!" Mr. Steiner said. "You know, Alex, the more people I meet here, the more it seems that everyone in California is from somewhere else."

"Really?" Alex cocked his head in polite interest.

"Oh, yes. In my few months of living here, I've met some interesting people, like you and your mother, but also some strange characters." Mr. Steiner shook his head.

Eve's eyebrows went up. "Strange characters?"

"Like the erstwhile professor from Harvard who tells kids to 'tune in, turn on, and drop out,' or something like that. He did all those experiments with LSD. Strange stuff."

"You mean Timothy Leary?" asked Alex, who looked slightly bemused.

"Leary. That's his name. He came into the gallery today. Just about knocked my socks off. He said he's living here. Opened a bookstore down the street called Mystical . . .

something or other."

"Mystic Arts World," said Eve. "Yes, it's down by Taco Bell. I do know about it. But it's not so much a bookstore as it is, well, a bohemian shop."

Alex gave Mr. Steiner one of his wry smiles. "That's what my mother calls the hippies—'bohemians.'"

Mr. Steiner smiled and looked at Eve, "So it won't be competition for you, then?"

"Oh, no," she said with a laugh. "I peeked inside his shop just last week—out of curiosity. So many colorful clothes and strange incense smells and items that I can't even begin to name. As far as books, the odd title, *Psychedelic Prayers*, seems to be their best seller."

"Hmph," said Alex. "'Only in California,' as they say."

Just then Eve caught sight of the high-haired lady and her daughter as they were leaving. She waved to them, and they all exchanged hearty Happy New Year good-byes.

"I really have to get going now," said Alex. "Nice meeting you Mr.—"

"Call me Sam, please, and that goes for you too, Eve," he said turning to the proprietor. "I don't like this Mr. Steiner business. Maybe for New York, but it's too formal and stuffy for California. Besides, it makes me feel like the old man that I am."

Alex chuckled. "All right then, Sam. See you later." He waved as he left, the bell jangling after him.

Eve turned to walk Mr. Steiner—Sam—to his favorite table at the back of the shop, the Van Gogh table, which displayed a postcard-size print of Van Gogh's *Irises* under the glass top.

"Your son has that film star kind of face," Sam said with a smile.

"I know. I'm terribly afraid it will dawn on him someday."

Sam laughed. "By the way," he said as he pulled out a chair, "I've almost finished *The Naked and the Dead*. You were right about matching me up with Norman Mailer." He paused, holding onto the back of the chair. "In fact, I could use some more of your advice on what to read next. If you have the time, that is." He paused again. "Would you have a cup of tea with me?" He gestured to the empty seat across from him. "Is that kosher—for the proprietor to sit down with a customer?"

"I'd love to. My feet would be especially thrilled," Eve said with a nervous chuckle. "Let me just get the tea, or perhaps Karen will—" She looked around for her employee. "I think Karen is on break. I'll just be a minute with the tea, and then we'll have a sit down. And talk books."

* * *

"It's true. Tea can change a person's whole life," said Eve to Sam Steiner after a half hour of talking about everything but books. "Take me, for example. My happiest memories of England are of drinking tea on the Strand while discussing Simone de Beauvoir with other women—women who actually wanted to converse about things beyond child rearing tips and recipes for puddings. That started the whole thing, really, the entirely impractical dream of this shop."

"And that's why you decided, at long last, to paint your dream?" Sam placed his cup on the saucer and looked directly at her.

"*Paint* my dream?" She set down her own teacup and inclined her head.

"Sure," he said, "like your Van Gogh here." He pointed to the print of purple irises under the glass table top. "Vincent—that's how he signed his paintings—he said something like, 'I dream of painting and then I paint my dream.'"

Eve took in the words as if they were Belgium chocolate. She repeated the phrase back to Sam as if that would make it last. "I like that, Sam. I thought I knew all the pithy Van Gogh quotes, but I somehow missed that one. I think I'll put it under the glass, next to his *Irises*." Eve smiled into eyes that smiled back.

"And speaking of art . . ." Sam said, and then paused to pour himself another cup.

He started to refill her cup, but she placed a hand over it. "I feel like I'm swimming in tea. And speaking of art . . . ?" she prodded.

Sam nodded and gestured with his cup toward the tea display behind the counter. "The tea wall over there—I see you've added several new pieces."

The "tea wall," which separated the main room from the kitchen, hosted various teapots, teacups, and a variety of tea accoutrements, all for sale. The china pieces from estate sales, jumble sales, and antique shops, were deftly intermingled with tea tins from Taylors of Harrogate, Twinings, and PG Tips, all of which sold so well that the shelves were always revolving and changing. Eve was particularly proud of her present display.

"Yes," she said, glancing at the shelves as if she had not seen them before. "The teapots are from an antique shop in Orange, and the new cups and saucers are from an estate sale in Newport Beach. Do you like them?"

Sam Steiner took a sip of tea and looked toward the tea wall again, as if pondering the question. Finally, he sat down his Lenox cup and pushed back his chair to stand. "Well, let's have a look-see." He moved toward the display and studied the assembled lot with arms crossed, tilting his head to one side and then to the other.

"Something's not right," he said shaking his head. Mr. Steiner exhibited a starkly candid style in his talk and gestures, as if his main philosophy might be "tell it like it is." While it might feel a bit hard hitting—as it did now—she was nevertheless drawn to it. So many of her erstwhile friends in Beverly Hills had smothered her with compliments they didn't mean or promises they never intended to keep. Sam Steiner's manner seemed more forthright, truthful (even if it did smart a little).

"If I were you," he said in the thoughtful manner of a professional, "I would set the orange cups right next to the pink teapot, see? That one on the right."

"Really?" asked Eve with raised eyebrows. "Bright orange next to the rose?"

"Oh, definitely. And I would separate the cups—all of them —from their respective teapots."

"Really?"

"Sure. Mix 'em up. Like you do when you mismatch the cups and saucers for customers."

Eve felt her insides smiling. He had noticed this little thing.

"A display of perfect harmony will be pleasant enough, sure," he went on, "but it won't provoke much interest. It's the contrast you want. Like your English flower gardens that I always hear about, the ones that mix up all the colors in a hodgepodge. It's the hodgepodge that people like, a dash of dissonance here and there. That's the thing about art, Eve. It's the surprises that make it interesting. And if you want people to buy on impulse, then you have to appeal to their more creative, even whimsical sides."

"I see. Yes, of course. You have both artistic and business sense, Mr. Steiner. Would you care to help me re-arrange the display? Do you have to hurry home?" She immediately wished she had held her tongue. This was so inappropriate, and he might even have a wife waiting.

"Only if you call me Sam. I really wish you would call me Sam."

Eve remembered his request, but it was hard to change once you called someone by a certain name, and "Mr. Steiner" felt . . . *safe*.

"Sam it is, of course." Eve looked back toward the starburst clock above the door, and then turned to Karen, who had just appeared carrying a sponge to clean the tables.

"There you are, Karen. You may lock the door now, but Mr.

Steiner—Sam—will be staying past for a few minutes to help out with the tea display."

Karen shifted from one foot to the other.

"It's all right, Karen, you can go on home. I don't want to keep you late if you have to be somewhere."

Karen's eyebrows furrowed into a near pleading look.

"Are you feeling all right, dear?"

"Can I talk with you . . . in the kitchen?"

Eve shrugged an apology toward Sam. "I'll just be a minute."

"Eve," said Karen over the washed teapots, "I'm feeling kind of nauseous. I've been running back and forth between the kitchen and the bathroom. Sorry you had to make your own tea."

"You should have told me you weren't well. I would have made you go upstairs and lie down, or sent you home—"

"I'm better now." Karen took a deep breath. "Eve, I've been trying to tell you all afternoon, but the time was never right. But now I just have to." She paused. "I'm going to have to leave the shop. My husband says that I need to stay home now."

"Now?"

Karen nodded. "Now that I'm expecting."

"Expecting? Karen, that's brilliant news! Why didn't you tell me?"

"Well, it's just that I wasn't sure, not until yesterday. Steve and I talked about it last night, and he really wants me to quit work. But it's a great afternoon job and I know you'll have no trouble finding a replacement." She took another breath. "Sorry about the short notice."

Eve van Gelder barely knew what to say, given that she had long suspected Karen's husband to be quite domineering. She imagined him in her mind, a humorless man with squinty eyes and a rather droopy moustache. He had only been in the shop twice in all the months his wife worked here. Eve grimaced at

the thought of him. She started to say, *But what do you want,
Karen?* but she held her tongue.

"Well, dear, if you think you need to leave, then . . . when?
When do you plan on leaving us?"

"Today, actually. I have to leave you today."

Chapter Four

Madeline re-sharpened her Number 2 pencil for the third time, as if the perfect point would produce the perfect word. But all that emerged from the chaos of her scribblings were three lines, which was apropos, she thought, given that it had been three days since the phone call, i.e., the final blow that had precipitated the collapse—was she being too dramatic?—of her entire world.

> Teetering now, cracking, falling, smashing—
> uprooted by death's indiscriminate fury,
> the forest has been assaulted . . .

She winced at the words and rested the pencil on her old homework desk. The pencil instantly rolled off the edge in defeat. *Absolute crap.* She could do better. Hadn't she written poetry in college? Hadn't Ben called her anti-war poetry "insightful and passionate"? But try as she might, her personality was not cut out for the "poor-me-ness" of confessional poetry, apparently the only poetry people wrote these days.

It all seemed to her like self-absorbed muck; or in the case of the ultra popular, clean cut, V-neck-sweatered Rod McKuen, *sentimental* muck. All the really good poets were dead, she thought. Well, not all. There was Robert Lowell. She liked Lowell, especially since he had joined the anti-war voices. And of course Ginsberg was still going strong, albeit balding and paunchy, ringing little Buddhist bells and *Ommming* the world into a great Oneness. Another of the Beat generation writers,

Jack Kerouac, had disintegrated into alcoholism. But he had already lost favor at the Berkeley coffee houses because of his falling out with Ginsberg, calling the chubby, middle-aged poet "unpatriotic" for protesting the war. Alcoholism could be tolerated; calling Ginsberg names would not.

Poetry was a form of protest, she had always believed, that is, if it ever got beyond the self-absorption that seemed to be infiltrating her generation. Other than those insightful few who could see beyond their own navels, people basically wrote cathartic crap—like the words staring back at her.

But then she was not trying to be some great poet, was she? She was just the sister of a dead soldier, trying not to implode. She put her needle-sharp pencil to the paper.

> *Engulfed by the indifferent surge,*
> *I fall into pieces of questions and laments that drift—*

The pencil lead snapped, breaking off a huge chunk. But it didn't matter. This was crap all right, but at least it was honest crap. *Put your pain on the page*—isn't that how Ben put it?—so you can observe it rather than just be tossed about by it. But it sure as hell wasn't working now.

"Maddy! Breakfast!" Kate Prescott's authoritarian voice from the bottom of the stairs sounded just as it had when Madeline was a kid. Was she, then, back where she started? Had her life in Berkeley been nothing but a dream?

She tossed her would-be poem on the lead shavings in the trash and leaned back on the hard desk chair, fighting the urge for a cigarette. She could, she sighed, sum up her thoughts in one word: *driftwood*. Why not just say it? *I feel like a pathetic piece of driftwood*. Not as sexy as Dylan's "Rolling Stone," but it had truth going for it.

She thought of the driftwood at Crystal Cove when she would visit Grandpa Abel and Grandma Daisy at their beach cottage. She and Sean would gather up the smaller pieces, so smooth and cool and hard—almost like stone. And there were the mysterious bamboo pieces that came from god-knows-where. Sean had said China and Madeline, being the big sister, insisted on Japan. Neither of them knew exactly where these countries were on the globe, but they were only playing—brother and sister under the endless sun, building driftwood forts by the sea.

But maybe the problem was the metaphor, she reasoned, tapping her pencil on the desk; something was wrong with the metaphor. Driftwood doesn't have much self-determination. Existentialism is lost on driftwood. But she wasn't saying she was, in fact, driftwood; only that she *felt* like driftwood.

Or maybe she was thinking about driftwood simply because she was missing the feel of the actual wood in her hands. Of course! Missing Crystal Cove. Missing her grandmother. *Missing her brother.*

She slumped back into the chair, closed her eyes, and replayed yesterday's memorial service in her mind. She felt herself there, in the newly cushioned pews of New Hope Baptist Church, surrounded by people she knew and didn't know. The service was for Sean, the person, rather than Sean, the soldier, since the official military funeral was yet to come. The memorial had focused on the tight end on the football team at Anaheim High School; the little boy in Sunday School; the son, the brother, the freckle-faced friend. It was a tough two hours, which was how long the service itself took given all the mourners who kept popping up out of their seats to offer an affectionate anecdote, reinforcing in her the sad fact that she didn't know the adult Sean as they did. If only she had spent more time with him these last few years.

So many regrets.

Madeline wondered what her own funeral would be like—given her root-less, friend-less, god-less life at the moment. She stopped herself. She couldn't go down *that* road and survive this. Maybe someday she could rewrite her crappy poem, so that she was not so helpless like a teetering tree, toppling into the ocean, but grounded and . . . free. Like an Existentialist: thrown into the world to create one's own meaning. She had felt the thrill of the word "free-will" when Professor Franzwa had batted it around. How liberating it had sounded, opening up all kinds of possibilities that Pavlov's Dog and Clarence Darrow's determinism had tried to squash.

But now the concept of free-will felt very much like anxiety. If every choice you made was completely free, she reasoned, then how could a person function without being overwhelmed with anxiety? And guilt, too. Existentialists, with all their giddy freedom, must feel heaps upon heaps of guilt, because at least half your choices were probably the wrong choices. Hurtful choices. Insensitive choices. Stupid choices. Like getting involved with a guy who looks like Trotsky.

Madeline could use just a little fatalism at the moment. Then she wouldn't feel the need to do anything but lie in bed and eat one See's chocolate after another while Fate worked away in the night. And she couldn't feel guilty at all, since whatever she did—eat bon-bons until she popped or write a great poem— would have been determined beforehand, if not by God, then by the mechanism of a cold, closed universe.

She shivered. She would have to find out if those were the only two options—unfettered free-will or cold, hard determinism. One produced anxiety; the other, apathy. Wasn't there something in-between, and a tad more . . . hopeful? If so, she'd like to fall into that crack right now. Maybe she would land on some new way of seeing herself and the world. It would sure beat falling like a teetering tree into an ocean of massive heartbreak. And hopelessness.

Hope was at stake here. Hope, for God's sake. *How could she save hope?*

She began to tear up against her will. Sean was gone and she was left behind, the child who seemed to disappoint—

Stop! she chided herself. Grief was one thing, but self-pity was inexcusable. Grief she could not control, but self-pity was a choice (or at the very least, a perceived choice). All philosophical issues aside, the grim reality was this: She, Madeline Prescott, must face this monstrous loss of hers without Mike, without Berkeley. Without her identity.

Who was she now, anyway?

She felt a slight constriction in her chest. She sat up and breathed slowly. Once she felt her breathing under control, she tried another technique Ben had taught her. Inhale for seven seconds; exhale for ten. She counted: *1-2-3* . . . As she breathed out the numbers silently, she affirmed inwardly that she was the granddaughter of Daisy Prescott, and that would never change; it was something to hang on to. "Self-pity is our *worst* enemy," Daisy would always say, never failing to quote Helen Keller at the first sign of whining. Grandma Daisy's reverence for Helen Keller was a thing you knew and understood and respected. She had taken Madeline, as a young teen, to see *The Miracle Worker* on stage in Los Angeles, and then again to the movie theatre to see Patty Duke play this brave little girl.

Grandma Daisy was on her mind often these days—the Grandma Daisy of her childhood that is, not the bent, arthritic shell of a woman from the year or two before her death. She remembered her now as the honey-haired, energetic woman who loved to read and hike in Laguna Canyon and quote famous people. She had said that to get herself "out of the doldrums" she would read quotations from people whom she admired, like Eleanor Roosevelt or Anne Morrow Lindbergh, and of course, Helen Keller. Madeline remembered how Grandma Daisy would send her greeting cards featuring famous quotations, for no particular occasion. She still had one hanging on the pegboard in this very room. She sat up in her chair and looked at it as if for the first time. It was a picture of a smiling woman in a huge red hat. Underneath was a quote by William

James,

> *To change one's life: Start immediately. Do it flamboyantly.*

Now that is what Grandma Daisy would do. Madeline slipped on her soft chenille robe and her pink slippers and breathed in the faint smell of Folger's wafting up the stairs. Perhaps today would be survivable after all.

* * *

John Prescott sat at the kitchen table, still looking pale and very much his own closed universe, but he managed a ghost of a smile for his eldest daughter. He handed her a section of the *Santa Ana Register.* Sean had made the front page earlier in the week, and now the spotlight rested on a young man from Tustin, Lt. Robert G. Jones, who was "killed in action," a catch-all for horrors best left unimagined.

"Is Jilli up?" asked Madeline, filled with a sudden need for her sister's buoyancy.

"She's still asleep," her father said without looking up.

Madeline thought of her little sister asleep in her room—a tiny sanctuary filled with Monkees' posters and Flower Power Barbie Dolls—dreaming of her "sort of" boyfriend. An awkward age, thirteen.

"Oh, there you are," said Kate Prescott as she emerged from the downstairs bathroom wearing her coffee-stained robe, which should have been burned ages ago (along with her pill box hat). "The egg casserole from Mrs. Gregory is warming in the oven."

"I don't think I can handle eggs this morning," said Madeline. "Maybe just some of Mrs. Mahaney's poppy seed bread and a cup of coffee. But I'll get it, Mom."

Kate lifted a hand to stop her daughter. "I need to keep busy or I won't make it." Madeline's mother retrieved the foil-wrapped poppy seed bread from the refrigerator and set it on the table. "I still can't get over the crowd yesterday at the church. I've never seen the church that full, even on Easter." Her voice wavered.

John said something in acknowledgment, but Madeline had already burrowed into the paper, studying the classified section.

Kate brought over the coffee pot, and Madeline could hear her sniffling, fighting emotion.

"Drink it while it's hot," John Prescott said to his daughter. He poured himself a cup and reached to fill his daughter's cup before returning to the business section of *The Register*. He paid no attention to his wife—who was, just then, pulling a wadded Kleenex from the pocket of her robe.

Madeline took in the familiar scene of two people on opposite sides of the emotional universe, but learned long ago that she could not do a single thing about it. Except get away from it. Escape. Which is why she shut out everything but the classifieds before her. She took a sip of coffee while her eyes scanned the job openings in Orange County, with an eye to anything near Crystal Cove, where a cottage sat empty—waiting for her.

There was an ad for a secretary in a Fullerton insurance office, a pet store clerk in Tustin, and a vague entrepreneurial opportunity for "energetic self-starters" at an unknown location in Huntington Beach. She sighed, imagining her own post: *Berkeley graduate seeking minimum wage job.* But her finger pressed onward down the page. A tiny ad caught her attention, a part-time job, afternoon hours, at Van Gelder's Tea and Books in downtown Laguna Beach. (*Perfect.* Five minutes—maybe ten to downtown—from Crystal Cove.) The job would involve general assistance with books and the serving of tea and scones. Tea and *what?*

"What in the hell—I mean heck—are scones?" she asked no one in particular.

"I think they're like biscuits, but with raisins or currents or something," her mother said, evidently in control of herself now. "Why do you ask?" Kate turned from cutting the egg casserole (as if someone would actually eat it).

"Have you heard of Van Gelder's Tea and Books in Laguna? They serve scones there."

Kate looked interested. "I remember seeing something about it in *The Register* awhile back—a review I think. I've been meaning to try it out, but I never get down to Laguna anymore now that Daisy's gone and your Grandpa isn't at the cottage." Kate's voice trailed off as she sipped her coffee. With sudden crescendo, she added, "And why is that of any interest to you? Good heavens, Maddy. How can you think of scones with a refrigerator full of cakes and breads?"

Madeline's father spoke from the depths of the sport's page. "Aren't scones just a little too *bourgeois* for Madeline Prescott?"

(Did her dad just say 'bourgeois'?) "Dad, I'm impressed," she said with a smile. "You must be a New Lefty after all."

"Not on your life," he said with a snort. And he meant it. In a strange way, Madeline felt comforted by this remark. Her father was a Goldwater Republican and that was that. She abhorred his politics, but at least she could count on it—their polar opposite views on everything—and she needed *something* to count on at the moment.

The kitchen settled into quiet now, with only the ticking of the grandfather clock from the hallway. Madeline stared at the ad; the job had possibility. She had experience with the coffee house at Berkeley. Yes, it could work. *It must work.* She knew she couldn't stay long in the depressing atmosphere of her parents' home. And she couldn't return to Berkeley—that was out of the question. The cottage at Crystal Cove would give her proximity to Jilli and her parents, yet space enough for herself.

"I need to call Grandpa," Madeline blurted into the silence.

Kate looked up from a little church devotional book, one that she kept tucked in the napkin holder. "Maddy, yesterday was hard on your Grandpa. He's very fragile, especially his mind. Couldn't it wait?"

"Sorry, I keep forgetting about Grandpa's mind, but I have

an idea that I think you and Daddy might like." (Would calling him "Daddy" help?) "I just need to get Grandpa's okay . . . or yours, I suppose."

"Oh?" her father said, attempting to rouse himself from the Dow Jones Industrial Average.

"I know you don't think much of my Berkeley connections"—she shifted in her seat—"and frankly, at the moment, I don't either." Kate and John glanced at each other. "In fact, I thought I'd send for my things. I don't have much there, really, just some clothes and albums and a few odds and ends." She felt hot and flustered as she spoke. Not wanting to reveal too much—the hurt was still raw—she jumped to the point with all the dignity she could muster. "What I'm trying to say is that I think I need to stay in this area for the time being."

Kate closed her devotional book and leaned back in her chair. "Maddy! You're really not going back to Berkeley? But what about—"

"Mom," Madeline interrupted. She could not bear to hear the name of the man—that whining, self-absorbed, round-spectacled louse of a man. "I can't go back *now*, when we don't even know when the service will be. I mean, the military one." She wanted to say the one with all the guns and flags and, well, the body. The casket. *The remains.* But all this seemed too brutal for the tender morning sunlight streaming through the kitchen window. "I *have* to be here for that. And besides, I've been thinking about . . . the cottage."

"The cottage?" Kate raised one round eyebrow. Madeline could see that her mother was pleased. Kate Prescott sipped her coffee with a careful show of nonchalance, trying to hide a ghost of a smile behind the cup.

What was her mother thinking? That her lost-sheep-of-a-daughter might finally be coming home?

"You want to go down to the cottage this time of year?" her father asked, folding the business section and looking directly at his daughter. He was fully engaged with her for the first time since the tragic news.

Madeline was pleased that she was being taken seriously. "I know the cottage has been empty for a while, and I could take care of it."

"For how long?" her mother asked.

"For a while. I don't know. I could work somewhere nearby, just for a few months. Maybe even through the summer, or until I figure out what I want to do next. What do you think, Daddy?"

Her father folded his arms and sat back in his chair. She held her breath while he tapped his fingers against his arm, a familiar gesture that reminded Madeline of more carefree days. Before the world fell in.

Kate took advantage of the pause. "Maddy, you can't just stumble around in low-paying jobs all your life. We didn't pay for you to have a first-rate education in order for you to—"

John raised a hand to silence his wife, an authoritarian gesture that normally annoyed Madeline; but not now that the argument was going her way.

"You know," he said looking at his daughter, "that actually sounds like a good idea. For once, you're making sense." Her father looked pleased. Was it because of Grandpa's cottage? Or was it because he could finally get his wayward daughter away from what he called "that mad crowd up in Berkeley"?

"So it's a yes? Do you think Grandpa would mind?"

He shook his head. "Grandpa's mind isn't up to thinking about it. But it would ease my mind. There are squatters to worry about, and with all those goddamned hippies around Laguna—" He shot his wife an apologetic glance. "Sorry, Kate."

Kate offered a moral wince but seemed otherwise unscathed.

He looked back at his daughter. "All right, Maddy. The cottage is yours, at least until you figure out something on that teaching certificate, or whatever you're going to do with your life."

Madeline smiled. "I promise to take good care of it . . . for Grandpa." Was she sounding too happy so soon after the memorial service? She calmed her voice. "And Jilli could come down and visit. And you, too—both of you." She looked back and forth between her parents. She took a sip of hot Folger's and sliced a hearty hunk of poppy seed bread. "Who knows?" she said, throwing a smile at her father, "I might even take up a liking for scones."

Chapter Five

The ad in the paper said to apply in person—probably, Madeline thought, to weed out the hippie types. A whimsical image of Jerry Rubin and Abbie Hoffman serving tea to blue-haired ladies and Orange County debutants entertained her while she dressed. She slid on her forest green A-line dress with a back zipper that required acrobatic feat to zip without help. One last tug and it was done. Except for the hook and eye clasp at the top, which she would forgo. She had brought the dress from Berkeley in anticipation of a New Year's party, but instead wore it to Sean's memorial service. The zipper felt cold against her skin.

She borrowed her mother's three-inch heels, a half-size smaller than her own, and they pinched in the toes. Still, they added height (a faux confidence at best). She brushed back her mass of curls, tied on a cream silk scarf, and stood at the mirror, turning this way and that.

Bourgeois, indeed.

Nervously, she smoothed on a coat of peach lip gloss with her fingers, the extent of her normal make-up routine. But her mother had again come to the rescue with a make-up bag full of items Madeline could not even name. Her eyes, puffy from a week's worth of crying, could use a little something. She applied mascara; her eyes immediately began to water. *Great.* She dabbed at the resulting smudges and stood back to assess the damage. Definitely a Maybelline challenge. She rifled through the odds and ends in the bag to find sky-blue eye shadow, but paused. Given her half-swollen lids, she imagined it would only accentuate them. Better go light with the makeup and just smile a lot. Teeth were the only thing in the world, it seemed, unaffected by grief.

* * *

The drive through Laguna Canyon in her yellow VW Bug felt like heaven—that is, if heaven existed. But it *must* exist, Madeline thought, so that she could see Sean again. And Grandma Daisy, too. Of course heaven must exist. But would God have to be there? How about Pastor Bob and the Brugeman twins? But that sounded more like hell in Sartre's play, *No Exit*: trapped in a windowless room with people who endlessly point out your transgressions.

She mused on what "to-each-his-own" Pastor Bob's heaven would look like. The Blacks would have a separate-but-equal heaven, equal being a euphemism for "not really equal" because everybody knows God is white. The Catholics would be the janitors and cooks, that is, if they made it in at all. For according to Pastor Bob, only the "saved" would get through the Pearly Gates. But saved from what? From thinking too much? From other points of view? In Pastor Bob's mind, all the Jews would be left outside, pounding on the door. She thought of Ben Schwartz, the wisest person she had ever known. Such people would be damned forever in Pastor Bob's heaven. That would mean—if you thought about it—that God must look a lot like Hitler. But then, she sighed, we were back to the evils of thinking too hard.

Shaking off the image of Pastor Bob's Third Reich heaven, she tapped the steering wheel to the sounds of *Sgt. Pepper's* on her eight-track player. Another thought struck her. What about reincarnation? That idea was now gaining ground in the West after The Beatles' trip to India. But that was hardly comforting, given that Sean might return as someone else (or something else). And the few friends she had at Berkeley who believed in that stuff were just too weird to take seriously. But, she sighed, who was she to say what was weird? She was ignorant on these matters, and didn't everything seem weird to an ignorant person?

A red corvette careened around a bend in the road, going too fast for this dangerous stretch. Her heart skipped a beat and she focused again on her surroundings, deep in the heart of Laguna Canyon with its sudden rush of hills and grazing cattle. She always forgot what it was like to come upon this place after driving the busy freeway. The sudden change hit her like something out of *Star Trek*, as if she were driving through a worm hole in her little VW Bug and discovering a whole new universe on the other side. She understood why the hippies chose Laguna Canyon for their hideout from the world. She imagined those communes tucked away in the hills with women tending gardens in long granny dresses and beads while the men, with their unwashed hair and scraggly beards, chopped firewood. She preferred this Rousseau-like image to the more likely reality: stoned college drop-outs tripping on dirty mattresses on the floor.

Passing the Laguna Art Institute on the right, she knew she was getting closer to the town itself, and to the beach. And to heaven on earth. She could smell it: the salty clean air, already beginning to cleanse all the sorrows from her soul. She changed gears to accommodate the traffic on Broadway and caught sight of the familiar boardwalk. And just beyond it, the wild sea dressed up in liquid azure blue.

That first glimpse of the sea always had an effect on her, an overwhelming sinking into serenity—even joy. Any ocean view would probably do, but Laguna Beach had a special effect on everyone, like fairy dust. The "Jewel of Orange County" was not only the most picturesque beach in Southern California; it was also a refuge for free spirits. Painters set up canvas here. Artists, writers, free-thinkers—even Democrats—were welcomed here.

As traffic slowed she glanced around. A woman in a fringed jacket and straight black hair came out of a shop and flashed a peace sign at the man in the car in front of her. The car, a midnight blue '66 Mustang, honked and the peace sign was returned. Madeline reached to turn up the volume on her stereo. *What would you think if I sang out of tune* . . . . She hummed along with John Lennon and Paul McCartney and felt her confidence surge. Nine times out of ten her sudden capricious decisions were disasters, but not this time. *Not this time.*

She parked on Broadway, fed the meter, and walked down the sidewalk past an overpriced surf shop. She hesitated at the door of her destination and looked around. She knew nothing about scones. Or tea. *What in the hell was she thinking?* She heard a familiar voice in the distance. She looked in the direction of Forrest Avenue.

Mr. Larsen, The Greeter of Laguna, stood on his corner like a sunbeam in motion. Waving wildly to a passerby with one hand, he leaned heavily on a cane with the other. Eiler Larsen was a local gardener by morning and "The Greeter" by afternoon. From the looks of him now, frail and stooped, he was probably long retired from planting and weeding. He had been a fixture in Laguna for as long as she could remember, a magical wizard-like character in her childhood. He had taken the place of old Joe Lucas, Laguna's first Greeter, a Portuguese fisherman who only spoke English by swearing (so goes the story). But gentle Mr. Larsen came clear from Denmark, spoke several languages fluently, and recited poetry to children.

Vowing to stop by and say hello afterward, she smiled and opened the door to Van Gelder's Tea and Books. Greeted by the homey jingle of a bell, she was immediately taken-in—even enticed—by the smell of recent baking mingled with the pleasant mustiness of old books. The rectangular room was lined with oak book shelves, filled nearly to capacity, a library ladder at one end. Sandwiched cozily between the long walls of books were tables dressed in bright blue linen cloths and adorned with canary yellow sugar bowls in the center of each. The glass tops laid over the blue linen would surely make easy clean-up (her practical mind mused).

At the far end of the long room was a counter on which sat a large glass cake stand filled with what must be the scones— looking less forbidding than she imagined. At the other end of the counter sat a basket filled with colorful packets and a sign that read, with British spelling, "Favourite British Biscuits." Next to the basket sat an empty oriental vase. Behind the counter and the cash register was a wall of display shelves filled a dazzling array of china pieces, all mixed up, as if playing a joke on your eyes.

While the Berkeley coffee house was very groovy with its Jefferson Airplane posters, it did lack in aesthetics. But this shop exuded an artistic, even loving, attention to detail. There was a touch of the feminine here; not the frilly, cloying kind, but tasteful and intelligent.

The woman behind the counter was busy showing a couple something from the display—a china teacup, it appeared. They were asking questions, giving Madeline time to peruse the shop.

She noticed a young man with a Beatle hair cut and a Nehru jacket hunched over one of the back tables near the library ladder. A consumptive-looking poet type, he looked up shyly and offered an awkward smile before returning to his yellow legal pad. Yes, she thought in amazement, this is definitely a place to write or read and let the whole world—its napalm bombs and riots and heartbreaks—disappear.

She meandered, examining the bookshelves, since the woman, presumably the owner, was occupied. She let her fingers feel the binding of a beautiful book by Steinbeck on display in a section called "California Writers." As she was about to pick up the volume, she heard a hello that sounded more like "Hallo" from behind the counter.

Madeline turned to see the woman craning her neck to see around the tall man in front of the counter. "I'll be with you in moment. Please, make yourself at home." The woman's tidy dark hair hosted a few dramatic waves of gray that, on her, only added to her olive-skinned elegance. She spoke with an English accent, a polished one at that, but with a subtle Germanic edge— Dutch, Madeline surmised from the name on the door.

She pulled out a chair at a window table and sat down to observe the quotes under the glass top, all printed neatly by hand on white paper, standing out against the blue cloth. (Oh, wouldn't Grandma Daisy love this?) But her eyes were drawn first to a clipping from the *Santa Ana Register* dated January 20, 1967, a review article titled, "Van Gelder's Tea and Books: An inviting mix of old world charm and casual California warmth."

After perusing the flattering review, she noticed next to the clipping a quote from *Portrait of a Lady* by Henry James.

> *There are few hours in life more agreeable than the hour dedicated to the ceremony known as afternoon tea.*

Henry James. Wasn't he the brother of William James, her Grandmother's sage of "flamboyance"? If she weren't an agnostic, she would swear that this must be a sign from some-where that she was on to something.

She overheard the woman with the intriguing accent telling a story that ended with, "The poor woman thought she was buying a teakettle. When I told her, 'No, dear, this is a teapot,' she said, 'So, what's the difference?'" This was evidently hilarious, given the guffaw. Madeline's stomach clinched. What exactly *did* make a teapot different from a teakettle? There would be a test on this, she was sure.

For a moment she toyed with the idea of just being a customer. She could look for a job somewhere else, maybe the surf shop next door. But before she could decide what to do, the woman emerged from behind the counter, accompanying the smiling couple to the door. She wore a butter yellow turtleneck sweater and a flowing skirt of green and yellow flowers. Her shoes were casual—low-heeled—unlike Madeline's three-inch heels. She suddenly felt awkward with her too-small borrowed shoes, her toes nearly numb.

The woman, presumably Mrs. Van Gelder, had an air about her, an air of intelligence and graciousness. A sense of confidence. A sense of herself. She was a happy woman, yes, a woman who (unlike herself) knew exactly what she was about in this world. And as the bell on the door jingled farewell to the customers, the woman's self-possessed brown eyes turned their attention to Madeline.

"Sorry to keep you waiting," she smiled. "What beautiful hair! Can I get you a cup of tea?"

Madeline returned the smile. "No thanks. I mean, that would be nice, but I'm here because I saw your ad in *The Register*."

The woman stopped short, as if surprised. "Oh, yes, of course. The advertisement . . . I'm just surprised to get such a speedy response." She smiled warmly. "Why don't you come back with me to my favorite table and we can talk between customers. I'm afraid it's the best I can do at the moment."

"Thank you, Mrs.—"

"Not 'Mrs.' Not any more. Call me, Eve, please. Eve van Gelder. I'm the owner. And you are—?"

"Madeline Prescott."

Once seated at a cozy table near the back, the woman asked, "And are you from around here, Madeline? I would have remembered the hair, I'm sure."

Madeline blushed, fully aware of her ice-breaker hair. "I'm from Anaheim. Originally, anyway. Then I went to school at UC Berkeley, and now I'm going to be living here. Or actually, at Crystal Cove."

"Crystal Cove? You mean the *plein air* artist haven just down the road, with all those quaint cottages? I know people—artists, especially—who would beg, borrow, or steal for one of those beach cottages." Apparently intrigued, the woman crossed her arms on the table and inclined her head, eyes bright and probing. "So, my dear, what possessed you to answer my ad?"

Madeline swallowed hard. "Well, I need a part-time job for at least a few months. Maybe longer. It's hard to say because I'm . . . well, I'm in transition. For the time being, anyway." She wondered if she sounded like some kind of directionless flake. Like a hippie from Laguna Canyon. Like a rolling stone. Like her pathetic driftwood metaphor. But she couldn't tell this stranger about her brother. Not yet. "I don't have much experience with tea *per se*," she continued, mustering a confident tone (and didn't *per se* make her sound sophisticated?), "but I worked at a coffee house in Berkeley, so I know about serving customers."

"A coffee house in Berkeley? I'd like to hear all about that. Were there poets and folk singers?"

"Oh, yeah, a lot of folk singers. Joan Baez was there, more than once."

"Really?"

The woman was easily impressed, thought Madeline with relief.

Eve van Gelder then asked about her studies at Berkeley and plans and dreams for the future. She told the woman, who reminded her just a bit of Audrey Hepburn (what was it? her carriage? her accent?) all about her undergraduate studies in history and her current interest in philosophy. When it came to future plans, all she could muster was, "I'm not sure yet. It all depends . . ."

While Madeline was striving (and failing spectacularly) to articulate her goals for the future, she heard the bell jingle. She looked around to see the towering figure of the Greeter making his way through the door, hook-handled cane in one hand and a bouquet of flowers in the other. His long mass of white hair flowed down to his shoulders in a wild disarray; the unruly beard took it from there, adding another ten inches or so of snowy white eccentricity. One would almost expect someone like that to wear flowing robes, too, like the gurus of Haight-Ashbury. But Mr. Larsen could not be pigeonholed so easily. He wore slightly baggy brown trousers with an equally loose jacket that always, *always* bore a fresh flower in the buttonhole of his lapel. Today it was a red carnation.

The flowers he carried were bright white daisies. She wondered rather wistfully if the daisies might be another sign from Grandma Daisy that this was the right place for her. (Signs from the afterworld? Was she suddenly turning into some far-out mystic? At this rate, she'd be wearing beads and Birkenstocks by Easter.)

"Helloooo!" the Greeter bellowed. Mr. Larsen's "hello" always stretched out like verbal taffy. Madeline smiled back and waved, as if still a child. Did he remember her? Surely not. He had scads of kids around him all the time.

"Hello to you, Mr. Larsen." Eve greeted the old man like a VIP, standing with a quick "excuse me for a moment" look at Madeline.

Mr. Larsen moved toward the counter with a mixture of elderly fragility and childlike ebullience. "Beauty for the beautiful!" he said, handing them to Eve with a slight bow.

"Ah, brilliant," Eve said with a sigh of satisfaction. "It's a day for daisies." She took the flowers to the counter and placed them gingerly in the oriental vase. "I'll need to add some water. Have a seat with us, Mr. Larsen. I'll just get you a chair."

The Greeter turned to Madeline. "I remember you, young lady. Where on this good earth have you been?"

"I've been away at school, Mr. Larsen. Berkeley."

"Berkeley," he said and paused, looking as if that reminded

him of a story. "You know, I went through there on my travels. I lived up in Carmel for a bit."

"Really?"

"Ever heard of Robinson Jeffers? Built a house up in Carmel. Met him once."

"The poet? He's huge in Berkeley. In fact, he's enjoying a revival right now, especially among the anti-war poets."

"Is that right?" The Greeter tilted his head as if his interest in the matter were piqued.

Eve brought the old man a chair and helped him settle into it, hooking his cane on the back of the chair. "Would you like your tea now?" Eve asked.

"In a moment, dear lady," he said.

Eve left to fill the vase and then joined them. The three of them chatted and laughed uninterrupted, except to wave good-bye to the writer who departed with a shy half-wave, yellow legal pad tucked protectively under his arm.

As it turned out, Mr. Larsen had indeed remembered Madeline, but he needed help with her name. It was, as she imagined, her hair that he remembered. They talked about the possible reasons for the scarcity of redheads in the area. Aside from the exotic women whose families came from Hawaii, the Far East, or Latin countries, all of whom tended toward the darkest hair colors, there was also a prevalence of very blonde women in Southern California.

"Partly the Germanic influence, don't you think?" Eve said. "Or could it be from your part of the world, Mr. Larsen— Denmark, isn't it?" Then she added, almost to herself, "But then, who really *is* blonde? I mean, it's hard sometimes to sort out the real blondes from the derivative ones."

Derivative ones? A strange choice of words. There was something in the older woman's voice that betrayed a strong aversion to unnatural blondes—just a subtle clip of her words.

Mr. Larsen told Madeline that his own hair had been red.

"Once. A long time ago. A *verrrry* long time ago," he said with another taffy stretch of a word, and then returned to the subject of poetry. "So, you say Robinson Jeffers is making a comeback up in Berkeley?"

"Well, he is at *my* coffee house," Madeline said. She realized her mistake instantly, a slip that might lead her possible future employer to think she may not have cut her ties with Berkeley. "I mean, the place where I used to work. When I lived in Berkeley. But I don't live there anymore." She felt herself stumble, but Mr. Larsen broke her fall—

"So, young lady, at this coffee house, you say they read all the old poets?"

"Blake, Emerson, Dickinson—they were all big, but the California poets like Robinson Jeffers reigned." She chuckled, "Whenever I heard a reading of his poetry, I'd get so caught up that I might forget what I was doing and spill the coffee."

Eiler Larsen roared with laughter, but Eve seemed pre-occupied and wandered from the table. Madeline wished she had not added that last bit. *Spill the coffee? Damn.*

Eve van Gelder returned with a hardback book, missing its jacket and beginning to wear on the binding. She set it down between Madeline and the Greeter. "I'll make some tea."

"Ah! This is one of Jeffers' best collections," Mr. Larsen said, opening the volume to the title page.

Madeline watched his sapphire eyes brighten and shimmer like the sea when the low sun turned the surface of the water into diamonds. With a kind of reverence, he turned the pages. His look of exquisite respect—eyes wide and hungry and shining—seemed to exclude everything around him. It fascinated her, the man and his poetry. Like a study in love. Wasn't the lover supposed to lose all peripheral vision for a time and toss everything else out the window and see stars, like the ones in Mr. Larsen's eyes? Perhaps then—and this one distracting thought intrigued her—she had never really been in love with Mike Riley. Nothing went out the window in favor of him; he was more of an add-on, really. In his presence, she never felt her own eyes turn into shining diamonds, or her face light up. (Nor did his, come to think of it.) She was not in love with Mike Riley and had never been; she knew that now, in this very instant. Here before her *was* true love, even if of a different sort: a bearded and ancient lover moving his old gardener's fingers across the pages of the beloved, touching the scattered words only lightly, with a tenderness that spoke of intimacy. She could not keep her eyes off him, even when Eve van Gelder returned with the tray of tea.

Mr. Larsen ignored the steaming tea in favor of these words, which he read aloud:

> *Does it matter whether you hate your . . . self? At*
> > *least*
> *love your eyes that can see, your mind that can*
> *hear music, the thunder of the wings. Love the wild*
> > *swan.*

Madeline felt the words float through her pores and settle lightly on her heart, as if Mr. Larsen had chosen these lines for her alone, as if he knew her inner need to get beyond her own skin. Beyond the suffocation of her grief. She felt a lump forming in her throat and disciplined it to behave, refusing to allow this moment to descend into mere emotion.

Mr. Larsen's voice, craggy and raspy with age, sent out sparks of something more than itself, something bright and hopeful and wise. His was a voice that seemed to know the words behind the words, a kind of spiritual knowing that she, Madeline Prescott, yearned for. For whatever this eccentric old man possessed—love, intimacy with words, faith in something beyond the tragedy of this life—this she must find and name for herself.

Chapter Six

"Hang on," Eve said into the phone, squeezing the receiver between her neck and shoulder while flipping through a tiny notebook. Alex would just have to wait. Hiring was her affair, her business, her decision, was it not? She had jotted down entries about each applicant, but it was the first one, the redhead, she wanted to tell him about. (Or was it to gloat that she had attracted a top class applicant with a degree from Berkeley?)

"All right, then," she continued, reviewing her scribbled words underneath the heading, The Redhead. "Yes, this one is well-educated, which means she's vastly overqualified and will probably move on to bigger and better things—teaching or something of the sort. But still, I was quite taken with her manners and her poise, and the way she interacted with Mr. Larsen. Not to mention, she has some actual experience behind her." Feeling the twinge of a headache coming on, she switched the phone to the other side. "Yes, I jotted down that she worked at a coffee house in Berkeley where they recite poetry and strum guitars, that sort of thing. But she doesn't look at all like a beatnik."

"Mum," Alex said with a chuckle. "I thought you called the hippies 'bohemians.' Now you're calling them 'beatniks?' You know that term went out with the Fifties."

"Didn't I say 'bohemian'?"

"No, you said, 'beatnik.'"

"Well, I meant bohemian," she said irritably. "I've just a bit of a headache, that's all." Eve's aggravation was more with herself than her son, for she prided herself on language. Her facility in language had bought a ticket to England; it had, in fact, saved her life. But since "the change," that odd euphemism women whispered among themselves, she felt these slips once in a while. Fatigue stalked her as well; and, on occasion, sauna-like sweats. Perhaps it would pass, she thought, but it was a nuisance. Just when she needed every last ounce of mental agility and physical strength to run her business—her "painted dream" (as Sam Steiner would put it)—her body seemed quite in revolt.

Eve gathered herself. "She—the redhead—is clever and quick and quite lovely. That's what I'm trying to tell you. She's perfect. Except . . ."

"Except what?"

"It's nothing really. Just that I picked up a kind of sadness in her eyes. Of course, I didn't want to pry, but I suspect it's grief. It's all in the eyes, you know." (And wasn't she an expert on the matter of grief?) "But, I must say, she has an extraordinary head of hair—gorgeous red curls. Not frizzy, like those ghastly home permanents. Madeline's hair—that's her name, Madeline Prescott—is utterly *au natural*. The color reminds me of a striking red-gold Laguna sunset."

"Hmph," said Alex. "So you're judging the applicants' qualifications by the color of their hair. Perfect."

She could picture him, shaking his head, rolling his eyes. She didn't mind, not really. Despite their prickly chats and mutual annoyances, sometimes out-and-out rows, she was connected to her son in a way she was not to her daughter. It wasn't that she loved Becca one iota less, and there was never a cross word between them during their trans-Atlantic chats. But then, she thought, wasn't it easier to get along with children who lived far away?

"Maybe," she said, "I am a bit too focused on hair color, but names are difficult to remember. It helps to have visuals. Blame it on my new color telly." The maple wood console television on the other side of the living room emanated with the best color available, even though it often needed adjusting when the faces began to look too red. Or green, which was decidedly worse.

With the sound turned down she was lured in by the visuals. A smiling mother with perfect white teeth held up a can of Campbell's Tomato Soup. Then the screen switched back to Mr. Cronkite who, unlike the mother, looked serious—even grim. She knew that look; she knew what it meant: that blasted war. The picture changed to an overseas war correspondent, an earnest young man called Dan Rather, and then to a stretcher bearing the bandaged figure of a soldier. Three men with helmets topped with camouflage foliage ran alongside the stretcher toward a helicopter. It happened every night, these ghastly film clips in hazy green tones (which had nothing to do with her set) showing guns and helicopters, accompanied by the bombastic staccato of machine gun fire. Every night, the same thing: young men falling headlong into the depths of a hellish fate. And this while her own son—safe and sound—sat chatting away with his mum in the bosom of Orange County, California.

And now, back to Walter Cronkite. His face evoked an immediate sense of comfort. It was not a handsome face, but it was an honest face, a trustworthy face. His temples were turning gray and she hoped Mr. Cronkite would never resort to that hideous hair dye men (like her ex) used to try and recapture their youth. It would utterly ruin her faith in him. Mr. Cronkite, with his open gray eyes—now sporting wire-rimmed glasses— was someone she counted on at the end of the day. She could, even with the volume turned down, follow every nuance of his facial expression to clue her in to the news behind the news. Was the world, on this day, dissolving into irretrievable madness? The answer lay in Mr. Cronkite's eyes.

"Are you there? Mum, are you all right?" Alex's voice seemed far away.

"Sorry, I was distracted. What were you saying, then?"

"I said, why don't you have the sad-eyed redhead—this Madeline . . ."

"Prescott."

"Yes. Have Madeline Prescott come back in for a second interview and I'll try to be there."

"I am perfectly capable of choosing my own employee," she said defensively.

"I know you are," Alex said, "but let me at least suggest that you take her on for a probationary period, say, two weeks or even a month. After that time, if she proves to be what you're looking for, then hire her permanently—with a bit of a pay hike. That's how it's done in the business world. It really is."

She agreed it was an excellent plan, but his proffered advice evoked a silent sigh. Alex was well-meaning, of course, except that he tended to hover a bit too much for her liking, as if she were some doddering old mum who needed help. Perhaps he felt he needed to watch over her since the divorce. But Colin never hovered like this; he wasn't home long enough. After his wartime stint in the R.A.F., he could never stay grounded, always flying off to California, and then, once they actually moved to California, he was off to France or some other exotic location. Even when he was home, lying around their pool with a script in one hand and a Scotch in the other, he still seemed to be flying about in his mind, never quite touching the ground of their relationship.

"And Alex," she said, now with her own clever idea, "since Madeline won't be working when you're here on Sundays, you must stop in on another day during her trial period. Pretend you're just a typical customer. You know, like those restaurant critics. I'd like to get your honest opinion. I really would."

"Right. And Mum, one more thing—"

"I know what you're about to say," she said. "You and Becca want me to hire someone full-time so I don't get so worn out. We've been over this."

"Exactly. You need full-time help, you just do."

"But can I afford it? That's the rub, isn't it?"

"Yes. You can afford it. I'm your accountant, remember?"

* * *

Madeline had to catch her breath when she heard Eve van Gelder's voice on the phone. She was expecting a call from her father at work about some details she'd wanted to talk over before her move to the cottage. But hearing the exotic voice pushed all other concerns to the side.

The usual pleasantries were exchanged while Madeline's mind raced ahead: Eve must need a formal resume. Or a second interview. That must be it. What would she wear? She had only the one dress. God, this could be complicated—

"My dear, I really enjoyed chatting with you, and I know Mr. Larsen was enchanted, but I must tell you that we—or I— have had a change of mind about the position."

"Oh?" Madeline's racing mind screeched to a halt. She really, really wanted this job, especially after her talk with Eve and Mr. Larsen. And there were the daisies . . . .

"Would you consider full-time?" Eve van Gelder asked. "Now I know it's not what you interviewed for, and I would understand—"

"Full. Time?" Madeline's voice squeaked out. "I'd love full-time! I'd prefer full-time." Her mental engine once again roared, racing with ideas of what she could do with the extra money. The woman went on to discuss appropriate attire, hourly wage, and about how the shop was closed on Mondays, and that Madeline would have Sundays off as well. They opened at 10:00 a.m. sharp and locked the door at six, but never rushed out the customers, so she would have to be somewhat flexible on that end.

"I'm very flexible," Madeline assured, smiling into her princess phone (which had now redeemed itself). She accepted the month-long probationary agreement with alacrity. "Yes, I'll be there on Tuesday morning. Nine sharp."

"And, Madeline, I do hope you're not allergic to cats."

"Cats? I don't think so. I have a little asthma—mostly, it's smog that sets me off." She didn't mention that military dress uniforms with white belts and shiny shoes also set her off.

"Still, just to warn you, I do have a cat on the premises. He was upstairs in the flat when you came before, but he does wander downstairs from time to time—much to the consternation of my son. I'll introduce you on Tuesday."

"To your son?"

The woman laughed. "No. To the cat."

* * *

That evening Madeline drew a bath, tossing in massive handfuls of her mother's Calgon bath beads. The steamy water smelled heavenly as she lowered herself into the lilac-scented bubbles. Once ensconced in suds, which suddenly smelled too much of lilac, she allowed images of Mike and Sarah to usurp her happy anticipations of her new job. It was almost as if these hungry images lurked, waiting for a free moment to pounce. Against nauseating images of the two making love, she imagined Sarah in Mike's shirt, standing over the stove in the tiny kitchen stirring scrambled eggs with Madeline's own special whisk. She tried to *whisk* the images out of her mind, but she supposed it was either this or thinking of Sean. And this was kindergarten pain compared to that.

She had to remind herself that Mike had made it clear from the beginning that long-term commitment was off the table, as he was trying to deal with his doctoral work. And wasn't she supposed to be rebelling against what Mike called, "petty bourgeois marriage"?

She splashed her face with soapy water, trying to ignore the gagging lilac perfume that refused to die with the bubbles. Okay, she told herself, forget about petty bourgeois marriage. The reality was less ideological. It was just a simple case of betrayal and hurt. It happened all the time. She pictured Sarah—her short dark hair and curvy figure. Her breasts were huge, when Madeline thought about it, as if it had just dawned on her. She glanced down at her own stick figure and the nearly imperceptible mounds that passed for breasts.

She sighed and pushed back her falling curls that slipped from the hair clip. Her hair. All she could crow about was a head of red curls that needed nothing but a good brushing and a bottle of Prell, unlike her friends who resorted to tortuous brush rollers, Dippity-Do, hair tape, sticky hair spray, and burning peroxide dyes. Her hair was her "crowning glory," so to speak. But what good was that in a world where men, in any given bar, could be heard saying, "I'm a leg man," or "I'm a breast man," but never, "I'm a hair man"? And never, ever, "I'm a brain man, myself."

She could almost feel the scales falling from her eyes, and she hated what she saw. Is this all women were about in the world? To please men, type their papers, cook their eggs, serve their carnal needs—now she was sounding like Pastor Bob— only to be discarded like old shoes? She thought of her friend, Amanda, who had tried to get her involved in a "women's solidarity" group on campus, as if women needed to ban together to become "liberated" from their stifling roles— something from Betty Friedan's book, the one she never got around to reading. She had thought them crazy at the time; not so crazy now. She turned the water as hot as she could stand it, ran a wash cloth under it, slapped the steamy cloth over her face, and leaned back. She would give up men for the time being. Maybe forever.

Her vows of celibacy were interrupted by the sound of voices and the squeaky floorboard in the hallway. The squeak had been quite useful as a teenager, seeing as her mother could never sneak up on her, allowing time to throw a cigarette stub out the window.

"Jillian Ann," she heard her mother say sternly, "I don't want to see that awful white lipstick on you, ever again. Do you hear me, young lady? You look like, like . . . you look sick."

Like death warmed over. That's what her mother was going to say, Madeline thought. But of course, she couldn't say it. Madeline had seen the colorless Yardley Slicker lipstick on Jilli's dresser, that perfect accessory to the cadaverous Twiggy look, and wondered how long it would be before the fireworks.

Predictably, she heard Jilli's door slam, not hard enough to call in the cavalry, but just hard enough to let her mother know that she wasn't a kid anymore. Madeline, practiced in the nuanced art of door slamming herself, smiled ruefully at the thought of her little sister holed up in her room.

Then the squeaky board in the hallway let Madeline know that her mother had retreated. She sighed as she splashed the tepid lilac water over her shoulders one last time. She would have to spend more time with her little sister; maybe that would get her mind off her troubles. At least that's what Grandma Daisy would say—she was sure of it.

* * *

"And then, you see, after you place the teacups just so, you pour the first cup." Eve van Gelder poured the tea in demonstration, catching the leaves in a silver strainer. She then set down the pot and lay the strainer aside. To Madeline's amazement, the wet tea leaves in the strainer had expanded and morphed into what looked like brown clumps of seaweed.

Madeline wasn't at all sure she was cut out for this new world—or rather, old world—of English tea. But here she was, her first day of tea training, serving invisible customers in her new J. C. Penny jumper and brown suede boots (low-heeled and plenty of room in the toes).

"That way," Eve continued, "you can show the customer how the tea strainer works, so they won't be afraid to use it themselves. I've found that people like to be in control of their tea, not wait until they can catch your eye for a refill as they do in coffee shops. That's why we leave the pots on the table. But, of course, the pot can be refilled if requested."

Madeline nodded dutifully, but was inwardly trying hard to pin down the whole idea of tea, which for her was like a foreign language with confusing syntax. "But isn't there an easier way, like, well, tossing a tea bag or two in the pot and be done with it?"

Eve's eyes grew wide. "Of course you could do that, but tea bags, well, they're *out* as far as this shop is concerned. The bags, you see, are filled with nothing much but tea dust—swept up leftovers."

"Swept up leftovers? That's what Americans drink?"

"The bottom of the barrel, quite literally. Most Americans are not even aware of it." Eve shuddered slightly as if tea bags symbolized the crumbling of Western Civilization. This woman was serious about her tea, and Madeline took note of this for future reference.

Eve, with a perfectly manicured nail, tapped the glass top of the very table they were using for practice, calling attention to the yellowed clipping displayed underneath. "Mr. Orwell, him-self, is our authority on the subject."

"George Orwell? You mean, as in *Animal Farm* and *1984*?"

"The same, yes. He was passionate about ideas, that one, even when it came to tea." Her finger scanned Orwell's words in a brief essay entitled, "A Nice Cup of Tea," from something called *Evening Standard*, dated January 12, 1946. Eve read aloud where her finger stopped. "'No strainers, muslin bags or other devices to imprison the tea. . . . If the tea is not loose in the pot it never infuses properly.'"

Madeline grinned at her new boss. "I've got it now: leaves,

free to expand and escape the prison of Big Brother's oppressive, all-seeing eye."

Eve threw her head back in laughter, which pleased Madeline, who had to admit she was enjoying the lesson, however weird it seemed. It was an education, sure, but she wondered what her former co-workers at the coffee house in Berkeley would say if they could see her now, surrounded by all this quaint tea paraphernalia, or tea *accoutrements* as Eve had said with a flawless French accent. (Madeline wondered if the woman ever felt like a fish out of water—all that cosmopolitan sophistication in Orange County, California.)

Just then the door bell jingled announcing a customer, an older man, elegant by sartorial standards, but with a gappy smile. Eve greeted him with her voice just a hair too high and strained in comparison to the way she spoke to other customers. Madeline could see that her employer's perfect composure was now subtly, but surely, rattled. She liked the man already.

* * *

Madeline's drive down Pacific Coast Highway from the shop to her new cottage digs at Crystal Cove took only ten minutes. The lazy orange sun waned over Laguna's landscape, relaxing her wired nerves. She had survived her first day, even if she had almost crossed a line by bringing up tea bags. She turned off Coast Highway and wound down the steep dirt road to the wooden garages located halfway between the cliff top highway and the beachside cottages. Her anxieties over the new job were behind her now, and a sense of tired repose set in—

Until she saw the taillights of her Dad's white Olds, parked in front of her garage.

Something was wrong, she knew it. Her dad would never show up uninvited. He was not a spur-of-the-moment type of dad—except for the time he showed up unannounced at Berkeley, early in 1965. The Free Speech Movement had come to a head by then, and some of her classmates were actually going to jail. To her horror, her dad had driven up from Anaheim to take her home, away from all "these misguided, rabble-rousing kids." But Madeline dug her heels into the soil of her college-born freedom. A battle won, albeit a Pyrrhic victory.

She parked behind his Olds, noting her mother in the passenger seat. She set the parking break, turned off the key, and jumped out. As she approached the driver's side, her father lowered his electric window. Madeline thought, not for the first time, that if they were going to put these ridiculous windows in cars, they should make them go up and down faster. She could now see her mother clearly. Tears rolled down Kate Prescott's randomly rouged cheeks, as if she had been determined not to go out without make-up, yet not having time to put it on properly.

"Dad, what's happened? Why are you here? Mom, what's the matter? Is Jilli all right?" She spoke too quickly and almost lost her breath.

"Jilli's fine. Slow down, Maddy, or you'll bring on an asthma attack," her father chided.

"Then why in the h— Why are you here?" She opened the back door of the Olds and slid in, closing the door. "Dad, please turn off the car and tell me what's going on."

John Prescott rolled up his electric window—a task which, again, moved at turtle speed—and then turned off the motor. Madeline put a hand on her mother's shoulder.

"I'm sorry," her mother sobbed, "I just can't go through with it."

"With what? You can't go through with what?" What was with her slow parents and their slow windows?

Her father sighed heavily as he felt for something in his jacket pocket. He pulled out an envelope and handed it to his daughter, hands trembling.

Madeline's heart seemed to stop. Her dad's hands never trembled. Never! They were strong hands, a father's hands, and she realized how much she depended on the very steadiness of them.

"What's this?" she heard herself ask, even while knowing full well what it was. Her eyes locked onto the word FREE scrawled in the upper right hand corner of the envelope. All soldiers in Vietnam had this perk: free postage.

"It came today," said her father. "It's addressed to you, so we thought you should open it. We were going to be here when you did." He glanced over to his wife and then back to his daughter in the rearview mirror. "But we've changed our minds. I need to get your mother home."

Madeline sat staring at the envelope bearing her brother's large, expansive handwriting.

> To: Maddy Prescott
> C/O: John Prescott
> 23 Ball Avenue
> Anaheim, California 92801

She was at a loss. Should she let her parents just leave like this? Open the letter right here in the back seat of the Olds? The moment was enormous. And cruel—as if they hadn't had enough suffering, for God's sake.

She glanced out the back window to see a man in an orange windbreaker jumping out of a Nash Rambler to open his garage door. The wooden door opened with a squeak and a thud, not unlike the sound of the screen door on Christmas Eve when she found herself staring at preternaturally shiny shoes. The sound of the Rambler idling was like a ticking bomb, pressuring her to make a decision. Or explode with emotion. She glanced back at her VW, parked behind her father.

"I'll move my car and let you out," she said.

"Do you want me to walk you down to the cottage?" her father asked.

"No, I'll be okay." Madeline carefully slipped the envelope into her sweater pocket and awkwardly touched both of her parents on the shoulder before she got out. Kate sniffed and dabbed at her eyes, but didn't say a word. The three of them knew the thin envelope edged with red, white, and blue stripes held too much pain to face. But it had fallen to her, the eldest child, to be the strong one—like it or not.

"Are you going to be all right, Maddy?" her father asked at the last minute, trying to keep his composure, but obviously conflicted with what to do or say.

"Of course. I'll call you soon, I promise," she said, climbing out of the backseat.

* * *

As she walked down the steep dirt road from the garages to the cottages, she felt a heaviness, as if a ton of bricks lay in her pocket instead of an air-thin letter. Half-way to the cottages she met a plump woman wearing a red bandana headscarf with dark frizzy curls escaping on each side. She was dressed in baggy overalls and red Keds. Panting, she apparently had stopped to catch her breath.

"Whew! What a climb! " the woman said with a breathless Southern accent. Madeline nodded, forced a smile and started to move on, but the woman said, "I saw you movin' your things in the other day, you and the little blonde—you're little sister, was it? Sorry we didn't come over to give you a proper welcome," said the woman, apparently oblivious to Madeline's body language, "but my boys were off fishin' with their dad. I'm glad to finally make your acquaintance." The chunky woman held out a hand. "I'm Biddy Gelson."

"Nice to meet you, Betty—"

"Biddy."

"Biddy." A strange name. But her smile was warm and honest and graciously Southern. And wholly unwanted at the moment.

"I'm Madeline. It's my grandfather's cottage. I'm just keeping an eye on it for now."

"Oh, yeah?" said the smiling woman, with an accent different from Mrs. Mahaney's, not as slow and graceful. Still, Madeline was not about to ask this Biddy person where she was from, for she imagined another ten minutes slipping away.

The woman slid her hands in the pockets of her overalls, as if relaxing into a long conversation. "We—that is, my husband and the twins and I—are down at Number 25." She gestured with her eyes in the general direction of the cluster of cottages to the right of the Crystal Cove Community store. "Just until August, that is. My husband is on sabbatical from the University of Texas at Arlington."

So it was Texas. *So what?* She wasn't interested in hearing any more about this woman, her twins, her husband, or her state—Lyndon B. Johnson's state, it occurred to her. But this woman looked innocuous enough, so she hated to judge the entire state of Texas by the decisions of one man, the man she held responsible for the brick in her pocket.

The woman's jolliness grated against her inner turmoil. If only she could get into one of those transporter machines on *Star Trek* and instantly disappear and reappear in her cottage, without all this chit chat to get through. *For God's sake! Didn't this woman see that she was about to implode with emotion over a dead brother's letter and a father's shaking hands?*

The woman, as if finally catching on to Madeline's body language, said, "I should let you get goin'."

They said their good-byes, and Madeline rushed down the road to the boardwalk which led to the cottage. Under other circumstances, Madeline might have enjoyed this plump and chatty Biddy Gelson from Arlington, Texas, whose husband was on sabbatical.

Yes, under other circumstances she would enjoy a lot of things.

Almost to the cottage, Madeline noticed that her ears seemed hypersensitive to the sounds surrounding her: the cry of seagulls, the insistent pounding of the waves against the rocks, the click-clack of her low-heeled brown suede boots on the boardwalk. A walk that seemed interminable. And yet, part of her did not want to arrive—and face it. Open it. Read it.

Salt in an open wound.

Chapter Seven

The Prescott cottage rested in the shadow of an enormous shale bluff, imposing with its jagged beauty, but geologically fragile compared to the stalwart granite rocks jutting out of the sea itself. The cottage below looked like a friendly beggar sitting with hat in hand at the gates of a great palace. Except the beggar was not alone. One of forty-six ramshackle dwellings, the cottage sat farthest to the south, on the edge of the community. Grandpa Abel's singular brown shingled cottage with bright turquoise trim had evolved through the years from a small shelter with a canvass roof back in the '20s, to a cabin in the '30s. By the '40s, when Grandpa Abel and Grandma Daisy moved in, it had matured into a full-fledged cottage with a small kitchen in the back, two bedrooms, an indoor bathroom, and a sea wall to protect it at high tide.

The bathroom was, oddly enough, a conversation piece, as the former renovators did not bother to remove the outside shingles on one wall when they upgraded from an outhouse, giving the indoor bathroom a tacked-on appearance. For Madeline, the mud-brown shingles on the bathroom wall reminded her that the cottage had history; it had lived and breathed and evolved through endless tides and moons, embedding within its rustic wood and shingles all the memories of its lucky occupants.

The original sash windows offered picture-postcard views of a seashore that ignited childhood imagination: huge black rocks like chunks of dark chocolate, hosting birds and lichen and green sea grass; capricious white-capped waves carrying heady surfers for brief moments of glory; long-billed pelicans clubbing together on rocky islands just off shore like so many school kids at recess; gray and white seagulls dipping and squawking against a clean blue sky.

On clear days, Catalina Island could be seen stretching out in the distance with its hazy blue promises of celebrity yachts and glass-bottom boats. Closer in, one might catch sight of funny little seals, and some big ones, too, paddling along with heads bobbing and whiskers glinting in the sun; sleek dolphins could be seen leaping into the wind, or a gray whale might just go spouting off. The whole picture screamed of primal beauty, and the Prescott Cottage was there to bear witness.

The congenial community of Crystal Cove, as with any good neighborhood, watched out for one another, rendering John Prescott's fear of "those damned hippie squatters" utterly baseless—if not laughable. (But what was the harm in Madeline's father owning this bit of fiction, if it gave her more reason to "look after" things?)

The morning could not have been more alluring—cool, crisp, clear—and because Madeline had only slept intermittently, she was up with the sun, already settled into the old deck chair with its sagging rubber slats. She sipped strong coffee, holding the steamy cup close to her face to warm her cheeks.

Biddy Gelson walked along the beach with her twin boys and waved to Madeline shyly, as if unsure of her welcome. Madeline returned the wave with a tinge of guilt for brushing the woman off last night, but would probably do the same if she approached this morning. Biddy wore the same overalls, her two boys dressed in jeans and windbreakers. These two miniatures of Biddy, plump and smiley, had a definite air of "double trouble" about them—something about their cowlicks. The trio moved on, clambering over rocks to an adjoining alcove, disappearing from sight.

She was alone again with the view, a wild beauty that seemed over-eager in its tug at her skin and nostrils and eyes, as if bound and determined to get inside her and take hold. But the more it tried, the worse the stinging pain behind her eyes. She blinked tears and the scene before her blurred into a kind of impressionist painting. She fumbled for a Kleenex in her sweater pocket, but there was no tissue, only the letter—opened and read and re-read and analyzed a dozen times throughout the sleepless night.

She would look at it once more before heading off to work. Then she would tuck it away and move it to the edges of her mind.

15 December 1967
Da Nang

Dear Sis,

I'm writing to you in hopes Mom and Dad will forward the letter or give it to you during Christmas break. Hope you don't mind, Sis, but I need to spill my guts to someone—and, well, you're it.

Maddy, it's like this. I feel I'm on the edge, like I'm going crazy or something. "Nervous in the service"—that's me. At first it all seemed like we (me and my buddies) were a part of something real important. All the guys in my platoon and me—we were like instant best friends. But now I see them die and I can't make sense of it. Dan and José are gone. Those guys—good guys—were in my squad. Dan's legs were blown to smithereens by a land mine and he died right after, but not soon enough from what I hear. And José—he was cut down by a sniper while on patrol.

The only real good buddy left is a guy from near home, Joey. He's a tough character, but he's good as gold and he's going through the same thing as me. It's just that we can't talk around the other guys. Some GIs are adjusted to this place—doing their duty without question. I respect that. Others are already around the bend and I hate to think about them going home and trying to adapt to regular society with wives and kids and such. I guess I'm somewhere in between, like I'm struggling to keep my soul inside my body. Does that sound crazy?

I feel bad saying all this, but I thought you might understand since you've been protesting the war up in Berkeley. I used to think you were unpatriotic to do that, and that's why I haven't written you (sorry!), but now things are changing inside my head. Maybe the VC (Vietcong) are godless Communists and all, but I'm having serious doubts about our mission here. What exactly are we doing here? I get the feeling we're in somebody else's civil war.

These are probably just coward's words. I'm scared out of my mind—I admit that. I mean, this place seems like a hopeless hell—not just the smell of death, the leeches and mosquitoes. I'm talking about something deeper. This place robs your soul, Maddy, your soul! The way I figure it, to stay alive you have to check your soul at the door. You just hope and pray that it will still be there on your way out. Or you have to pretend it's a game, like something at the arcade. You hear it all the time: how many "Gooks" did you get today?

Like I said, some of the guys can adjust to all this without a problem and will probably go home to be great citizens. I admire these guys—I really do. But I'm not cut out to be a warrior, at least when I don't see the point of it all. I just can't seem to adjust, that's all.

Take what happened last week: We ambushed the VC in an offensive that we knew would be dangerous. By some miracle, we didn't lose any of our guys, but we killed 14 VC. It looked unreal to me, Maddy—all those bloody bodies lying in this one spot in the jungle. Then we stripped the bodies *from the waist up, took IDs and such, and confiscated their AK-47s (real good weapons). Then we dragged the bodies without ceremony to a huge net spread out on the ground in a clearing. We tossed the bodies into the net on top one another. By the time we finished, the bodies on top the pile would slide down like slippery fish. (These guys looked like 12-year-old boys compared to us big Americans.)*

I was in charge of getting all the bodies within the parameter of the net. I had to look straight at them. Some of the dead guys had eyes wide open and I wish I'd closed them or something, but I was afraid to touch them anymore than I had to. I looked at each face and asked, "Did I kill you? Was it my weapon that did this to you?" I wanted to say I was sorry, and I guess I did with my thoughts. I can't shake those faces, those small, limp bodies all squished together. There was an indignity about it, Maddy, a real indignity.

So there was this big heap of them—lifeless legs and arms and faces all scrambled up into a pile. And then they hooked the ropes up to the helicopter that finally hoisted the whole sad lump up into the air. There it was, swinging above me in the sky—this huge net full of human bodies. I swear it looked like a net of fish up there. I half expected some flapping around or something. All I could do was retch my guts out.

Anyway, they were carried off to a mass grave somewhere to be counted so that people back home could see how many we killed. That's the way it is here. No prayers. No funeral. Nothing but body count, body count, and more body count.

You guys at home have no idea what goes on here, even with TV and all. It's so far from normal life that I can't even remember what it feels like to be a regular guy, just thinking about cars and girls and going to the movies. Sometimes I think I'm already dead and this must be hell.

I've tried, honestly, to be a good soldier, but I seem to lack something. Courage? The warrior spirit? You're the smart one, Maddy. You know who you are. I'm feeling pretty lost. But if I'm not a soldier, then what am I? My commanding officer sent me to the chaplain and he talked to me awhile and I guess it helped, but before I left he told me to write my thoughts down in a letter to someone who would understand, somebody back home. Well, I chose you, Sis. I know your thoughts on this war and I know we've disagreed about it and all, but if something should happen to me I want you, of all people in the world, to know these things about me.

Am I a coward, Sis? Sometimes I think I am, but then other times I think, no, I'm just trying to hold on to my soul. Which is it? Am I good soldier or a bad soldier?

I signed up—didn't wait for my number to come up— cause I wanted to do what Dad did for our country. I wanted him to be proud of me. Pretty pathetic, huh? I'm not smart like you, but I thought I could do this and make a difference, like Dad. But now—I don't know how much longer I can go on like this.

(Please don't show this to Mom and Dad. I don't think Dad would understand, not with his fighting in the Pacific and all—back when going to war made some sense.)

Give my love to Mom and Dad and Jilli—how's she doing?—and Grandpa Abel, that is, when you're home for Christmas. I wish I could be there. Wow, I've written a book.

Write me, Sis.

Love,

Sean

She folded the letter, slid it carefully into the thin envelope, and tucked it into her sweater pocket. She wiped the tears with her sleeve, heaved herself out of the droopy lounger, and went inside to wash her face. She must get hold of herself; her second day of work was still ahead.

* * *

"Madeline, dear, are you all right?" Eve noticed something

amiss the moment she unlocked the door. The downcast image before her—puffy red eyes and lackluster smile—clashed with the image of the happy girl who had left the evening before.

Madeline looked to be paralyzed by the question, her eyes moist, unblinking.

Eve relocked the door, as it was still well before opening time.

"Come, sit," Eve said gesturing toward the Van Gogh table where she was having her morning tea.

"You've had a loss," Eve said once they were settled. She folded her arms and waited, giving Madeline time to gather herself.

"How did you know?" Madeline looked surprised.

"Oh, I know grief when I see it. Who—may I ask?"

"My brother."

"Oh." Eve's hand instinctively went for her heart.

"He was a marine," Madeline went on quickly, in a faraway monotone. "He was killed in action in Vietnam. We were told on Christmas Eve. That's why I'm here, really, instead of Berkeley. I need to be close to my family."

"I'm so very sorry for your loss, Madeline. I know, you see, what it's like—" She paused, sat back, and regrouped before going on. "I knew you had suffered a loss the day you came in for the interview. It was in your eyes."

"Look, Eve," Madeline said, removing her sweater as if to end the conversation and get to work, "I know we need to get busy. I don't want to cry or get emotional or anything." She looked around as if half-expecting a roomful of customers. When she looked back at Eve, her valiant attempt at stoicism crumbled and the tears fell like raindrops onto her blue turtleneck.

Eve offered her a napkin to wipe her tears and blow her nose. She looked at this young woman, so clever and lovely and well-educated. And so very distraught. Eve could see the pain of a fitful night written on Madeline's face, for she knew all too well the monsters of regret and guilt and grief, all of which planned their assaults for the wee hours.

"I'm going to bring you a strong cup of English Breakfast and a warm scone. I just took them out of the oven. And then, we'll talk."

"But I can talk while I work—really!" protested Madeline.

"We might do that, too, but for now I want us to just sit. You see, I need a little break after my early morning routine. I've been up baking since six, so I like to sit here and rest my feet with my own cup of tea, just the last half hour or so before opening. And now you can join me in this little ritual. How's that?"

Madeline nodded gratefully, dabbing at her eyes with the napkin.

Eve went to prepare the tea, which was easy enough since she had already put on the kettle for herself. As she poured the boiling water over the dry leaves, she felt the significance of such a simple ritual. The very act was like a thread of history, linking Eve to her mother and to past generations, all of whom found comfort from the woes of life—toothaches to heartaches—with a calming, reassuring cup of tea. But Becca, her own daughter, was not all that fond of a companionable sit down with a cup of tea; she preferred the comfort of a day at Harrods. Eve had longed for her daughter to sit and talk, but Colin always intervened with cash in hand. That was Colin's way of dealing with the little aches and pains of life: buy something.

When Eve returned with the tea and a plate of warm scones, Madeline was leaning down, stroking Earl Grey's silky coat as he lay curled up on her boots. "Earl Grey has way of showing up when someone's upset," Eve said. "He's uncanny in that respect." She began to pour the tea for her new employee—eyes red as her hair. "I gather you didn't eat breakfast."

"Thank you. No, I couldn't stomach a thing."

"Well, then," Eve said, pouring her own cup, "you must eat. And tell me, when you're ready, about your brother."

Madeline took a bite of scone and put the cup to her half trembling lips. She barely took a sip before words tumbled out: "I thought I was doing all right—I really did." She appealed to Eve as if trying to convince someone. "But then last night . . . I got a letter." She bit her lip in an effort at composure.

"A letter from . . . ?"

"My brother."

Eve felt a shiver down her back. "Oh . . . Oh, my." She set her teacup down gently as if the cup itself were grieving.

Madeline nodded. "My parents gave it to me last night when I got home from work." She sighed. "It was written not long before he was killed. Very personal. His feelings about the war—really distressing feelings. Doubts, that kind of thing. And he specifically addressed it to me. He chose me to tell, and I can't respond. Or share it with my parents."

Eve leaned in. "And why, dear, can't you share it with your parents?"

"Because he asked me not to. He didn't think they would understand. And he's right, they wouldn't." She paused and shuddered as if chilled. "It's just a lot to take in, that's all."

"Take it slowly. Your heart has its own timing."

"I know," Madeline said with forced brightness and a valiant return to her scone and tea.

The two sat in quiet repose, Eve wanting very much to find out more but not wanting to push.

Then the girl set down her cup, crossed her arms on the table, and gave Eve an inquiring look. "You said, just now, that you know what it's like—and then you stopped. Did you also lose a brother or sister? Is that what you were about to say?"

Eve paused, reluctant to open the door to her own past. "Yes," she finally said. "I lost a brother. And a mother and father." Eve noticed Madeline's expression move from curiosity to mild shock. She continued her litany of sorrow. "And grand-mother. And cousins and aunts and uncles. Yes, gone—my entire family—in one fell swoop."

Madeline's eyes widened. "World War II? The camps?"

Eve was not surprised at the girl's quickness. "Yes . . . the camps." She almost said *Auschwitz*, for the young woman with a history background would surely know of it, but the very word stuck in her throat, an ugly, vile word. She went on quickly. "I was in England studying English at King's College when Hitler invaded my country."

Madeline nodded, unblinking, apparently transfixed. "I'm sorry," she said.

Eve smiled ruefully. "Madeline, survivors of war have more to deal with than one might suppose. I am the only survivor in my family. Not an easy thing, that." She set her cup and saucer aside and folded her arms on the table. "You see, there is a kind of guilt that's attached to it, albeit an irrational one, even after these twenty-odd years of trying to come to terms. It crops up every now and then—this difficult feeling." Eve began to feel a heat rise up from her torso and into her face as if the temper-ature had suddenly turned mercurial. Was it the discomfort of this chat, or simply one of those bloody heat flashes? She blotted her forehead with a napkin.

"Are you okay?" Madeline looked concerned.

Eve nodded reassuringly as she glanced to the starburst clock above the door. She saw that it was coming up on 10:00 a.m. and already a shadow loomed at the door. Matthew Hanson, the budding writer, always showed up early. She got up to unlock to the door and greeted him with a particularly warm smile as the cool ocean breeze swept across her cheeks.

Chapter Eight

On the morning of Sean's military funeral, John Prescott looked up from *The Register*, peering over his dark rimmed reading glasses to say to anyone listening that the USS Pueblo had been seized by the North Koreans. The news barely registered with Madeline, who normally would have snatched the paper from her father and devoured the article. But she had, for the time being, quit reading the newspaper—quit caring about the world that had taken away her brother.

By 9:00 a.m. Madeline's family, subdued and well turned out in their Sunday finest, piled into the Olds and drove to Sunny Grove Rest Home to pick up Grandpa Abel and his aluminum walker. Abel Prescott was a tall, frail looking man with a shock of white hair, deep-set eyes, and shaggy eyebrows. His once impressive 6'4" frame had shrunk at least four inches, leaving him still tall, but gently stooped, bending further toward the ground year by year.

Grandpa Abel was a kind man, a lively soul, and a proud veteran of WWI. But now he suffered a cruel form of dementia that made it hard for him to remember much. At times he was lucid and full of great stories from the past, about working in the orange groves and riding his old paint horse, Cornelia, in the canyons and hills of Orange County. But it was painful for Madeline to visit him in the rest home because he kept calling her "Gertie," the name of his long dead sister. It broke her heart. There was some question, at least in her mind, as to his ability to withstand the funeral at the Los Angeles National Cemetery. The trip alone would take at least 45 minutes, depending on traffic. But her dad assured everyone that his father was fit to go, at least in body.

Grandpa Abel now stood waiting by the automatic doors of the rest home, grasping his walker and accompanied by a stocky black female attendant dressed in white. His wispy hair blew straight up in the breeze like cotton candy, revealing a scalp riddled with age spots. He looked vulnerable and fragile and unknowing, smiling brightly as if heading to a family wedding. With practiced skill, John and Kate helped Grandpa into the front seat of the Olds, while Madeline and Jilli folded up his walker and placed it in the trunk.

So there they were, thought Madeline, as they set off for the military cemetery: John Prescott driving his beloved Olds with its electric windows, accompanied by his aged and confused father, two remaining children, and a wife calmed by a hefty dose of Valium. A mutually understood silence overtook the mourners—a reverent, almost church-like stillness, far removed from the noisy freeway of life-as-usual outside.

After all the waiting and red tape, Sean's casket had finally arrived home on Thursday. Only Kate and John had been allowed to meet the body at El Toro Marine Base. Madeline wasn't sure if that were true—that only the parents were allowed. She suspected that John Prescott wanted to shield Jilli in particular from the encounter, one that would possibly entail seeing her father in tears.

Sean was to be buried next to other fallen soldiers of wars gone by. And according to the pamphlet given to the family, two famous dogs were also buried there: Old Bonus, an adopted pet of residents in a soldiers' home, and Blackout, a war dog wounded in the Pacific during World War II. She and Jilli would have to find those special burials someday, when they brought flowers for Sean. And they would do that, of course. It might even lend some levity to the whole matter of visiting the dead, imagining these dogs in uniform. But then she supposed such levity would be inappropriate. Then why, she wondered, did people often have an uncontrollable urge to giggle at funerals, as in a solemn church service? Maybe levity was something you could call a "coping mechanism." That's what Ben would call it.

She was looking for another word, though, as she so often did when Ben threw out his clinical definitions of things. Perhaps levity in the midst of sorrow was something like a "merciful tickle" to break the intensity. But "merciful" implied a merciful God. And for an agnostic, which Madeline was, God—merciful or not—was the Question-at-hand. She sighed and resolved to talk to someone soon about such things as God and mercy, someone outside the confines of the New Hope Baptist Church. After all, wasn't it the duty of an agnostic to hunt for truth? Or at least for a good metaphor?

They turned off the 101 onto Sepulveda Boulevard and drove slowly into the green, well-groomed cemetery grounds. The administration building of white stucco and red Spanish tile looked more like a mission than a military building. Vivacious pink rose bushes and climbing bougainvillea offered a soothing effect to mourners of lost soldiers. The cemetery spread end-lessly, acre after acre, like the expanse of the sea: the signif-icance lying beneath.

Madeline looked sideways at Jilli, who was staring out the window at the endless rows of white crosses and grave stones, and took her hand. Madeline turned to her mother and started to take her hand as well, only to find her asleep, her head bobbing up and down as the car inched over the bumpy road.

"Mom, we're here. Wake up," Madeline prodded gently.

"Wha . . . ?" her mother mumbled, blinking hard.

"We're at the cemetery."

Kate gathered her dignity as she palmed and patted her overly sprayed flip, which had not budged a hair since they left the house.

The car finally came to a stop at a verdant patch of ground where impressively dressed military personnel stood ready to open the door of the Olds. It was all very reassuring, thought Madeline. These men, seven in all, were part of the detail honor guard, marines from Camp Pendleton where Sean had undergone his basic training.

"What in the world?" Jilli said as she emerged from the car with the help of a white gloved marine.

"What's wrong, Jilli?"   Kate turned quickly toward her youngest, now fully awake and anxious.   Her Valium had probably run its course.

"That's Gary Littleton, Tim's brother. He's got his trumpet."

"That's a bugle," interjected John Prescott with a little pride in his voice. "It's a tradition to have 'Taps' played, but there aren't many buglers around. I couldn't stand the thought of a recording, so I talked with the funeral director and he found this kid who plays in the high school band."

There had been no visitation at the funeral home because the casket could not be opened. The dark-suited funeral director, Bob Tucker of Tucker and Son Funeral Home (who wore the shortest tie Madeline had seen since 1961), had said in a solemn home visit that he was "very sorry, but the most skilled reconstruction attempts had failed to produce results."   For God's sake, she thought at the time—and thought again, now—what could have happened to create such a mangle of flesh that even Tucker and Son, the biggest funeral home in Anaheim, could not create a respectable showing of Sean Prescott's lifeless body?

This disturbed Madeline, since she thought that seeing the body would give the family something shrinks like Ben called "closure," a final good-bye that would be more meaningful than just staring at a flag-draped coffin and imagining his body inside. And, what if it wasn't there? What if it they put the wrong body in the casket, got them mixed up? But what could she do? Like her parents, she had been too stupefied to think what to ask poor Bob Tucker, the son of Tucker and Son, who was only doing his best to comfort the family.

Madeline glanced around the crowd gathered on the green lawn. Some who attended the memorial at the church had come for the military funeral: Mrs. Mahaney, the Gregorys, Pastor Bob, and some of her father's co-workers from Rockwell. Most apparent were a number/Sean's old high school friends sitting together, buddies from the football team. Even teachers. Mr. Lee, her old science teacher, offered an acknowledging smile. She returned it and swallowed hard at the sight of such a showing on behalf of her brother.

There were various military men and women in the crowd, too, probably from Camp Pendleton, which was only about two hours south of Los Angeles. Among the group of uniforms, a dark-skinned marine stood out—probably because he was staring at her. His face was badly scarred on one side, a deep slash reaching from his left ear to his mouth. His worn, leathery skin made it hard to determine his age: he looked young and old at the same time, as one who has seen too much trouble, too much sorrow, and possibly a bar fight or two. He offered a bleak smile and a nod, as if he knew her. But she didn't know him.

There was something irrationally disturbing about this marine with the scar.

Madeline helped Grandpa Abel edge his way to the reserved seating in the front, his walker supporting him. He stopped suddenly and looked about the cemetery, at the men in uniform, at the flowers, and it was as if he finally recognized the reality of his destination. Madeline watched the tears roll down his aged face. All she could do was reach down into her macramé purse and fish around for the little pack of Kleenex.

Draped with the bright, crisp Stars and Stripes, the casket rested on a platform over the grave—albeit, a grave hidden from sight—in dignified repose, demanding everyone's rapt attention. Madeline's mother could not look away, her gaze frozen on the unfathomable sight in front of her. Suddenly she drooped as if to faint. Her husband of twenty-five years caught hold of her and held her up, his arms around her shaking shoulders, his hand grasping her arm.

Kate Prescott sobbed inconsolably.

Madeline squeezed her eyes shut at the sound of her mother's discomposure. *All this pain. All this inconsolable pain for a freckle-faced brother who could not check his soul at the door.*

The jolting sounds of the 7-gun salute shook her out of her dark reveries. She grabbed Jilli's hand with a protective tightness.

Then, four of the white-gloved marines moved toward the casket and lifted the corners of the flag. They held the four corners in a reverent way, and she felt a rush of gratitude toward these marines. To Madeline Prescott, the flag, suspended as it was above the casket, looked like a merciful umbrella—a protective cloak to shield Sean from a garish sun.

Gary Littleton began to play "Taps" on his shiny brass bugle. Madeline looked over to see Jilli's face distorted in grief. She felt eyes on her, too, and glanced over her shoulder to see the dark marine with the scar on his face. He looked straight at her and she thought she saw tears in his dark eyes. She looked away from him and back to the four marines with their bright white hats and belts gleaming in the sun.

The bugler suddenly cracked on a note near the end, not uncommon for a young brass player, but here in this place of sorrow and reverence, it sounded the vulnerability of all goodness in the world.

And then it hit her. The unthinkable.

~ Part Two ~

Heraclites' River

Chapter Nine

On the first day of February, Eiler Larsen turned from his empty teacup and grappled for his cane on the back of his chair. As Eve helped him with his coat, she noticed his hands, especially his fingers, long and large and slightly swollen in the joints. But somehow, she thought, these hands still managed to wave to children, drink from delicate cups, and turn the pages of poetry books. This afternoon the Greeter of Laguna had drunk two pots of Earl Grey at the George Orwell table, perused a volume of William Blake, and talked at length with several young bohemians who had caught sight of him through the window. They had come inside to "rap" as they called it.

Eve winced inwardly at this questionable use of language (was "chat" not a perfectly good word?), but she was nevertheless thrilled at the way Eiler Larsen, just by being himself, attracted customers. Even the bearded, beaded youth of Laguna had money, or "bread" as they called it, for used books. And they all seemed to "dig" the gray tabby that roamed from sandal to sandal only to plop down over a white-socked foot sporting Birkenstocks. Earl wasn't the only one drawn to these cork and leather sandals adopted by the bohemian crowd. Eve, more than once, looked down at them, longingly, imagining them on own feet after a long day on the floor.

But now the colorful youth were gone—even Earl Grey had disappeared through the cat flap—and the day was gently winding down. The Greeter of Laguna moved hesitantly, relying on his cane, while Eve went ahead to get the door. Madeline, closing out the cash register, waved her good-bye from behind the counter.

As Eve opened the door, Sam Steiner appeared in the early darkness, all smiles and greetings. He grabbed the door and held it wide for the old man and his cane. Sam's presence at this late hour caught Eve a bit off guard; it was closing time, after all. Her feet, not having the benefit of Birkenstocks, were aching in the arches. She was looking forward to her usual date with Walter Cronkite, followed by a simple omelet, a hot bath, and a nightcap with Agatha Christie.

"Closing up shop?" Sam asked, barely inside. His eyes looked expectant, like a boy of ten instead of the gray-haired business sophisticate he was. He nodded his hello to Madeline.

"Closing, yes," said Eve, "but for you—" She motioned him to follow her to the Van Gogh table, his usual place.

"No tea for me," he said.

"No tea?" Eve said, stopping in her tracks, hoping her half-relief, half-disappointment didn't show.

He shook his head. "What I really want is for you, Eve, to join me for a cocktail at Hotel Laguna. It's Happy Hour—a great American custom. Are you game?"

Eve was startled by so forward an invitation. Was this the way busy professionals socialized in America? And what was all this "are you game" business? It certainly felt like a game, all this tiptoeing through the minefields of etiquette. She must think up an excuse. *Quickly*. She had to feed Earl Grey and finish with the clean up. And, of course, there was the small matter of that gold band on his finger.

"Eve," Madeline said from behind the counter, "I'd be happy to close up by myself."

Eve stared at her employee with a lifted brow.

"Don't worry. I know how to lock up—you gave me a key. You guys go on."

It was two against one now, no graceful way out of it. "But Earl Grey . . . I need to feed him and get a wrap—" Eve looked at Sam. "Give me ten minutes?"

Sam beamed his Omar Sharif smile. Eve smiled back nervously, hiding a multitude of doubts.

She started up the stairs to the flat. This was a bad idea. It might give Sam the wrong idea, of course it would. Why had she agreed, for goodness sake? She would, after all, be breaking her date with Walter Cronkite. And Mozart. Alex had given her a new recording of the Amsterdam Concertgebouw performance of Mozart's *Jupiter*, and she'd not had a chance to give it a good listen. But then, when she got home from her drink with Sam, she would need both her cat and Mozart to reassure her of her moral integrity.

Earl Grey lay sprawled in front of his cat dish, tail thumping in anticipation. Sam and Earl really got on, she thought with a smile, opening a can of Starkist Tuna. The cat seemed especially keen on Sam's Italian loafers with their irresistible tassels. Sam liked cats, she could tell, and she wondered if Sam also liked Mozart. It didn't matter, of course, because he was obviously married. Or separated. And even if he were free as a bird, it still didn't matter—his taste in music or anything else—because she was simply not in the market for a new husband. Or even a . . . what was the word these days? A "relationship"? She threw off the whole idea of it as she washed her hands, checked her hair pins in the bathroom mirror, refreshed her lipstick, and grabbed a coat before turning off the lights.

"Wish me luck, Earl," she said into the darkness, to a cat in the midst of a bath.

* * *

"Eiler's quite a character," Sam said as they began their self-conscious journey down the street. Eve was still busying herself with the buttons on her camel colored coat. The night was chilly with a wind off the ocean.

"Who?" asked Eve, distracted by nervous energy.

"Eiler Larsen," said Sam. "He's a true original."

"Quite," said Eve. "Madeline and I look forward to late afternoons, in hopes of seeing the famous Greeter of Laguna walk through the door." She wanted to say, *and you, too. We look forward to seeing you, too.*

"Very generous of you, taking care of him like that," Sam said, putting his hand on the small of her back to guide her across the street at the intersection.

"Not my generosity at all. It's his. We have a trade, you know, an understanding. He provides flowers; I provide tea. We trade books as well. Some of our best poetry volumes come from Mr. Larsen. I don't think I've ever seen anyone of such small means give so much."

Sam smiled. "He restores my faith in humanity, that's for sure."

Eve felt especially exuberant in the crisp air that rumbled with early evening street chatter. "Not to mention," she continued, "the man's a magnet. He brings in the young people—interesting ones at that." She chuckled. "It's especially gratifying given that my son assured me I would be catering only to elderly women and British expats who vaguely remember the quaint concept of tea."

Once inside the softly-lit lounge of Hotel Laguna, with its relaxing bossa nova sounds and candles glowing sensuously on every table, Eve began to feel off balance. And just a little dull. The place was full of sharply dressed business people, some colorfully dressed ones, too, all obviously enjoying what Americans called "Happy Hour." She was self-conscious in her conservative skirt and unexciting penny loafers. *Why had she not at least thought to change her shoes?*

A sudden rush of insecurity fell over her. Perhaps it was the bossa nova beat, which reminded her of martini parties in Beverly Hills, with women "friends" who eyed her lackluster fashion sense in a way that made her feel always the outsider.

Was being out of place—a constant foreigner—her lot in life?

All the tables were occupied, so they settled onto cushioned leather stools at the bar and ordered wine, Eve, a Cabernet, and Sam, a Chablis. She noted his wedding ring again, as if it might have magically disappeared. But there it was: a thin gold band that both annoyed and assured.

"And how's Madeline working out?" Sam asked with easy congeniality.

"Oh, she's a dream. I really can't believe my luck on that one. She's a Berkeley graduate, you know."

"I do. A history degree, I hear. And a budding philosopher. Maybe even a poet, judging from her chats with Mr. Larsen about this poet or that. And she strikes me as a responsible young lady, so"—he leaned in to avoid a loud-mouthed man on the seat next to him—"when you want to leave, to get away for a break, you can trust her to hold down the fort."

Was Sam hinting that he wanted her to leave the shop more often? *With him?* She noticed the bartender fiddling with the portable television perched up high behind the bar. Walter Cronkite's face appeared. It was odd seeing that face in this place, and in stark black and white hues—outside the security of her green leather lounger with Earl Grey curled on her lap. What would Mr. Cronkite think of her? Here she was with a married man in a bar full of rather loud people and sensual music. She felt as out of place as her shoes and wished she hadn't come.

The wine arrived. She took a drink of the Cabernet as if it were a glass of water and shook her head at the sting of it against her throat.

"So, Sam,"—she had to raise her voice to be heard above the inebriated laugh of the man sitting on the other side of him—"how do you like the new Norman Mailer book? *Armies of the Night*, the one I sent home with you the other day?"

Sam smiled. "We're on the same wave-length, Eve. That's just what was I was about to tell you. I can hardly put the thing down. Reads like a novel. Biting, too—edgy. He's a real New Yorker after my own heart."

Eve wondered at Sam's own New York edge. The way he spoke, the accent, the frankness. She caught herself close to daydreaming further (she must slow down on the wine!) and set down her glass. "Alex said the book is wildly controversial and everybody's reading it."

He turned to her as if she'd spoken magic. "Exactly. That's what gave me this idea, something I want to talk over with you."

"And what idea is that, Sam?"

"Reading Mailer," he said, "I realized how great it would be to talk about it, I mean to really—"

"Please, don't say 'rap,'" she said in a sudden fit of giggling (was it the wine?). "Sorry, go on, Sam."

"Okay, I won't say 'rap.' But wouldn't it be *groovy*,"—he chuckled at her expression of mock disapproval "if we talked about it in a group. You know. A book club—that's my idea. In your shop, of course."

Eve felt a sudden sobering. There it was then: a book club. Sam wanted to start a book club. How innocuous! Yet, wasn't she slightly disappointed that it was not more than that? Perhaps she really was dull in her middle years. Perhaps he was not at all attracted to her; but then, that was good, wasn't it? The last thing she would ever want to be was "the other woman," putting her on the same plane as Colin's peroxide blonde, Marcela Blankenship. She celebrated a brief moment of moral clarity and relief as she sipped her wine, a blood-red Cabernet that had somehow lost its zest.

"Think about it, Eve," he said, "your cozy shop would be perfect. And *Armies of the Night* could be our first book. Like Alex said, everybody's reading it."

Eve inclined her head in a half-nod. A let-me-think-on-it

brow shot up.

"Oh, you wouldn't have to do a thing," he went on, reading her look. "I would coordinate it—even lead the discussion—and put a notice in the *Laguna Post-News*. Who knows? If it's a success, it could turn into a regular thing. And talk about publicity for the shop!" He looked like a man possessed. "It would bring in people who wouldn't ordinarily go in for tea—"

Eve lifted a hand as if to say, *slow down*. "I do like your enthusiasm, Sam. I would be up for it, yes—yes, of course—but only if you keep your promise to coordinate the whole thing."

They talked about how to proceed. The date would have to be set, but that could wait until he got back from his trip to New York.

"New York? You're going back to New York?"

"For just a few days . . . business. And family." He said this last with a sigh.

Eve held her breath, as if waiting for more explanation regarding "family." She opened her mouth to prod, but he went on—

"That's why I wanted to talk with you before I left, so I could think about it on the trip. Something to keep my mind occupied on the airplane. I could even get some of the gallery folks interested—" He stopped, unable to continue because of a distracting noise that neither of them could avoid.

They turned toward the TV at the bar. Framed on the small square screen were chaotic, disturbing images: bodies strewn about some kind of building, another body being dragged crudely through a street . . . General Westmoreland speaking . . . smoke, fire . . . a father running with his infant . . . .

The hip looking bartender with long sideburns turned up the volume, and it seemed as though, within seconds, every conversation in the lounge had come to an abrupt end. Eve squinted up at the tiny screen. She heard the voice of Walter Cronkite narrating the horror, but the comfort of his voice was no match for the image of a small child's bruised face and burned leg. She felt her stomach churn, the acid from the wine mixing with anxiety.

So much for "Happy Hour" and book clubs, she thought. This was not just another night of war-on-television. Something significant was happening on the other side of the world, something that suddenly rendered shameful her worries of men and wedding rings and dull shoes.

Seeing the interest, the bartender turned up the volume even louder and went back to polishing a glass with a white cloth while watching the screen. The loud-mouthed man sitting on the other side of Sam shouted over the voice of Cronkite, as if talking back to the television, "But LBJ said we're winning the goddamned war. Didn't he just say that in the State of the Union speech?" The heavy-set man, hair plastered to his head with sweat, pushed up his thick-lensed glasses and railed again at the television. He leaned over to Sam, as if just now realizing that the television would not talk back, and spoke with liquored breath: "He did say that, didn't he? That we're winning the goddamned war?"

* * *

The call came at 11:40 p.m. the next evening, disturbing Madeline's sleep. She reached to grab the receiver from the night stand and yawned an unenthusiastic hello.

It was the operator. "I have a person-to-person call for Madeline Prescott from Mike Riley. Go ahead, please."

"Hey. It's me—Mike. I know you don't want to talk . . . ."

It took a moment for Madeline's mind to break through the fog of sleep. "How'd you get this number?" she finally asked with unconcealed annoyance. She didn't associate the cottage with Mike Riley, and it irked her that his voice had now contaminated her new space. Her new life. At least this time he didn't have the effrontery to call collect.

"Your little sis gave it to me. Look, I know you're pissed at me and I understand—"

"Do you know what time it is?" She pulled the illuminated face of the clock close to her. "Some of us have to work in the morning."

Ignoring her, Mike plowed on. "I just wanted to let you know what's happening here in your old digs."

"You mean, with you and . . . *Sarah*?"

"No, Red." He took a nervous breath. "She . . . we aren't together anymore, but that's not why I'm calling."

"You're wishing me a happy Ground Hog Day, then?"

He laughed too loudly. "Damn, you always make me laugh. No, I was just thinking of you, and wanting to hear your thoughts on Tet."

"My thoughts on Ted?" Madeline was in no mood for this. "Ted, who?"

"Not *Ted*." Mike's voice inflected a familiar patronizing tone. "*Tet*, the Vietnamese New Year."

"You called me in the middle of the night to ask my thoughts on the Vietnamese New Year?"

"Man, you've been out of it, Red. Haven't you even looked at a paper?"

"No," Madeline said coldly. "I've been on a news diet. And quit calling me Red."

"Well then . . . *Madeline*, let me be the first to tell you that all hell just broke loose in Nam."

Madeline bristled at word, "Nam," as if Mike Riley had intimate knowledge of the place, as if he had just returned from a tour of duty.

"Not interested."

Mike ignored this remark. With his usual bull-in-a-china-shop approach to human interaction, he rattled on—something about a huge, well-organized Communist offensive against thirty cities in the South on the eve of Tet, a day that was supposed to be a cease-fire. Even the embassy in Saigon had been attacked.

Of course Madeline had known something was up. *Of course* she was aware of the chatter around her, but she tried hard to block out anything related to Vietnam because Vietnam was Sean. *Write me, Sis,* she kept hearing in her head like a bad TV jingle. Her feelings on the issue of "Nam" were too raw at the moment to be touched.

"So I take it," Mike said, "you didn't see the execution footage on the Huntley-Brinkley Report tonight."

"The *execution* footage? What are you talking about? Who was executed on TV?"

"A Vietcong prisoner. The thing about it, Red . . . I mean, Madeline, is that it showed a Vietnamese General—one of *our* allies—shooting this prisoner execution style in the head, up close and personal. It was brutal. And on film. It was in all the papers yesterday—the photo, that is. I still can't believe you missed that. You need to start reading papers. Anyway, that's the state of things over there. Outta control. It looks like LBJ's song and dance routine last month at the State of the Union— you know, about how we're winning the war, battle by battle and all that shit—is no longer gonna fly. The credibility gap is just too damned wide."

Madeline remembered that Mike had a fondness for the expression, "credibility gap." She must have typed it a hundred times in his papers. What the White House was saying about the war, and the war that people were seeing on their televisions— well, it just wasn't jiving. There was a gap all right, she sighed. And Sean Prescott had fallen headlong into it.

"Yeah," she said, conscious of the rhythmic sound of the waves outside her bedroom window, "I'd say the credibility gap is about the size of the Pacific Ocean." She paused. "But wait a minute. You say a film crew from NBC and a photographer were just standing there while this general shot a prisoner in the head? So why didn't they put down their cameras and try to stop it, I mean, if it was so morally outrageous?"

"I don't know . . . oh, that's not the point," Mike said with irritation.

She turned in her bed, stretched the phone cord to its limit, and looked out the window into the night. But she could see no stars.

"Are you still there?" Mike asked, now sounding exasperated.

She let the pause linger, just to annoy. Then she said lazily, "So, what does this mean?"

"It means you need to get your butt up here. Everyone—the Vietnam Day Committee, the SDS, half of San Francisco—they're already organizing for a massive protest. Even the acid-heads in Haight-Ashbury are sobering up." He chuckled, but Madeline held silent.

"Anyway," he rumbled on, "rumors are already flying that Westmoreland is going to ask for more troops. The guy had the audacity to play this whole thing down on television, turning the truth on its head by saying that the offensive was a bust because all the offenders were killed." He punctuated this last statement with a cynical grunt.

"The body count theory," said Madeline. She felt sick, remembering Sean's letter and the way dead bodies were netted like fish and then dumped into mass graves.

"Yeah. Body count. And then there's the election in November to think about," continued Mike. "I guess you haven't heard, since you've been on your *news diet,* that Dick Nixon just entered the race for the Republican primary. That bastard could just win if we don't get a good anti-war candidate to rival LBJ."

"Uh huh," Madeline said, wondering just where this conversation was headed.

"They say Gene McCarthy is going to run in the New Hampshire primary."

"Yeah, yeah, okay. Gene McCarthy. So what are you trying to say?"

"That you have to come back to Berkeley."

"I'm not coming back."

"Man, how can you say that? How can you just abandon The Movement? You've got to come back. It'll be great Red . . . *Madeline*. Like old times."

"Old times? You think I'm hankering after old times?"

Ignoring this, he said, "Hey, you'll love this. A sociology prof and I are interviewing students about their reactions to Tet. I mean, if Berkeley can't put pressure on the government, then who can? But we need you." He paused. "I mean, I need you."

Madeline Prescott sensed another paper coming on—a paper in need of a *typist*. Her cheeks felt hot. "You sound almost happy about all these people dying and that the war is out of control."

"Of course I'm not happy about it, but this will galvanize the anti-war movement here, don't you see?"

"I've got a job, Mike. Commitments."

"I've still got your albums," Mike said, as if holding Joan Baez hostage.

"About that," she said, taking a deep breath. "Could you box them up with the rest of my things and send everything down here? I miss my albums. And my history books. And the Camus novels."

"Oh, Red." (He'd quit trying to make an effort with her name.) "You don't mean that. We're a team, Red—a *team*. Believe me, Sarah and I . . . it was a damned stupid mistake. How many times do I have to tell you that I'm sorry?"

"How many times? Just when *did* you say you were sorry?"

"Well, I'm telling you now—"

"I really don't care, Mike. I don't love you. You don't love me. It's ridiculous, all this. Just let it go."

"I never said—"

"Just let it go, Mike. You can demonstrate and plan protests and canvass the crowds all you want. Without me." She paused. "For all the good it does."

"What in the hell do you mean?" Mike snapped.

She could imagine his perfectly round Trotsky glasses steaming up.

"Has it changed anything, Mike? All that, '*Hey, Hey, LBJ, How many kids did you kill today*?' Has it stopped the war? Did it save . . . my *brother*?" She wished immediately she could reel that back in. Reel in her anger, her grief. She could never share these deeper feelings with him, and especially not that terrible fear: that unspeakable thought that hit her like a punch in the stomach at the military funeral. She could never share this with a man so lost in high-minded abstractions that he couldn't cope with the feelings of those around him.

"Okay, I know. I *know*. You're . . . grieving. I am sorry for your loss. I hope you know that."

"What I do know," Madeline said, "is that you're a day late and a dollar short." She paused, surprised at her own words. Had she really used a cliché that was probably as old as the cottage? She half wondered if Grandma Daisy were somehow still present, whispering in her ear, guiding her every word.

When she finally hung up, well after midnight, she felt peevish and hungry and wide, wide awake. She got out of bed and went to the tiny kitchen at the back of the cottage and filled the teakettle. She hoped the chamomile tea Eve sent home with her would help her sleep. While waiting for the kettle to boil, she grabbed the Vanilla Wafers from the cabinet and began eating them out of the box. They were soft and tasted like cardboard, but she kept shoving them into her mouth. It was this or a cigarette, she reasoned, and she had to quit smoking. She just had to.

She drank tea now, for God's sake.

Chapter Ten

///"The storms of youth precede brilliant days,'" Mr. Larsen read aloud from his poetry book, as Madeline poured him a fresh cup of Darjeeling. She was familiar with the verse, but only in the context of Berkeley and protest flyers. Coming from a man who looked like a prophet (albeit, a baggy suited, carnation-bearing sort of prophet), the words took on a wiser tone.

"That's Lautreamont, isn't it?" Madeline asked, setting down the pot.

He nodded, wide-eyed and obviously impressed. "Young Lady, let me tell you something." The old man tapped the book with knotty fingers. "Poetry is alive. It's never the same one day to the next. I first read these words years ago, but today it looks very different to me." He took a sip of the hot tea, his intelligent blue eyes smiling through the steam.

"Like Heraclites' river, I suppose," said Madeline, recalling a lecture from her philosophy class. "What was it he said? Something like . . . 'You can never step into the same river twice.' So, maybe, then, you can never step into the same poem twice."

Mr. Larsen looked pleased at that response. He nodded thoughtfully. She wondered at his age—approaching eighty, was he? Even with his current bronchial problems, he had, by his own account, lived an energetic life. He'd traveled the world. He'd fought in The Great War, his entry into American life and loyalty. But Madeline found that image hard to swallow, this gentle man fighting in any war. But then, that was a lifetime ago. People change, like Heraclites' river. Perhaps, she thought, this was the way of life. One is born into a river of change, and one *becomes* a river of change.

And hadn't she changed, too? Even within the space of a single month? A refreshing sense of her own life's movement swept over her. And to think that Mike wanted her to step back into the same old stale water. *Impossible.* Heraclites said it himself; she had Greek philosophy on her side.

She returned to the kitchen, releasing the metaphors of the day to the back burner of her mind while she focused on her work. She stopped to look back at Mr. Larsen. His long tresses flowed over the side of his face, so that all she saw was massive white hair and the tip of an aquiline nose pointed toward his book. For a poetic existence such as his, she mused, a cup of tea, a little conversation, a book: the perfect benediction to the day.

Her serene meditation on the old man's profile was interrupted by the jangling bell. In walked one of the best-looking men Madeline Prescott had ever laid eyes on. She immediately disliked him. He was what she and her friends at Berkeley would refer to as the "Ken Doll" type. These were overly gorgeous, overly confident men who thought every woman should fawn and beg for their attention. They were always brainless narcissists. Always. This particular Ken Doll, tanned and chiseled, had a cleft in his chin—the worst kind. She would be cool towards him, so as not to give him the ego strokes that such faces craved. But, on the other hand, he was a customer, so she must be courteous.

The man was in his late twenties, maybe thirty. His dark eyes and olive skin contrasted in a most aesthetically pleasing way with his golden, sun-bleached waves of hair. It annoyed her to no end. His chinos and golf shirt gave him an athletic look. *Probably never cracked a book.* However, she was forced to note that he bore a newspaper under his arm. At least he read something.

Then he smiled.

Her knees nearly gave out in response to that smile, a shy, bemused sort of smile. A smile of the eyes, mostly. Brown eyes. Eyes that shot out sparks of light. It was as if his mouth and eyes were of different personalities, one diffident and reserved, the other bright, confident, gregarious. Which was he? she wondered.

"Hi," she said with her voice a bit too perky. "I've got a table right by the window, if you want."

"Thanks, but I would really prefer one of those tables . . . over there, if that's all right." He gestured toward the Steinbeck table, near the California Writers section of books.

He smiled again. Her knees went weak again.

His English accent piqued her interest, too. Was it real or affected? Did he have some kind of 007 routine he used on women? She would need to keep her distance from this one.

The man walked toward the table but then turned to pat Eiler Larsen on the back. The two shook hands as if they knew each other. That was not unusual, as everyone knew the famous Greeter of Laguna, but it did mean that the stranger was local. She had hoped he was from far away—the just-passing-through kind of lady killer.

The man sat down and asked for tea, specifically PG Tips, and a scone. Madeline knew instantly that his accent was real because, according to Eve, only true Brits ordered PG Tips.

In the kitchen, she put together the perfect tea tray: a plain, flowerless china teacup with matching saucer, a scone from the warm oven, boysenberry jam and an extra large dollop of Eve's special clotted cream on the side. When she returned to the Steinbeck table, he looked engrossed in his newspaper. He offered a polite "thank you," but didn't look up at her while she poured the tea. She preferred not to be watched and was glad when she could move on to serve other customers.

Eve was attending to some business upstairs in the flat, leaving her alone for the first time. Perhaps it was some kind of test, she thought, to see if her new employee could actually manage on her own. Madeline would have to hustle to meet the demands of a Saturday, but she enjoyed the challenge.

She refilled a teapot for the young hippie, Simone, a regular in the shop. Simone wore a long cotton dress that looked vaguely Indian and fell down to the tops of her sandals. Her dark brown hair hung straight down her back, and she sported tiny wire-rimmed glasses in the style of John Lennon. The glasses sat on the end of her nose, giving her the look of a middle-aged reader when she must be only eighteen or so. She was presently thumbing through a copy of *Siddhartha*.

Madeline engaged Simone in light conversation about her own preferences for books. She surmised that Simone might not be so intrigued with Hermann Hesse's *Siddhartha* as she was with Matthew, the Neru-jacketed writer who sat at the table near the general fiction section. Matthew, with his shaggy Beatle hair cut, looked exactly the same as he did on Madeline's first day in the shop, still scribbling away, probably hoping to be the next Jack Kerouac.

Still discussing books with Simone, she glanced over at the Steinbeck table, just to check her dimpled-chin customer, but his face—and dimple—were hidden behind his newspaper. While she was still looking, the paper began to lower, and when his eyes met hers, he shoved the paper up like something from a bad spy movie.

She greeted another customer coming through the door, a hippie with sun-streaked once-brown hair flowing down to his shoulders, and a long, unkempt beard of biblical proportion. His jeans and baggy poet shirt somehow added to the effect of one going for the Jesus look. He declined tea in favor of perusing the poetry books.

As she started back to the kitchen, she had the feeling of

being watched. She turned to the man with the newspaper, and again he shoved the paper up like a drop-out from spy school. Why would he be staring at her? Was she really that fetching in her green jumper and brown suede boots? She imagined his "type" in women. And she wasn't it.

When she returned from the kitchen, the Jesus look-alike was gone, but she saw something, a little booklet, lying on the table next to where he had been standing. She started to run after him until she noticed the title on the front of the booklet, "Where Will YOU Spend Eternity?" A religious tract? Now the hippies were getting high on Jesus? She heard there was a "far-out" church in Costa Mesa and that the pastor baptized hippies at the beach. Curious, she thumbed through the tract, a simple four-step plan to reserve your place in heaven. At the end, you could be saved by saying a particular prayer—conveniently written out for you. Instant salvation, she thought with a sigh, to go along with instant coffee, Tang, and foiled TV dinners. *Had the Big Questions really been reduced to this?* She tossed the tract in the trash with the biscuit wrappings.

"Madeline, could I get a biscuit to go with my tea?" called Simone from her table.

"Sure. What kind do you want? Chocolate or shortbread?" Madeline gestured toward the basket of "Favourite British Biscuits" on the counter.

"No, I want a *biscuit*, like his." She pointed to the Thoreau table, to Matthew and his half-eaten scone.

Matthew looked up. Simone had finally managed to catch the writer's eye.

Madeline held back a smile. "Those are called scones, Simone. Remember, it's a British shop. "Cookies are biscuits; scones just look like biscuits."

Simone looked thoroughly confused.

"I'll bring you a scone," said Madeline with a smile. "Want it warmed?"

Simone nodded and went back to her tea and *Siddhartha* and stealthy glances toward the sensitive looking guy in the Nehru jacket.

Madeline noticed the Greeter grappling for his cane on the back of his chair. She rushed to help him to the door. He looked down longingly at his book.

"Take it with you, Mr. Larsen. Go ahead. You can bring it back next time." The old man smiled and thanked her. By the time Mr. Larsen left with book in hand, the only customers remaining were Simone, Matthew, and the Ken Doll spy, who was now heading towards the cash register.

"Was everything all right?" she asked, as she did with all her customers.

"Everything was great," he said, laying exact change on the counter. "I'll be back again soon. You can count on it."

She put his money in the cash register and gave a polite good-bye. He opened the door and then turned, offering one last nod and one more devastating smile. Soon after he left (and her knees had recovered) she said good-bye to Matthew and his yellow legal pad, noticing that Simone had timed her departure to match his.

* * *

Setting herself to the task of cleaning tables, Madeline noticed the spy-man had left his newspaper folded neatly next to his teacup. Like the hippie's religious tract, she picked it up with curiosity. It was *The New York Times*, the same paper Sam Steiner often brought in to read alongside the *L.A. Times*. It seemed that those two papers summed up the world, sandwiching the rest of the country between them. But the odd thing was the date, February 1. Why was this guy reading a paper that was two days old? And more to the point, why was he staring at her behind a two-day-old paper? Maybe he wasn't actually reading it, but using it as a prop, like in the movies. Maybe he was in fact spying on her, or at least checking her out.

The idea made her laugh.

She started to toss the paper, but then stopped, captured by a picture near the top of the front page. It was a big man pointing a gun to the head of a small, frightened man with bound hands. Point blank range. A shiver of revulsion shot through her. The little man—so young!—with bound hands was about to be shot out of existence. His dreams, his loves, his world, his history: all about to be obliterated in a deafening moment. The terror on his face bore into her. This must be the execution that Mike had seen on the Huntley-Brinkley Report.

Despite her present aversion to Mike Riley, he was right about one thing. Vietnam was a quagmire, an endless death mill that would surely grind up thousands more brothers and fathers and sons. As she stared at the executioner—the chief of the national police, according the caption—she thought of a phrase from Nietzsche, "the will to power," that ugly human obsession that squeezed the trigger, endlessly. *Squeezing, squeezing, squeezing . . . all the poetry from the world.*

Madeline shook off these dark thoughts, threw the paper in the trash, shuttled the dishes to the kitchen, and grabbed a clean rag and a bottle of Windex on the way back to the tables. The Oscar Wilde table needed attention. It was her favorite table to clean since there were dozens of his witty quotes under the glass. She closed her eyes and moved her index finger on top the table like an Ouija board, as if seeking some random wisdom. She opened her eyes and looked at the quote beneath her still finger:

The world is a stage, but the play is badly cast.

Ha! Badly cast is right, she thought, squirting the glass with the blue cleaner. If the world was a stage, LBJ needed to be yanked off with the proverbial shepherd's crook. Someone needed to stop this war. But the only anti-war candidate who could beat LBJ in the primaries, at least to Madeline's mind, was Bobby Kennedy. *Only* Bobby Kennedy. *But he wouldn't even try.* He had closed the door. Eve, who was not on a news diet, had informed Madeline days before that Senator Kennedy had spoken: he would not be contesting Johnson. For a moment, she stopped polishing the glass and closed her eyes as if praying, as if willing Bobby Kennedy to change his mind. He just had to change his mind now, after this Tet thing, or . . . or what? More LBJ? More endless war?

She took a deep breath and moved to the Thoreau table (Matthew, the writer, always left crumbs). She wished she didn't feel so passionate—even enraged—about things, all these larger issues of war and peace and justice and meaning. But she did. *She just did.* It may, she thought, be a curse not to be able to live happily ensconced in one's own private world, tripping with the hippies at Mystic Arts World. *What? Was she actually envious of acid-heads?*

If she had just listened to her parents and stayed home that Sunday night, back in 1961, the day Martin Luther King came to Orange County to lecture at Chapman College, she wouldn't be so easily agitated by the injustice of things and the sheer stupidity of violence. But Dr. King's powerful voice had changed her, lit a fire under her, and there was no going back. No rewind button. His philosophy of non-violent change had come to be the closest thing she knew to be a religious feeling. As long as King was preaching against racism and poverty—and now, against the war—she would have her own prophet-of-sorts.

She sighed heavily over a *Walden* quote:

> *If you have built castles in the air, your work need not be lost; that is where they should be. Now put the foundations under them.*

Perhaps that was her problem, she reasoned. She had the castle-in-the-air thing down, but no real foundation—no concrete plan of action. What would her brother think of her? Here she was, selling books and pouring tea and discussing poetry and trying to figure out the mysteries of life while the world went up in smoke. *Damn it all.* Part of her did wish she could go back to Berkeley.

She would have to do something.

But what? Ben would know. Ben Schwartz would understand. Hadn't he helped her before? Didn't he share her views on the war? Yes, she would find her old college counselor and talk things over with him, even if it was only on the phone. Maybe she could talk to him about what was bothering her, about Sean's death. And that unspeakable fear that must, somehow, be spoken.

* * *

"You're scrubbing that table top to within an inch of its life," Eve said, startling Madeline. "Would you like to join me for a glass of wine upstairs?"

Madeline, rag in hand, turned to look at her employer. "Wine?"

"A reward of sorts. It was your first day by yourself, and you were brilliant from what I hear."

"How did you—?"

"But I realize," Eve cut her off, "that it's Saturday night, and I'm not the most exciting company for someone your age."

"Wine sounds great," Madeline said, torn between wanting to rush home and call Ben Schwartz and this unusual invitation. She shrugged to herself. Ben could wait.

"Good, then." Eve looked pleased. "I'll just lock the door."

Madeline followed Eve up the stairs to her flat with Earl Grey bounding ahead. He shot through the cat flap while Eve fished around in the pocket of her skirt to find her keys. The two women entered into the warmth and charm of the upstairs flat to find Earl thumping his tail in front of his cat bowl.

Madeline surveyed the apartment with a curious pleasure. The shiny hardwood floor featured a Persian carpet patterned in apricots and greens. Above the television was a framed print of

Van Gogh's *Sunflowers*. The main room was small and cozy with just enough furniture: an antique chair by the door, a sofa (plastic free) in soft beige, and a green leather easy chair with books strewn about on the lamp stand. In front of the easy chair was the television, a large console TV—color, by the looks of it.

"Have a seat. I'll bring the wine." Eve gestured around the room. "You see that it's rather 'cozy' as the real estate people like to call it."

The kitchen was open with only a bar separating it from the living room. Madeline started for the sofa but then stopped to watch Earl Grey stretch his paws on Eve's flowered skirt as the whir of the electric can opener signaled imminent satisfaction. She liked how the sleek gray tabby dug into the fish with gumption and thought she could hear him purring while he ate, as if he wanted to burst with pleasure. Her pensive mood had past and she was ready to enjoy this new experience.

"Earl must be good company," Madeline said, bending to offer the cat a few strokes. His fur was slate gray, soft and lux-urious.

"He's a terrible bother," Eve said unconvincingly, beaming down at the cat, "but at least he's not a man. I can say that for him."

Madeline stood up. "Eve, do you mind if I ask you some-thing?"

"It's about Sam, isn't it?" Eve said this as she perused the choices of wine in the wooden rack on the cabinet. She turned to look at Madeline. "That is what you were going to ask—am I carrying on with Sam?"

Madeline smiled. "I know you're not 'carrying on' with Sam. But it's curious. He wears a ring and yet, I never hear him say anything about a wife. What do you make of it?"

Eve picked a bottle of wine and set it on the cabinet, "I was going to ask you the same thing. He didn't say a word about a wife the other night over drinks, but then we were so rudely interrupted by all that business in Vietnam. The Cronkite report was on, and there was a loud-mouthed man next to Sam and, well, we didn't stay long after that."

"You need to ask him, Eve. Just ask him."

"But then I'd be showing my cards, cards that I don't want to play. But still, I've never had a male friend like this, and I'm not sure what the rules are. Do American women have friendships with married men? Or am I in dangerous territory?"

Madeline inclined her head. "Do you want my honest opinion?"

"I do."

Madeline noticed Eve's hair coming out of its pins and the heaviness of it drooped over the back of her turtleneck, the same butter yellow sweater she had worn on their first meeting. Her neat French Roll was starting to unravel; the woman, it seemed, shunned Aqua Net. In fact, Eve van Gelder looked quite vulnerable, quite different from the confident professional woman who interviewed her that first day.

"Dangerous territory, that's what you're into now, Eve. I think before you go on any more Happy Hour excursions, you should ask him about the ring. It's that simple."

"But Madeline, he and I aren't on such personal terms, not really. It's not like—"

"Having drinks after work constitutes personal," Madeline said with authority. "And you have every right to ask him. Promise me you'll do that?"

"Well, I can't promise, but I do think you have a point . . . " Eve trailed off as if completely at a loss in a world that a younger woman knew so well.

"Here's my theory," said Madeline, enjoying herself. "I've thought about it while drying endless—and I do mean endless—cups and saucers: He's getting a divorce. He's left his wife in New York. She doesn't want to move to California with all its hippies and radicals and weirdoes. She would miss the high life in New York—the theater, the opera, weekends in the Hamptons. And then to make matters worse, he's falling for the lovely lady at the tea and book shop. So, he's going back this weekend to talk to his lawyer and get a divorce. That's what I think."

"Oh, my!" said Eve with an extravagant laugh, uncorking the wine bottle with a soft pop. "You've cooked up quite a little drama while drying the teacups. Remind me to keep you occupied out on the floor."

"But what else could it be?" Madeline asked. "She's obviously not with him, or we would have seen her by now, or he would have said, 'Oh, I should tell my wife about that,' or 'My wife would like this teapot.' He's that sort of guy, Eve. Very thoughtful, I can tell. So, if his wife were here, we'd have known by now. Right?"

"I don't know. There must be some other explanation," Eve said, pulling out a plate of cheese cubes from the refrigerator and handing it to Madeline. "I've got it. Sam is really some mysterious Mr. Rochester with a mad wife hidden in the attic."

Madeline laughed. "So you like him, don't you? And by the way, it's very American to come right out and ask such questions, so I will not apologize for what you English might call 'impertinence.'"

"Madeline, I think you've read too many nineteenth-century English novels. We're just like you Americans, really . . . well, maybe a bit more reserved."

"So?"

"Oh, all right." Eve turned and smiled with mock exasperation, arms folded over her yellow sweater. "Yes, I am fond of the man. Very fond. But I am not in the market for a husband. I just got rid of one."

"Sounds like you put arsenic in his tea."

"I didn't have to. He left me for a younger woman, a platinum blonde called Marcela." Eve spoke these words with the casual air of one speaking of someone else: *Oh, he left his wife for a platinum blonde, you know.* But Eve was speaking of herself —her own betrayed self—while she reached for two fat wine goblets from the cabinet.

"Oh. I'm sorry," Madeline said, slightly shocked.

"Don't look so serious," Eve said. "It happens. Some men, like Colin, need reminders of their lost youth. They're terrified of getting old. They get these bloody awful dyes to cover their gray. They get sports cars. They take up with young things like Marcela. There's a word for it now. It's called, 'Mid-Life Crisis.' I read about it in *Life* magazine. My daughter has taken it all quite to heart. She's still embittered over the whole thing."

"Really? Why?" Madeline felt a wicked curiosity. Eve van Gelder suddenly seemed much more than just a boss. Her life— even at such an age—was filled with surprising intrigue.

"Her father married a woman who looks almost as young as herself—probably because she *is* almost as young as Becca." Eve rolled her eyes for effect. "Anyway, Becca was always . . . well, the apple of his eye. I think my poor daughter is actually more devastated about the whole thing than I am."

"So his affair didn't bother you that much?"

"Of course it did. And I don't mean to trivialize our marriage. Or any marriage for that matter. It's just that we had already grown apart, far apart, so the affair—when it finally came to light—was what you might call 'the last straw.'" She gestured toward the tiny drop-leaf table in the kitchen. "Please, dear, pull out a chair and sit down. Try the cheese."

Madeline popped a cheese cube into her mouth, pulled out a wooden kitchen chair, and turned it to face Eve. "But was it really that easy for you? To see him fall for this . . . Marcela person?" Madeline couldn't seem to let this go, for she still felt her own oozing humiliation at the thought of Mike and Sarah, and hers was no marriage—not by a long shot. Surely Eve must have been more devastated than she was letting on.

"Not easy," Eve said, handing Madeline a glass of wine. "You have to understand, dear, that the really terrible thing was not the affair itself. It was our marriage. That was the real tragedy. Ending it was like lancing a boil so that it could finally heal. You see, Colin and I struggled against each other for years. I wanted a more independent existence, and he wanted a glamorous 'show wife' to entertain his friends and be, well . . . *amusing* at parties. It just wasn't in me to be that woman."

"But you were married a long time, right?"

"Oh, yes. Young war bride and all that." Eve sat down with her wine and reached for a cube of cheese. "You've heard it before, I'm sure. We really didn't know each other when we got married, but war does that. You're afraid the world is about to end." Eve concluded her sad fact-of-life lesson with a quick sip of wine. Then she smiled and took a bite of cheese. "It's an aged Gouda—needs the wine to bring out the flavor."

Madeline took another cheese cube, and then with sudden spontaneity, lifted her glass towards Eve's own. "To women!"

"To us!" joined Eve with exuberance, clicking her glass against Madeline's.

They took simultaneous sips of wine, as if making a pact of solidarity. And the moment seemed cleansed somehow of all men who betrayed their women.

Chapter Eleven

It was past eight o'clock when Madeline finally left Eve's flat and arrived back at Crystal Cove. She managed by stealth of darkness to dodge the loquacious Biddy Gelson, who was engaged in lively conversation with neighbors on the boardwalk.

It was probably ridiculous to call Ben now. No shrink wanted a call on a Saturday night. It would make her sound desperate—a real Looney Tune. But she was still too wound up to settle into the new Norman Mailer book, so she called information and requested a station-to-station call, feeling her heart beat wildly as the operator connected her.

"Ray Dobson here."

Ray Dobson? "Uh . . . I might have the wrong number. I'm looking for Ben Schwartz."

"I'm his roommate, or his former roommate, that is. He's just taken a position at UCLA. I've got his number here somewhere if you want to hang on—"

"Yes, thanks," she blurted, unable to contain her excitement. *Ben Schwartz in L.A.?* Minutes away. She took the number from Ray Dobson, thanked him profusely, and dialed Ben. Moments later she heard the familiar voice of comfort and sanity.

"Ben, it's Madeline. Madeline Prescott. From Berkeley."

A slight pause. "Not the redheaded radical who writes poetry—"

"The very one. But I've given up poetry. Can't seem to find the right metaphor."

Ben laughed. "Madeline Prescott. Great to hear from you. Are you still living in Berkeley with . . . ?"

"Mike. And no. I'm not even living in Berkeley. I'm in Orange County."

"You? Behind the Orange Curtain?"

She laughed. "Not as bizarre as it sounds. I'm in Laguna Beach with all the artists and free spirits. It's great." She took a quick breath before launching into her reason for calling, a reason she wasn't quite sure about until it tumbled out. "Ben, I'm sorry to call you at home and on a Saturday night, but it's important. It's . . . my brother." That was all the redheaded-radical-would-be-poet could get out of her mouth. The familiar emotions welled, tugging at her like the force of a rip current.

"Can you talk about it?" Ben Schwartz spoke in his usual way, soothingly and direct. She could picture his huge dark—not unattractive—eyes searching hers, his leaning in toward her with hands patiently folded in a listening gesture, as if she were the most important person in the world. But she was spoiling it now, paralyzed with emotion. She wished she hadn't called. *Another impetuous decision gone awry.*

After a time, Ben said gently, "Madeline, how far are you from UCLA? Could you drive up and see me? Or I could come down there. I think we need to talk in person, don't you?"

She willed herself to speak without a waver. "Yes, I do. I'd love it if you came down here. I'm working in a bookshop—a British-style tea and bookshop right across the street from the beach. And Ben, you'd love it, the beach, I mean. It's a kind of refuge from smoggy L.A. And we'll have tea in the shop. Real tea—not in bags or anything—and cookies that are called biscuits and biscuits that are called scones."

He laughed. "How about tomorrow afternoon?"

When she hung up the phone she immediately picked up the receiver again to call Eve, just to forewarn her that she was bringing a guest to the shop on her day off.

* * *

Feeling confident in her favorite turtleneck and cords, Madeline took a step back when she met Ben Schwartz in front of Van Gelder's Tea and Books. He looked well-kempt and utterly clean shaven—a small disappointment. She had forgotten his high forehead, or was it a receding hair line? He was, after all, somewhere in his early thirties by now—almost elderly by her generation's standard. He wore a pressed shirt and a jacket with elbow patches. Quite the academic. Quite unlike the unshaven, slightly tattered, non-conformist grad student she remembered. She wasn't sure what she thought of his transformation, but then, she reasoned, he was part of The Establishment now, with a professional position. At least he still wore the same dark-rimmed glasses on his prominent nose, giving him that air of authority in all matters psychological.

He opened his arms wide and hugged her like an old friend rather than a client, leaving her dizzy in a rush of awkwardness and exuberance. He opened the door for her and she walked inside the shop with the sense of stepping into a different world, a different river altogether.

They sat down at the Greeter's favorite table, the George Orwell table by the window. Because it was Madeline's day off, she and Ben could be waited on like real paying customers, even though Eve had insisted that their tea would be "on the house." Madeline could hardly wait to show off her old friend to her new boss, a boss who, despite their age difference, was becoming a new friend.

But she panicked when Eve did not greet them at the table. In fact, no one greeted them. Then, rounding the tea wall from the kitchen was a man with a tea towel slung over his shoulder. She recognized him instantly. Her jawed dropped and a dumb stare came over her.

"Hello, Madeline," said the Ken Doll before he even reached their table. "I'm Alex. Alex Moore, Eve's son. I help out on

Sundays." He wore a sheepish look, unlike his former non-chalance. "I believe you waited on me yesterday."

"Yes. I. Did."

"Right . . . well," Alex stumbled, "Mum wanted me to observe her new assistant. She, of course, thinks you hung the moon, but we thought I should play it incognito, you know, like a restaurant critic . . . of sorts."

"Of sorts," Madeline muttered, still off balance by this sudden revelation of the man and his dimple. His dark gray turtleneck seemed to accentuate the deep cleft in his chin. And his square jaw. Nobody had a right to look that good. It made the rest of the world, at least her world—her own self, to be exact—feel too Plain Jane. She was most annoyed by his mouth, the way his lips curled in a restrained effort to hide a smile, as if he had something hilarious on you, but wasn't telling.

But this was Eve's son, so she forced a half-smile.

Suddenly she remembered Ben. "Oh, this is Ben, my friend from Berkeley."

She could tell that Ben was aware of the tension. The two men shook hands.

Alex looked back at Madeline. "I'm really sorry if I made you feel uncomfortable or—"

Madeline lifted a hand. "Not at all. I just hope I made the grade."

"Oh, you were brilliant." He turned to Ben. "She was brilliant." Back to Madeline. "And, as it happens, I recommended a pay hike."

She smiled and felt herself begin to relax into a near-human state. "By pay hike, I guess you mean . . . a raise?" He nodded smugly. "Thanks," she said. "Thanks . . . Alex. By the way, where's Eve?" She was anxious to change the subject.

"She's on a long-distance call. My sister in London."

"Okay then, Ben and I will just take a quick walk and come back in a few minutes."

Alex looked troubled.

"We'll be back soon," she assured.

* * *

"That was tense," Ben said, once they were outside the shop.

"Oh, let's forget it. Let's just enjoy the walk. I want to take you up to the park overlooking the ocean—Heisler Park, it's called."

They crossed the street and walked along on sidewalk lined with exotic trees.

"What's that strange looking tree that has all its roots above ground?" Ben's hand went toward his chin as if stroking an imaginary beard. "Intriguing. Like the unconscious surfacing."

"Only a shrink would say that about an Ombu tree. That tree is where the Greeter likes to sit—usually drawing a crowd of children. You know about the famous Greeter, don't you? Eiler Larsen?"

"I've heard of him. Hasn't everyone?"

Madeline wondered with amusement what a shrink would say about Eiler Larsen. A crazy old man with a prophet complex?

She stopped suddenly; she had forgotten her sunglasses. She must have left them on the table. *Damn!* She didn't want to go back and face Alex Moore.

"Are you all right?" asked Ben.

"Oh, just my shades—forgot them. I'll survive." She led the way up the stairs and onto a meandering path bordered by deep green palms and blooming bird-of-paradise plants, quite a contrast to their previous meetings in the poorly lit campus office with a pot of dying brown ivy lurking in the corner.

"It feels a little weird—meeting you off campus like this," she said, catching her breath midway up the path.

"Feels nice," Ben said, dodging a teenage girl clad in ultra wide bell-bottom pants.

Nice—but weird, she thought "Ben, I want to pay for your

visit like a regular appointment, something above and beyond the tea and scones. I'm not a student anymore, so free counseling is a thing of the past for me."

"What are you talking about?" said Ben, turning to her. "I'm here on my own, because I . . . I want to be here."

"Okay," she said. Was he attracted to her, she wondered? She hoped not. And hoped so. But she wasn't sure if she could ever see Ben as an equal. He was too "up there," too "all-knowing," too much *her shrink*. Still—

"Madeline, let's sit over there," he said a little out of breath, pointing to a sun-drenched bench near the edge of the rocky cliff.

Madeline sat close—but not too close—and gazed out to sea, shading her eyes with her hand. This particular view never failed to engulf her with feelings of awe for the vastness of it, the mysteries that lay below, and the endless sky above. It was a different vantage point from her sea-level cottage. On the beach, it's as if one is a part of the landscape itself, alongside the rocks and the birds and the starfish in the tide pools. But up here on this high cliff, taking in the expanse of beauty in a hundred different expressions, it was like being an unseen observer of the world, less entangled by it all. More contemplative. It was just the place for someone to sit and search for a metaphor to live by.

She had once seen the librarian who frequented the shop, May-ling Wu, sitting cross-legged on the grassy edge of the cliff just beyond where she and Ben sat. May-ling's eyes had been tightly closed and she looked deep in meditation. At the time, it didn't seem right to interrupt her, but Madeline asked her about it later, when serving her tea.

"Do you have a secret for your meditation? Some . . . mantra?" (At least she knew the lingo.)

"The sea sings; I listen. That's all," May-ling had said, touching her ear for emphasis.

Now, thought Madeline, the sea sang with a heady rhythm

that calmed her mind, and nothing seemed as urgent as it did earlier. All anxious thoughts receded with the outgoing flow of the surf. Settling onto the warm bench, they shared the panorama of blue and turquoise, the smell of salt and sea, the feel of the cool wind on their skin.

After a few moments of drinking in the landscape, Ben draped one leg over the other and looked squarely at Madeline. "I brought you something." He reached inside his jacket pocket and pulled out a news clipping.

"What's this?" Madeline said, taking hold of the clipping and smoothing it out as it flapped about in the breeze.

"An article from yesterday's *New York Times*."

"Hey, doesn't anyone read the *L.A.Times* anymore?" she said with mock irritation.

"My family gave me a subscription," Ben said, "so I don't lose my East Coast moorings. It's an opinion piece. Look at the name on it."

"Robert Kennedy."

Ben nodded. "Read it and weep."

Madeline's eyes swept over the piece entitled, "The Malaise of the Spirit." She skimmed the article, reading to herself. "Oh, this is good," she finally said. "He's saying that we measure our actual worth as a country solely by the Gross National Product" —she pulled the paper closer to read aloud—"'which does not include the beauty of our poetry, the strength of our marriages, the intelligence of our public debate . . . . It measures neither our wit nor our courage, neither our wisdom nor our learning, neither our compassion nor our devotion to our country. It measures everything in short except that which makes life worth while.'"

Madeline closed her eyes in a sigh. "This is beautiful, Ben. But it makes me sad, too." She looked at him. "This is the man who should be running the country."

Ben looked out to sea dreamily. "I remember how we used

to talk politics after your sessions. It always came back to JFK and RFK, didn't it?"

She smiled. "JFK, RFK., a.k.a. Tragedy and Hope."

Ben smiled and moved into his familiar listening posture, leaning forward with elbows resting on his legs, hands clasped in a casual manner. He set his brown eyes on hers. "Speaking of brothers, tell me about yours."

Madeline folded the news clipping, slipped it into her macramé purse, and turned back to her companion. "Sean was killed in action. Right before Christmas."

"Oh, no . . . I'm so sorry." His voice tumbled down deep and warm. He reached for her hand. Ben's hand on hers did not feel contrived, nor did it feel like a romantic gesture. Rather, this felt like something rare, a kind of human to human expression of solidarity—at a level too deep for words. Gratitude swept over her.

"Helloooo!" The familiar voice broke though the moment. Eiler Larsen, wild hair and beard blowing in the wind, labored toward them, cane in hand.

They stood to greet him. "Ben, meet Mr. Larsen, the famous Greeter of Laguna."

Madeline took a step back, shielding her eyes from the sun, observing the men talking as if they'd known each other for years. One loomed tall, wild, eccentric. The other, shorter and tidier. But both were wise and precious to her.

She noticed that, although Mr. Larsen's eyes were just as blue as her own, his were not squinty and watery. But then, he was a tough old bird with years of wandering about without the aid of sunglasses. The Greeter was a good friend of the sun, she reasoned; she, categorically, was not.

Mr. Larsen turned toward her and bowed. "She walks in beauty," he said with all the gravitas of Lord Byron. He turned to Ben. "She takes care of me in the book shop, bringing me pots of tea and my favorite books."

"Are you coming by this afternoon, Mr. Larsen?"

"I just might," he said. "But I've also been invited down to the Cottage Restaurant for supper."

"Well, celebrities are like that, always booked," she said.

As the Greeter moved on, she closed her painful eyes. When she forced them open, she saw Mr. Larsen turning back for one parting gesture with his cane.

"I like your friend," Ben said. "The old man reminds me of something Rollo May—the eminent psychologist—says about the difference between the normal adult and the creative adult."

"I assume Mr. Larsen is in the creative category?"

"To the nth degree," Ben chuckled. "You see, Rollo May says that the normal adult escapes anxiety through the comfort of conformity, but the authentic, creative adult approaches the anxiety of life with courage. That's how I see your Greeter. Authentic. Creative. Courageous, even."

She liked that; and she liked Ben for seeing Mr. Larsen that way. A flood of affection ran through her. "Speaking of anxiety, Ben," she said, motioning for him to sit down, "you were a huge help to me at Berkeley. I was a mess, wound tighter than a ball of yarn. I needed a lot of untangling at the time."

Ben sat down close to her. "And what about now?"

She turned toward him, her face away from the sun so she could look him straight in the eye. "I'm coping. The job has helped to distract me. Eve and Mr. Larsen and Eve's friend, Sam, they've all been great. But they're all so much older, and well, it's just so good to have you here, someone more my own age . . . well, relatively speaking."

"And do you know anything about what happened . . . regarding your brother?"

She stiffened. *She must hold it together.* "That's just it. I'm unsettled about it, Ben. Something's not right, or maybe it's just that it's hard to let it go."

"What do you mean, 'not right'?"

"It was a closed casket, which isn't so unusual I suppose; but it was upsetting—especially to the imagination. And then there was the letter."

"Letter?"

She nodded. "His last one. At least to me. Dad brought it to me right before his funeral. And there was something in it, something he wrote that made me wonder if . . ."

She took a deep breath and looked out toward Catalina Island for courage.

"If what?"

"Oh, it's a crazy notion, but he was unhappy, really disillusioned about the war. He wanted out, Ben." She turned to look at him, hoping he would understand. "I suppose you shrinks would classify his condition as a nervous breakdown."

"We don't say 'nervous breakdown' anymore. We call it clinical depression."

"Whatever it is, he said something that haunts me." She gulped. He waited. A seagull squawked above them and the landscape seemed too painfully beautiful for such dark thoughts. *But it was now or never.* "He said . . . he didn't know how much longer he could go on. I figured that meant he might be tempted to go A.W.O.L. or something. But then, at the funeral, it hit me . . ."

"Okay, Madeline," he said, touching her arm. "You don't have to spell it out. A gun. A depressed guy. A closed casket. But you're jumping to conclusions, you know. They told you he was killed in action—right? And he was a trained marine, not just any guy with a gun."

"I know. But they wouldn't tell us if he'd done away with himself; they'd use the generic 'killed in action,' wouldn't they? To comfort the family. To avoid bad press. I'm not naïve, Ben. I don't trust anyone in authority anymore." She squeezed her watery eyes shut. "Part of me wants to forget it, but another part of me desperately wants to know what happened. To know the truth. And after this Tet thing—the Tet Offensive, you know—I feel like I need to do something."

"The activist in you," he said with a knowing smile.

"Partly, but it's more than that. I feel like I want to do something . . . for Sean. For his memory, I guess." She relaxed and stole a glance at him through her sun-scorched eyes.

God, she needed a cigarette. This was like sex, a release of mounting tension.

"We'll just have to think of something, won't we?" Ben said, with a squeeze of her hand.

*   *   *

When they arrived back at the shop for their "Take Two" attempt at tea, Eve was waiting for them, smiling and welcoming, her usual self. During the introductions Madeline kept glancing about the shop for Mr. Dimple, critic "of sorts." Alex Moore was nowhere to be seen.

Simone—hippie glasses perched precariously on the end of her nose—sat in the back at the Thoreau table across from Matthew. Madeline felt a stab of sympathy for the writer, who looked less than engaged. Matthew, she knew, preferred to be left alone to write. She imagined that he thought of himself as the solitary café writer, an American-style Albert Camus, with all the fine romance of that image. It was a small demand, a subtle expression, something you just knew and understood by the way he focused his attention on the yellow tablet, the way he held his pen, the way he didn't speak unless spoken to. But Simone was not one for subtleties.

Eve led Ben and Madeline to their table, already arranged for them. Madeline was surprised at all the formality. Instead of the George Orwell table, Eve had pulled together the two center tables, the Jane Austen and Oscar Wilde tables. They were already set with teacups and packages of biscuits and empty plates promising scones. Madeline's errant sunglasses sat folded above her plate where a place card might be. In the middle of one table sat a little package, dressed in slick green paper and white ribbon.

After she and Ben had settled into their seats, Eve caught Madeline's eye and gestured toward the package.

Madeline followed her gaze. "What's this?"

"We're celebrating your pay hike," Eve said.

"You mean I'm really getting a raise?" She looked at Eve and then to Ben, as if he could somehow verify this. "Do I deserve this?"

"You certainly do, my dear," Eve said proudly. "It's been one month, and you've already outdone your employer in the number of books sold and teapots served."

Madeline laughed. "You've counted?"

"My son has. Alex is a stickler for details, obsessively so. I worry about him," she said with a chuckle, turning toward Ben. "I really think he needs analysis, but then it would most probably point back to me in the end. Isn't it always the mother?" Basking in Ben's laughter, Eve put her hands together and looked at her employee as if to say, *I approve.*

So Alex did give her good reviews after all. As she thought of him (with mixed reviews of her own), he appeared from the kitchen sporting the same dishtowel over one shoulder, greeting them as if nothing uncomfortable had passed between them. He stood hovering over the table expectantly.

Simone somehow pried herself away from Matthew's artistic presence and sauntered over to the group.

"I dig presents," the hippie said, pulling up a chair next to Eve.

"So do I," said Madeline, tearing open the wrapping, "especially this one." She stared down at the book with the title, *To Seek a Newer World.* "Bobby Kennedy's new book, the one I've been wanting." She turned to Ben and back to Eve, and then to Alex. "Ben and I were just talking about RFK."

Ben said, "I have that book. It's great, especially the postscript. It's from his famous speech in South Africa. You really have to read the postscript."

Madeline looked to Eve. "Thank you, Eve. Really. But, how did you know I wanted it?"

Eve raised her eyebrows and shrugged as if it was just one of those mysteries of life. But not Alex Moore, who looked just a bit smug. She didn't remember talking with *him* about books yesterday as he sat behind his newspaper, spying on her with all the panache of Don Adams in *Get Smart*.

Simone stood to leave, flipping back her long braids, explaining that she was starting a night job at Taco Bell and would have to "split."

After Simone left, Madeline, still giddy with gratitude and surprise, turned back to her companions. They talked about how best to go about inaugurating Ben to "real" English tea. But before they could order the tea, the door jangled. Madeline turned, hoping it would be Mr. Larsen. Then, the day would be perfect.

But it wasn't Mr. Larsen.

It was the opposite of Mr. Larsen, the opposite of warmth and light. It was as though a cold chill had swept into the shop. The two young men who entered brought with them dark looks, suspicious glances, as if just on the edge of paranoia. Like soldiers in the land of the enemy.

Chapter Twelve

Eve was utterly taken aback by the manner of the two young men who entered the shop. They scowled—they actually *scowled*—with eyes scanning the shop before landing on her and her guests. She offered her usual hello in her most gracious voice, a voice that never once failed to elicit a smile. But the two men, one tall and gangly, the other short and stocky, only nodded without smiling—as if they didn't smile on principle.

The tall one with a buzz hair cut and horn-rimmed glasses walked slowly toward the counter, pausing to look down at Madeline's book, which lay in full view on the table. He approached the counter, but not as if he wanted to buy a package of biscuits or get a better look at the scones. No, Eve thought, it was more like he was selling something. She noticed a bundle in his hand, some sort of flyers, it appeared. She supposed he was advertising something, although in her experience such peddlers were always friendly to the hilt. Why would anyone buy anything from a scowler? If they are sales-men, she thought, they aren't very clever at it.

As she walked toward the counter, she noticed the shorter man with precision-parted blonde hair looking too full of Brylcream (and wasn't that greasy look supposed to be going out of fashion?). As physically different as the two men were, they looked about the same age, late twenties she guessed. The only commonality was that they were both dressed in suits: the shorter man in a near-black suit with a narrow black tie, the taller man in a dark brown ill-fitting suit, his pants too short for his frame.

The stocky man with the clean part and oily hair veered off from his partner and began to peruse the books.

"May I help you?" she asked the taller man as she moved behind the counter.

"I want to leave some literature with you—for your customers." His words were cordial enough, but his eyes held an odd intensity. "We'd appreciate it if you could put these flyers on your counter, as a public service to the community."

"I'm sorry," she said, "but we don't—" *We don't what?* She wasn't sure what to say because the young man somehow put her off. Intimidated her. Perhaps he was from one of those religious groups that went around proselytizing. His eyes were opaque blue—nearly colorless. And cold. Like ice in an Amsterdam winter. Disquiet washed over her. "Are you a business or—?"

"We're from the Orange County chapter of the John Birch Society." At that, Eve caught the sound of someone sighing; she saw that it was Madeline, looking in her direction, now rolling her eyes (a gesture the girl was fond of) as if to signal something about the man. He handed Eve one of the flyers.

She took it, looked down at the paper in her hand, and read aloud, "The John Birch Society invites you to the Anti-Communism Christian Crusade." Before she could read on, she again caught sight of the redhead, this time with a stop-everything! wave of the hand. The fiery redhead bounded out of her seat and rushed toward the counter, leaving Ben and Alex to gawk. She moved wordlessly, authoritatively, like a school teacher getting control of her class. She stepped behind the counter alongside Eve, snatched the flyer out of her hand, and handed it back to the man.

"Thank you," Madeline said, "but we're not interested."

Eve was taken aback by Madeline's steely take-charge

manner—a new side to her celebrated employee.

The tall man's sharp chin rose in a kind of self-righteous defiance as he turned his attention to Madeline, assessing her through the bottom of his horn-rimmed glasses. He said with a contemptuous smile, "I saw your book on the table, the one by Robert Kennedy. He's a Communist sympathizer, you know."

"No," she snapped, "he's *not* a Communist sympathizer."

Eve let Madeline take over while she kept her eye on the shorter, Brylcreamed man with the neat part, now eyeing Alex's prized first edition display copy of *Tortilla Flat*.

Her son lept up as the man opened the book.

"Sorry, it's not for sale," Alex said coolly as he took the book from the stocky man and set it back in the display holder.

The man shrugged and walked away from the bookcase, stopping at Matthew Hanson's table where the young writer sat with his yellow pad and pen. The oily man stood with folded arms and cocked his head, staring at the writer, as if provoking him to look up. It was like one of those Westerns on TV, Eve thought, gunslingers strutting into a bar, scaring everyone dumb. And yet these young men had no weapons other than their scowls and their air of self-importance. She bristled at the man's rude stare at Matthew, for she felt rather protective of the young man who was much too shy for such obnoxious personalities as these.

"Do I know you?" Matthew asked, looking up from his yellow pad at the husky man bearing down on him.

"Ha! I don't mix with—queers." He said this in a derisive half-whisper, but Eve didn't miss it.

She stepped out from behind the counter. "Sorry, but I'm going to have to ask you to leave. Both of you." She shot a look at each man in turn. The oily man shrugged, apparently his main form of communication, and motioned his partner toward the door. They turned to walk out, sharing an amused glance between them, as Eve held the door. And her breath.

Madeline stood next to Eve, shoulders almost touching in a wall of solidarity, until the door jingled behind the two strangers. Ben and Alex looked at one another, awestruck. Matthew sat with open mouth, pencil mid-air.

"Well done!" Alex said after a moment, shooting his amazed look back and forth between his mother and Madeline. "Well done, the both of you." He turned to Ben, who nodded in agreement.

But Eve was perplexed. "Who were those two, Madeline? What is this . . . this John Birch Society?" She returned to the table overcome with questions and not a little anxiety. She had never before asked anyone to leave her shop, and her heart still beat wildly. She glanced over at Matthew, who was scribbling on his yellow pad, seemingly undeterred by the interruption.

"They're complete nut cases, that's who they are," Madeline replied as they settled themselves again at the table. "But usually they're more polite than that—at least while promoting themselves." She shook her head as if shaking off the image of the two men. "Anyway, the JBS—the Birchers we call them—are right-wing wackos who believe there's a Pinko under every rock."

"But those days are over—the McCarthy years, I mean," Eve said. "Aren't they?"

"Not in Orange County." Madeline said, rolling her eyes again.

Ben said, "I've heard about the JBS, but never encountered them myself." He leaned back from the table and crossed his legs, a gesture that seemed to relax everyone at the table. "The Birchers have a strong following in Orange Country, don't they?"

"Probably the strongest chapter anywhere in the country," said Madeline. "Don't forget, we're sitting at the center of the military-industrial complex, the most conservative spot in the nation, only we forget about it because we're in free-spirited

Laguna Beach."

"But they called Robert Kennedy a Communist sympathizer," Eve said, still bewildered. "How can anyone do that?"

Madeline sighed. "They called President Eisenhower a Communist sympathizer."

"No!" Eve laughed incredulously.

"Oh, yeah. In my history classes we used the Birchers as a handy example of the conspiracy theory of history—Communist conspiracy, that is—beginning with Franklin Roosevelt on down. And you've seen the bumper stickers, 'Support Your Local Sheriff,' right? It's the Bircher's slogan. Comes from their contempt for public protests and civil disobedience and union organizers, like César Chávez and the farm workers."

Eve swallowed hard but didn't respond. Alex and Ben nodded, as if everyone in the world knew about the John Birch Society but her.

"And guess who they think is behind Dr. King and the Civil Rights Movement?" Madeline continued.

Eve shrugged. "The Communists, I suppose."

Madeline nodded. "Now you've got it. In a nutshell. With emphasis on the nut."

"Right," Eve said. "Then just who, may I ask, do they consider . . . well, *not* to be a Communist sympathizer?"

"That would be Barry Goldwater," Madeline said, "even though the Birchers make Goldwater look like a flaming liberal."

"It's all true, Mum," interjected Alex. "They actually think President Johnson is a dupe of the Soviets and the Chinese, and that Martin Luther King is a puppet of the Kremlin. They're bloody fanatics."

"Alex," she said as if scolding him, "How do you know about this group, these . . . these . . . Birchers as you call them? Have they approached you?"

"I approached them, as it happens. They have a huge bookstore in Tustin where they sell extremist literature. Some of them are not just anti-Communist and anti-Civil Rights, but anti-Semitic, too. It put me off, I'll say that. Oh, and they're against the U.N. Can you believe it? They claim the United Nations is plotting with the Communists to create a one world socialist government. Really, I kid you not."

Ben and Madeline nodded as if this were a well-known fact, and they all began to speak at once, each one eager to share an anecdote about the JBS while the others chuckled in turn. The three of them seemed to be taking it all in stride.

But Eve felt a cold chill. She looked firmly at Alex and interrupted the conversation. "But why would you even go into such a place, Alex? Was it just one of your random book hunts?"

"Sort of," he said, shifting in his seat. "I was dating a girl in Tustin at the time. I was on my way to collect her, but got there early and saw the bookstore. You know how I am, Mum: I see a bookstore, I stop. It's what I do." He smiled and said in mock snobbery, "It's the reason we have such a discriminating col-lection of books all about us." He gestured at the ceiling-high bookcases chocked full of his discriminating taste.

Despite her son's airy tone, Eve's disquiet now bordered, however irrational, on dread. How could these people invade her world? Was this John Birch Society a dark secret of her beloved Orange County, the underside of all this beauty and affluence? If so, she would just as soon have remained ignorant. She wished those two men, with their cloud of paranoia, had never come into her shop. Or was she just projecting on them memories of Hitler's brown-shirted youth?

Eve looked at Ben with sudden interest. "Ben, what do you make of these people? From a psychologist's point of view, that is."

Ben sighed with a shake of his head, as if even he were baffled. He crossed his arms. "A book comes to mind, *The True Believer* by Eric Hoffer. It's a rather chilling study of extremist groups. Came out after the war. An attempt to explain the psychology of how a small, tangential group morphed—almost overnight—into the monstrous Nazi movement that rampaged across Europe."

"You're saying these young men are Fascists?" Eve said evenly, trying not to reveal her own fears.

"No, no, not like the Nazis, but they are on the extreme end of things, at least for our country," Ben said, learning in as if to calm. (Could he sense her anxiety?) "But Hoffer does suggest that the extremist mentality that we see in both hard-line Communism and zealous anti-Communism is actually two sides of the same coin. You see, it appears they are at the opposite ends of a pole, but in reality, they're at the same pole."

"How's that?" Alex asked.

"Well, psychologically speaking, they may hate each other's guts, but with a kind of brother hate. They're bound by their fanaticism, you see. Both sides have the same fanatical make-up. This makes them more alike than different."

"But why the fanaticism?" asked Eve. "What creates that mentality? Nature? Nurture? What's your diagnosis, Ben?"

"I think," said Ben, "it has something to do with profound insecurity. The extremist personality needs something to cling to, so they're drawn into groups that give them all the answers, in black-and-white. Like the John Birch Society. Or it could be a fundamentalist religious group, or a combination of politics and religion, as in the case of the 'Christian Anti-Communist Crusade.' But it could be any group that believes it alone possesses absolute truth. It all comes back to insecurity."

"But isn't there more to it than that, Ben?" asked Madeline, suddenly serious. "I mean, you're right of course about in-security, but let's face it, we're all insecure. All of us. Since the Cuban Missile Crisis, nobody feels safe anymore. We're all living under the shadow of the Bomb, but not all of us become fanatics or join weird fringe groups." She paused, shaking her head in thought. "No, it's not mere insecurity; it's more like . . .

like one's response to insecurity, isn't it?" She turned to look at Ben, whom she obviously held in great regard. "I mean, it's a kind of an irrational all-consuming fear—Fear with a capital 'F'—that makes people so paranoid and intolerant, don't you think?"

Ben was about to respond, but Alex jumped in. "Fear? Or is it ignorance?" Alex sat directly across from Madeline with Ben to his right, his head resting on one hand in a thinking posture. He seemed to be focused intently on Madeline, blocking out the others.

"Ignorance is part of it," said Madeline, "but fear perpetuates ignorance." She spoke with confidence, looking directly back at Alex, matching his stare, as one who loves debate.

"Or does ignorance perpetuate fear?" Alex countered.

Eve knew this could go on all day. "It's the chicken and egg quandary," she broke in. But that did nothing to stop the two from volleying their assertions back and forth. Neither Ben nor Eve could get in a word edge-wise since Madeline and Alex seemed fixated on one-upping the other. It was as if Eve and Ben were simply onlookers at a ping-pong tournament.

Madeline said, "But if you're afraid of ideas, then you can't learn, so fear comes first."

"But ignorance has to come first, or there's no basis for fear in the first place."

"But you can understand something intellectually and still fear it."

Finally Eve held up her hand. "Yes, yes. I can see that this discussion is going to take some time and some thought—and some caffeine."

Alex broke eye contact with Madeline, as if suddenly aware of his surroundings. "Sorry," he said, tossing an apologetic smile to Ben. "We almost forgot the tea."

* * *

Madeline loved the cry of seagulls in the morning: the call

of life's urgency, as if the raucous gulls reproached the world for sleeping itself away. *Get out of bed and move!* they seemed to cry. And she had obeyed.

Get on with it! Onward and upward! they now called. But upward, where? she wondered. What was the meaning of it all? Where was everything headed? She had to quit asking so many unanswerable questions.

But it was hard, lounging on the old deck chair, book in hand, not to look out and philosophize on all this beauty, especially in the midst of a world so heartbreakingly sad. As the high tide burst onto her beloved chocolate rocks, saturating them with rushes of frothy white, it seemed to Madeline Prescott that the whole world was breaking upon those rocks. But perhaps— just perhaps—it was breaking and cleansing itself at the same time, as if the breaking gave birth to some wild, raw, cleansing power.

It was Tuesday morning, the first day of her work week. She felt lighter and a bit heady as she replayed her Sunday afternoon with Ben. Everything had been perfect. Everything except for those idiot JBS guys who descended on the shop with their cloud of anti-Communist religious fervor. She just hoped that those Birchers would stay out of Laguna, and definitely out of Van Gelder's. She would rather have Timothy Leary walk into the shop peddling LSD, for God's sake, than to see those two Birchers again. They were delusional. And bigoted. Alex was right about that.

But then, had she not deluded herself into believing that a man with a face like Alex Moore's could not be smart and well-read? A bigotry of her own? She thought back to their debate at the teashop, and felt again the thrill of it sweep through her. Was it the thrill of actually talking about things that mattered? Debating the Big Questions? Or was it that Mr. Dimple had actually held his own?

She took a breath of salty air and smiled down at the book

by Robert Kennedy, resting patiently on her lap. Curious about the postscript that Ben had mentioned, she decided to read it first. A particular passage screamed out at her like a seagull's urgent cry:

> Each time a man stands up for an ideal, or acts to improve the lot of others, or strikes out against injustice, he sends forth a tiny ripple of hope, and crossing each other from a million different centers of energy and daring, those ripples build a current that can sweep down the mightiest walls of oppression and resistance.

She re-read the passage and felt herself suddenly light and expansive. She thought of Einstein, about his passionate quest to answer the single question: What would it be like to ride on a beam of light? A passion (she remembered from physics class) that led him to the theory of relativity. And now, as ocean waves crested and fell before her, she wondered what it would be like to ride a ripple of hope. *Riding a ripple of hope.* What if she held on to that passionate desire like Einstein and his beam of light? Where would it lead? She took a breath and sank into the metaphor. Her whole body tingled as the ripple turned into a wave. She felt herself riding that wave. The vague discomfort of the droopy lounge chair vanished completely, and she felt herself (in some weird way) spill over the lines of her body, becoming part of the air and sea and sand.

Then it occurred to her: Perhaps this was what one might call "a spiritual moment," free from the heavy baggage that often came with the word "God," but still, somehow transcendent. Expansive. Spacious. She sighed into the beauty of Bobby Kennedy's metaphor, closed the book, then her eyes. She lay still in a moment of peace, taking in the sound of the waves, rising and falling and rising again. Nearly asleep from the hypnotic rhythm, she suddenly felt the sun warming her face and realized that it must be late. She heaved herself out of the droopy chair, stretched, and made her way into the cottage to prepare for another day of work.

* * *

Shades of soft orange morning light streamed through the dormer window of Eve's bedroom, high above the shop. A dapple of amber light settled happily on Earl Grey, a sleepy curl of gray fur, every subtle stripe fully delineated. His body felt warm and comforting against her own. Without disturbing the cat, she reached to her nightstand to turn off the radio, which she set as a wake-up alarm. She loved to wake up to the beautiful classical music out of L.A., but this morning there was a dissonant modern piece that she could not name, one of those atonal horrors.

Just as well, this morning she needed quiet. She thought for a moment that she might just resort to her frozen stock of scones and have a good lie-in with her favorite furry companion. She was especially tired and emotionally drained. Since the visit on Sunday from the strange creatures called Birchers, she had felt uneasy. All that talk afterward about extremists and Nazis left a cloud over her. For two nights her sleep had been fitful, full of nightmarish images of concentration camps: her mother and father and brother, Elias, in stark and desolate barracks. She never let her mind go any further. It would be unbearable.

She wondered if past evils were still with us, like stalking ghosts—a hateful sort of energy—just waiting to materialize again into flesh and blood. She shivered and stroked Earl Grey.

But then she thought of her papa, his laughter, his warmth, and realized that if past hateful energy still lurked about, then so must past loving energy still heal and comfort and guide. She must remember that, of course. *Yes*. But still, on days like this, when memories surfaced, the past seemed all too menacing.

The only refuge from those dark thoughts was work. Work was her salvation, was it not? She started to run through the day mentally and felt much better with her mind engaged in the simple banalities of a work day. Then she realized (a stimulating thought) that this was the day Sam would return from his trip to New York, at least she thought so. *Hoped so*. Would he come by to see her? Would he be, as Madeline said, foot loose and fancy free with no wedding band on his finger?

Would she really want that?

Chapter Thirteen

Sam Steiner, silvery gray hair backlit by the sun, walked into Van Gelder's Tea and Books at 4:00 p.m., smiling as if he'd swallowed the canary. Skipping all but compulsory greetings, he presented Eve with an enormous book, an elegant volume of Van Gogh prints with a number of color photographs. Expensive, she thought. *Too expensive.*

She nodded—a loss for words—staring down at the prints, absorbed by each luminous page. She forgot Sam altogether as she smiled down on the cozy *Bedroom in Arles* before she spotted her *Sunflowers*, the image that graced her flat. Then she turned to see her beloved *Irises*, the rich green-blue stalks and vibrant purple flowers. The print was much grander than her postcard-sized print that accompanied her morning tea at the Van Gogh table. In this larger version, she noticed the one white iris standing alone, apart, as the painter himself must have felt. As she, too, felt at times. Different, out of sync, yet somehow deeply connected to the whole.

She turned the pages highlighting the many self-portraits, and was grasped by the knowing eyes of the man in the straw hat, vibrant brush strokes in yellows and blues. A short but vibrant life, she thought—an Iris sort of life. And was there not something to be said for vibrancy? For quality of life over quantity of years? Could she say this of her vibrant, loving parents and her talented brother? Could that assuage her guilt of having survived to the ripe age of fifty-two, when they were denied all these years? As she looked at the artist in his hat, a surge of pride welled within her.   Here was her fellow Dutchman, a seer of sorts, who illuminated the world, catching beauty's ripeness just on the cusp of perishing.   He saved moments for eternity, this man. He made her weep. He made her weep for Amsterdam, for her mama and papa, her grand-ma's cocoa, the sound of her brother's violin.

But letting emotion get the best of her was precisely what Eve van Gelder would not do in the presence of Sam Steiner. She steadied herself before speaking. "He's the Mozart of the art world, that's what my papa said." She smiled up at Sam. "It's brilliant. Thank you, Sam. Really, thank you."

"I picked it up at the Strand, my favorite bookstore. Next to this one, of course."

"Of course," she said with a laugh, feeling lighter now. "We missed you around here. So much has happened while you were in New York."

"Oh? What did I miss?"

"Well, Simone took a job at Taco Bell. Madeline received a pay hike, or I should say 'a raise,' as you call it here" (and now she felt herself babbling but couldn't stop) "and Mr. Larsen brought us two Louis Untermeyer poetry books. And, let's see, oh yes, we had some strange political group who thinks the world is one great Communist conspiracy. And Ben came to tea."

"Ben?"

"He's Madeline's friend, a clever psychologist from Berkeley, but he's now at UCLA. We had a grand time dis-cussing the vagaries of human nature. Wish you could have been here. But now I need to get your tea."

"And yours, too, I hope. You will join me?"

Eve felt herself blush like a schoolgirl. She nodded.

Eve and Madeline worked together in the kitchen preparing tea and carefully arranging the silver-rimmed Lenox china, the one reserved for Sam.

"He's not wearing a ring," Madeline whispered excitedly, as if Eve had not noticed.

"I know . . . *I know*," Eve said, plopping haphazard dollops of cream and jam next to a warmed scone. Just as she left the safe haven of the kitchen, she glanced back at her employee whose expression held all the mischief of a child. Eve tried, but couldn't hold back a conspiratorial smile. It was rather exciting.

Not long into the tea, Sam asked Eve if she would join him for dinner on Tuesday evening. "I'm dying to try that new place in Newport Beach, Antonio's. If you'd join me, we could nail down some details for the book club."

Antonio's was one of the most expensive restaurants in Newport Beach, right on the harbor. And, if Eve remembered correctly, one of her customers said they had gondolas, for heaven's sake.

"They have gondolas," said Sam.

Gondolas at Antonio's seemed a great jump indeed from drinks at the Hotel Laguna. What would be next? A trip to New York for bagels and lox? She looked at him with raised eyebrows and a smile. She could always pull off a smile; smiles were easy. But her tongue was undergoing an untimely paralysis.

"You okay? Did I say something wrong?"

"No, Sam, it's not that." She paused and said, "I'd love to have dinner with you, but first, I need to ask you something."

"Anything. Go ahead, shoot."

Just then, Madeline interrupted to say that Alex was on the phone. Something about a book order. By the time Eve returned, the moment had passed.

* * *

The weather was too chilly for gondolas, Eve thought, adjusting her silk shawl around her shoulders and peering out the window of Antonio's. But the gondolas nevertheless swayed in the shining sea, lit by floodlights, giving the whole view a festive brilliance. One boat swayed a bit too much as an extraordinarily large woman stepped aboard, sitting down hard, making the other side of the boat rise up perilously. After a good deal of awkward commotion on board the tiny craft, two men—perhaps her husband and grown son?—finally sat down on the other side of the craft, balancing her weight. In spite of Eve's compassion for the unfortunate woman, the little tableau was simply too funny to let pass. Eve turned to Sam who was also watching, and they struggled to hold in the laughter, but without success.

A tall, dark, and extremely charming waiter appeared at the table and offered wine menus.

"Probably an actor," said Eve *sotto voce* as he left the table. At least in her experience of California, most good-looking waiters were really actors waiting for their big break.

The waiter brought Chianti and uncorked the bottle. Eve watched as he poured the wine for Sam to taste, wondering why the man was always assumed to be the wine expert. But no matter. She was glad to watch the richly gray-headed Sam in his light blue turtle neck and navy jacket taste and judge the wine. He nodded his pleasure, and the waiter filled both glasses with as much finesse as her own tea-pouring skills.

After a few sips of wine, she felt more relaxed and just a little brave. Time for tact was over. She needed a dose of Madeline's American . . . what was it? *Say it like it is* approach. She wanted to feel comfortable with Sam tonight, especially if he got into his head that they would paddle about in a gondola.

"Sam," she said with a directness she wasn't accustomed to, "I still need to ask you something that has . . . puzzled me for sometime." He nodded, as if knowing what she was about to ask. "I assume since we're here, that you are, well, not married or involved, but you have worn a ring—up until now. And . . . so . . . are you divorced? Separated? Or—?" She left it hanging.

Sam, matching her directness, leaned in toward her and said, "Eve, I'm a widower."

"Oh—" Eve sat up straight, adjusted her silk shawl, and regrouped. "I'm sorry." She wondered if Madeline had been here, what the redhead would have said: *So, Sam, did you do her in last week? Throw her off the Empire State Building? Is that why you left with a wedding ring and came back without it?* Eve pressed her fingers to her lips as if she might smile at her own thoughts, which would be a disaster. But she did want to laugh out loud. It was the relief of it all. *The sheer relief.*

She steadied herself and asked with great solemnity, "How long?"

"Two years in April. I should have told you before, but it's just something I've had trouble talking about. I know that I need to, but finding the right person to talk to isn't so easy."

"You can talk to me."

He smiled. "I know." He crossed his arms on the table as he often did in the teashop. "The long and short of it is that my wife—Jo was her name—died of cancer, and frankly, I couldn't cope. I tried. I threw myself into work at the gallery, the family gallery in New York. But one day I found it hard to get out of bed. Couldn't eat. Just stared at the walls. My analyst said I was 'frozen' in grief. He said I needed to move on to the next stage of grief. They have stages for these things now, you know."

The handsome waiter arrived to take their order, but Sam told him they weren't ready. The waiter nodded discreetly and left them alone.

"I thought that if I gave up my grief," he continued, "I would be giving up my love for her, like my grief was the only thing connecting us. Sometimes I felt like Heathcliff in that novel—what was it? *Jane Eyre*?"

"*Wuthering Heights*," she corrected him with a smile.

He laughed. "That figures. My approach to grief worked

out about as well as my knowledge of English literature." He looked out the window now, the candlelight falling on his face in a way that made him look vulnerable—exposed.

Eve wanted to reach out and touch that face—his arm, anything—just to give a sense of her presence. Raw human presence. Wasn't that more important than words? But she held back.

"So there I was," he said, "in my apartment, falling deeper into despondency. And making a wreck of things at the gallery. So my two sons suggested we branch out and open a gallery on the West Coast. I was, at first, really indignant that they wanted to ship me out like that—putting the old man out to pasture. But the more I thought of it, the more the idea grew on me."

"What changed your mind?"

He paused, tilting his head in thought. "I guess you could say that *art* changed my mind. I mean, the art world was no longer a source of joy for me. I'm old fashioned, I suppose, but I just don't get the *avante-garde*. Just when I almost—and I mean *almost*—made peace with Jackson Pollock and the whole splashy abstract expressionists painters, then along comes Andy Warhol." He looked at her, shaking his head. "Tell me, Eve. Are Campbell soup cans really art? And Brillo boxes in 3-D?"

Eve laughed. She had read in *Look* magazine about this Andy Warhol, the "Pope of Pop Art." She rather liked some of his celebrity paintings of Marilyn Monroe and Jackie Kennedy, but she wasn't too crazy about his earlier supermarket themes and knew that to someone like Sam, it must seem that the world of art had lost its soul.

"So, it eventually made sense for me—a refugee from the New York art scene—to come out here. Laguna is one of the last frontiers for beautiful landscape art. And I thought it might help me get . . . well, thawed out." He gave a deprecating chuckle.

"So has it worked for you, then? All this beauty?"

"It has," he said as he reached for his wine goblet, not

meeting her eyes. He seemed quite raw still, as did the narrow ring of colorless flesh on his ringless hand, now resting on the table. She found herself studying the exposed white skin.

Sam followed her gaze. "When I came out here I decided to leave everything behind reminding me of my life with Jo, except for her picture of course. And the ring . . . the ring was the rub. Seemed to be holding me back. But on my trip back to New York I did some thinking; I talked to the kids and to my all-knowing analyst. And I decided once and for all to take off the ring, as a kind of—oh, I don't know—symbolic gesture of my moving on. I guess she would understand."

"That you need to get on with your life?"

He nodded. "That I will love her for all eternity, but I can't live in the past." He looked utterly embarrassed now and sipped his Chianti.

"She must have been a wonderful woman," said Eve gently.

"She was," he said, now more animated. He opened his menu. "And I'll tell you all about her, but let's order. I'm starved, and that waiter looks like he'll go out for an audition if we don't order something fast."

* * *

"So did he serenade you in the gondola?" teased Madeline, sliding another tray of scones into the oven. Today was Valentine's Day and a surge of customers was expected—or at least hoped for.

"We didn't exactly get round to the gondolas," said Eve. "We just watched the little boats glide past our window booth as we talked and ate and talked some more. And ate some more. Oh, I'll never eat again! In fact, I can't even stomach a scone. You'll have to test them for me."

"Gladly, but what about the . . . you know . . . the *wife*?"

"Oh that," Eve said with feigned nonchalance. "He's a widower."

"Great! I mean, not that he's a widower. You know what I

mean."

"As I told you, Madeline, I'm not looking for a husband. I'm just getting to know myself."

"But?" Madeline prodded, unable to stop herself.

"But, yes, I am glad. I'm glad that I'm not in cahoots with a married man." She smiled shyly. "We talked about his past, about his need to move on and to let go of his grief—a two-year-old grief, as it happens." She paused and added, "Which is the same length of time that I've been divorced. So, we're two peas in a pod, both at loose ends and needing some companionship. That's all it is."

"You're sure?" Madeline knew that she was going too far now, but she, a slave to curiosity, was no longer in control.

Eve began filling the first of the four kitchen teakettles with fresh water. She glanced at her employee with what looked like bemused exasperation. "I know it must be a disappointment for you, but I made it clear to Sam that I'm just getting my sea legs with this business, and that I just want friendship. Nothing more."

"But did you actually *say* that?" pressed Madeline, probably at the point of risking her employment.

"Not in those precise words, no, but I hinted rather strongly."

Madeline forced her lips together, but the smile came anyway.

"What?"

"Eve, you need to understand that men, at least American men, don't get hints. They have no concept of hints."

"Madeline," Eve said firmly, "I do think you must have your own romantic interests to keep you busy enough. Ben is a nice young man. Very clever."

"Ben? He's my shrink, and he's not so young. Besides, like you, I'm not in the market for romance. I'm keeping my distance from men, even though . . ."

"Even though what?"

"Even though it's hard. And I want to believe in them—in men—but the whole romance thing is so overplayed. Love doesn't have any staying power anymore. No sense of commitment. I'm watching my step, that's all."

Eve turned off the water, set the last heavy teakettle on the stove, and turned to Madeline with a worried expression. "Have I . . . did I . . . add to your disillusionment with my own overly cheerful divorce story?"

"Don't worry, Eve. I was good and disillusioned before I even met you." Madeline pulled the scones out of the oven with thick insulated mitts and began to turn them onto the cooling rack.

Eve, who looked unconvinced, turned on the gas burners, each of the four burners hosting a separate teakettle, as if tea drinkers would be lining up at 10:00 a.m.

"By the way, Madeline, how are you with signs?"

Madeline grabbed a hot scone from the cooling rack and juggled it in her hands. "Signs? You mean like signs from God or something?"

"No, I mean signs, literally. Words on cardboard. Are you artistic at all?"

"Not particularly. Jilli is the artist in the family." She paused to take a bite of the scone. And another. "And these scones. They're perfect. Extra light with that flour you sprinkled on top at the last minute. Nice touch. And what's all this about signs?"

"Sam and I have set the date for the book club, the tenth of March. I want to put a poster board sign on the door, something that will attract a younger—" Her words were cut off by a loud knock at the door. "That's funny," she said, "it's too early—even for Matthew." She headed toward the shop door, Madeline close on her heels.

"Mrs. Eve van Gelder?" said the thin man with stringy hair

escaping from behind his ears. He held a glass vase filled with deep purple irises.

"Not Mrs., but yes. Are these for me?"

"They sure are, ma'am." The young man handed her the enormous bouquet.

Madeline sidled up. "Valentine *irises*?" Odd, she thought, but then, Sam—and they must be from Sam—was the artist type. You could never tell about artists. "Is there a card?"

Eve seemed not in a hurry, but thanked the delivery man, set down the arrangement, and coolly re-locked the door.

"The card!" Madeline said. "Open the card or I will."

Madeline watched Eve as she plucked the tiny card from the flowers and opened it. The expression on her face was something Madeline could only define as an odd mixture of delight and dismay.

* * *

Jilli told her sister that it would be "far out" to help make a sign for the door of the shop, especially on a Sunday (giving her a good excuse to skip out on church). The nearly finished poster sign that lay on the kitchen table—smelling to high heaven of Magic Marker—had a simple, enthusiastic message:

VAN GELDER'S BOOK CLUB BEGINS!
Join us for tea and a discussion of:
Norman Mailer's Armies of the Night
Sunday, March 10, 7:00 p.m.

But this simplicity was bordered with an array of psychedelic peace signs, set off with flower appliqués in each corner.

"Very groovy," she told Jilli, but wondered what Eve would say about a sign that looked more like an album cover for The Doors. Eve did say she wanted young people—

Suddenly she noticed her father with his empty beer bottle, apparently back for more. "Norman Mailer," he read aloud over her shoulder. "Isn't that the writer who was arrested at that anti-war protest?"

"Well, yeah, back in October. That's what the book is about, The March on the Pentagon. An insider's view, written like a novel. It's getting rave reviews."

He gestured a mock apology. "Well *excu-u-use* me."

"Dad, what's your problem?" Madeline asked, irritated. He looked strange, disheveled, shirttail sticking out the back of his pants.

"Mailer," he said as if the name was some tropical disease. "He made a fool out of himself. I know about him. You think I don't know, but I keep up with all your peacenik baloney."

"Dad, this isn't a protest. We're just going to discuss a book, that's all." She considered the discussion closed and picked up a colored pencil from the table and shaded the border. Jilli followed suit, both ignoring their father, hoping he would get his beer and get out.

But John Prescott did not go away. He hovered over them, beer breathed, watching them. Then, without warning, he slapped the table with the flat of his hand so hard that colored pencils bounced and fell to the floor. Jilli looked like a frightened bird. Their father had a temper, of course he did, but not like this—not with the slurred speech of a drunk. In fact, he rarely drank because their mother was so dead set against alcohol. Madeline wished her mother were home from church.

Jilli sat stock still. Madeline was glad that her father's blustery vehemence was aimed solely at her.

"It's enough that you're turning on the memory of your brother with your goddamned peace and love and flower-child malarkey," he said into Madeline's passive face, "but you can't drag your sister into it. I forbid it, Maddy. Not here. Not in this house."

Madeline said nothing, for how could one argue with a drunk? Jilli began to cry.

John turned to the child. "I . . . I didn't mean to lose my temper like that, but you should be at church with your mother."

Jilli looked at her father, no tears now, just an air of defiance. "So why aren't *you* at church, Dad? You just quit going after . . . after . . ." Flustered, she got up, shot her father a resentful look, and ran out of the kitchen.

Madeline turned to her father with his beer breath and his haggard appearance. She wanted to slap him. John Prescott did not look his eldest daughter in the eye, but opened the refrigerator, reached for another Budweiser, and popped the cap. She stood watching him, her arms crossed, her body rigid. *Would he not speak to her?*

She sighed at the sorry sight. He was already drunk and getting drunker. There was no talking to him now, even though there was so much she wanted to say.

She looked at the clock over the table. "I have to get back now. Mom will be home any moment. Drink some coffee, Dad."

John Prescott leaned over his beer, granting his daughter only one shame-filled nod. She picked up her poster and walked out of the kitchen and out of the house, the screen door squeaking and then banging against the frame. She walked out into the sunlight of the coming spring and headed for her VW Bug, a lump in her throat.

Her dad was actually drunk. *Her dad.* His shaking hands bearing The Letter had thrown her, naturally, but . . . *this*? What in the hell was happening to him?

She decided to sit in her car and wait for her mother's station wagon to pull into the drive before leaving her sister alone with . . . what was supposed to be a father. She gazed on her house, a traditional house with trellises of bougainvillea. A decent house, a well-kept house. A house whose inhabitants were all lost, unable to speak to one another. Unable to laugh. *The House of* (No) *Mirth*, she thought, remembering a chat about Edith Wharton's book over morning tea with Eve. They had been debating whether Wharton's complex character, Lily Bart, had actually intended suicide. Or was it just a tragic accident?

Her mind shifted to Sean, to unanswered questions. "For God's sake!" she shouted aloud into the abyss of her macramé purse as she rummaged for an "emergency" cigarette. She found one and stuck it clumsily between her lips. She fumbled again in near desperation until her fingers wrapped around the cold, smooth, familiar Zippo lighter. She lit up and puffed urgently until her mother's wood-paneled white station wagon came into view.

~ *Part Three* ~

The Tea Goddess

Chapter Fourteen

On the tenth of March, the Book Club at Van Gelder's Tea and Books was launched. Eiler Larsen arrived first, with a fistful of yellow daffodils and a white carnation in his buttonhole. Shortly afterward Sam Steiner burst through the door, wearing a sweater vest over his turtleneck and an expectant smile. To Madeline, he looked like a liberated man, unfettered as George Orwell's tea leaves, free from the constraints of business attire, eager to dive into his new role. She noticed, too, that his eyes lit up like sparklers when looking in Eve's direction.

More book lovers arrived, the continuous jingle of the door promising a festive night ahead. Among the strangers was a jolly man, plump and fair-skinned with a warm, affable expression. His old-fashioned horned-rimmed glasses framed happy eyes, eyes that danced around the room, taking in everything. Then he moved to the tea wall where he stood contemplatively with hands behind his back, as if looking at an art exhibit. Madeline noted his gray-flecked hair bearing telltale signs of having once been bright red like her own. He had the intellectual air of a professor, that ineffable quality of curiosity, as if life held one discovery after another.

"Do you like the display?" she asked, sidling up to him.

He nodded. "You know," he said, glancing at her and back at the tea wall, "I like tea, I really do. But I didn't think a place like this existed, not in this country. It's a find, this shop, a real find." He then turned to her and extended a hand. "I'm Henry Graham."

She was taken aback by his soft Scottish accent. (Or was it Irish? She could never tell the difference.) She thought of something Sam always said: *Everyone in California seems to be from somewhere else.*

"I'm Madeline Prescott. I work here."

"Is that right? You're lucky to work at such an establishment." Then he tilted his head as if an idea had just struck. "Madeline Prescott, I think we must share Scottish relatives, at least from the looks of it. My hair used to be as coppery and shiny and thick as yours."

She smiled. "My paternal grandparents are all descended from Scotland, as far as I know. How about you? You don't sound like a native Californian."

"Scot all the way. I came to California from Edinburgh as a young man, on a USC scholarship. Fully intended to return, but the Mediterranean climate—not to mention a certain young lady—kept me here. Except for a brief stint in Chicago for graduate school."

"*Graham.* Are you related to the guy who invented Graham Crackers?" Madeline felt it a silly question, but the man in front of her seemed to have a buoying effect on her. With the growing tension between her and her father, this jolly man, looking the age of John Prescott, seemed like therapy to an aching daughter's heart.

"No, but some might call me a cracker." He laughed as one who enjoys self-deprecating humor. "But you're not far off. My family tree traces back to one James Graham, an eighteenth-century medic in Edinburgh, who became rather infamous for his practices, a nut by standards back then."

"A nut? How so?"

"He was an early champion of vegetarianism—tried to promulgate such 'heresy' on his patients. Thought it would make them better, healthier. Imagine that, vegetables making one feel better! He was called—and I quote from his peers—'a quack, and possibly a madman.' Thus, I am descended from the Mad Vegetarian of Edinburgh."

Madeline laughed with the man whose joviality seemed infectious. "Quite a legacy you've got there," she said. "And what do you do, Mr. Graham? Don't tell me you're a doctor, like your Mad Vegetarian ancestor."

"Call me Henry, please. No, I'm not a doctor, at least not in that sense. My doctorate is in something quite unrelated. But I do work with patients."

"A psychologist, then?"

"No, but close. I'm a hospital chaplain."

"Really? Like a minister? So it's Reverend Graham, then. Or Reverend Doctor Graham, or—"

"No, no. I prefer Henry. I really do." He looked at her in earnest, as if he'd been down the appellation road before.

"Okay, Henry. Are you a theologian, then?"

"I suppose it looks that way on paper, but I warn you, I'm a bit of a heretic. I have to be, you know, just to keep up with my unorthodox ancestor."

Madeline's mind raced with questions she would like to ask, but by that time Mr. Larsen (another character specializing in unorthodoxy) had made his way to Henry, locking the shorter man into a bear hug.

"So you two know each other?" Madeline asked, looking from one to the other.

"We're great pals," said Eiler Larsen. "He came to visit me in the Veteran's Hospital, when I had that last bout of pneumonia."

"Oh, of course," she said looking back at Henry. "I guess that's what chaplains do."

"But tonight I'm not a chaplain. Just a book lover."

"Are you a fan of Mailer, then?" she asked as the Greeter

and his cane swept past them.

"Oh my yes. Big fan," said Henry Graham, "but I'm especially keen on William Sloan Coffin, the chaplain at Yale who helped organize the March on the Pentagon. He's in the book, you know. I met him once at a conference, and we really hit it off."

"That's great," she said, glancing toward Sam, noting that he looked eager to begin. "Well, we're about to start so I better get your tea."

By the time she returned with Henry Graham's tray, she noticed the room was filling up with guests. She shot a glance at Eve. A moment of mutual panic connected them. They had not expected a full house. Who would have guessed? Serving so many would take all night. They should have planned for refreshments afterward, but it was too late.

Eve walked toward her with an air of perfect efficiency under pressure, her knee length skirt swishing elegantly. (Madeline noticed Eve was wearing heels tonight.) She gave brisk instructions: "I'll stay on the floor to greet guests as they arrive. You offer tea—since we've already started serving—but not by yourself. Enlist Alex."

"Alex?" Madeline glanced around.

"He should be here any minute. He went to collect his date, but date or no date we'll have to put him to work until everyone who wants tea is served. On the house. And, of course, don't forget that May-ling brought an enormous batch of brownies." Eve gestured toward the kitchen. "They're in the foil wrap on the counter." Even as she finished speaking, she turned away, headed toward arriving guests.

"Okay," Madeline said to Eve's back.

Simone, one of the first arrivals, followed Madeline back into the kitchen as if she were a paid employee. "I can serve the brownies," she offered.

"You're a life saver," Madeline said to the braided, beaded

Simone, her hippie glasses barely attached to her nose. She added, "I noticed Matthew is here. Are you going to sit with him?"

Simone grimaced. "He's brought a friend—a *guy* friend." She seemed mildly dispirited; no doubt she had hoped to have him all to herself, sans yellow legal pad.

Sam began with introductions while Madeline and Simone rushed around trying to get everyone served. Still, no sign of Alex. But Simone was the perfect server, and not a little intriguing with a platter of brownies in hand—an Alice B. Toklas tableau if ever there was one.

"*Armies of the Night* chronicles, in a novel-like way, Mailer's own experience as a participant in the protest," she heard Sam say with his strong New York voice. "This book deserves special attention since the Tet Offensive has turned up the heat on the issue of Vietnam." He paused as two more guests entered and found their seats. "And as you know, the poet, Robert Lowell, walked with Mailer during the march. Mailer included Lowell's poem at the beginning of his book."

Madeline knew that Sam had already lined up Mr. Larsen to read, so she wasn't surprised when Sam said, "I want to introduce Mr. Eiler Larsen—the illustrious Greeter of Laguna—who will read the poem."

The Greeter heaved himself from his chair, lumbered toward Sam and stood, taking a moment to catch his breath. He looked down at the book as if about to read, and then handed it back to Sam. Madeline's heart sank. Had he changed his mind? Did he not feel well? Then he began, not reading, but reciting the words of Robert Lowell by heart.

> *Pity the planet, all joy gone*
> *from this sweet volcanic cone;*
> *peace to our children when they fall*
> *in small war on the heels of small*
> *war—until the end of time*

to police the earth, a ghost
orbiting forever lost in our monotonous sublime.

Madeline set down her teapot and began the applause, her heart leaping: partly for the beauty of the words and partly for the magnificence of the Greeter's vocal interpretation. It struck her that the words never changed. Yet with every reading— different time, place, listeners—it became something unpredictably new. Heraclites' river, she mused. *Never the same, but wildly alive.*

During the applause, three hippies sauntered in, a man with a blonde pony tail and another with sideburns and glasses. The woman in the group wore a granny dress with bright orange beads. Madeline pegged them as members of the commune in Laguna Canyon before she panicked at the realization that there was nowhere left for them to sit. She gestured for the three "bohemians" (as Eve would call them), to follow her to . . . the floor. (Where else?) Dressed in her standard—and suddenly practical—cords and turtleneck, she joined them on the hardwood floor. She had given up on serving more tea and it seemed to her the right time to settle down and give Sam due attention.

Another jingle at the door caught her attention. In walked Alex Moore, looking apologetic. Behind him was a stick-thin blonde of the most polished variety, hair ratted to high heaven.

Madeline faced Sam, who was reading some passages from the book, but she managed a sidelong glance at the couple. She saw what kind of girl Alex Moore was interested in: the perfect kind. The kind with chin held high like a debutante, possibly to avoid looking at the hoi polloi down below. Madeline noted the striking contrasts. On her level—the floor—sat hippies with old clothes, pony tails, sideburns, and beads. The rest of the crowd, she noted with a discreet sweep of her eyes, wore mostly casual wear. Then there was Miss Barbie Doll, with her high Sassoon do, exotic eye make-up, double-breasted navy jacket with gold buttons, and a white pleated skirt. And, of course, stilettos in bright red. *Did she think she was going to the yacht club?*

Madeline, slightly ashamed at her thoughts, wondered why such perfect women made her feel so . . . so *basic*, like a Simplicity pattern next to an Yves Saint Laurent design. She, Madeline Prescott, lacked glamour. She never thought about it except when put next to one of these Barbie Doll types; but the fact was, she would always be a Midge, Barbie's lackluster friend.

A few more minutes into the discussion, she fell prey once again to temptation and stole another look at Alex's date. Someone (to her dismay) had given up his chair for the Perfectly Dressed One, who sat with ankles crossed like a Miss America contestant. The woman also looked intensely bored, examining her nails as if she were counting down the minutes until her freedom.

Reproaching herself, Madeline returned her attention to Sam.

Sam read with half-moon glasses, which gave him the look of a distinguished scholar. "'Certainly any war was a bad war which required an inability to reason as the price of retaining one's patriotism.'" He finished the passage and took off his glasses. "What are your thoughts on that? Anyone?" He looked at Madeline, as if pleading for help.

"I agree," Madeline said, clearing her throat. "That's what makes me so frustrated with this war. People are not allowed to think, to question, to reason without being accused of being unpatriotic. There's no real rationality about Vietnam."

Alex, still standing near the door, spoke out, "But war isn't rational, is it? It seems to me that people are more brutal and irrational than they are reasonable. That's why we have wars. It's human nature. I think Vietnam was inevitable—even if regrettable."

"That's rather cynical, isn't it?" retorted Madeline, against her will. "I mean, what about the Cuban Missile Crisis? We avoided all-out catastrophe then, didn't we? Didn't sanity prevail in that case?"

"Good point," said Henry Graham, jumping into the fray. "In that crisis, cool heads prevailed. But of course, it's all in the quality of leadership, don't you think?"

Discussion flowed with debate over Mailer's diagnosis of America at war in Vietnam. Then Sam added fuel to the fire by giving another prompt from the book. "Here's a line for you to chew on, from page 187, 'The burning of villages by napalm might be the index of our collective instability.'"

May-ling Wu spoke up. The librarian's blunt cut chin-length hair looked like black silk, and her skin seemed to mysteriously repel the ravages of the California sun. She spoke with excellent English, but with a deliberate cadence that made her sound wise, Confucian-like. "Like the fire of napalm, violence feeds on itself. Violence always breeds violence. Why do we not see that?"

"Yeah," said Matthew's friend, a thin young man with high cheek bones and swept-back hair, "but what would happen if Vietnam fell to the Communists? Wouldn't that be a greater disaster?"

There were low murmurings around the room. A number of people spoke up. Some, notably a man in an old-fashioned trilby hat, seemed to think all civilization would collapse if America pulled out of Vietnam. Madeline held her tongue, enjoying the debate.

Finally, the hippie with the pony tail spoke up. "Vietnam is a bad trip, man. I mean, we're stuck in a no-win situation. McNamara and Johnson are escalating the war when we should be gettin' the hell out."

Still more murmuring. The middle-aged man in the trilby hat—the kind with a feather, the likes of which Madeline had not seen since before the Kennedy administration—spoke up, "What else can we do? We have to escalate now, since the Tet Offensive. We can't afford to lose this war. We've never lost a war."

Madeline could not hold her tongue any longer. "Didn't you hear Cronkite's report after his trip to Vietnam? He said something like, 'With each escalation, the world comes closer to the brink of cosmic disaster.' I think history would bear him out."

"How's that?" asked Mr. Trilby Hat, crossing his arms on his stomach.

"Take the invasion of Sicily during the Peloponnesian war," she said. Madeline glanced around and thought she caught the slightest crumpling of the Barbie Doll's perfect posture. She wished she hadn't opened her mouth. She would just sound like a know-it-all, and no one was interested in a history lesson.

Alex cleared his throat. "Go on. What about Sicily? You're the historian here," he said.

Madeline felt a sudden flush in her cheeks, but soldiered on. "You all know about Athens and Sparta, right? The Peloponnesian wars?" A few people nodded. "During that time, about 2400 years ago, Athens got involved in a long-standing civil war in Sicily because they thought that getting a foothold in Sicily would be a real boon to their empire in the face of their mortal enemy, Sparta. The war was going badly. I mean, they had no understanding of the Sicilians when they went in. And the enemy was better organized than they imagined. So what did they do? They escalated like mad—ratcheting up the war, even when they knew it was hopeless—because they were too bull-headed to admit defeat." Madeline paused to shift her position.

"So, what happened?" Alex asked. "I assume the escalation was a disaster?"

"Not just a disaster," Madeline said. "A *catastrophic* disaster. Thousands of Athenians were killed or sold into slavery. The navy was destroyed, and all the other nonaligned states sided with Athen's enemy, Sparta. Within a few years, the famous Athenian democracy had collapsed, and Athens, the greatest city-state of the ancient world, had been conquered by Sparta."

Alex's eyebrows shot up. "So you're making the analogy that the United States will destroy itself if we keep on in Vietnam? I doubt many Americans would agree with that."

Eve spoke up, not giving Madeline a chance to retort, as if peace-making between these two was her role in life. "Well, it seems that Mr. Mailer himself is quite the historian. He seems to think—if I'm reading him right—that if we pulled out of Vietnam, Communism might spread initially, but would eventually weaken on its own accord. But of course, we human beings are not famous for our patience, are we?"

Mr. Trilby Hat spoke up. "I'm still not convinced that a history lesson will help us here. Not that I don't see your point, young lady," he said looking at Madeline, "but the Greeks were not dealing with the Reds. And," he said, turning now toward Eve, "I'm not so sure the menace of Communism would die on its own accord. It could very well reach our shores, and then where would we be?"

The whole room began buzzing with different "what if" scenarios.

The hippies on the floor were murmuring among themselves but seemed reluctant to speak up, as if joining in a conversation with people over thirty might taint them in some way. But finally the pony-tailed hippie, evidently the spokesman for the group, said, "War is not the answer, man, and like she said"—he glanced to Madeline—"we might end up like Athens. Self-destruct. Poof!" He made a Houdini-like gesture. The other hippies nodded and murmured in agreement.

Madeline looked at the "bohemians" in a new light. She wondered if her past judgment that all hippies were apathetic acid-heads might be in need of revision. Maybe they were starting to come around and actually get involved in the real world.

"So then," said Sam, "that begs the question: are *all* wars wrong?"

That open can of worms spurred the pony-tailed hippie and Mr. Trilby Hat into a philosophical argument with no end in sight. The hippie was—no surprise—on the side of absolute pacifism while Mr. Trilby Hat, who had fought in Korea, challenged that notion with conviction.

Sam finally held up a hand. "We'll come back to this philosophical issue later, but here's another controversial statement that I want to throw out. Mailer seems to think that, and I quote, 'the center of America might be insane,' and that 'the average good Christian American secretly loves the war in Vietnam.'" Sam splayed the book on the table, took off his half-moon glasses, and waited for reaction. He looked to Madeline, as if assured she would jump on it.

But Madeline looked at the chaplain with questioning eyes, curious about his response.

Henry Graham caught her inviting look and put his thumb to his chin in the style of Ben Schwartz. "Well, it's a provocative statement, yes, but he has a point. Societies can become insane, even ones that claim to be Christian. I'm reminded of Martin Luther King's sermon last year at Riverside Church—a speech that got him into trouble, by the way. He said a nation that continues year after year to spend more money on military defense than on programs of social uplift is approaching spiritual death. That might be part of what Mailer is getting at."

Madeline smiled. Henry Graham, descendant of the Mad Vegetarian of Edinburgh, proved her theory that the New Hope Baptist Church was not the only game in town. And that Pastor Bob, with his shaking jowls of disapproval and absolute certainties, was not the only picture of the religious face. But more than that, this brief foray into spiritual matters landed on an aching spot inside her. She wasn't too keen on organized religion, given her severe allergy to the church of her childhood, but she was heartened to see so many diverse faces of religion in the room. There was Henry Graham, probably a Christian of some liberal variety, and May-ling, a Buddhist she supposed. Eve and Sam were both Jewish, and the hippies next to her were most likely of the "LSD Saves" variety. And then there was the Seeker, the Quester, which was herself. Every person in the room had a different view about life, God, and the world. A different angle. And didn't white light refracted through a prism at different angles create a full rainbow of colors? Who was to say which color is best when they're all part of the same beam of light. Was this not a metaphor worth pursing?

These lofty ideas restored Madeline's sense of hope in herself as a thoughtful human being, as opposed to her small and petty judgments of Miss Barbie Doll who was, Madeline observed stealthily, still meditating on her perfect nails.

After a pause and some general murmuring, May-ling raised her hand.

"May-ling, please," said Sam with alacrity.

May-ling nodded respectfully before speaking. This woman did not seem to be in a rush, as if her meditations on the singing sea had created a calm and measured mind. "On the news this evening, I saw Mr. Chávez breaking his fast on behalf of the migrant grape workers. Senator Robert Kennedy was standing at his side. I'm afraid I cried at the sight of it. It's not about the war, but it fits Mr. Mailer's book. I think if we take protest seriously, then we need to stand with Mr. Chávez, like Senator Kennedy." She emphasized her words with a raised index finger, as if instructing children at the library. "This is some-thing we can do to change things in a non-violent way. Refuse to eat California grapes until the farm workers are treated with respect."

The hippies began to clap, and May-ling blushed with pleasure.

Simone called out from near the kitchen, "Hey everybody, May-ling made the brownies!"

Enthusiastic applause ensued as Simone passed the brownie plate for one more spin around the room.

Madeline beamed as the brownies were passed to her. She loved the bright energy that emanated from so many free spirits in one little teashop full of books and genteel subversion.

While Madeline chewed the most delicious brownie she had ever eaten, Henry Graham's eyes caught hers and gestured discreetly toward Mr. Larsen. The Greeter dozed serenely with Earl Grey curled in his lap. As if sensing he was being watched, Eiler Larsen roused with a jolt that sent the cat flying. Madeline, Simone, and the group of hippies giggled first. Soon everyone caught sight of the cat as he scampered like a wild panther up the library ladder to the top of the bookcase, where he poised himself over the crowd. It was not just laughter, but a sort of giggling that overtook everyone, a silliness that would make outsiders looking in the window wonder if those brownies were spiked.

Even the Barbie Doll laughed, the first crack in her frosted lips all evening.

Sam held up a hand. Once order was restored, further discussion ensued on topics related to the author's view of dissent and the American soul. Finally, they approached the end of the book. Sam looked at Madeline and asked her to read something aloud. And, if she wouldn't mind, to come forward and read it from where he stood, so everyone could hear.

Madeline got up from her place on the floor rather awkwardly, as her right leg had gone to sleep. She felt her face flush in self-consciousness as all eyes were on her, but Sam's smile and the way he held out the book to her, lured her onward. She took Sam's well-worn copy of the book, and her eyes skimmed the page until she latched on to the paragraph Sam had marked in brackets. She cleared her throat.

> *Brood on that country who expresses our will. She is America, once a beauty of magnificence unparalleled, now a*

beauty with a leprous skin. She is heavy with child . . . she will probably give birth, and to what?—the most fearsome totalitarianism the world has ever known? Or can she, poor giant, tormented lovely girl, deliver a babe of a new world brave and tender, artful and wild?

Chapter Fifteen

The wind blew Madeline's red curls with abandon as she rested her arm on the car door and breathed in the brightness of spring popping out in graceful yellow waves of mustard blossoms.

Glancing at her front seat passenger, Eve said, "Are you sure that wind isn't too much for you? You could roll up the window."

Madeline turned to volley the question to the back seat, where sat Sam Steiner and Eiler Larsen. "Is the wind too much for you, Mr. Larsen?"

"I like it," said the old man with coarse gray hair flying across his face. "Makes me look smarter, like Albert Einstein."

The four laughed as they left Laguna Canyon Road and merged onto the 5 freeway. There was reason to laugh. Not only had Madeline rounded up this little coterie from the shop for the getaway down to San Juan Capistrano, but she had also just learned from the *L.A. Times* that Bobby Kennedy had changed his mind. *Bobby Kennedy had changed his mind.* The book club itself had already reinvigorated her hope in humanity. Now there was this new hope afloat in the wind: Bobby Kennedy as President. "Motoring" (as Eve called it) to the mission for the annual celebration of the return of the swallows to Capistrano made for a fitting celebration.

Alex Moore—a.k.a. spy, lady-killer, cynic, faithful son— volunteered to mind the store so that Madeline, Sam, and Mr.

Larsen could educate Eve on the one cultural festival that she had somehow missed in her four years of living in Southern California.

Madeline took in deep breaths of clean coastal air and imagined Bobby Kennedy as President. She could almost envisage the soldiers coming home from Vietnam and the huge outpouring of money that had gone toward the war being funneled into more humane enterprises—like LBJ's forgotten Great Society, a country where poverty would be a thing of the past. She pictured Sean's face relieved and happy at the news, as if he might somehow *know*.

The Festival of the Swallows at Mission San Juan Capistrano had been something she and Grandma Daisy had shared, an annual grandmother/granddaughter event. And now she was going with an odd assortment of "new" old people. *Old people who were her friends* (a dastardly renunciation of "Don't trust anyone over thirty!"). And traveling in style.

Madeline looked at Eve. "This Jag is really spectacular. What year is it?"

"'61, I believe. But you might change your opinion if the engine decides to lie down and die; it's notoriously unpredictable. I don't know why I keep the thing, except that Marcela—the new Mrs. Moore—would have it if I hadn't fought for it during the divorce. I feel rather obliged to hang onto it." She sighed heavily. "But I have to admit, the bloody thing is like an albatross around my neck."

"Now, what kind of language is that?" Sam teased from the back seat.

"It's true, Sam," she said loudly into the rearview mirror, negotiating traffic and trying to speak so that he could hear. "The mechanics at Laguna Imports have probably made enough money off this car to buy a dozen more."

"I swear, Eve, when you say my name you sound exactly like Audrey Hepburn in a movie I saw back in New York. *Wait until Dark*, I think it was called."

"So I'm not the only one who thinks she sounds like Audrey Hepburn?" Madeline asked.

Eve shook her head of thick, dark, gray-streaked hair, which today she wore down around her shoulders with only a white stretch headband holding it in place. Madeline thought she looked years younger this way.

"Well," said Eve with mock resignation, "I guess there are worse things in life than being compared to Audrey Hepburn."

Madeline laughed. No shadows or worries today. Maybe the worst of her grief was behind her. Like stars, millions of willowy yellow mustard blossoms greeted her on every side.

Mr. Larsen noticed, too, commenting on the fields and hills saturated with yellow blossoms. "Have you heard the story, Madeline?" he said from the backseat.

She turned her head and leaned back as far as she could to hear the old man so he wouldn't have to strain his famous Greeter's voice.

"What story, Mr. Larsen? You mean about the swallows?"

"No, I mean the story about the mustard seeds and the missions." Eiler Larsen rolled up his window and she followed suit, to gain some hearing between them. "Mustard seeds," he said. "The padres scattered mustard seeds all along El Camino Real so that people could follow the yellow flowers to reach the different missions. Those little yellow mustard blossoms waved the pilgrims on to their destination, making the roads easier to follow."

Madeline smiled. "Like 'follow the yellow brick road'?"

Sam turned to the Greeter. "How many missions are there in California, anyway?"

"Oh, about twenty-two up and down El Camino Real, so that's a heck of a lot of mustard seeds they had to plant."

Madeline's neck was failing under the strain of craning it backwards, so she looked forward again noting the endless yellow landscape. A pilgrimage lined with beauty, she thought, from seeds left by those who came before: like Grandma Daisy, leaving behind seeds of memory and wisdom for Madeline to follow; Sean, too; people who have died waving on the living— their guidance, their love, their wisdom still blooming wildly in the world. It occurred to her that here was the perfect metaphor for a poem—that is, if she were a poet.

But of course, she was not.

Inside the pepper-tree lined adobe walls of the Mission, the four pilgrims began to meander around the cloistered space with its gardens and ponds and porticos and stone ruins. Madeline stood looking at the stone wall of ancient bells and smiled. It was all exactly as she remembered, as if nothing had changed in the world. This place had always satisfied the historian within her. The mission, consecrated in the year of America's Declaration of Independence, was the oldest structure in California still in use. Here was the perfect time capsule of forgetfulness in a world of suffering. Each year, the Spanish dancers and Juaneno Indians retold the stories of history, the irrepressible themes of tragedy and hope.

Madeline pointed out to Eve the main structure, the ruins of the old church. "It's called the Great Stone Church. The swallows begin arriving mid-morning and rebuild their mud nests in the ruins." She spoke as if lecturing a class on a field trip. "It was an architectural marvel in its time—not Spanish, like the rest of the buildings in the mission, but Greco-Roman in style. It stood five stories high with, I think, seven domes and a bell tower that could be seen for miles. You can see that the roof is completely collapsed now." The sun was already too bright, so she began the familiar ritual of fishing around in her purse for her sun specks.

"But why is this great church all in ruins?" Eve asked, with Sam listening in close beside her.

Madeline found her sunglasses and put them on. "It was

destroyed in an earthquake in 1812. I associate that date with The War of 1812. That's how I remember dates, by making associations."

Eve nodded. "And I will remember it by *The 1812 Overture* —Tchaikovsky." Just then the breeze caught a lock of Eve's hair and blew it into her eyes. As she fumbled with her hair in the breeze, Sam stepped in and brushed away the errant stands.

"Was anyone inside when it collapsed?" asked Eve, looking a little embarrassed by Sam's solicitude.

"More than forty worshippers were crushed to death," said Madeline. "They couldn't get out because the earthquake pinned the doors shut." This cruel knowledge was her first remembered foray into the Big Questions. It seemed to her, even as a child, that if there was a God—and wasn't an earthquake called an 'act of God'?—then God must be some kind of giant mean-spirited troll who hides under the bridge. Such images were silly now, even if the questions still lingered.

Sam was listening in. "And yet, there are swallows thriving in the ruins," he said, and motioned them forward. "Let's get a closer look to see if they've arrived." The path to the ruins was lined with red hollyhocks and yellow roses. Purple wisteria climbed the ruins of Great Stone Church as if trying to cover the wound of it, while ubiquitous bougainvillea vied for attention like shocking pink hot pants.

Elier Larsen pointed their eyes toward the little mud nests of the swallows, something that looked to Madeline like beehives made of mud.

"Are those the swallows?" asked Sam, turning to the Greeter and pointing up to a flock of small birds.

"Probably the scouts." Eiler Larsen squinted a bit into the sun, the lines in his weather beaten face accentuated in the light. "More on the way."

"But, where do the swallows come from?" Eve asked.

Madeline, feeling very much the teacher, jumped in. "They

arrive from Argentina like clockwork every year on March 19th, which just so happens to be St. Joseph's Day. And then they go back to Argentina on October 23rd."

"But I don't understand," Eve said. "How do the birds know how to calculate their flight to the exact day? That seems far-fetched."

Sam chimed in, "But it's true. I didn't believe it at first, either. Incredible little creatures." Sam's smile lingered on Eve.

Madeline turned back to the swallows that flitted around—so tiny and dark—and then disappeared into the roofless structure to feed on insects that inhabited this building with a tragic past. They all stood enraptured, gazing up at the old church dotted with mud nests to watch and wait for another glimpse of the birds, the creatures with a mysterious inner radar system rivaling anything at NASA.

"'Hope is the thing with feathers,'" said Mr. Larsen aloud to no one in particular.

A perfect day for the poet, thought Madeline, smiling to herself, glad she had invited Mr. Larsen. But then, it was Eve's voice completing the verse:

> *that perches in the soul,*
> *and sings the tune without the words,*
> *and never stops at all.*

Madeline stared at her employer in surprise.

"Well, I had to memorize poetry at King's College . . ."

While Eve chatted on about her English education, Madeline was distracted by a particular face in the crowd. It was *that* face: the very one she had seen at her brother's military funeral; a face scarred with too much experience for its age; a soldier's face.

He stood by the koi pond dressed in fatigues and boots, cigarette in hand. He exhaled a curl of smoke. Their eyes met. There they were, like two cats paralyzed mid-step by the sight of the other. Who would move first? Madeline excused herself from her friends.

"Do I know you?" Madeline asked as she approached the man, leaving the others wholly absorbed in finding swallows inside the ruins of the Great Stone Church.

The marine stood nursing his cigarette by the pond near the mission entrance—an incongruous figure next to the lily pads floating placidly on the surface. She approached him with half-fear, half-curiosity, heart in throat. The same scarred face, hard not to remember.

"No, but I know you." He paused. "Want one?" he asked, pulling out a pack of Lucky Strikes from the front pocket of his fatigues.

"I'm trying to quit."

His amused brow did not calm her inner collision of dread and curiosity. Something inside her, perhaps intuition—that mysterious way of knowing hidden away in swallows and women and poets—told her that this man held something for her, but it was something too awful to contemplate.

"Oh," she said after a pause, "just one wouldn't hurt, I guess." Despite the scar, his was not a bad looking face, just worn and hard and toughened. His hair was stubby and course in military style, his teeth small and yellowed by nicotine. She studied him with curiosity, watching him light her cigarette with his own Zippo lighter.

"Thanks," she said, looking around without success for a place to sit. The old mission now swarmed with far more people than swallows. She caught a glimpse of movement beside them, restless teenagers vacating a bench that wrapped around the koi pond. She gestured for him to sit.

Upbeat Latino music and dancing on the other side of the grounds softened her apprehension, but the noon sun drenched the concrete bench with a kind of fierceness; her wool turtleneck, which in the early morning had seemed perfect, now made her sweat and itch.

"I saw you at the funeral," she said, then took a nervous

drag on her cigarette. "I thought you must have known Sean."

"Ya look just like your picture," he said. "Can't mistake that hair. Ya have a sister, too, a blonde."

Madeline's heart nearly stopped from this sudden image of her brother showing off his family pictures to a buddy. She imagined him saying, *And this is my big sister, Maddy, the redhead, like me.* She looked again at the man, as if seeing him for the first time, or at least from another angle. He must have been Sean's buddy. But how? How, for God's sake, could someone who looks like he's done time in San Quentin find anything in common with her freckled-faced little brother? But then, she guessed, war made strange bedfellows. Her mind raced back to Sean's letter. There was some buddy from Capistrano . . . what was his name? John? Joe? Joey, that was it. But a little-boy name like Joey hardly fit the tough character in front of her.

"Are you, by chance . . . Joey?"

"Yeah," he said. "Joey Lobo. Named after St. Joseph him-self"—he gestured to their surroundings—"so my parents think I have to be here on St. Joseph's Day. I humor them when I can. When I'm not dancin' over landmines in Nam." He gave a cynical grunt and exhaled a swirl of smoke. "My parents are in the chapel right now lightin' candles." He gestured with his cigarette toward Serra Chapel, the ancient place of worship that Madeline thought of as the "red candle chapel." When she and Daisy would visit Serra Chapel, it always seemed toasty warm inside from all the red candle holders bearing light in the flickering hope of answered prayers.

"Hot as hell in there," he said, and then added with a cynical grunt, "Or Da Nang—take your pick." He settled back on the bench and crossed a boot over one knee. "So ya say Sean men-tioned me?"

"In one of his letters. His last one . . . "

"Yeah? Me and Sean were great pals."

"Joey," she said with unease, still finding his name at odds with his face, "do you know something about the circumstances of Sean's death that I should know? That my family should know?"

"What makes ya ask that?" His tone was wary.

"It's just that I get the impression that there's more to it than what we were told. Which was practically nothing. It was a closed casket, no explanation. A family wants to know . . . ." She wanted him to say that Sean had in fact died in combat, and died instantly, without knowing what hit him. If Joey could just tell her that—give her some reassurance—then she would never revisit this again.

"Sean told me you were the smart one in the family," said Joey Lobo, "a real smart gal." He smiled just enough for her to see his yellow smoker's teeth.

She imagined herself with those stained teeth. She put out her cigarette.

"So I'm right? There is something . . . something suspicious about the official story? Is that what you're saying?"

Joey Lobo fidgeted and looked around. He, too, tossed down his cigarette and ground it with his boot. After an interminable pause, he responded, but with a change in demeanor, less nonchalant: "I do wanna sit down with ya sometime, Maddy, sometime before September, when I go back for my second tour. It's just that I don't think I can talk about it right now. Not yet. And definitely not here." He looked around. "I'm just tryin' to get my shit together, that's all." He paused. "And I don't know how much I can say, even if I wanted to."

"How much you can *say*?" Her voice edged upwards; her whole body began to tighten and her imagination leaped to conclusions: Sean had gone over the edge. He had blown his brains out in the dead of a swampy night. God! *Stop it!* She couldn't go there. And yet, with her fiery curiosity on auto-pilot, the truth begged to be known, even while she willed it to stay down, stay hidden, stay deep in the murky "killed by enemy fire" territory of her understanding.

"Now just hold on there, Maddy. It's nothin' ya gotta be concerned about."

"But you've already let the cat out of the bag," she pressed, a little bruised from his rebuff, as if he were saying, *Don't worry your pretty little head about it.* Her anger empowered her. "Look," she said, meeting his eyes directly, "I know there's something you're not telling me, and I can't rest until I know. If you don't talk, I'll go straight to Camp Pendleton. I'll demand answers." She felt herself growing hot and frustrated. She wiped beads of sweat from her brow, as the sun was un-relenting.

Joey turned away, then back, as if not sure how to handle this. "Look, they won't tell ya a thing. Nothin'. Trust me. Just give me some time—a little time—okay? Just got to get my shit together, that's all." His eyes pleaded with hers.

What about me? she thought. My grief? *All I want is to know—to get it over with, for God's sake.*

But the guy did look tortured. Maybe he was shell-shocked, or whatever they called it these days (she would have to ask Ben about this). And the guy obviously needed time to get past it before he could talk about the war, let alone her brother's death.

"Just remember," he said with a no-bullshit look. "Sean was a damned good soldier. The best."

Of course he would say that.

On the other side of the pond, a chubby toddler with blonde curly hair reached his tiny hands into the koi pond as if to catch one of the golden, elusive fish. An older child slapped his hand and the little boy began to cry. Scream, really.

"I don't mean to push," she said, once the little boy's cries subsided. "I'm sure you've seen horrible things, beyond what I can imagine. It's just that—"

"Where can I reach ya?" he interrupted.

"I work in Laguna Beach, at a book shop on Coast Highway. Next to the surf shop. Please, come and see me. When you're ready, that is. Or just drop in for tea and we can—"

"Drop in for *tea*?" He laughed. "You're a teahead? Don't look the type."

Madeline blushed. She'd forgotten that the old beatniks used the term "tea" for marijuana, which made Joey Lobo seem even older. "No, actual tea, tea you drink. It's a British-style shop. Just come by, okay? In the meantime, how can I get a hold of you, Joey?"

"No, I'll come to *you*," he said evasively. With that he nodded toward an older couple coming toward them. "Gotta go, Maddy. My parents have lit their candles and said their prayers."

Chapter Sixteen

Madeline walked alone on the beach, just as the sun's rising began to burn through the misty marine layer. The bite of the salty morning breeze against her face matched the icy chill of the surf on bare feet. Her clam-diggers protected her legs from the wind, but the Berkeley tee under her sweater was feeling nearly thread-bare. She pulled the sweater tightly around her torso, stuck her hands in her pockets, and hoped to God for some time alone before the rest of the cottage community began to filter out.

After her disturbing talk with Joey Lobo, her mind couldn't stop screaming with what-ifs: What if she never saw hide nor hair of Joey Lobo again? She should have kept pressing. That's what she should have done. Of course, she could be jumping to conclusions about Sean, but the alternative possibilities for the closed casket—and Joey's need to "get his shit together"—were just as disturbing. What if Sean had been beaten to death by a fellow soldier who learned he was going to desert—was that it? Was Sean planning to go A.W.O.L.? Or, even worse, what if he'd fallen into one of those hideous Viet Cong traps, sharpened bamboo dipped in poison . . . .

She shivered away the images before they could fully form. *Stop! Just stop it!* She would wait for Joey Lobo to come to her. When he was ready. She could, of course, go straight to Camp Pendleton and make waves. Making waves was her forte at Berkeley. But, she reminded herself, this was the military, not a university administration.

Just then a pelican took flight from its rocky perch. She stopped to watch it glide over its prey, plunge into the water like an Olympic diver, barely splashing, and rise again with the poor fish in its beak. Looking back toward the cottages, she noticed that some of the artists were already out and about with their canvasses—one now at work on the bluffs—probably absorbed in beautiful thoughts. For a moment, she envied the *plein air* artist who could somehow transcend this world.

She plodded along close to the water in the wet firm sand, trying to open herself up to the peacefulness of the sea—its singing. So many metaphors hovered about her; yet they were as elusive as a slippery fish. She thought of the swallows and the mustard blossoms leading the pilgrims to the missions along El Camino Real, the stuff of poetry. And yet, she felt utterly at a standstill in the creative department.

"Hey there!" Biddy Gelson's plump figure loomed on the boardwalk. Dressed in her usual overalls and red Keds, she slogged through the dry sand toward Madeline.

"Morning, Biddy." Madeline felt a little ashamed for always trying to avoid her bubbly neighbor. But now, like the fish in the pelican's beak, she was caught.

"Are you all right, hon?" Biddy said, a little breathless. "You look a little down in the dumps, the way you're walkin' with your head down, like you're takin' on all the worries of the world."

"I'm fine. Really. How are the boys?"

"They're as ornery as all get out. They got into their dad's paints the other day and used it like war paint."

"You're husband, the engineer—he paints, too?"

"That's why we're here. You know Roger Kuntz, the famous *plein air* artist, who lives up there?" She pointed to one of the cottages on the hill. "My husband studies with him."

"But you're from Texas. I've never heard of *plein air* painters from that part of the country."

"Hon, we might just surprise you. We're not all cowboys and Indians."

Madeline smiled. "Are you an artist, too, Biddy?"

"Oh, I make sand candles and do a little macramé. And cakes—lotta cakes." She chuckled and added smoothly, "How 'bout you, hon? You look like an artist."

"I can't draw a thing, let alone paint."

"Bet you're a poet, then." She pushed back her dark frizzy bangs.

"Why do you say that?" Madeline's interest piqued. Practically everyone wrote poetry these days; but still, the woman seemed unusually intuitive—something in her penetrating gray eyes.

"I dunno. There's just somethin' kinda pensive about you that just screams 'poet.'"

"Well, I dabble in poetry. But right now"—the dabbler paused to sigh—"I'm suffering from . . . from writer's block, or something like that."

"Writer's block?" Biddy Gelson said in a tone of exaggerated disbelief, flinging out her fleshy arms as if to say: *Here*? *How could anyone but an idiot fail to see the poetry here?*

"I know," Madeline said, "I *know*."

"Don't worry, hon, just a few more walks down this beach should clear out the cobwebs."

Madeline nodded, shading her eyes with her hand. "Yeah. A few more walks should do it," she said without conviction.

* * *

"Mornin', Ben."

"Madeline—is that you?"

"*Shore* is," she drawled into the receiver, mimicking Biddy Gelson, who had, by some miracle, taken her *out of the doldrums* (as Grandma Daisy would have put it).

"Has anyone told you," said Ben in mock irritation, "that

you've suddenly developed a very bad case of a Southern accent? Especially for eight o'clock in the morning."

"I was just talking to my neighbor. She's from Texas. Her husband's a *plein air* artist. Did you know that artists come here from Texas, just to paint? She's got a really groovy accent. I think it must be contagious."

"Before I recommend a lobotomy, tell me what's going on with my favorite redhead. Anything wrong?"

"I'm fine," she said (vowing not to inflict Ben with her dark thoughts). "I just haven't talked with you since the big news, about Bobby throwing his hat in the ring. Incredible, huh?"

"Yes. Incredible," he said, but in a measured tone.

"I hear worry in your shrink voice."

"Not worry, just caution. You know as well as I that it's not going to be easy for Bobby to beat LBJ, especially coming into the race so late like this. And a lot of college students are already loyal to Gene McCarthy, so it's not going to be a walk in the park—"

"*I know*, but since Tet, don't you think people are hungry for real change? I do, Ben. I think Bobby might just ignite a revolution."

"It has to be a quick revolution then, if he's going to beat out LBJ and the Republicans." Ben sighed into the phone and Madeline struggled to keep up her optimism. "But like you, I think he can pull it off, if—and only if—he wins California."

"If he doesn't win here, he won't have a chance to win the nomination. I know that much."

"Yeah? Okay, then. You wanna be a part of somethin' big?" said Ben, with his own lame attempt at a Texan accent.

"You mean the campaign? Of course!" she said with rising enthusiasm. "Is it going to be headquartered in L.A.?"

"Yes, and Madeline, you wouldn't believe the number of people from right here at UCLA who are volunteering. Students, professors, staff, janitors. A lot of folks are jazzed."

"It's no wonder," she said. "It feels like a burst of hope just exploded onto a really dark sky. Like fireworks."

"Ah, waxing metaphorical again. Any poetry in the works?"

Damn. Why was everyone riding her about her poetry? "No, not yet . . . I told you, Ben. I haven't found the right metaphor."

"Madeline, there are no perfect metaphors, and if you try to wait for one, you'll never write. And poetry really matters right now. Even Eugene McCarthy's writing verse—"

"Look," she interrupted. "I appreciate all that, but I don't want to talk about poetry. Or Bobby's political rival. Or myself." Madeline knew that if she didn't change the subject she would blurt out her strange encounter with Joey Lobo (a subject for another time) and possibly sob into the phone, ruining her Biddy-induced bright mood. But even worse, they would be locked into a doctor-client relationship forever. Why couldn't he be a little less . . . wise?

"Okay, then," he said. "Come up to L.A. on your days off and we'll stuff envelopes or canvass neighborhoods or something. I'm setting aside a number of vacation days myself; it's that critical, I think. You're going to be a part of history, Madeline."

"My favorite subject," she said, smiling into the phone.

* * *

On her day off from the library, May-ling Wu had offered to bring a plate of her brownies for a late afternoon tea at Van Gelder's. Eve felt her saliva glands working overtime in anticipation. Madeline didn't help matters by constantly reminding her of the moist texture and rich dark chocolate flavor. Sam had been alerted by phone, thanks to Madeline, and was planning to leave the gallery early.

Simone, too, got wind of the upcoming tea party, featuring May-ling's "magic brownies," as Simone called them—a name that seemed to stick. The young bohemian was always in the shop these days, but never seemed to have any money—or "bread"—on her. Eve finally decided that if Simone was going to hang around so much, she might as well be put to work re-shelving books and tidying up in a fair exchange for tea and sustenance. Simone could not, of course, be counted on as regular help, as she had already lost her job at Taco Bell because of her easy-come, easy-go approach to things. The hippie mantra of "if it feels good, do it," did not strike Eve van Gelder as a good principle to live by because she knew of many things that felt good, but that she would not do. Eating a steady diet of May-ling's "magic brownies" would certainly feel good, but would not exactly be a brilliant idea.

Sam arrived just in time to help Simone pull together the two center tables while Madeline directed and set out napkins and plates. When May-ling arrived with a large sack—no doubt bearing warm brownies tucked in aluminum foil—Eve was ready with kettles boiling.

In the kitchen, May-ling pulled several things out of the sack, not only the much anticipated confection, but several packages of tea with Chinese lettering and six small, pale green ceramic cups, perfectly round with no handles.

"I hope you don't mind," said May-ling. "I do like your English tea, but today I want to share my own tea. From Taiwan."

Eve was intrigued, as Oriental teas were something of a rarity for her. She, and most Westerners, had been raised on black teas, primarily from India.

Everything Eve tried by way of help got a curt, "Okay, okay," from May-ling, who was trying to put together a tea tray in her own way. Eve finally realized she would be of more help if she let May-ling be.

"I'll make sure the brownies get to the table," said Eve. "You're in charge of the tea."

Eve went back to the table and visited with Sam, who wore a

tie of green and yellow paisley—one of his more "hip" sartorial additions. Eve noticed that Sam wore a different tie every time she saw him, and wondered how he kept them all lined up in his closet.

When May-ling finally arrived with the tea tray, she had two pots of tea on the tray encircled by small ceramic cups. Everyone stopped talking and looked to her, as children ready for their lesson.

"I want to offer you two kinds of tea," May-ling said. "You might like one better than the other." She set out the tiny cups with ceremonial care. "Now, the first tea is called 'Taiwan Beauty Tea.'"

"Will it make me beautiful?" asked Eve with a chuckle.

"You are already beautiful, dear lady," said May-ling. "It will make your skin soft and young, yes, but more important, it will help you feel beautiful inside yourself. And some say that it is named 'Beauty Tea' because the island of Taiwan—my homeland—was first the island of Formosa. Formosa means 'beautiful.'"

Madeline's hand went for the sugar bowl. "No," said May-ling with an index finger raised in her librarian manner. "Try it first without sugar, so you don't alter the taste."

Madeline took a sip and nodded a sparkling smile toward May-ling. Eve, too, sipped the little round cup full of amber gold liquid. It tasted good, refreshing, and not altogether strange.

"It's more coppery colored than black tea," observed Madeline, "but really mellow."

"This is a very fine oolong tea," said May-ling. Taiwan is most famous for its oolong teas." She smiled. "Very tasty with brownies, too."

Sam reached for the plate of brownies. "I'll be the judge of that."

"Now, when your teacup is empty, I will pour the most

special of all oolong teas. This one may take you Westerners some getting used to because it is very fragrant. The leaves themselves are very dark—I will show you in a moment—but it is not a black tea. It must be very carefully prepared. Water has to be hot, but never boiling. Never!" She waved her index finger again, this time as if warning a child of the dangers of a hot stove. "And be careful not to steep too long."

As if performing a religious ritual, May-ling carefully poured the steamy liquid into the tiny cups. "First, take time to smell the tea. Let the fragrance enter your nostrils. It will calm you. Then taste."

Everyone obeyed. Eve watched Sam out of the corner of her eye. He held the tea up to his nostrils, as if testing wine. She took his cue and breathed in the startling aroma before tasting. She closed her eyes. The tea reminded her of grassy fields after an English country rain. She took a sip and felt a clean, peaceful warmth flood her body. Or was it the warmth of sitting here with Sam and her friends that made the tea so extraordinary?

She opened her eyes and watched Simone's eyes grow wide.

Finally, the young hippie spoke, "Yeah, it's calming all right. Smells like weed. I think I could get into this."

Madeline burst out laughing, which only egged on Simone.

"It's intensely fragrant," Eve said, trying to quail the un-abated laughter, which had spilled over to Sam as well. "What is it called?"

"It is called Ti Kwan Yin, 'Tea of the Iron Goddess of Mercy.'"

Madeline looked curious. "Iron Goddess of Mercy? I'm sure it has an interesting history."

"Here," May-ling said with eager eyes. "I brought you some of the leaves because I knew you would not believe me. Here, look." May-ling poured out the strange black leaves into Eve's hand and then into Sam's, Madeline's, and Simone's.

Simone sniffed at the tea leaves. "Can you roll it and smoke it?" she asked, causing another wave of giggles at the table.

Eve ignored this, as she was wholly absorbed in the charcoal colored, tightly curled leaves, so different from any tea leaves she had ever seen.

Sam looked puzzled. "So, is this tea from the same origin as, say, Earl Grey or Irish Breakfast? Is it all the same tea plant?"

"Yes," said May-ling with authority. "*Camilla Senesis.* That is the botanical name for all tea, as Eve can tell you, but it tastes different because people all over the world cultivate it and prepare it in many different ways. There are many levels of fermentation as well. Black tea is highly fermented, but oolong, not so fermented. Green tea is the least fermented of all. Tea is universal, but it is also . . . what is the word?"

"Particular? Specific?" offered Madeline, who seemed as enthralled with the conversation as Eve.

"Yes. Specific," said May-ling. "Every culture has a specific way with tea, and to taste another's tea is to taste another's culture—to understand a people in a way you cannot through books and conversation. Tea is more personal; it goes inside you and feeds your senses. Then you can know a people much better. It is a way of knowledge, to taste someone's tea. It is like learning another's language."

Like learning another's language. A thought struck Eve. She glanced over at the George Orwell table by the window, the table where the Greeter loved to sit, but which was vacant now. *Forgive me, Mr. Orwell,* she thought, *but you were a bit short-sighted.* Perhaps even the great George Orwell was only re-flecting the biases of the British Empire when he said that "a nice cup of tea" only referred to Indian tea. She had never ques-tioned that point of view. Never—until today.

It occurred to Eve that, even in middle-age, life kept opening up, as if she were still in the blooming stages of life. She had always thought that once you reached a certain stage in life, you would attain a fully-baked view of the world that would never really change. You simply lived off it and shared it with others, like a loaf of bread. That was supposed to be wisdom. But perhaps wisdom included the drinking of exotic teas and thus entering worlds yet unknown. Maybe this kept one from going stale, even if it meant one had to, on occasion, toss out hidden biases—biases exposed in a single sip of tea.

"So tell us the story about this tea, May-ling," Madeline pressed.

"Okay, okay. I will tell you the story of the Iron Goddess of Mercy."

Everyone grew quiet and sipped the fragrant tea.

"Centuries ago there lived a poor farmer in the Fujian Province of China. He lived in an area plagued by drought and poverty and every calamity, a very sad place. But in this place was a temple, an old run-down temple that needed care and upkeep. Inside the temple was an elegant iron statue, that of Kuan Yin, the Chinese Goddess of Mercy. Many Buddhists, like this poor farmer, would pray to Kuan Yin for enlightenment. So the farmer would go into the temple and sweep up all the twigs and dust around the beautiful statue.

"One day the farmer came as he had for many years, dusting and sweeping. He lit incense for the goddess because he thought she would like this. Suddenly, the goddess appeared to come alive! The farmer fell to his knees in great shock, and the goddess whispered in his ear, 'The key for your future is just outside this temple. Nourish it with tenderness; it will support you and your family for generations to come.'

"The local farmer took a few moments to recover from the shock. Was it a dream? Or had the goddess *really* spoken to him? Unable to contain his curiosity any longer, he went outside the temple, and there he found a withered bush. The farmer watered it, brushed away the grass and weeds at its roots, and said to the bush, 'You are a gift from Kuan Yin. I shall treasure you.'

"The next day and everyday for weeks, the farmer cleaned the temple, lit the incense, and watered the plant. Soon the bush was rich and full, its glossy green leaves healthy and thick. The farmer discovered that the leaves, when mixed with hot water, made a refreshing drink. As the bush grew, he cut away branches for his neighbors to plant and nourish, and soon the whole area of Fujian was full of these magical bushes.

"And so the farmer began to experiment with the leaves, and dried them in a stone wok; they soon turned a smooth charcoal black. When he tasted the black leaves, he fell in love with the fragrance and the sweet taste. The farmer called his drink Ti Kuan Yin–tea of the Iron Goddess of Mercy."

May-ling smiled when she finished her story and bowed slightly, as a non-verbal The End.

"That's a beautiful story," said Madeline, the ever curious one. "But how did Kuan Yin, the Goddess of Mercy, get her name in the first place?"

"Kuan Yin actually means, 'She who hears the cries of the world.' That is why Chinese Buddhists love her so much. You see, she is the Chinese goddess who forsook enlightenment in order to help those still struggling with the confusion and suffering of this life. There are many tales of Kuan Yin, of course, but this one I told you—it is my favorite."

Eve felt the world to be suddenly a peaceful and good place, here with the Goddess of Mercy. And her friends. She stole another look at Sam and noted a playfulness in his eyes, as if he enjoyed this moment as much as she. She took another sip of tea, settled into it fully, and pronounced inwardly that the whole calamitous world must have suddenly found peace. And that nothing could possibly happen to shatter it.

Chapter Seventeen

Early on the first Thursday of April, Eve smiled into the phone from the comfort of her lounge chair, waiting for the kettle to boil. Earl Grey was busy lapping up his morning cream. Becca's voice bubbled brightly from across the world. Eve so loved to talk—or more accurately, listen—to her daughter chatter on a mile a minute. For Becca, it was already afternoon in London with too many cups of coffee behind her.

"And what about this new man in your life, the customer called Sam?" Becca asked in a half-teasing voice.

"You know about Sam?"

"Alex told me when I rang him last. Some sort of art dealer from New York, I recall. What is he like, Mum, I mean on a personal level?"

"He's very blunt about things—I guess that's the way of New Yorkers—very forthright, no beating around the bush. And he loves books. And he thinks I remind him of Audrey Hepburn." Eve laughed. "I'm afraid I don't get it, but who's to argue with that?"

Her daughter laughed. "Well, I'd say you've got quite a charmer on your hands."

"Oh, but Sam is only a friend—"

She was interrupted by a knock at the door below, the private entrance beneath the stairs opening onto the parking lot. Alarming given the hour, barely six-thirty in the morning. She wasn't dressed to see people.

"Becca, I have to ring off now. I hear a knock downstairs." Becca must have sensed Eve's disquiet for she begged her mother not to hang up, but Eve knew the expense of a trans-Atlantic call.

She hurried to the bathroom to find her robe. As she tied the sash, she heard the knock below grow more insistent. Her anxiety mounted as she descended the stairs and approached the door in the poorly-lit entry way. She should have put in a peep hole by now, she chided herself, as she raked a hand through her hair. She cracked the door, chain lock still in place.

"Good morning, ma'am," the deep voice said. "Sgt. Duane Thomas, Laguna police."

"Oh dear . . ."

More than anything, it was the holstered gun that took her breath away. She was used to English Bobbies, for heaven's sake. The policeman reminded her of the motion picture gun-slinger, John Wayne, who, she was told, resided in nearby Newport Beach.

But this middle-aged man was decidedly not John Wayne. What stood before her, besides the gun, was a razor-close crew cut and dark glasses (were they really necessary at this hour of the day?) and a policeman's blue uniform with black belt and boots.

An armed policeman. Here? For a moment she wished Becca was still on the line. She felt the need for a strong connection, even a trans-Atlantic one, just for the sense of support.

"Are you Mrs. Van Gelder?" he asked in a husky voice.

She took off the chain and opened the door. "I'm legally Mrs. Moore, but I go by Van Gelder, my maiden name, you see." She mentally slapped herself out of her bumbling and stood a bit straighter. "I'm Eve van Gelder, yes."

"I'm sorry to bother you so early, Mrs. . . . ma'am . . . but there's been some vandalism on your property."

"Vandalism?" Eve clutched the lapels of her robe.

The officer suggested that she dress and meet him at the shop entrance door.

In the manner of Earl Grey, Eve darted up the stairs, heart pounding. She yanked an old green pull-over shift off a hanger and grabbed her slip-on sandals. Not very smart looking, but anything else would have taken eons to put on. All she could think of was to hurry. *Hurry!*

As she dressed, her mind chased questions. *Vandalism.* What did he mean, exactly? A break-in? Theft? Someone must have broken in to raid the cash register. Thank God Earl Grey was with her the whole night! Everything else could be replaced, except for some of her antique china teapots, but who would want those? Or did they take Alex's treasure, the first edition of *Tortilla Flat* that he had on display? A million half-baked scenarios rushed through her mind like a modern abstract painting: splashes, impressions, random colors, nonsense.

She started down the stairs, but turned on the landing and hurried back up to the flat, remembering Earl. She plucked the well-fed sleeping cat from the sofa and set him down, against his will, on the cold floor of the bathroom and closed the door. She didn't want him following through the cat flap, for God only knew what waited below.

She raced back down the stairs, dizzy with all these confusing thoughts, but when she reached the bottom, she stopped short and steeled herself for what was about to unfold. She opened the interior door to the shop haltingly, taking in small bits at a time. She looked first at the floor. No glass. No broken china. But of course, she would have heard . . . . She looked at the counter. All was in perfect order. She then moved her eyes toward the tables and book cases. Nothing out of place. *What, then?* A moment of relief swept over her. The policeman must be mixed up. He probably meant the shop next door had been vandalized. It was rather confusing the way the shops and private entrances were laid out—

Then she saw it, disbelieving.

Here in this little coastal town of artists and beachcombers and Cornwall-style cliffs was the last place on earth one would expect such a thing as this. Huge and black and menacing: a swastika. It glared backwards at her from the shop's glass door. *Her* door. Like the eyes of a genocidal madman. She crossed her arms, hugging herself protectively, and stood still against the shock of it.

Sgt. Thomas, showing impatience with his knocking, jolted her into action. She moved forward, fumbled with her keys, and finally, with shaking hands, opened the door for the officer to enter.

After a cursory look around, he said, "I think the only damage is to the door."

Only damage?

Then he spoke again, but the only words that registered were, "No sign of a break-in."

Satisfied, he opened the violated door—she could not bear to touch the thing—and they moved out onto the sidewalk. The morning traffic was light, but a woman in a Mercedes Benz slowed down and shook her head in disgust at the obscenity. A young man walking his dog on the other side of the street stopped and stared with mouth agape. Eve turned back to look at the full brunt of it and covered her face with her hands. *A bad dream, this.*

"Are you all right, ma'am?" Sgt. Thomas asked, grabbing on to her arm in a professional manner, as if he did this routinely for women about to faint.

She nodded and brushed away his assistance. She stood there hugging herself, shivering in the cool, cloudy, marine-layered morning. She gazed inside the widows at the pretty yellow sugar bowls on blue table cloths. She pictured Eiler Larsen sitting there at the George Orwell table, reading poetry and looking out at the lovely view of Main Beach. But now the coveted view was besmirched by the worst form of profanity. She shivered and stared. Beneath the Nazi emblem were three words, one underneath the other in stark black capital letters:

JEWS

COMMIES

QUEERS

Onlookers began to appear, early bird tourists on their way to breakfast and shop owners arriving for a new day of business as usual. Eve was only vaguely aware of the sounds of shoes on pavement, barking dogs, murmurings of shock and revulsion.

"Ma'am, it's only spray paint," said Officer Thomas with a note of gentleness.

Only spray paint?

"We'll clean it off for you," he said, still getting no response from Eve, "but first we need to get some pictures for the file. The Anti-Defamation League will no doubt want one, too. I've already radioed the precinct for a photographer, and then we'll get this vile stuff off your door. . . . Are you sure you're all right, ma'am?"

She nodded without speaking. *Not possible. Not here. Not in this neighborhood. Not in this country.* Was this the way the Negro people in the South felt, she wondered, when ugly, violent words were painted on their homes and churches? Crosses burned in their yards?

She saw the glass door now as a kind of motion picture screen from which leaped strange images. She saw her own reflection—but not her. It was her mother she saw in the reflection, the woman who always wore simple cotton dresses like the one Eve was wearing. Then she saw her papa and her sweet brother, Elias, with his violin. Then she saw them all, naked and cold, shivering against the bitter indignity, moving listlessly toward the "showers" with the dark, foul smoke—the color of the spray paint—rising high to cover the whole sky.

She felt light headed. Nauseous. And then, nothing.

* * *

When the phone rang, Madeline was toweling her freshly washed curls and basking in the news that everyone was still talking about: LBJ's dramatic announcement that he would not seek re-election. News couldn't get any better than that—at least for Bobby. She grabbed the receiver on the second ring, expecting Ben to call about directions to the RFK campaign headquarters.

"Madeline, Sam here. You need to get here as soon as you can. It's—Eve."

"Sam? What's happened? What's wrong? Is Eve all right?"

"There's been a . . . an incident." He took a breath, while Madeline's own breath stopped in mid-exhale, waiting for him to finish. "Eve fainted," he finally said. "She's all right, but shaken."

"But why? Why did she faint? What *incident*?"

"She's *all right*," he said with too much inflection, which meant she was certainly not all right. "She's had a shock. Just get here when you can. Alex is already on his way."

Madeline pulled on the skirt and sweater she had already planned to wear for the day's work, grabbed a silk scarf to pull back her damp curls, and left Crystal Cove with heart in hand. She made record time in her little VW, but the crowd gathered around the shop door told her something was terribly wrong. Someone with a camera was taking pictures. Of what? *For God's sake, what's happened?*

She wheeled into the alleyway that led directly to the employee parking lot behind the shop, only to find that her usual parking spot next to Eve's Jaguar was taken. By the time she parked on the side street, fed the meter, and got to the door of the shop, the crowd had dispersed, except for two touristy-looking onlookers and a police photographer.

Then she saw it. Her chest began to tighten, and she forced herself to breathe. This was no time to have an asthma attack.

Eve needed her. Eve, who had taken her under her wing, now needed comforting. She explained hurriedly to the policeman who she was, unlocked the defiled door, relocked it behind her, and ran up the stairs to Eve's flat, taking two steps at a time. The door stood partially open. She heard voices coming from within and gingerly knocked.

"Madeline, sorry about this," Eve said, waving her inside. She sat in her favorite lounge chair with her feet up on the ottoman. She looked pale and small, her hair disheveled. "It seems I fainted, like some Victorian with the vapors." She pointed toward the men. "Sam and Sgt. Thomas are making a big to-do about it."

Sam moved toward Madeline. He wore his usual dress clothes, but his tie was haphazard.

The policeman, much older and heavier than the one at the door, nodded his hello, rather grudgingly it seemed, but then, he was trying to talk to Eve. He finally grabbed a dining room chair, set it between Eve and the console television, and pulled out his notebook.

"I've got the teakettle going," said Sam, following Madeline into the kitchen, leaving Eve and the officer alone to talk. Then he dropped his voice to a whisper. "Thanks for coming. I didn't know what to do. The officer called me just as I was leaving for the gallery." He sighed, leaned up against the counter and loosened his tie even more, as if at the end of a work day. But Madeline picked up in his voice a tinge of satisfaction that Eve had given the officer his name. Still, he looked nervous, raking his fingers through his hair, the way people do when they're not sure what to do next. "I guess you saw the obscenities."

"Oh, yeah. Hard to miss," she said, shaking her head, still in a state of disbelief.

"I'm worried about Eve," Sam said. "When you came in, she put on a brave face, but she's obviously very upset. She fainted on the sidewalk. Of course, she refuses any medical attention."

While Sam helped her with the teacups and milk, Madeline measured the tea, PG Tips, the first box of tea she spotted in the cupboard. Earl Grey bobbed his head around the corner of the door shyly. Sam scooped him up.

Madeline carried in the tea tray just as Alex appeared at the door wearing a suit and tie, but not his usual devastating smile. He offered only a curt nod in the direction of Madeline and Sam as he moved to peck his mother on the cheek. He sat on the arm of the sofa, folded his arms, and listened intently to the officer. Worry covered Alex Moore's face, Madeline observed (not diminishing his looks one iota, as it would with normal mortals).

"Thank you, dear," Eve said, removing a stack of books so Madeline could set the tray down on the table beside her chair. "Just what I needed. A cup of tea."

Madeline watched as Sam attempted, without success, to place a squirming Earl Grey on Eve's lap. The feline wasn't in the mood for it just now, not with all the commotion.

"Oh, Earl, you're such a scaredy-cat today," Eve said, her eyes following the cat's escape, his little bell jingling away down the hall. "But that's all right, we're all a bit frazzled." She turned to the police officer. "I will be ever grateful that you caught me, Sgt. Thomas, before I hit the cement and cracked my head."

"Glad I could help," said the officer with a look of pride, as though catching falling ladies-in-distress was the best part of his job.

"It was a shock, that's all," Eve said, "a real shock."

"Now, Mrs. . . . Miss . . . ma'am," said Sgt. Thomas, seemingly uncomfortable with how to address Eve, "I don't want you to worry. We'll be getting back to you, but in the meantime, make sure you keep things locked up and let us know if anything else happens."

"Nothing else will happen," interjected Madeline, glancing at Sam and Alex. "We'll see to that."

Chapter Eighteen

By 6:00 p.m. the worst was over. Someone from the city had come to clean off the spray paint from the glass door; there was not a trace of the swastika or the foul language anywhere. Except that it wasn't gone, Madeline thought, not really, not in the mind of anyone who had seen it.

Eve was sequestered in the flat with orders from Alex to rest. Thankfully there were scones neatly bagged in the freezer, ready to be thawed in a warm oven.

With the day winding down and the shop door locked, Madeline felt weariness set in, but an awkward nervousness, too. She was not alone. She glanced sideways at Alex, who had removed his tie and rolled up his shirt sleeves. He had called his office to say he would be taking the day off due to "a family emergency." She hated to admit it, but despite his unfortunate taste in women (i.e., Book Club Barbie and her perfect nails), his fierce protectiveness of his "mum" was something that she found attractive. There seemed to be more to him than met the eye (ruining a perfectly good stereotype).

Sam had gone to his gallery shortly after the police left, but he had returned at five o'clock to check on Eve, climbing the stairs with a sleek brown sack that looked suspiciously like wine. He was probably pouring her a glass now. The mother hen, Madeline thought, was now the baby chick. At least for the day.

With Eve and Sam upstairs, Alex and Madeline bandied about possible motives for the obscenities on the door of Van

Gelder's.

Madeline looked at Alex, whose hands were immersed in hot water. "Do you think the 'Queer' jab was for Matthew, the writer?" she asked. "I take it he's not fond of girls. Even Simone, with all her flirtatious attempts, has finally come to that conclusion."

"I suspect that's the case," Alex said, "but most people in Laguna are pretty tolerant. That's what puzzles me. This is the most open-minded place I've ever known. Whoever did it must be from outside Laguna, somebody who sees this place as a hotbed of subversives." He handed Madeline a wet teacup.

She took the cup and began to dry, mulling over his last statement. She liked his phrase, "hotbed of subversives." She liked it very much; in fact, the phrase alone changed the way she looked at the man with the too-perfect face. And he was tolerant, even comfortable, talking about a subject that would have set Mike off. (Her erstwhile lover, for all his Trotskyite bravado about equality, could not tolerate "queers.")

There was a depth to Alex, too, an intelligence and wit that she never imagined could accompany such perfect outer perfection. But his face wasn't all that perfect, not really. She noted a slight misalignment in his nose, as if it had once been broken (by a jealous boyfriend?). Yes, she thought, the nose was off, slightly askew at the bridge, and she liked him better for it. Maybe, if she tried, she could find more flaws.

She gathered her own wits as she sat down the dry teacup and took another from Alex. "You know what I think," she said, "I think our vandals were those guys who creeped us out that day in the shop."

"What guys? What day?"

"You know, the Bircher Brothers, the day you and Eve gave me the book. The chubby guy in the suit and the other one—"

"Buzz haircut and horned-rimmed glasses," he finished with a nod of his head.

"Yeah. He was the one who called Bobby Kennedy a Communist sympathizer. Ben Schwartz was here that day, remember?"

"How could I forget?"

Her mind firmly set on the idea, she urgently poured out the theory developing in her mind. "They were pretty pissed when Eve told them to leave. Probably put her on their 'hit list' right then and there. And maybe they saw the sign on the door about the book club, or the notice in the paper. To them, Norman Mailer would be the devil incarnate. In fact, they might have had their eye on the place for a long time."

"So you think they might have been spying on us, then?" His lips curled into a smile. (Her knees, now getting used to the sight, kept steady.)

"Creepy. But, it's possible."

"Possible, yes. I suppose I should mention that to the police." Alex wiped his brow with the back of this hand. The kitchen was a sauna from the kettles going full blast throughout the day due to an onslaught of customers; some of them, no-doubt, curiosity seekers.

Given the intensity of the day, Madeline sensed they needed a change of subject. "By the way, Alex, I've been meaning to ask. How did you know that I wanted that particular book by RFK? Or that I even liked Bobby Kennedy?"

"I heard you talking with your chum, Simone, the day I did my own spying. You mentioned something about the book, that you wanted it. A good spy has good ears." He looked at Madeline, again wearing that familiar wry smile. "And no, the Birchers and I were not mates at spy school."

She was unable to suppress a smile. "Okay, I remember now. But Simone is not what I would call a *chum*—as you put it. She's a customer, and I do like her, but I don't have a lot of what you'd call real friends in the area anymore. I've been away so long."

"Hmph," said Alex. "But what about your friends from Berkeley, besides Ben, that is. Do you ever see them?"

"No, never." She did not want to elaborate.

"You want to know my theory of friendship?" asked Alex.

Madeline shrugged. "Okay."

"The more you have—friends, I mean—the more experiences you have, and the bigger you get. Having friends makes you bigger."

She looked at him warily. "You must be suffering from heat exhaustion. Or too many scones. Are you saying that friends make you . . . *fatter*?"

Alex laughed out loud for the first time that day. He, too, seemed in need of a break from the morning's ugliness. Madeline wondered if this was more of that *merciful tickle* that she felt at her brother's funeral, as if laughter could somehow stitch together the wounds of the day, making them bearable.

"Fatter is good, yes," he said with a half-exhausted laugh. "But it's an inner fatness, you see, even though I can't quite articulate it."

"You mean like a fat soul, something like that?"

"A fat soul? That's it, that's what I'm saying." Still smiling with self-satisfaction, he motioned for her to move while he crossed the kitchen for more china dishes in need of a scrub. She stared at this man she barely knew, full of strangely-put ideas.

"I mean," he went on with a quick tilt of his head, seemingly energized by this turn in conversation, "say a friend goes to Japan, and you can't go with him for one reason or another. You see his slide show or snapshots, and hear about his first time eating sushi. It's a way of seeing through the eyes of someone else. It makes you bigger somehow, more real, weightier—your existence, I mean. Sort of like expanding as far as you can, taking in as many experiences through as many people as you're able."

"So you mean *vicarious* experiences?" she asked, trying to

make heads or tails out of his idea.

"No, it's deeper than that. You care about their experiences; you really care."

Madeline countered, "But taking on the experiences of others has its drawbacks, doesn't it? I mean, there are awful experiences, too, like when your friend finds out he's dying of lung cancer. Then, you're taking on a lot more than slide shows of cherry blossoms. It gets . . . serious."

"Well, there you go," he said. "Be big and suffer, or be small and cold and barely alive."

"Touché," she said. "But aren't you, in your own weird way, simply describing what we all know to be 'empathy'?"

Alex shrugged. "I guess so," he said slowly as he adjusted the hot water tap. "Yes, empathy. But what I don't like about that word is that we always associate it with sadness, you know, feeling the pain of others. But it also means feeling the excitement and joy of others as well. So, yes, if my mate, Joe, comes down with cancer, then I'm going to feel sad, but if he gets the Nobel Prize, then I'm on top of the world with him."

"But that's a little simplistic, don't you think? You've missed the whole thing about flaws."

"Flaws?"

"Yes, flaws. We're all so horribly flawed that we end up hurting each other all the time, and that makes your whole fat soul philosophy near impossible."

"Impossible? Now you've lost me."

"I said, 'near impossible.' Say you've got really great friends. You'd trust them with your life. They form a sort of buffer around you, protecting you from the brutal reality out there." She picked up one of Eve's oversized oven mitts and brandished it for effect. "A protection, like insulation from the pain of life. But then, these buffer people stop buffering, and you get burned. How can you ever open yourself up again to that big fat feeling you're talking about? No one can be so large and expansive as that."

"A bit cynical," he said, that smile tugging at the corners of his mouth, his brown eyes shining with mirth. (He was distressingly appealing.)

"Just answer the question."

"Well, yes, we all get hurt, but you go into it with the understanding that you will hurt each other—at some point or other. But you don't give up on your 'buffer' people. You . . . you forgive them, I suppose. Or you find new ones. Either way, you don't stop having friends altogether. That would be daft. It really would."

He looked at her knowingly, and she hated what she knew was coming—and wasn't she asking for it?

"So," he said, "would I be stepping over the line here if I suggested that you're speaking from experience, about being hurt by friends, I mean? Maybe even . . . a lover?"

"No!" she said too quickly. And emphatically. She felt her cheeks burn red with embarrassment. She quickly turned to place cups and saucers in the cabinets, avoiding eye contact. *He would not see her flushed cheeks.* "I'm not talking about myself," she said with her back to him, "just about things in general. Anyway, I want to get back to Bobby Kennedy and the book you and Eve gave me."

"You're quite besotted with Bobby Kennedy, aren't you?"

"Besotted?" she laughed, pausing to shoot him a look over her shoulder. "Well, that's a word I don't hear every day."

"You know what I mean, smitten."

"Smitten? No. Don't hear that word either."

"Right, then, you really . . . *dig* Bobby Kennedy."

"That's better, but it sounds like some hysterical Beatles' fan."

"Well, isn't it true? He affects people that way. Like a rock star, from the looks of it."

Her mirth vanished and she turned to look at him, arms

crossed. "What are you trying to say?" She straightened her back. "Are you saying that I'm nothing more than a political *groupie*?"

"No. I didn't mean that at all. I know you're taken with his ideals and his way with words, but you have to admit he's also quite youthful and dashing. Certainly not old and haggard like Mr. Johnson. And he *is* JFK's little brother."

"So?" she demanded in a tone of rising accusation.

"It's just that my dad is in the motion picture business. I hear things, you know, like how the women in Hollywood tend to throw themselves at the Kennedys."

Like you, she wanted to say. *Look in the mirror. Women must throw themselves at you on a daily basis.* "So you're saying that you can't run for president if you have youth and good-looks? You might accidentally attract movie stars? Is that your argument?" She knew she sounded sarcastic, but she couldn't stop herself. She plowed on, even though Alex looked eager to respond. "My God, Alex, have you read his book? Have you followed his career and seen the incredible things he's done? His work in the slums of New York—do you know about that? And how he kept us from a catastrophic nuclear war with Russia during the Cuban Missile Crisis—"

"I believe you," said Alex with hands lifted in surrender. "I really do."

She felt foolish for her diatribe but, like a fast moving train, her passion could not slow down easily. "Now I admit," she went on, "the Kennedy brothers were both wrong on Vietnam— initially—but Bobby's not afraid to change his mind, to grow, to evolve with the circumstances. He stood up in the Senate just last month to apologize for his part in it. To stand up and say you were wrong—that has to be a first for a politician. Who would do that but a very . . . well, a very big man? A man with a very fat soul, I'd say."

"Quite," said Alex, glancing at her with those eyes that

belied an ongoing amusement, even when talking about something as serious as this.

It irritated her, his lack of seriousness when she was becoming increasingly red-faced and flustered. *Why was everything so damned amusing to Alex Moore?*

"It's true, all of it, I'm sure," he said, "but it's also clear to me that you not only love his ideals, but you idealize the man. You're such an idealist, Madeline. I've never encountered such an idealist as you. I'd hate to see you, well, disappointed, that's all. Maybe you need to separate the two, the man from the ideals, so as not to be disappointed in case he doesn't follow through."

"But you can't sift out the ideals from the person. That's ridiculous! Then the ideals are just hanging out there in the air, invisible and useless. Ideals have to be embodied in flesh and blood."

Alex paused, but only briefly, handing her a delicate teapot, freshly scrubbed and rinsed, "Maybe. But what about 'flaws,' as you say? Don't you think he might just have a few of those?"

"Of course. He's human. We all have flaws. He won't be a perfect president. His own brother made the Bay of Pigs mistake, but we still believed in him." She began to dry the lid of the pot, a delicate and difficult task.

"True enough. And yet in regards to . . . friends—and *their* flaws—you seem to think that risks are not worth taking. Do you see a contradiction there?"

Wait a minute, she thought in a kind of mental slow motion. He wasn't supposed to see contradictions. People who looked like Alex Moore weren't supposed to see, touch, taste, or smell contradictions; it was . . . a Law of the Universe. Was he trying to dismantle her neatly drawn stereotype? Cut and cube it liked a Picasso painting?

"Very clever," she said, recouping, "but I could turn it around. You—with your Fat Soul Philosophy—aren't so magnanimous when it comes to people in the larger world, like politicians and people with power." *She had him now.*

Alex's eyebrows rose, as if pleased to accept the challenge. "Madeline, I find it hard to trust people who wield a lot of power. Presidents. Prime Ministers. The whole lot. Power corrupts, even the best of men. You're the historian. Am I not right?"

"Well, that's generally true, but . . ." *But what?* He flummoxed her, this man with the damned dimple in his chin trying to argue her into a corner. "You don't seem to be a big Bobby Kennedy fan," she said lamely, regretting it even as she spoke. She would never make it as a serious philosopher, not at this rate.

"You're wrong," he said. "I like the man—I really do. I hope he wins. But . . ."

"But what?"

"Well, from what I hear, he's got death threats hanging over him—you know, all that business with Jimmy Hoffa when he was Attorney General—so I don't think it was particularly wise to put himself out there like that, not after what happened to his brother. He's like Icarus. I mean, don't you think he's flying a bit too close to the sun?"

He turned to look at her and must have noted her bleak expression. "Sorry, I didn't mean—"

Alex didn't have time to finish. They both turned to see Sam standing at the kitchen door, a bit breathless.

"Come quick," Sam said, running his hands through his thick gray hair. "You're needed upstairs, both of you. Something else has happened."

Madeline dropped the damp dish towel, and without a word the three of them rushed up the stairs to the flat.

* * *

Eve sat upright in her easy chair, staring at the television, her hair neatly pinned, dressed in casual stretch pants and a pink

Seersucker blouse. She would have looked perfectly fine except for the hand covering her mouth and the tears rolling down her cheeks. Madeline thought of her mother, the way she'd covered her mouth when the marines came to the door with news of Sean.

Someone had died. Oh, God, she thought, don't let it be Bobby. *Don't let it be Bobby!*

She crossed the room to see the television screen. It flickered now from Walter Cronkite to a live report. There was Bobby Kennedy. Alive. Wearing a dark overcoat, he descended the steps of a plane with grave deliberation. Then he was in front of a microphone, up high, as if on a podium, except that it looked more like the back of truck. Eve's television set was off-color again with all the faces washed out. Or was it that Bobby's face was ashen with distress? Except for the light of the camera, it was pitch dark—probably his campaign tour in the Midwest where it would be two or three hours later—and the wind was blowing his hair.

Bobby Kennedy brushed back his unruly hair, twice. He then said to the waiting crowd, "I have bad news for you, for all of our fellow citizens, and people who love peace all over the world, and that is that Martin Luther King was shot and killed tonight."

Sudden screams of shock and moans of despair erupted from the dense crowd. Anguish took hold of the faces—mostly black—who had obviously been waiting for a word of hope from this man with the wind-blown hair. Instead, they got the worst news possible. Madeline, herself, could not seem to take in the shock of it all at once, but stood stock still by Eve's print of Van Gogh's *Sunflowers* while Bobby Kennedy continued to speak to the distraught crowd. He said something about having a member of his own family killed, and the crowd grew as silent as the night.

"My favorite poet is Aeschylus," he said to the crowd. "He

wrote: 'In our sleep, pain which cannot forget falls drop by drop upon the heart until, in our own despair, against our will, comes wisdom through the awful grace of God.'"

* * *

That evening, Madeline Prescott sat on the edge of her bed in the cottage, looking out at the stars through the bedroom window. Tears, standing in her eyes, created little rings around each star, like halos.

Numb and saddened, she felt a torrent—like a wild wave— loosen the foundations inside her. *When would it end, all this death and dying? The hatred. The death of dreams, the cutting down of great men, great ideas . . . .*

In the torrent, lost words seem to break loose, and she said them aloud, the verse from Shakespeare, now remembered in its entirety:

> *. . . and when he shall die*
> *Take him and cut him out in little stars,*
> *And he shall make the face of heaven so fine*
> *That all the world will be in love with night*
> *And pay no worship to the garish sun.*

Juliet had said these words about her Romeo. Bobby had said these words about his dead brother.

She stared up to the stars and picked out one for JFK and one for Dr. King. And one for Sean: She chose the brightest star for him.

~ Part Four ~

The Poet of the World

Chapter Nineteen

Mystic Arts World stood in all its "bohemian" glory directly across from Taco Bell at the bottom of the hill that separated the exclusive downtown from the free-spirited stretch of Laguna's Pacific Coast Highway. A boxy free-standing building with frowzy display windows, Mystic Arts World seemed to gloat in its unadorned hippie humility: a beacon of rebellion against bourgeois society. The gravel parking lot itself was a proletariat free-for-all with no marked spaces. Madeline's VW Bug lurched up over a half-curb onto the rough gravel while Simone sat in the passenger seat, hippie glasses bouncing to the very tip of her nose.

The news that the vandals had also hit Mystic Arts World came as a great shock. "Goodness," Eve had said over morning tea, hand to her heart. "Why would they choose our two shops out of all the shops in Laguna? I have nothing to do with Mr. Leary. Or his shop."

"Look, if the police are right," said Madeline gently, "that the two JBS guys did this—and they must have, since they were spotted by the night crew at Taco Bell—then it makes sense. In the eyes of the Birchers, hippies are the mortal enemy, the worst sort of . . . "

"Communists?" Eve supplied wryly.

Madeline smiled, a welcomed lightness, cutting through the grief that hung over everything since Dr. King's assassination. She offered to pay a visit to Timothy Leary—on behalf of Van

Gelder's, of course—to compare notes, commiserate, and to find out if he planned to press charges. Eve probably saw through her offer. It was the perfect excuse to meet the notorious LSD guru who had decided to retire (i.e., lay low) in Laguna Beach, a temptation Madeline could not pass up despite her eye-rolling disregard for Leary when he led the "Tune in, Turn on, Drop out" charge at Berkeley.

Truth was, Madeline didn't know what to do with the hippies and their psychedelic philosophy (if you could call *tripping* a philosophy). During her four years as an undergrad, the gulf between the politicos, who wanted to change the world, and the hippies, who wanted to escape the world, was a given. Disdain in equal measure. But as the Vietnam War continued to rage, there were signs that the two streams of rebellion could meld together in a more powerful river of protest against the war.

Madeline thought about this promising metaphor as she got out of the car and walked carefully toward the door, her boots unsteady on the pebbly surface. Besides, she liked some of the hippies—Simone, a case in point. Hippies added a splash of color and levity to an otherwise grim world. And, she thought, patting her purse, they made great macramé.

An enormous peace sign of psychedelic colors in Day-Glo paint greeted them in the widow, behind which a hodgepodge of tie-dyed shirts and head bands were loosely, almost apologetically displayed, as if to say: *Be cool, man. No pressure to buy here. We're not capitalist pigs.* As they walked through the door, smells of incense and candles blasted Madeline's nostrils.

"Hey, is Tim around?" Simone asked the clerk behind the counter, as if Dr. Timothy Leary were her best friend.

"No, but he'll be by later." The young man's long, dark hair hung limp, uncombed, in agonizing need of a bottle of Prell. He smiled at Simone in her jeans and fringed jacket, and then glanced at Madeline with her conventional skirt and blouse, his expression shifting from pleasure to boredom.

"I hear you guys had some vandalism Friday night," Madeline said, sidling up to Simone.

"Yeah," he said looking back and forth between the two women. "When I saw the mess, I thought I was havin' a bad trip, man." He gestured behind him to the X-taped window on the side of the building, not visible from the front. "Yeah. It took all the friggin' day to pick up shards of glass. Only my second day here, too."

Madeline imagined he must have been quite put-out, having to actually work after only two days here. (The term "energetic self-starter" did not seem to apply.) "And you are . . . ?" she prodded.

"I'm Kevin." But he said this to Simone, not to Madeline.

"Well, Kevin," Madeline said, taking the reins, "I'm Madeline and this is Simone. We're from a shop up the street, Van Gelder's. They got us, too. That's why we're here. It seems we're the only two shops that were vandalized."

"Yeah? Did they throw a rock through your window, too?"

"No broken windows, but really nasty graffiti. We just wondered if you've talked with the police. You know, about pressing charges against the two guys."

The young man's large-pupiled eyes opened wide. Evidently the word 'police' sent instant waves of anxiety through Kevin, who finally managed to eek out—

"I don't talk to the fuzz, man. I just sell books and beads and incense and dried fruit. Ever tried dried mangos?"

"Look," Madeline said, "if Dr. Leary comes in, could you give him the number of our shop?"

The clerk nodded and pushed his hair behind his ears (the most energetic show so far). He then struck up a conversation with Simone while Madeline fumbled inside her purse for a pen. Simone sauntered over to the incense sticks, Kevin close on her heels, while Madeline jotted down the number of the shop on the back of a stray receipt on the untidy counter.

Then, behind her —

"Is that hair for real? Or am I'm having an ecstatic vision?"

She turned quickly to see a tall, lanky, thin-lipped man in a white cotton Indian-style tunic, matching white pants, and Birkenstock sandals. With his sandy-haired Beatle cut, small dark eyes, a sharp chin that looked perpetually defiant, and a prominent nose that could pass as a ski slope, she knew exactly who he was. All that was missing were the love beads.

"Oh. Mr. . . . Dr. Leary. I'm Madeline."

"Call me Tim. We're all brothers and sisters here. How can I be of service, Madeline?"

"Well, it's about . . . I'm from Van Gelder's, up the road. It seems we share something in common." She gave a nervous chuckle. "Our shops were both vandalized, so I'm just here to see if you've heard anything more from the police—you know, compare notes and all."

Leary made a dismissive gesture, as if the whole business was of no importance, and motioned for her to follow him behind the counter. Madeline noticed the open door, which looked like it might lead to an office.

"We can talk back here," he said in a whisper, turning back to her. "I don't want to alarm the customers."

Madeline glanced around to see only one so-called customer, Simone, mingling in the garden of incense sticks with the unkempt Kevin. She felt her stomach lurch with the full brunt of too many smells: jasmine, gardenia, patchouli. Especially patchouli.

She wondered if she should mention that she was from Berkeley, just to break the ice; after all, Leary earned his Ph.D. from her alma mater. But then, he would probably ask her about the Human Be-In last year in San Francisco, when he and Jerry Reuben tried to unite the Berkeley radicals and the Haight-Ashbury hippies. She and Mike had boycotted the Be-In on principle. In fact, Mike had it in his conspiratorial head that the CIA was behind the whole LSD craze in order to discredit and diffuse the anti-war movement. It seemed silly now, but still, she held firm in her resistance to the philosophy of retreating to the faux world of White Lightening and Orange Sunshine (specialties on the acid color wheel) while serious students were putting their education, their freedom, even their lives on the line for the sake of peace.

And now, here she was, magna cum laude in history, meeting one-on-one with the person some considered the craziest, most dangerous man in America. *What in the hell was she thinking?*

Yet, Tim Leary had a quality about him, an unnerving intensity mixed with striking charisma. She realized the emotive or psychic—or even spiritual—power he must wield in the hippie community, and she could half-understand how one might be swayed.

Leary led the way behind the counter and through the door into a modest, square room, made larger by the absence of furniture; instead, it sported only rugs and mats scattered around the tile floor between unlit sand candles and lava lamps. The walls were covered with dizzy psychedelic art posters featuring brightly colored spirals that she supposed transported many a seeker of transcendence into the hypnotic realm of . . . something. She wasn't at all sure.

Leary motioned for her to sit. Madeline was not dressed for sitting cross-legged on a rug, so she sat gingerly with feet skewed to one side, awkwardly arranging her skirt. She felt out of place, overdressed—not unlike Barbie Doll, Alex's date the night of the book club. The comparison made her a bit nauseous. (Or was it the damned patchouli?)

"I don't want to take up your time, Dr. Leary . . . I mean . . . Tim." She felt intensely uncomfortable, not only with his name, but with his person. This was *not her scene*, not her scene at all.

"It's all right," Leary said. "Time is not important. Living in-the-now *is* important. So these young men who broke the window—I know who they are. Don't you?" His odd look bore through her.

Madeline nodded. "Yeah, they came into the shop—"

"They're just two lost souls," he said, cutting her off, "who need to expand their consciousness, get in touch with the Universe, learn how to be free. Do you know what I mean?"

Madeline shrank back. "I'm not sure."

She vaguely wondered if she should seize the opportunity to interview him about his philosophy of drug-induced mind-expansion. Did he not claim this to be a spiritual path? Was this not the very room where the so-called Brotherhood of Eternal Love, an LSD sort of church, gathered? In secret? At least that was the rumor, a story Simone relished in the telling.

She and Simone should return immediately to Van Gelder's —yes. But then, it was the end of the day, and how often does an opportunity like this come along? This was Tim Leary, *the* Tim Leary. How could she walk away now? And, what was a Quest, anyway, if not research into other philosophies (weird as they might seem)?

Leary motioned for Simone, who now stood at the door of the psychedelic-ridden room with enormous eyes, incense sticks in hand.

"Come, sit," he directed, like someone used to people following him like zombies.

Simone wore an expression of utter awe, as if she had landed an audience with the Maharishi. The young hippie moved as in a daze and arranged herself on an orange mat next to Madeline's green square of shag rug.

"Dr. Leary," said Madeline, still not comfortable with "Tim," "While I'm here, could I ask you about your . . . philosophy? I mean, do you really think LSD is the way to spiritual enlightenment? Your way to . . . well, to God or something?"

Leary's demeanor changed. "Are you a journalist? Are you from *The Register*?" His eyes had a wild, defensive, Mad Professor look about them.

"Oh, no. No. I'm just an amateur philosopher, that's all."

His face now relaxed back into guru mode. He closed his eyes and placed his hands on his crossed legs. Was he going to begin "Ommming"? Was he seeking some higher wisdom before answering her question? Madeline looked at Simone with a What-in-the-hell-do-we-do-now? expression.

Leary opened his eyes and looked up at Kevin, the clerk, who stood learning against the door frame, the young man's brown eyes lingering on Simone. "Kevin, could you bring us some punch for our guests?"

Madeline wanted desperately to exchange another glance with Simone, to get her take on the situation, which was growing weirder by the minute, but Leary's eyes locked onto hers. She wasn't sure whether to laugh or shudder.

"We really can't stay," Madeline said. She cast a sideward glance at Simone, who looked crestfallen.

"It's the end of the day, my friends," Leary said with open hands. "Can't you stay for a while? We can talk about God."

Madeline sat up a little straighter. She could stay for a while, of course. At least it would be a way of getting her mind off everything. It had been a sorrowful week since King's murder, right on top the vandalism. (She hoped tragedy didn't come in threes.) Particularly depressing were the pictures on the news of cities all over the country rioting and burning in the aftermath of the assassination. Eve had invited Madeline upstairs almost every night and Madeline went, not only for the news but for the comfort, the companionship. The wine. If ever she was in need of diversion, the time was now. And besides—she stole a glance at her companion now in a full lotus position—Simone would never forgive her for pulling her out of the "inner sanctum."

"Mr. . . . Tim, about God—" She took a breath for courage, "I'd really like to know how you personally conceptualize God." She knew this was the wrong tack but said it anyway because she wanted to talk with Leary in a rational way, the way she was taught to do at Berkeley. But Timothy Leary was obviously not "hip" on rational discourse, despite the appellation of Doctor. He was a mystic—a drug-induced mystic at that—who had left his rational mind back at Harvard, his last academic post. Now he was telling kids to drop out of school, for God's sake!

But wasn't there something to mysticism? Isn't that what she felt when she read poetry? Didn't most of the world's religions have some version of mysticism in their practices? Of course there was more to life than argumentation and refutation. But a life devoid of rational discourse would not make sense either. All these thoughts swirled around as she waited for Leary to answer her question, but Leary did not seem to hear, or at least regard, her inquiry. He busied himself with the punch that his employee had just brought in, tiny paper cups arranged on a tray.

Finally he said, "Let us not discuss God. Let us *experience* God." He looked down at the paper cups. "There is only enough here for a very short trip. Are you hip with that?"

Simone nodded enthusiastically. Madeline's jaw dropped and she felt not only conventional, but stupid. Naïve. Had she thought he was just being hospitable with a cup of punch on a warm day?

What was she so afraid of? She had smoked pot plenty of times, the only damage being an insatiable appetite for pizza and moon pies. Grass was different though. Most artists and intellectuals smoked grass these days. It was somehow part of the whole existential ennui. But hallucinogens? That, she thought, was better left to the weirdo mystics. That's where she, Madeline Prescott, drew the line. What if they scrambled her brain? No. This was not her scene . . . .

But then again—

"You must experience God in order to know God," he said, as if sensing Madeline's indecision. "Are you ready to know God, Madeline?"

Madeline accepted the tiny paper cup from Leary's hand, her own hand apparently not listening to her head. She stared into the unearthly red liquid inside. Leary and Simone were engaged in a pre-trip chat of some sort, giving Madeline a few moments to writhe in indecision. Her mind veered from one extreme to the other. *Curiosity killed the cat, yes . . . but, it also discovered DNA.*

She looked up and noticed that Kevin had left the room, closing the door behind him. She studied the orange and pink spiral on the back of the door, as if it would put her in the proper mood for consciousness expanding.

Doors, she thought, remembering a book title. Didn't Aldous Huxley find some kind of spiritual bliss behind the psychedelic-induced "doors of perception"? Hallucinogens didn't seem to impair *his* mind or turn *him* into an empty-headed frolicking idiot. Perhaps she should consider this one—and only one— foray into the psychedelic world to be a sort of research project. Yes, she resolved, she would be a kind of "existential researcher."

She stared at the bright red liquid in her Dixie cup, as if it were Socrates' hemlock. Simone was sipping hers, but Madeline still hesitated. Where were the sugar cubes? *Weren't there supposed to be sugar cubes?* Or little tabs that looked like postage stamps? She'd never heard of taking a hit of LSD in Hawaiian Punch. This was odd, but Leary was odd—perhaps even mad. Maybe, she reasoned, the punch was his way around nosey policemen who were constantly trying to bust him.

She felt a twinge of guilt (and excitement?) over the illegality of the stuff. Though it had long been used for psychiatric studies, in 1966 the state of California declared it an illegal substance. But, as she remembered from her Berkeley days, that law only made the stuff more appealing to those disposed against Establishment rules. Would she be thrown in jail? Could she plead "existential researcher" and get off?

She sipped the sickly sweet liquid slowly while Leary talked about strange things concerning the mind's journey into true reality, dissolving into Oneness with the All.

Simone, eyes closed, nodded at every pearl of spiritual truth falling from Leary's lips, her hippie glasses slipping clear to the end of her nose. (If her tiny nose were not tilted upward, Madeline thought, her glasses would be swimming in the punch about now.) Simone, Madeline guessed, was like a candle in the wind, easy prey for just about any philosophy that breezed by. She wondered if there was any truth to what Leary was saying, or if there was just enough truth to be dangerous. She listened quietly and tried to analyze his words, but her powers of mental acuity were not steady—not steady at all . . . .

A tingling sensation started in her legs. Had she sat on her boots too long? She changed position, but the tingling was still there. Then she realized it wasn't only her legs that tingled, it was her arms. Her whole body, in fact, began to tingle, and she saw the colors of the posters take on a brightness that wasn't there before. She looked around the room at the vibrant posters, each color bouncing out like balls, undulating, circling, falling— oranges and reds and greens—as if the colors themselves were alive. For a moment she could swear she had on 3-D glasses, the kind she had worn in movie theaters as a kid. She felt herself to be light and swimming through the air, the whole room swirling about in a lake of colors.

Then she heard Leary say, "Let go . . . dissolve. Become One." His voice seemed to be inside her head, and yet mutating with overtones of highs and lows.

Now the colors in the room were actually making *sounds*— odd, slippery sounds, like an out-of-tune violin. But then:

Euphoria swept over her and she perceived herself falling away into the ocean of bright colors. She felt light and free, as if the boundaries of her ego had been stripped away.

Then a single round swath of orange from the vortex-like spiral on the door started turning in mad circles—faster and faster—as the sounds coming out of the colors morphed into an odd kind of voice. Who—what was it? The voice sounded slow and deep, like her eight-track tape deck when the tape got warped and the voices slurred. The bright, welcoming colors appeared to turn on her. What was the weird, slow voice saying? *Help* me? No. *Write . . . me . . . . Write . . . me . . . Sis.* Madeline's heart raced, and she barely heard herself calling Sean's name.

She heard Leary say, "Breathe deeply now. Count to eight. You're all right. Breathe . . . . Breathe . . . ."

But the orange-colored voice would not stop. *Write . . . me . . . Sis* continued like a low slurred plea—a last gasp of the dying. Madeline began to feel herself desperate for the sinister swirling orange color to stop. She felt sick to her stomach. Her heart beat wildly in her chest and she let out a tight scream.

"Breathe, my sister," said Leary in a soothing monotone. "You're in a safe place. Just breathe . . . ."

Chapter Twenty

The next morning, Madeline woke to the bright sun shining mercilessly through the slats in the blinds. She sighed at the day ahead. Normally she would have wanted to skip Easter, as it meant going to church with her family and having to face Pastor Bob and his ridiculous sermons. However, given her excursion to Mystic Arts World (a bad trip in every sense of the word) her image of Pastor Bob's sparsely populated head gleaming under the pulpit light was beginning to look tolerable.

She winced at the thought, the regret, the sheer embarrassment of the day before. She and Simone had ended up sitting out the trip on Main Beach until well after dark, in the hazy afterglow of Leary's magic punch. The mortification of the whole thing—the way she must have cried and gone on about Sean, and how she needed to be "brought down" by Leary—made her want to stay under her grandmother's quilt for a very long time.

To add insult to injury, Eve had called later that evening to inquire about the visit and why Madeline never returned to the shop. All Madeline could manage was a pathetic, "Sorry, Eve. I didn't feel well. All those incense smells made my asthma flair." It felt rotten to lie to Eve. *Really rotten.*

But she couldn't tell Eve that she'd been on "a trip." Eve would never believe it. She couldn't believe it herself, for that matter. She'd heard of bad trips and hers must have been textbook. But surely the problem was her state of mind, her grief over Dr. King. Still, she was smarter than that. Simone had reminded her—after the fact—that "you should never, *ever* trip when you're bummed out." Madeline knew that, but there was no stopping her insatiable curiosity, *her damned impetuous decisions*.

She pulled the quilt over her head as if that would absolve her from yesterday's sins and stupidities. Perhaps, she thought, there were other ways, other paths to some transcendent hope in this world, some sense of spiritual aliveness. Hadn't she felt something like that when absorbed in the beauty of nature? Aldous Huxley aside, LSD was too unpredictable—scary, even. And there was something that didn't feel right about dismissing rational discourse altogether, as Leary would have it. Was spirituality nothing but a mystical experience devoid of any rational thought? Wasn't there a place for the mind inside one's soul? What about a fusion of sorts, a kind of friendship between the mind and the heart? The soul, she mused, the moral and spiritual part of a person, must be large enough to contain both the heart and the mind, feeling and thought. There must be room for both. Yes, she thought with growing clarity, why not just make the circle bigger? *Fatter*?

She thought of Alex—Mr. Dimple, himself—and his odd Fat Soul Philosophy, but that would never do in her already confused and raw state of mind. Was she actually drawn to him? This lady-killer? This Ken Doll who, much her to consternation, had a depth to him that ruined her most cherished biases? Everything seemed upside down; her head was beginning to hurt.

* * *

"The Monkees are going off TV," said Jilli. She lay sideways across her bed, which was covered with stuffed animals.

Madeline lounged on a bean bag chair surrounded by Flower Power Barbie and Barbie's friends, Ken and Midge. "Pleasant Valley Sunday" bubbled out from the record player, a much needed lightness after Pastor Bob's insufferable sermon, followed by the tense family meal in the dining room. The only other bright spot was visiting Grandpa Abel after church. He actually seemed to know who she was (at least he didn't call her Gerty this time). Her father was no longer angry—or drunk, thank God—but he barely spoke, never made eye-contact, and left the table in favor of football before the ice cream was served. Was he ashamed of his drunken behavior over the book club poster? Or just shutting out the world in general? Grief, thought Madeline. It had to be grief. *Losing a child was the worst thing*, Ben had told her when she finally spilled the beans about her family. Ben said to give him time. *Time*. Sure.

"The Monkees—going off T.V.?" she said, now focused on her little sister. "But that's your favorite . . ."

Jilli teared up in a sudden teenage mood swing. Madeline got up, grabbed a box of tissues, and sat down on the bed next to her bird-like sister.

"Jilli, it's just a TV show. It doesn't mean the Monkees are splitting up or anything." She didn't know if this was true, but it seemed the only thing to say.

"I know," she said with a sniffle.

Madeline handed over a tissue as she studied the vulnerable blue eyes beside her. She knew that Jilli's tears were more for a brother lost—a childhood lost—than it was for the loss of seeing Davy Jones shake his tambourine.

"I've got an idea to make you feel better," Madeline said cheerily. "Presents. We never opened our Christmas presents. Here it is Easter, and the presents are going stale on the shelf in the hall closet."

"But I don't think Mom—"

"Oh," said Madeline, waving off any argument, "we don't have to make a big deal of it. I could sneak in there and get your present without Mom even knowing."

Jilli's face brightened. "Only if you get the one I picked out for you."

A few minutes later, Madeline and her sister sat on the bed, unwrapping their presents in conspiratorial glee. Jilli tore open the gaudy wrapping, seeming to forget all about the demise of the Monkees.

"A Polaroid *Swinger* . . . far out!" (You'd think she'd been given the moon.) "The pictures pop right out of the camera. All my friends have one."

Madeline helped her load the film, and Jilli took a picture of Madeline holding up her own unwrapped gift. The mechanism made a loud noise, and the square film popped out, curled and black.

"It'll take a few minutes to develop," Madeline said, opening her own present, an eight-track tape, *Smiley Smile, The Beach Boys*. She scanned the list of songs. "'Good Vibrations,' my favorite. This is great, Kiddo!" She looked up at her little sister, who beamed from ear to ear. An idea began unrolling with her words. "Hey, Jilli, would you like to drive down to the cottage with me and spend your Spring Break vacation there? We can listen to the Beach Boys on the way down."

"Really?"

"Sure. I do have to work, but you could come in and help me or hang out on the beach. And we could have a picnic."

"I'll bring my new camera and take pictures of the beach and everything. Do you think Mom and Dad will let me?"

She looked so desperate that Madeline vowed inwardly to kidnap the poor child if nothing else.

"I'll make sure they do." Madeline smiled and pointed down to the thin, curled Polaroid photo, a black and white version of herself slowly materializing.

* * *

Eve's face turned fully toward the sea as she welcomed the cool, salty spray on her cheeks. She wasn't quite sure which was headier, the spray or the squish of wet sand between her toes.

This was lovely, *really lovely*, she thought with a rush of euphoria, a place of such beauty where one can simply seep into
the very fabric of it all. She now understood why the landscape
painters lived for such spots as this, a hidden little paradise with
stately cliffs and ragged boulders scattered about, as if protecting the fragile wildness.

Madeline had invited her to Crystal Cove for a beach picnic
as a parting gesture to Jilli, whose last day of Spring Break
needed something of a send-off. Jilli was supposed to have gone
home on Sunday, but had negotiated with her parents for one
last day, given that Madeline had Monday off. It was just the
girls, so Eve hadn't bothered with make-up or her hair. It felt
good to be so casual, free, unencumbered by convention.

And by Sam.

Sam. He had shown such care and comfort after her fainting
spell, a hoverer like her son. She appreciated it, yes, but it scared
her, as did his ringless hand.

And yet, there was his smile, that gap between his teeth, that
imperfection.

She shook him off in favor of the beauty around her, its
sensations so direct and heady. Soothing. Healing, too. And
there was much healing to be done: grief over the death of Dr.
King, the swastika on the door, memories cracked wide open.
And out of that crack arose that familiar darkness, her guilt.
Why should she be alive? Just because she was lucky enough to be
in England when Hitler invaded her country? Would it ever
leave her, this bleakness that hovered about? At times, it seemed
to spread over her, like wings of darkness. But she would not
think of it today. Not when the sun was drenching her back.
How she loved the sun!

She took a deep breath. A seagull landed directly in front of
her and squawked, as if scolding her for dark thoughts. *Look
around you*, the bird seemed to be saying, *goodness and beauty are
alive and well in the world!*

This was Eve's first experience at Crystal Cove, so different from Laguna's bustling Main Beach across the street from the shop, with its volleyball nets and folk singers and rows of oiled-up tourists. Here, with the few scattered beachcombers, there was a sense of keeping things as they were, of letting the landscape simply *be*. Even the community of demure cottages barely intruded on the rustic sense of peace.

Eve waved at Jilli and her friends, twin boys, as they built a sand castle. The twins' mother watched them and occasionally intervened with funny interjections like, "What in the Sam Hill are ya'll doing?" Eve realized that, even with what she thought to be impeccable English language skills, Southern English—or at least Texan English—was still a complete mystery to her. That and Simone's strange hippie talk. She would have to create flash cards for the new lingo: rap = chat; bread = money; dig = like. She was getting too old for yet another language! *Old?* Was she getting old? she wondered with a feeling of sudden panic.

She turned her attention to Madeline, the young and lovely Madeline with her whole future in front of her. The girl reclined in a battered old lounge chair on the cottage deck, wearing huge sunglasses and completely absorbed in a book of poetry, Rilke's *Book of Hours*, a gift to the shop from the Greeter. Eve hoped it would inspire the girl to write a poem or two, for there was to be another book club meeting soon, and it would center on poetry —the reading of poetry—with special emphasis on original poems.

Eve walked further down the beach, away from the girls, as the sun tilted toward the West. The bracing water overtook her feet without the least objection from their owner—too cold for a swim, but perfect for toes.

What was it about this girl, Madeline? Her own daughter, Becca, would never pick up a book of poetry, not in a million years. Her passions lay elsewhere—*Vogue* magazine perhaps?— which was fine. But this redhead reminded Eve of her own young adulthood: her passion for books and knowledge and history and a sense that everything was possible. If only she, Eve van Gelder, had not given up her independence so soon. It had been so much easier to simply be . . . subsumed.

She had not married for love, she was ashamed to admit to the seabirds squawking about on shore. No, she corrected to the inquiring birds, she was in love—at least she supposed she was—but how much of that was simply fear disguised as love? She had lost all hope of seeing her family, for heaven's sake. But it was fear after all: fear of the war, fear of being alone in the world, fear of everything, really. It was simply easier to disappear somewhere under Colin's dominating personality. And then came the trap of the 1950s housewife: subsumed forever. Many women were still there, still trapped, she thought with a shiver. Climbing out of the shadow of a powerful man was the accomplishment of a lifetime. She could never go back. She looked around her and, with the salty breeze, felt a rush of freedom, a rush of accomplishment—albeit, a silent one. No accolades for a divorcée in this world. But things were changing, were they not?

She took a deep breath as frigid foam washed up to her knees, bringing her back to the present. She didn't exactly know how she had moved so far out into the surf, but there she was, standing knee deep with soaking wet peddle pushers.

And then she thought she heard someone call her name. She turned and saw Sam Steiner half-running along the beach toward her. *Sam?* Wasn't this supposed to be girls-day-out? What on earth? She felt for her hair. (She must look a mess.) But there he was, the usually elegant Samuel A. Steiner of New York, clad in Bermuda shorts, a Hawaiian shirt, and a straw hat. She'd never seen his spindly, slightly bowed legs before, and in that hat and get-up, he looked rather . . . endearing, and just a little comical.

"I didn't know you were coming!" Eve called back, moving

awkwardly toward him, trying to keep her balance in the strong backwash, which seemed determined to pull her back into that dreamy place.

"Madeline called me," he said, eyes squinting into the sun. As he came closer, he added, "You look great, by the way. Your hair—I like it that way."

"It's a mess," she said, grabbing and smoothing her hair self-consciously, wishing she had brought along a scarf. And a tube of lipstick.

As they lumbered through the sand toward the cottage, she saw that Madeline had left the poetry book on the sagging lounge chair and was now giving instructions to her little sister. The waif-like child was apparently much stronger than she looked, for she was heaving a huge picnic basket down the cottage stairs. On the beach in front of the cottage, lay a big plaid blanket thrown haphazardly over the rippled sand.

* * *

Madeline sensed an anxiety in Eve, not unhappiness, but a quiet restlessness. Sam, on the other hand, was buoyant, as if he'd never been on a picnic before in his life.

"So what's the story behind these beach cottages?" asked Sam, looking up the hill as he put down the plate of sliced green apples and white cheese. "Any more tea, by the way?" he added quickly.

Madeline pulled out the thermos of Darjeeling and refreshed everyone's cup, except Jilli, who preferred her beloved Fresca.

"The cottages go way back," she said, "to the Roaring Twenties. And during prohibition, this place was a secret harbor for rum runners. Really neat stuff, the kind of history I adore. The subversive kind."

Sam laughed and nudged Eve. "Are you awake and hearing all this subversive history?"

Eve lay comfortably on the blanket with hands behind her head, eyes closed, as if lost in thought. She roused and propped herself on one elbow and joined in—

"Quite. I heard everything about the rum runners."

"We still find old bottles of rum," said Madeline, "washing up on shore from some ill-fated run." She looked at Jilli who was downing a deviled egg that Eve had brought. "Hey Kiddo, do you remember that story Grandpa Abel used to tell about the shipwreck on Balboa?"

"No, I missed out on everything. By the time I was old enough to remember anything, Grandpa and Grandma were too old and sick." Then, apparently bored out of her skull, she changed the subject. "Hey, why didn't you buy some Fritos? I'm hungry for Fritos."

"Because, Jilli," Madeline said, half-annoyed, "the seagulls love Fritos. They would never leave us alone if we had Fritos."

Just then, as if catching wind of the word "Fritos," a snow-white seagull squawked and landed near their blanket.

"It's the Frito Bandito!" said Jilli, pointing to the bird, causing Eve to break into a hearty laugh, her first real laugh of the day. Then they all laughed, as if in a contagion. Not so much because of the seagull, but because the sun-drenched day simply called for it.

After she got hold of herself, Eve looked at Madeline. "Wait, go back. What about the shipwreck on Balboa Island?"

"A big schooner, nearly 300 feet long, wrecked on Balboa just north of here. Sometime in the Twenties—1927, I think. Before the shipwreck, the only habitats in Crystal Cove were tents. Lots of tents. But when all that lumber from the old schooner started washing up, people used it to build the cottages. Like an instant lumber yard." She turned to Jilli. "Grandpa's cottage was built with the very wood of the wrecked ship. Neat, huh?"

"Neat," Jilli mustered, obviously uninterested in both history and grown-ups.

Sam looked at the child. "Say, Jilli, did you have a good

time this week with your sister?"

Jilli lit up. "It was really neat. We got our ears pierced and everything."

Eve smiled and turned to Madeline with an inquiring look.

"A crime of passion," Madeline said. "Mom will kill both of us, but especially me for letting Jilli put holes in her ears."

"Your ears, too!" Jilli said, unveiling her big sisters ears behind the curls. "See? Matching ear studs."

Madeline rolled her eyes. "I'm not sure it was such a great idea." She fingered her tender ears. (Yet another impulsive act to be regretted in the morning.)

"Jilli, you look lovely," said Eve. "And when your ears are healed up nicely, then you can wear all kinds of fun earrings— little lady bugs and turtles and the like. I've seen the young girls wear them."

Jilli looked at her big sister. "I know, but I really want peace signs."

Madeline raised her eyebrows, knowing that Jilli wearing peace signs would go over in the Prescott home about as well as the ghastly Slicker lipstick.

After more conversation and food, sleepiness began to descend on the picnickers. All but Jilli. She roused the group with her Polaroid *Swinger*. She had carried the clunky camera all day with the attached elastic band, the mechanical marvel bouncing from her wrist (thus, the name "Swinger"). She had gone through several packs of film, and the constant high pitched whir of the camera shooting out film every few minutes was starting to make Madeline wish she had bought her sister another Monkees album.

Jilli instructed Eve and Sam to smile and get closer as she stood with the camera to her eye. "No, closer!" she would say, oblivious to what Madeline saw as Eve's growing discomfort. Eve complained that her hair wasn't right for pictures—"a rat's nest," she said. They assured her that her hair was fine. Sam, on the other hand, beamed out his gappy smile.

"Now, you get in the picture, Maddy," said Jilli.

Each one took turns snapping pictures until finally, thank-fully, Jilli ran out of film.

"Well, that's it, Kiddo," Madeline said. "We've got to get you back and face the music." She touched the lobe of one of Jilli's newly impaled ears.

"Say, hold on," said Sam. "Before you go, I brought a little something for Eve that I want to share with the two of you as well. It's on the porch."

Eve looked startled. "What's the occasion? It's not my birth-day."

"Well, you have to have a birthday sometime," Sam said, as the four began cleaning up picnic remains. Eve helped Madeline fold the picnic blanket while Sam and Jilli walked ahead.

When they reached the cottage porch, Sam presented Eve with a large rectangular package while the others looked on. Eve gave a nervous laugh and untied the string.

It was a painting, pungent with the smell of fresh oils.

"Oh, my!" said Eve. But that was all she said.

Madeline jumped in. "It's Main Beach—right across from the shop. Did you get it from one of the *plein air* artists, Sam?"

Before Sam could answer, Jilli said, "Don't you like it, Eve?"

All eyes turned on Eve.

"Let me see it in the light." Eve took the canvass and walked out beyond the shade of the porch, onto the deck and turned it toward the sunlight. Everyone followed and huddled around it. "It's remarkable, really," Eve said. "There's the Hotel Laguna, right there." She pointed, without touching, to the mission-like tower in the middle of the landscape. And the birds! Oh, the seagulls and the pelicans are stunning. Who did it, Sam? Who is this fine artist?" She looked up at him.

Sam pointed to the signature at the bottom right and stood back while the other three crowded in to look.

Eve squinted. Madeline shook her head, giving up on the scrawl.

"It looks like "D-i-n-e-r," said Jilli, spelling it out. *"Diner?"*

"Steiner," said Sam with a chuckle. "I'm afraid I haven't mastered the art of the signature yet."

"You?" Eve said, turning sharply to face him.

"Yeah, Sam," said Madeline, "you never let on that you painted."

"Wow," said Jilli. "You're good. Those pelicans look real."

Eve's mouth stood open, wide like her eyes, and everyone looked to her expectantly. Finally she said, "A truly impressive work, this. How many like it do you have hidden away?"

"It's my first completed work," he said, "my first painting. I'm studying with the master himself." He pointed toward a cottage at the top of the hill. "Roger Kuntz."

Madeline remembered this to be the artist Biddy's husband studied with.

Eve shook her head, as if unable to take in this new revelation.

Madeline glanced from her to the beaming Sam Steiner, gallery owner and *artiste*, and back to Eve.

"But I can't accept it," Eve added firmly. "Not your very first work. You should display it in your gallery, Sam. You really should. Or give it to your children. I simply can't accept your first piece. And something so grand."

Madeline looked back at Sam. His face seemed to deflate like a cake falling, as when the oven temperature is set way too high.

Chapter Twenty-One

"Why didn't Eve want the painting?" asked Jilli, breaking the silence in the VW on the way back to Anaheim.

"Oh," sighed Madeline, "I don't know. Maybe she felt uncomfortable accepting it—I can't say. Grown-ups are complicated."

"Like Mom and Dad."

"Like Mom and Dad," Madeline said, glancing behind her to change lanes, or attempt to, with rush hour traffic pressing in. The VW Bug finally fit snuggly between a VW van filled with long haired guys (smoking who-knows-what) and a yellow Mercedes. "You know, Jilli," she said, relieved to be in the correct exit lane, "we haven't talked very much about Mom and Dad, have we?"

Jilli blew out a sigh. "Not much to say. Mom just cries and mopes around the house. When she's not at church. She goes to church all the time now, even on Wednesday nights."

"And Dad?"

"He's just weird." She looked away, as if studying the traffic. "You know, like when we made the sign for your book club. Sometimes he yells and sometimes he doesn't say anything."

"Well, get ready, Jilli," Madeline said, downshifting as she slowed onto the exit ramp. "We're about to get our comeuppance over the earrings. Let me take the heat, okay?"

"But I wanted my ears pierced."

"No, Jilli. I insisted, all right? We have to keep our story straight."

Jilli nodded, as if agreeing to drive the getaway car at a robbery.

* * *

A heavily-oiled salad drooped despondently in the center of Kate Prescott's table. A pitcher of perspiring iced tea sat next to the salad, while four tumblers languished with half-melted ice cubes.

They were in trouble all right.

Kate, wearing a pink floral mu'u mu'u, hugged each girl perfunctorily, without warmth. No inquiries about her daughters' week together. "The casserole is probably too dry to eat now," was all she said as she put on her large red oven mittens.

"Sorry, Mom. We'll do the dishes." Madeline looked around. "Where's Dad?"

"Oh, he's in the garage," Kate said dryly. "He spends most of his time out there. When he's home." She motioned the girls to sit down, guiding them with her oversized oven mittens as if directing an airplane on a taxiway.

Madeline could not tell if her mother was annoyed at her for bringing Jilli home late, or if her dad was the source of irritation. But she definitely seeped resentment, as if from some vast reservoir of pent-up anger. Her teased hair was especially high and lacquered, as if compensating for her low mood.

"So what's Dad doing in the garage these days?" Madeline probed while pouring the tea.

"Jilli!" her mother said, ignoring the question. Her eyes shot back and forth from daughter to daughter. Madeline's curls covered her own ears, but Jilli's sin had nowhere to hide.

"Jillian Ann, are those studs in your ears?"

Madeline cut in quickly. "Mom, it's my doing. She's only going to wear little tiny earrings—lady bugs and turtles, that kind of thing. All her friends are wearing them. I got mine pierced, too. See?" She lifted her hair.

Kate did not see. She purposely avoided seeing, as she turned toward her bubbly casserole resting on the cold burner on the stove, testing it with a fork. "I don't care what you do to your own ears, but she's just a child." She paused. "You put holes in her ears." She punctuated each word, as was her practice when she put on her authority voice, but there was in her tone not so much a sense of parental objection, as of defeat.

Jilli's shoulders slumped, deflated, her entire little frame turning inward. *The domino theory of resignation*, thought Madeline, feeling her own shoulders caving in.

Kate kept testing the damned casserole as if determined to tear the whole thing apart, while Madeline sat still, recalcitrant, steeling herself for another psychic jab. Almost wanting it.

But instead of the expected dig, Kate veered off in another direction, as if the pierced ears were suddenly old news. She waved the fork laced with chicken casserole goo in the direction of the garage. "I'm at my wits end," she said. "Your father's got some woodworking project going on out there and the noise is maddening! I don't know how much longer my head can stand it."

The noise began, as if on cue. Madeline winced at the piercing roar from the garage, like an enormous dentist drill.

"It's called a circular saw," said their mother over the noise, throwing up her hands in aggravation.

"Mom, do you want me to tell Dad we're here?" Madeline said, once the noise subsided.

"No, I'll get him." Kate wiped her hands on the dishtowel. "The casserole isn't too dry after all, but it will get cold if we wait any longer." She went to fetch her husband, slamming the door behind her as if she meant it for John, not the girls.

Shortly, Kate returned to the kitchen with John on her heels. Her father was dressed in blue jeans and an old blue tee shirt bearing the Rockwell logo from the defense plant where he worked his long hours. He wiped his feet on the throw rug, greeted the girls, and started toward the kitchen sink to wash his hands. Then John Prescott began to whistle, some old tune that Madeline didn't recognize.

She was confused. He never whistled. He wasn't the whistling kind of dad.

* * *

"Alex, take these books back to . . . wherever you found them. I don't want them in my shop." Eve knew she sounded irritable, and maybe even unreasonable, but she couldn't seem to help it.

She sat, book in hand, at the Steinbeck table close to where her son was arranging a new shelf of California authors. She had been reading a copy of Alex's newest "find" between customers, becoming more incensed with each page.

"What books?" Her son looked genuinely nonplussed as he turned from his task.

"The very book you're presently arranging on the shelf, *The Teachings of Don Juan*. I don't like it and I don't want it in my shop."

"You don't mean that, Mum. These books are hot off the press, and I managed, not without some effort—"

"Sorry," she cut in, "but they have to go. Take them . . . oh, I don't know . . . take them down to Mystic Arts World where they belong."

"But this book is all the rage. Granted, it's not book club material. But it will sell; I can promise you that."

"I don't care if it sells. I don't like all that . . . that 'getting high' on peyote. Mr. Leary would be the one to endorse this, not me." She flipped through more pages. "And the way the author portrays women! Alex, he actually calls women 'devil's weed.' I find that more offensive than the drug-induced visions."

"But the author is an anthropology grad student at UCLA."

"I don't care who he is."

"But this isn't like you, Mum, to censor books."

Eve ignored her son and read aloud, "'The Devil's Weed is like a woman, and like a woman she flatters men. She sets traps for them at every turn . . . don't let the devil's weed blind you. She's hooked you already.'" She splayed the book on the table, took off her glasses and said, "He's prejudice against women, a misogynist, I'd say."

Alex sighed. "Mum, we all have our prejudices. Even you."

"What on earth are talking about?"

"You have your own blind spots, you really do."

"Me? How can you say such a thing, Alex? I deplore prejudice of any kind. You know that."

"Then why do you constantly demean platinum blonde women, as if they're nothing but—" He stopped and dropped his shoulders in a sigh. "Sorry."

She said nothing. All her powers of denial were busy vying for a word, but her anger had already given way to a sense of shame.

"No, you're right," she said, gaining composure. "You're spot on. Not that it's a full-blown prejudice, mind you. More of an aversion because of . . ."

"Marcela Blankenship," he said, stating the obvious.

"Marcela Blankenship *Moore*, you mean." She paused. (Thinking of Colin's new wife did nothing to improve her mood.) "I'm sorry, Alex, really sorry that it was that noticeable. And if I've insulted you on account of your girlfriend, the blonde . . . what's her name?"

"Tori, and she's *not* my girlfriend," he said irritably. "I don't even see her anymore. But let's not talk about her, all right?"

Eve held her tongue. She welcomed Sundays because Alex worked alongside her, usually niggling her about the state of the finances or lecturing her on how to organize the books. Even with their bickering, she always looked forward to his coming.

If only she could do that with Sam. *Bicker*. Yes, she thought wistfully, even an all-out row would be preferable to the awful politeness between them. He continued to stop in for tea, though less often. He had even purchased another book upon her recommendation. But the sense of intimacy had vanished since the picnic, and they were locked into a game of formal, awkward gestures.

"Look, Alex, I don't mean to pick a fight. It's just that I'm a bit out of sorts today."

"You are that," Alex said, looking over his shoulder, meeting her eye. "Do you want to talk about it?"

She sighed. "It won't help. I've really mucked things up, that's all."

"Mucked things up? What things?"

"It's the way I left things with Sam at the picnic. I feel like I should have accepted the painting. I really should have taken it. But at the time, well, at the time I just couldn't do it. I don't know why—a spur of the moment decision. It's been nearly two weeks . . ."

"Tell him you changed your mind, then. You really should, you know."

"It's not that easy, Alex. I need to think about what to say and how to say it. It's just such a touchy matter, that's all." She looked back at the little book in front of her and made a decision, at least about the blasted book. "Alex, you can keep your copies of *The Teachings of Don Juan* on one condition. You must sandwich them between copies of Simone de Beauvoir's *The Second Sex*"—she paused, enjoying the confused look on her son's face—"and Betty Freidan's *The Feminine Mystique*. You'll find them on the non-fiction shelf."

Alex smiled broadly while Eve set the book aside and went back to the kitchen. And to the battle within.

* * *

José Feliciano's "Light My Fire" pulsed from the car radio while Madeline maneuvered the Bug around a huge truck on the 10 freeway. The mild-mannered guitar version annoyed her; she preferred the original Hammond organ and the edgy voice of Jim Morrison of The Doors. She wished she could listen to her new Beach Boys tape (Jilli's sweet gift), but the eight-track player was on the blink, having eaten a Joan Baez tape earlier in the week. She'd have to ask her dad to look at it. But with all the tension between them, she wondered if she would ever see the day. It had been over two weeks since she witnessed him whistling in the kitchen. No communication. Nothing. Give him time, she thought. *Give him time.*

The air outside was bleak, stale, and smoggy. Her chest felt tight and she'd been congested for days. She glanced in the rearview mirror to see what the eye-reddening, murky gray L.A. air had done to her. Not a pretty sight.

She thought of the day behind her, an eventful day of canvassing for RFK. She and Ben had saturated the USC campus with flyers and talked with students about Bobby's great vision: to get the U.S. out of the war in Vietnam and channel those resources into the war on poverty—LBJ's stillborn Great Society. The students were receptive, but some criticized Bobby for waiting so long to jump into the race, and stayed loyal to Eugene McCarthy. But she had expected this, and was ready with persuasive examples of Bobby's record and experience.

As the afternoon waned, they had ventured off campus into the neighborhoods of Watts. By 4:00 p.m. they found themselves on Jefferson Street. She was met with a forest of black faces, some friendly—the older people especially. Many of the young men looked downright suspicious, as if to say, "What're you doin' on our turf?" Her heart pounded, partly from fear of seeing a switchblade and partly with the excitement of it all.

These were Bobby's people: the poor, the despairing, the unemployed. Getting them out of the trap of poverty—and Vietnam—and into jobs was Bobby's vision. Unemployment was the norm here; consequently, crime was high. Getting this neighborhood to vote was her job at the moment. They had passed out a number of flyers and a few voter registration forms.

She had been about to suggest they call it day when a hulking black man with a bulbous afro and an orange tunic approached them. He wore reflective sunglasses and a steely expression.

Madeline had felt her breath freeze inside her already-aching chest.

"Hey, man, what you got there?" The man's voice was not friendly, and it bothered her that she couldn't see his eyes.

Ben handed him a flyer with RFK's picture and cleared his throat. "Yeah, uh . . . Senator Kennedy wants to bring hope to your neighborhood, to bring jobs here, but he needs your vote on June 4th for the primary. Are you registered to vote, sir?"

The man didn't answer, but took the flyer and looked at it without so much as a twitch in his flint-hard face. Madeline tried to relax. She shouldn't be so afraid, she thought, but then, since King's death, many of the poverty-stricken black communities had lost patience with non-violence. At least Watts, still recovering from the riots three years earlier, had not exploded.

She and Ben exchanged glances. Ben looked uneasy. Even without the afro, the man was considerably larger than Ben.

The forbidding man had taken several seconds to read the flyer with no change of expression. Finally he said, "Yeah, I'm registered." Then his reflective glasses moved in their direction. "*This* white dude's all right, man. He's all right. I remember his brother, when he was shot in Dallas. I cried, man, cried like a baby that day."

Madeline thought she heard Ben sigh with relief, and she felt her heart slow down. The man, who now seemed more interesting than fearful, engaged Ben in an intense conversation about the disproportionate number of blacks who were dying in Vietnam. Ben was good at this, she thought, a first-rate shrink who knew how to put people at ease. As they turned to leave,

the man gave Ben and Madeline a toothy white smile displaying
one gleaming gold front tooth.

"You know, Ben, I think we've done enough for today," she
had said, feeling her eyes sting from the bad air quality. "I need
to start home before the freeway turns into a parking lot. I
promised Jilli I'd stop by the house on my way to the cottage."

They headed back to her VW parked near the USC campus.
Just before they got to the car, Ben suddenly stopped and turned
to her. A strange look came over him.

"What is it, Ben?"

Recalling this moment irritated her as she put on her blinker
to change lanes. She fumbled with the radio, trying to get a
better station.

"Madeline, do you have to drive back this evening?" he had
asked. "You don't work Mondays—right? We could come back
here in the morning. How about it?"

Why did he have to go and say that?

Madeline had looked at him in confusion. *Stay over?* All the
exhilaration of their work together was suddenly usurped by
anxiety. And an escalating war within. Part of her wanted to
say *yes,* to exchange the danger of canvassing a rough neighborhood for another kind of danger.

"No," she found herself saying. "I really have to get back.
Sorry." She smiled with what she hoped looked like regret, but
was actually a feeling of utter confusion, as when she stared
down at the LSD-laced punch in Mystic Arts World. She didn't
want to make another embarrassing mistake on the heels of that
one. She needed a break from catastrophe.

"It's okay, Madeline." Then Ben leaned in and kissed her
gently on the lips, but the feeling of it hardly registered for the
anxiety clawing away inside. She pulled away.

She had pulled away.

Now, as the light began to wane and things tended toward
reflection, she would love to have a glass of wine with Eve and

bend her ear. She wanted to forget about her confusion over Ben. And Alex.

For God's sake, why was she thinking of Alex? Since that day in the kitchen, the day of the vandalism, he just kept popping in and out of her mind. *Alex and his Big Fat Philosophy.* What was happening to her? Was she becoming one of The Shallow People? Did she actually have feelings for him? Or was it just a school-girl infatuation with a well-put-together face? It didn't matter. She could have all the feelings in the world, but she would never be his type. That blonde yacht-club nail-polished Barbie Doll was his type. Although, she hadn't seen hide nor hair of the woman since the book club. Still, the lines were drawn. She was Ben's type; Ben was her type. Ben had made the first move. And she had pulled away. *Damn!*

She was tired now, beset with confusion, and frustrated with the congested stop-and-go traffic, her foot working the clutch like a pump organ.

Weary and confused as she was, her VW seemed to find its own way down the freeway and onto the Ball Road exit in Anaheim, the half-way point between L.A. and Crystal Cove. She would get something in her stomach and check in with Jilli before returning to the cottage.

When she pulled into the driveway, the sun was setting and the view of the lawn and shrubs was clear enough. She noticed the yard was not as manicured as it used to be, milk weeds growing up among the pink geraniums. This was not like her *House and Gardens* mom. She felt a twinge of worry in her gut, but shrugged it off as her eyes landed on Jilli, who sat on the porch dressed in culottes and a sweater. She was not smiling. In fact, Madeline saw that Jilli's face was scrunched up. *Good Lord, she was crying.*

"Jilli, what's happened?" Madeline said, shutting the car door. She ran toward the front porch.

Jilli, hugging her knees, spoke with effort. "I've been waiting for you . . . I thought you'd never get here. It's bad . . . Mom and Dad are splitting up."

"What?" Madeline felt her head spin. She sat down on the porch next to her sister. "Mom and Dad? Never! They don't even believe in divorce. They're almost Catholic about it." She tried to make her sister smile, but Jilli would have none of it. "Hey, Kiddo, let's go inside. I could use a Coke."

"Maddy, you're not listening," Jilli said as the screen door creaked shut behind them. "Dad's gone. Mom's holed up in her room. She's got the door locked. She won't talk to anyone, not even me." She fell into her big sister like a rag doll; Madeline put her arms around her and stroked her hair.

"It's all right, Kiddo. It's all right. I'll find out what happened. It's probably just another one of their arguments. It'll blow over in a couple of days."

Jilli was curiously silent.

"Jilli, where did Dad go, exactly?"

"He told me to," she sputtered, "he told me to tell you that he was going to stay at a hotel. *A hotel*, Maddy. The Holiday Inn, I think, the one by Disneyland." Jilli looked like a little lost bird with sore red eyes that rivaled Madeline's own.

"He just needs time away. He's done that before. You weren't old enough to remember. It's just one of their fights, that's all."

"No. It's worse than that. Mom and Dad have been fighting over . . ." She couldn't finish for the sniffling.

"Over what? What have they been fighting about, Jilli?"

"Sean. They're fighting about Sean!" Now Jilli burst into furious tears.

Madeline led her over to the plastic covered sofa and sat her down. She let Jilli cry for a few minutes longer, patting her back for comfort. Then she left Jilli and went to hunt down Kleenex. On her way to the bathroom she nearly knocked on her mother's door, but decided against it. She could only handle one hysterical person at a time. In the bathroom she noticed that everything was untidy and dingy. Towels were lying about; the waste basket overflowed; the tissue box, empty. She grabbed a wad of toilet paper and started back to the living room. She stopped at the kitchen door and saw pots and pans that needed soaking tossed carelessly in the sink.

Her chest tightened. She began to wheeze.

She hurried back into the living room where her Twiggy-thin wisp of a sister lay curled up on the sofa. She must find her purse—find her inhaler. *Find her inhaler.* She felt the breath go out of her while she searched the bottomless pit of her purse. She couldn't find it. Where in the hell is it? she thought with mounting panic. *Jilli needs me. Mom needs me. Dad needs me. The whole damned world needs me. Breathe, breathe!* she told herself. But the more she fought it, the worse it became. Her chest felt like a lead balloon.

She ran down the hall to her old room to get the emergency inhaler from the nightstand drawer. She retrieved the inhaler, positioned it, pushed, and . . . *nothing.* It was empty. She threw the useless thing on the bed and raced back into the living room.

Jilli saw Madeline's distress and yelled, "Maddy, where's your inhaler?"

Madeline dumped the entire contents of her macramé purse—a purse her dad called "a potato sack"—onto the living room floor. Jilli got down on hands and knees with her, and the two sisters searched frantically through the scattered contents: Zippo lighter, hair brush, billfold, Hershey's bar, Kleenex, address book, RFK button, the odd cigarette . . . .

"It's not here, Maddy, it's not here!"

Chapter Twenty-Two

Madeline awoke to a feeling of irritation in her newly pierced right ear. Her first thought was that she forgot to take out her earrings before she went to bed. But, on second thought, this wasn't her bed. Raised metal bars greeted her on each side. Reality dawned when she felt the tug of an oxygen tube clipped to her nostrils. She heard murmurings, familiar voices. She turned her face upward to see worry lines staring back at her. Her mother's face. No make-up. Puffy eyes. Her teased hair jutted, bulged and drooped in mangled configurations.

"Mom," she said, her voice thick, her mouth dry. "Sorry. No inhaler in my purse—"

"Don't try to explain," Kate Prescott said with tears floating in her eyes. "I heard you girls—well, I heard Jilli—screaming and it got me up. The ambulance must have been right around the corner, thank the Lord, because almost as soon as I put the phone down, they were walking in the door." She sniffled. "You gave us quite a fright, Maddy, like you did when you were little. But you're all right now." Kate closed her eyes, squeezing them shut, while tears escaped down her cheeks. She rubbed her daughter's arm with an affection Madeline barely remembered. Madeline knew she was thinking of Sean, of the possibility of losing two out of three children. And perhaps, too, of her Holiday-Inn husband.

She felt the touch of another hand and looked to the opposite side of the hospital bed where Jilli stood with large, blue, sleepless eyes.

"It was real scary, Maddy. I was so afraid . . ." Her voice broke.

Madeline squeezed her hand. "Thanks, Kiddo. Sorry I scared you."

Kate handed her daughter a plastic cup with a bent straw and insisted she drink. The water seemed to get the cobwebs out of her mouth, at least enough to persuade her mother to take Jilli home. The two of them desperately needed to rest, since, according to a bosomy blonde nurse who appeared out of nowhere (a third head peering down over the metal bars as if she were a baby in a crib), Jilli and her mother had both stayed the entire night, each taking turns on the vacant bed in the room. Also, according to the nurse, Madeline would have to stay put for the day, at least until the doctor officially released her.

After they had gone, she lay watching TV images of a soundless soap opera—what was it? *General Hospital*? Here she was, she sighed, a patient once again at Anaheim Memorial Hospital with her two old friends: the oxygen tube and industrial strength antihistamines dripping into her veins. On closer inspection, her hand had only a bandage where the IV needle had been. So the crisis was over, and she had missed it all in some drug-induced sleep.

She jumped at the knock on the open door and turned to see a middle-aged man lighting up a shadowy doorway with a smile.

"Hello there. I didn't mean to wake you."

She blinked several times, her eyes gritty and dry and not quite focusing. She suddenly realized it was the Scottish chaplain from the book club, the round and happy man who impressed her as being something of a heretic.

"You're the chaplain from the book club . . . the descendent of the Mad Vegetarian of Edinburgh." She heard him laugh with satisfaction as she tried to sit up. He moved to help her with the pillows. "Henry, isn't it? Henry Graham."

"Yes," he said with delight in his voice. "Very good of you to remember my name, and especially my mad ancestor. I've been meaning to stop by for tea and a good chat." His eyes smiled behind his old-fashioned glasses.

"What are you doing here in Anaheim?" she asked. "This isn't your beat, is it?"

"Well, as a matter of fact, it is my 'beat,'" Henry said. "My home base is South Coast Medical, near Laguna, but on Mondays and Wednesdays I shuttle between two other hospitals in Orange County, this being one of them. The circuit-riding chaplain, I am."

"Is this Monday?" she asked herself out loud in an attempt to orient herself. When he nodded, she felt relief that she wouldn't be missing work since the shop was closed. One less thing to worry about.

"So, how are you feeling, my dear?"

"Okay, I guess. A little groggy." She paused. "But how did you know I was here?"

He chuckled. "I was walking by a few minutes ago on my way to the chapel when I caught sight of your red locks through the open door, and I stopped in my tracks. 'It's the Scot!' I said to myself. 'The redhead from the book club.' The nurse at the desk gave the okay to come in. It's Madeline, isn't it?"

She nodded, self-consciously raking her fingers through her wilder-than-usual curls. "Sit down and talk. Please. Do you have time?"

"For you, of course," he said with an open smile. He pulled up a dastardly institutional chair. At her request, he lowered the metal bar so she didn't feel like a sideshow in a cage. "You had a rather serious asthma attack, I hear," he said finally. "Tough stuff. You're lucky you weren't alone when it happened."

Madeline nodded and adjusted the oxygen tube. She looked up at Henry's warm round face and everything seemed to spill out: "If my parents hadn't been fighting—that's probably why I had this attack, that and the smog—then I wouldn't be here. I've been in L.A.where—"

"Slow down, now," he interrupted gently with a wave of his hand. "What's this about your parents? Anything serious?"

"I'm not sure. But my dad has moved into a hotel. I haven't had a chance to talk to either of them yet, but I know they haven't been dealing very well with my brother's death."

"Your brother? An illness?"

"Vietnam."

"Oh," Henry nodded. "I'm sorry to hear that, Madeline, really sorry. So our discussion of Vietnam at the teashop was pretty close to home for you."

She nodded. "I remember thinking you were pretty unorthodox, at least not like a lot of stuffy religious people I know. So what are you, then? What denomination, I mean?" He looked ready to speak. "No, on second thought," she said, "I don't want to know. I mean, it doesn't matter because I have this allergy to organized religion. But just the same, I have questions for you. If you don't mind."

"And what question is on your mind at the moment, my dear?"

"Well, to start with, I'm having trouble with God."

"Okay, then," he said, linking his hands in his lap. "Tell me about this God you're having trouble with."

"It's just that it's so confusing," she said without a clue as to where she was headed, "all these different versions of God out there. They all seem to have the one and only way, you know. There's the Jesus People from the hippie church in Costa Mesa. They leave religious tracts at the shop." He nodded as if she were actually making sense. "And then there's the psychedelic spiritual enlightenment crowd at Tim Leary's place." Henry's eyebrows shot up at this, and she hoped her voice didn't reveal her regrettable dip into the waters of weirdom. She said quickly, "And then there's my parents' old-time-religion church with Pastor Bob's weekly altar calls to save your soul from the devil, by which he means drugs, sex, and rock-and-roll."

Henry chuckled, which gave her confidence to continue with whatever she felt like spilling out.

"I'm sure there are normal, sane . . . even beautiful expressions of religion out there somewhere," she said almost apologetically. "It's just that I keep running into the weird ones—the extreme ones, you know. I seem to attract them. It must be my hair or something."

Henry laughed exuberantly at this. She liked the man for his easy laughter, but mostly for his open acceptance of her irreverent, confused self. Pastor Bob, she mused, would be calling in an exorcist about now.

"So then," he said with his smiling eyes on hers, "God just keeps turning up like a bad penny."

She nodded. "You can see why I need professional help."

He paused. "Are you sure you feel like talking?"

"Oh, I'm fine. Really. I'm getting out today." But she felt her mouth dry from the drug and reached for the plastic pitcher. Henry intercepted, poured her a cup, and handed it to her, bending the straw to the proper angle. She thanked him and waited for him to set down the cup before she said, "Henry, the question I want to ask is this: how can you believe in God? I mean, in the face of all the evil and suffering in the world?" She added, not waiting for an answer, "I'm agnostic myself, at least at the moment—keeping my options open, I suppose. But now that my brother's gone, I find myself thinking about it even more. The spiritual side of life, I mean. Sean believed in God, but I can't seem to reconcile the horrors of . . . say, Vietnam, with a belief in God. I just can't believe in a God who sees these monstrous evils—war, violence, napalm—and who has the power to stop them, but doesn't. And what about the Holocaust?" She thought of Eve's family. "I can't believe in a God who would allow such atrocities. I just can't, Henry."

"Neither can I," Henry said, catching her completely off guard.

"But don't you believe in God?"

Henry readjusted himself in the bedside chair, an unforgiving metal horror probably meant to make visitors uncomfortable so they wouldn't stay too long.

"Yes, I believe in God," he said, "but not the one you just described. Not the God the philosophers love to bat around. Oh, I'm familiar with the arguments, yes. Something like: God is all-good, so God *wants* to stop evil; God is all-powerful, so God is *able* to stop evil. But evil exists. Therefore . . . well, therefore either God is not all-good or God is not all-powerful—or God does not exist."

She nodded. "Exactly! That's what I'm talking about. Is there a way to solve the problem . . . and still believe in God?"

"Well, some would argue that God is not all-good, at least not in any way that makes sense to us. These folks rage at God, fists in the air to protest God's capriciousness and negligence. In seminary, we called it the 'protest theodicy.'"

She sighed. "I'm all for protest, Henry, but how can I protest injustice in this world if God himself is some capricious, negligent tyrant? It doesn't make sense. And who would worship such a God? I mean, shouldn't goodness—or love or compassion or whatever you want to call it—be at the very *heart* of spirituality?" She felt herself clear headed now, her passion for the subject rising inside her.

Henry nodded. "I think so, yes."

"But then," she thought aloud, "the other possible answer, that God must not be all-powerful, can't be challenged. I mean, who would seriously question God's . . . omnipotence?"

"I would. In fact, I do."

"But isn't God, by definition, all-powerful?"

"That would depend on what metaphor you adopt."

She gave him a questioning look. "Metaphor?"

"Sure. We humans have to think in metaphors, don't we? Especially with a mystery as huge and exhilarating as God. Some do speak in terms of 'absolute truth' in spiritual matters, but I think that's a mistake—a dangerous one. It leads to delusional thinking and religious fanaticism. But a metaphor, you see, is not an absolute."

"What do mean, 'not an absolute'?"

"I mean metaphors have strong eyes, but weak backs: they help us see clearly, but when pressed too hard, they break down. That's the beauty of a metaphor. It helps us see things more clearly, yes, but it also keeps us humble. And if there's anything religion could use these days, it's a dose of humility."

Madeline smiled. "No kidding," she said with growing comfort in the presence of the descendant of the Mad Vegetarian of Edinburgh. It was as if they were on the same 'vibe.' She added, "Metaphors have a special appeal to me . . ."

"You're a poet, then?" He inclined his head with interest.

"Well . . . not at the moment." She wished she had kept her mouth shut.

"Are you sure you shouldn't rest now, Madeline? We can have a grand philosophical discussion over tea once you're feeling better—"

"No! You can't leave me hanging like this, Henry. I'm on a quest and your input is crucial."

He chuckled. "I can't turn down a redhead on a quest." He crossed his legs and continued. "Okay then, let's do it the Socratic way. Let me ask you a question. Give me a metaphor for God—the first one that comes to mind."

"Okay, that's easy. Policeman in the sky. No, dictator is better. The Dictator in the sky who wields all power in the universe."

"Ah, the Cosmic Dictator."

"You said to give you the first one that comes to mind. I didn't say I liked it. Oh, and he has beard, too . . . a long white one."

"Ah, very old and very . . . male."

"And very white," she added.

"Exactly. You'd think that women and people of color might be a little put-off by an exclusively white male image. It's a pretty impoverishing metaphor, all in all, wouldn't you say?"

She sighed. "Of course, and I don't get why I can't see beyond that dictator image. Why is it so hard to get past it, Henry?"

"Blame it on the Roman Empire!" he said with another warm chuckle.

"What are you talking about?" she said, curious where this was going.

"You're an historian. Think about it. Our Western religions —Judaism and Christianity—were profoundly influenced by the first Emperor of Rome."

"Caesar Augustus?"

"Exactly. With Caesar, omnipotence—having all power— was synonymous with divinity. Caesar was the divine, all-controlling power of the world. The idea seeped into the collective Western consciousness. Theologians began to speak of God's power as all-controlling, determining every last jot and tittle of history. As the philosopher Alfred North Whitehead put it, 'The Church gave unto God the attributes which belonged exclusively to Caesar.'"

"Isn't that a parody of something Jesus said? Something about giving unto Caesar what belongs to Caesar and unto God what belongs to God?"

Henry looked just a little surprised.

"I did learn something before I bolted from Sunday School." She took a sip of water and said, "But what's the alternative,

Henry? You know, the subversive one?"

"Well, Madeline, you could say that 'subversives,' like me, see the dictator's form of power as the lowest, most degrading kind. The most noble, the truest form of power does not manipulate from above, but empowers from within." He tapped on his chest for effect. "God's power, I believe, is not coercive and all-controlling, but persuasive and relational, the model for us all to follow. And this . . . this powerful divine energy within beckons us toward the good, the true, and the beautiful. But it's up to us to answer the call. We can refuse and mangle up our lives, but the wooing persists—"

"Wooing? That sounds more like . . . a lover."

"A lover, yes. Or a poet."

"A poet?"

"Sure," said Henry. "That's it. That's my favorite metaphor for God. Whitehead said it first: 'God is the poet of the world, with tender patience leading it by his vision of truth, beauty, and goodness.'"

"Poet of the world," Madeline said aloud. She liked the sound of it, as if the words had vibrations; a wave of something near to joy passed through her. Then, a radical thought occurred to her. "But poets suffer," she said. "Does God suffer, do you think, Henry?"

Henry Graham shifted positions, rearranging his arms about his midsection as if signaling that what he was about to say was significant. "I think God suffers more than we can possibly imagine. For example, I think the war in Vietnam breaks the heart of God—"

"Vietnam? Do you really think God feels the pain and suffering of the war?"

"I do. It's as if the whole world, you see, is God's body; and when one part of the body rages with an infection—like the ghastly infection of war—then God feels it, suffers it. So yes, I believe God feels the whole brunt of Vietnam. And the brunt of your grief as well, Madeline."

Madeline tried for a smile, but got a trembling bottom lip instead. While waiting for her lip to calm, she thought of a line from *The Book of Hours*, a book the Greeter had given her, a book she could hardly put down. God was speaking in the poem: "'Time is a canvas, stretched by my pain,'" she said aloud. Henry looked puzzled. "It's from a poem by Rilke," she said. "It suddenly makes sense to me." Was she stepping into that moving water again—Heraclites' river? "But, Henry, what does God do with all that pain?"

"Heals it, of course," said Henry. "And what better way to heal than to create? To re-imagine? Isn't that the only option for a poet? To take the wreckage of life and create something new out of it?"

Madeline swallowed hard. Her emotions swelled, for he was speaking to the huge hole in her heart. In order not to break down, she forced herself to think. To think like a philosopher.

"Okay, then," she said, "for argument's sake, let's go with your idea. Let's say that there is a God, and that this God is all-good, but not all-powerful, at least not in the form of a cosmic dictator. Understood. But doesn't this beg the question: is God weak? Isn't that the counter-argument, Henry?"

He uncrossed his arms and leaned in toward her. "Is love weak, Madeline? Is it weak to feel the suffering of the world?"

He asked this with such passion that she felt it herself, his own great feeling sweeping over her. Suddenly another line came to her, this time from May-ling's mouth: *She who hears the cries of the world.* The Tea Goddess. There was something particularly lovely—and deliciously subversive—about this female image of the divine. It seemed a companionable thought to The Poet of the World. She felt the thrill of something "clicking" inside her mind. And very possibly, her soul.

"No, love isn't weak, Henry."

He sat back in the chair. "But love is a word batted around

these days with such flippancy that I suppose I should use another word. You and I know that persuasive power is superior to coercive force, right?"

"Like Dr. King and the Civil Rights Movement," she said, quickly catching on to his line of reasoning.

"Yes, indeed—God rest his soul." Henry paused, as in respect for the man everyone was missing these days. "But I suppose I was thinking of King's own inspiration, Mahatma Gandhi in India. His concept of the highest power was 'soul-force.' Are you familiar with it?"

"*Satyagraha*—that's his word for 'soul-force.' I wrote a paper on it."

Henry smiled. "I'm not surprised. Then, you would agree that Gandhi was not a weak man?"

She chuckled at the question. "Hardly. He singlehandedly toppled the British empire."

"Is it any wonder, then, that King studied Gandhi, and Chávez studied King? Gandhi's legacy of soul-force actually works in the world because the world is relational by nature. That's why every act of kindness in the world is felt by God. And every act of cruelty, too. That's why what we do makes a difference in the world. For all eternity."

"For all eternity?"

"Sure. I believe everything of value is saved everlastingly in God. Our experiences of love and courage and beauty are saved in the Divine Heart. Nothing is lost."

"But all the suffering—how about all the suffering, Henry? I don't exactly want that saved-as-is, do you?"

Henry looked as if he could see right through her, right to the core of her grief. "Look, my dear, if God is eternally loving, then we can hope for an eternal healing—a grand healing of sorts—in the Poet's huge, huge heart."

"What would it be like, do you think—this grand healing?" Madeline pressed, her imagination soaring with thoughts of

Sean's soul in such a Heart as this.

"I like to think we will come to know ourselves more fully, as God knows us, no longer hiding behind pretense and ego— which could, all and all, be pretty painful for most of us. And yet, love can't by its nature be frozen in pain or guilt or in the anguish of our worst acts. Love presses on toward a deeper understanding, a deeper healing. Perhaps we will even participate in the healing of each other."

"The healing of each other?"

Henry nodded. "Perhaps our souls will expand into a fully realized empathy, but now we can only catch glimpses of—"

"Expand?" she cut in. "You mean our souls will get fatter?"

Henry laughed. "Well, yes, fatter—I like that, yes!—fatter, so that we can take in the joy of others. And the beauty. There is much beauty in the heart of God, I think." He paused, the humor returning to his eyes. "But don't quote me on it. After all, I'm just—"

"The descendent of the Mad Vegetarian of Edinburgh," she supplied with a laugh.

His hand went for the water pitcher. "I've talked too much, my dear." He refilled her cup. "Let's save some heresy for later. Over tea—"

The sound of someone clearing his throat stopped their conversation.

"Oh. Sorry to interrupt," said a voice from the doorway.

The very particles in the air seemed to stand still. Madeline could not see around Henry Graham, who blocked her view of the door. But there was no need. She knew that voice well.

Chapter Twenty-Three

"**D**ad." Madeline swallowed hard at the sight of him: haggard, pale, puffy rings under his eyes.

He bent to kiss his daughter's cheek and put his arms around her shoulders—somewhat awkwardly, but still, it was a valiant attempt.

Henry Graham bowed out graciously after shaking hands with her father. He bid his good-bye to Madeline, promised to drop by the shop for tea, and left.

She looked into her father's tired eyes. "I didn't do this for attention. I promise."

"I know," he said gently. "Jilli told me all about it. But I would have thought you could keep a stock of inhalers in that potato sack of yours."

She laughed at his attempt to cheer her, but underneath she felt bereft by his reference to Jilli, and not to her mother. *Were they not even speaking?*

"What happened between you and Mom?" she asked, as he sat down in the same torture chair Henry Graham had just vacated. She locked onto her father's gray eyes and would not look away until he answered.

He finally escaped her gaze, looking down.

"Daddy, what is it? Please tell me."

"I want you to hear it from me first. And since you're prone to asthma attacks when you get upset, I guess the hospital would be the safest place to tell you." A melancholy smile passed over his face.

"Tell me what?" She felt hot with impatience.

"Only if you promise to keep calm."

"I promise. I've got a back-up, anyway," she said, making a show of the oxygen tube that she no longer needed.

"Okay then. Now, I want you to be a brave girl."

What? Was he dying or something?

"Maddy," he said after a painful pause, "it's not your mother's fault, my leaving like that. It's just that . . ." He paused again, infuriating his daughter.

"It's just that *what*?"

"It's just that I'm . . . in love with another woman."

Madeline's eyes flew open. She willed herself to breathe. And to blink. She thought her father had said he was in love with another woman, but she must have been mistaken. That wasn't possible.

"You're joking," she said with a disbelieving chortle.

Her father didn't smile, but looked down; his face took on a painful expression, all the fatherly authority and self-assurance gone out of him.

"Dad. Explain. Please."

"Only if you promise to stay calm."

"I'm calm, I really am," she lied.

"Maddy, your mother and I have not been happy for a long time. Surely you remember the fights we had when you were young."

Madeline did remember. And for every distressing argument between her parents, she somehow managed an equally distressing asthma attack, which also brought her parents to their senses. There was some shrink word for it—psychosomatic, that was it. Uniting her parents through gasping for air: It sure as hell wasn't working now.

"Well," he said with a ghost of a smile, "that was the good part of the marriage. After you left for Berkeley, we slowly quit talking about much of anything. Let alone argue." He resettled himself in the chair, but his acute discomfort was still visible. "And then, the news about Sean . . . well, after that we just quit talking altogether. It was as if his name stood between us, but we couldn't . . . speak . . . his name."

His voice rose as he struggled for composure. Madeline reached out to touch his arm. A shudder of deep emotion— guilt? regret?—pulsated through her. If only he had come to *her*, his eldest daughter, they could have talked about Sean. Had she been so wrapped up in herself that she couldn't see her own father's need? She wondered in a flash if her dad, too, had suspected suicide. Or was that just her own deranged theory? Should she tell him about her uneasy feelings about Sean's death? About Joey Lobo? She watched her father struggle, his courage just on the cusp of failing.

"Neither of us could stand the tension," he went on with a glance at the ceiling. "So we went separate ways, your mom to more church meetings, and me to my sawing and hammering in the garage."

"But, Dad, where does this . . . other woman come in?" She withdrew her hand from her father's arm and waited with almost morbid curiosity.

"Maddy, you have to understand that because your mother and I were completely shut off from each other, I found my only means of comfort in Elaine."

"Who's Elaine? The only Elaine I know is your secre—" She stopped short, noting her father's barely perceptible nod.

"Your *secretary*? You're having an affair with your *secretary*?"

She glanced up at the soundless television screen as a diversion from knowledge she could not take in. On the tiny screen she saw a nurse with her prim white three-point hat speaking earnestly to a handsome doctor. She leaned in as if to kiss him, but at the last moment turned and walked away, rather too dramatically. Madeline thought that perhaps she was dreaming, and that this bizarre conversation with her dad was an episode from *General Hospital*. It was like that, unreal and so utterly ridiculous.

She looked back at her father, who sat looking thoroughly ashamed. No, she thought. It's real. She could never have dreamed up something so pathetic.

"But, Dad, having an affair with your secretary—that's so . . . *cliché!* I don't believe it, not of you, and certainly not of Mrs. Fisher!" Madeline could not believe that Elaine Fisher, her father's long-time loyal secretary—a matronly Korean War widow who sent them peanut brittle every Christmas—could ever pull off such a thing as being the "other woman." It made her sick to think of it, literally sick. She felt a wave of nausea.

"I think I'm going to be sick."

"I'll call the nurse," he said firmly, sounding again like her father.

"No, I'll be all right. I just need to rest."

"I'll let you sleep, then." He kissed her quickly, awkwardly, on the forehead. "See you later, Pumpkin."

He hadn't called her "Pumpkin" since she was in grade school. All she could muster was a curt nod. A smile seemed ludicrously out of place at the moment.

* * *

At noontime on Thursday, Eve van Gelder, busy proprietor, became Eve van Gelder, escape artist. With lunch bag in hand and a heart filled with purpose, she walked toward Heisler Park, the bluff overlooking Main Beach.

Having Madeline back in the shop, safe and sound after her terrifying asthma attack, gave Eve the freedom to get away with peace of mind. But she did worry about the girl. She looked thin and pale, and that hint of sadness in her eyes—the one Eve had noted on their first meeting—had returned. This time it was something about her parents, but the girl seemed embarrassed and Eve hadn't pressed. But neither would Eve leave Madeline to carry her sorrow alone. They had grown too close for that.

She slowed only for a moment to glance over to the Greeter's corner. There was dear Eiler Larsen, happily engaged with a number of tourists. He stood now with a child on either side while a woman snapped a picture. Eve would have to stop by on her way back and invite him to Poetry Night. She knew that, with all the poems bouncing about inside his head, he would be the centerpiece of such a gathering.

She moved on, across the boardwalk and up the steep path to the park where she found an empty wooden bench, sun-drenched and welcoming. She sat down with her lunch bag filled with apples and cheese, stretched out her bare legs from beneath her skirt, and slipped off her shoes. It felt like heaven, all this Van Gogh-like vibrancy surrounding her, embracing her. The sea frothed up with lavish energy. It intrigued her, all of it, the vastness of the sea teaming with unseen creatures roaming beneath.

Her attention was drawn to a few brightly dressed beach-goers below on the shore, all looking upwards with hands shading their eyes from the intense noonday sun. She followed their gaze upward and saw an enormous bird. A hawk. A huge, gorgeous, chestnut brown hawk with reddish markings on its wings—magnificent wings of jagged feathery perfection. It hovered on the wind like a living, stringless kite quivering in salty blue air. It moved her, transfixed her, this show-stopping creature in the sky.

Sam would enjoy this, she thought, remembering the birds in his painting of Main Beach—his lovely painting with its seagulls and pelicans and little gray dots of sandpipers on the shore's edge. *The painting. Oh, that blasted painting!* If only she could reverse time and accept the thing that kept them at arm's length.

She must not leave this place of beauty and light, she

resolved, until she decided exactly what to do about the whole mess—how to approach it, how to mend it. Someone had to break the icy politeness between them, and since the ice was, in fact, of her own doing, she must make the first move. Now for a plan. Yes, she must come up with a plan. And yet, with all her mental resolve, a lazy, devil-may-care feeling took over her body, and her mind flagged at the thought of any serious contemplation.

If only Sam could witness this beauty with her. She stopped herself as she knew her heart to be weak with desire for his presence, his sharing of this moment. She wanted that. Why, then, be so standoffish, hovering over the idea of him?

Perhaps, she thought, she had become like one of those amateurish confessional poets that Madeline derided for starting too many lines with "I," as if the whole world revolved around them. Perhaps she had become one of those "I" people, excluding all else. Self-enclosed. And why? For fear of repeating past mistakes?

Was she afraid of making a mistake? *Fear, there it was again.* Was she going to base her entire life on that four letter word? It occurred to her that she might, in fact, be repeating the past instead moving away from it. Could it be that her fear of getting involved with Sam was the same motivating factor—in a different guise—that threw her into the arms of Colin Moore? Fear can wear so many hats, she thought, but it was the same life-stultifying menace. Now, it was as if she feared being . . . happy—too happy. Ecstatically happy. It didn't seem right somehow. After all, she lived; the others . . .

She shook her head at the old images that forever haunted. And, with Sam, it was all so confusing, she confessed to the hawk still hovering in the sky. Had she secretly believed— somehow convinced herself—that she needed to stay small and compact and neatly encapsulated in her work, to avoid more pain in this very uncertain world? Happy, of course, but not too happy—not too . . . vibrant. She thought of Van Gogh. Would he stand for all her careful dullness? Should she dare expand this notion of herself? To include Sam? To move from the "I" to the "We"? To a larger and wider embrace of life? She asked this of the wild beauty still hovering in the sky. Here was Wider and Larger before her, and not just before her, but wrapping itself around her.

She studied the hawk for a long time and tried to emulate its stillness, its perfect balance and focus. She finally closed her eyes, taking a break from the sun, and after a few moments, she opened them. The hawk was gone.

She closed her eyes again and listened to the sound of the surf, its rising and falling. How she loved the sound of the sea— as if it were a kind of music, not just a pounding rhythm, but lush and orchestral with chords that penetrated the soul. The music of the sea was now vibrating deep inside her, rising and falling gently, like an adagio. She felt sleepy and settled her arms on the back of the bench for support. She crossed her legs, let her head fall to one side, and fell into a half-doze.

"Eve?"

She heard the voice, but she had drifted off and had to get her bearings. She sat up and blinked. It was Sam, nervously raking his hand through his hair, his mustard yellow tie blowing in the breeze.

"Madeline told me you were up here," he said. "I hope you don't mind my interrupting your lunch." He looked vulnerable, with an expression full of significance.

Jolted by his sudden appearance, and still in a sun-drenched dream state, she pointed to the sky. "Sam, there was a red-tail hawk, just over there, hovering over everything. You would have loved it. You could have painted it." Moving her brown bag she motioned for him to sit. "Come, sit down. I've got some rather warm cheese here and a few apple slices." She wanted to say: *Maybe we could re-do that picnic.*

Sam sat down and put his arm on the back of the bench in an attempt at nonchalance against the wave of strain between them. "It's gorgeous here, really perfection. That's why I painted it."

"You're a wonderful artist, Sam," she said looking at him now.

He chuckled. "I'm no Van Gogh, but I love painting. That's the important thing, Eve. To love what you do."

Eve looked out to sea and back at Sam. "Is it possible to have another look at it—at your painting, I mean?" she said tentatively. "I think I made an awful mistake not to accept it. I really wish—"

Sam held up a hand, shaking his head. "No, Eve, it was my mistake. I put you in an awkward position. It's just that you were my inspiration for the painting, so it seemed fitting to give it to you."

"Me? An inspiration?"

"Yes, you. It's not until I started coming into your shop that I began to paint. Paint my dream, you know."

Eve nodded at the reference to Van Gogh and offered a gentle smile.

"You did it, Eve," he said, looking at her and then back out to sea. "You proved to me that a dream could be waged, like war—only without the blood." He laughed and his eyes crinkled on each side, those magnificent lines of age and grief and laughter. "And so, since I'm not exactly getting any younger, I went out and bought the whole works: paints, brushes, canvass, turpentine, the whole set up. Just blew a wad of cash on the supplies and started painting right up there." He pointed behind and above their spot, to the highest point of the hill that made up Heisler Park. "That was my vantage point. Right there."

"Let's go up," Eve said, already putting on her shoes. "I want to see your vantage point. I really do."

They took the path up the hill to a flat area with more sunny benches and yellow rose bushes and a monument to something or other in the center.

"Here's the spot," he said, just a little breathless. "This is the very spot where I set up my canvass and gave my dream color and light—that is, after Roger Kuntz gave me a few lessons." Sam breathed out a self-deprecating chuckle.

He stood close behind her, leaned in, and put his hands lightly on her shoulders, the side of his face inches from hers. He pointed out all the sights that inspired him, including the Hotel Laguna's mission-like tower, where they had their first "date."

Eve looked out across the whole arc of Main Beach, with its rocks and pelicans and striped umbrellas and colorfully clad sunbathers—all of which looked like nothing more than dots of color from a painter's palette. But in this impressionistic vista each swimsuit was, in fact, filled with flesh and blood, each body pulsing with dreams as huge and deep and misunderstood as the ocean.

Eve van Gelder, independent woman and proprietor of Van Gelder's Tea and Books, fell prey to the moment. No time to stew or analyze or even reason out a course for her life. With this bird's-eye vantage point, where the world opened up in a panorama of beauty's contrasts and possibilities, she simply acquiesced. She wanted to cry—to sit down next to the rose bush half-full of tender blossoms and sob for the relief of it. But she settled on smiling and folding her fingers into the hand of an artist.

~ *Part Five* ~

The Fat Soul

Chapter Twenty-Four

Madeline sipped fresh, steamy morning tea while Eve carried the conversation with animation—and a hint of pure zest.

"So our next book club is set for Wednesday night, the fifth of June," Eve said. She took a sip of tea and set it down with purpose. "Poetry Night at Van Gelder's."

Madeline loved this time of day, the few minutes of chat at the Van Gogh table before opening time. Eve looked radiantly happy, finally free of that cloud that had hovered over her mood since the vandalism; there was something else, too, something she surmised that had to do with Sam Steiner. Madeline smiled at the thought, but didn't say a word. Eve would tell her when she was ready. (She had learned by now, not to push.)

She spread cream on her scone and ate, starving as she was, having gotten up too late for breakfast. She and Ben had worked late into the night with the other volunteers, stuffing envelopes for one last push before the primary.

And here was Eve, hovering over her like a mother hen, making sure she ate two scones, heaped with cream and Knott's boysenberry jam. She gladly ate and listened.

"I've talked it over with Eiler Larson," Eve continued. "He'll be reading—or reciting—several of his favorite poems. I'm encouraging original poems, of course, but I doubt I'll get very many of those." She looked at Madeline with pleading eyes. "Do promise you'll write something."

"I'll try," Madeline said dutifully, but with inner trepidation. She had begun a poem, an idea inspired by something Henry had said at the hospital, but she couldn't imagine reading it in front of living, breathing, actual people. "But remember," she added, "I asked you for that day off since I'll be celebrating— hopefully, anyway—late into the night on Tuesday."

"Celebrating? Oh, yes, you'll be at the Ambassador for the primary election. Right, I almost forgot."

Madeline hadn't forgotten. She was living for it.

"And Madeline," Eve said cautiously, "would you like to invite your parents, or at least your mother and Jilli? I would love to see that child again."

Madeline couldn't imagine her father attending anything called "Poetry Night." He would rather opt for a root canal, she was sure of it. "Well, maybe Jilli, but you know my parents have separated." Humiliation stopped her from saying anything further. There was no reason to tell people about Elaine Fisher— home wrecker/peanut brittle maker—not yet. Her dad would come to his senses, of course he would.

"I know it must be hard to see them separated like this," Eve said, slowly setting down her cup. "And your little sister in the middle of it all." Eve steadied her brown-eyed gaze on Madeline, eyes that reminded her of Alex's eyes—deep, brown, shining.

"I'm hoping they'll reconcile," Madeline said, setting down her own teacup, "but I don't know. Ben said that it's common for parents who lose a child to get divorced. Statistics are something like seventy-five percent—if you can believe it."

"It does seem high," Eve said with a sigh, "but it makes sense in a way. I suppose it would either tear you apart or bring you closer, depending on, well, on the state of your marriage in the first place. And how you grieve. But there's no way around it. Grief changes everything." Eve reached to refill Madeline's cup, and her own.

The two women sipped in silence. Madeline felt herself

suddenly beckoned by purple irises, the ones in the small Van Gogh print beneath the glass. She hadn't really taken notice before. When cleaning the table tops, she always re-read the quote, the one Eve had placed beside the print: "I dream of painting and then I paint my dream." She was, on the whole, more drawn to words than to art, but now it was the art that captured her. It was as if the irises invited her to yield all thoughts to them alone—all the messy clumps of thoughts in her head: her mixed-up parents, her dead brother, Joey Lobo with his dark secrets. Something seemed to capture her in the thick outline of those irises, the silky movement of the stems. Ever since her close-call asthma attack, she had felt herself on a mystical track, or at least an intensity of feeling: a vivid aware-ness of everything, even the edges of purple iris stems under the glass table top.

"Eve," she said thoughtfully, "Van Gogh . . . do you think he believed in God? I mean, his works seem so inspired by some-thing almost unearthly."

"Now I'm not a Van Gogh scholar, but I do remember reading a Dutch publication of his letters to his brother, Theo."

"Van Gogh had a brother?"

"He did, and thankfully so, because it was those letters, you see, where we get a glimpse of Van Gogh's deepest thoughts. And yes, he talked much of God. He even toyed with becoming a minister like his father. But he moved away from his original religious moorings—the very rigid, authoritarian views of his Calvinist father. He quite rebelled against it, I think."

"Sounds like my soul mate," Madeline said.

Eve smiled and continued. "As his life and art progressed, his view of God became more . . . more expansive, I'd say. He began to see God as a sort of struggling artist. A loving, suf-fering God—"

"God, a struggling artist? An artist like Van Gogh, painting dreams all over the world?" Madeline's questions tumbled out as she thought of Henry Graham's philosopher, Whitehead, and his Poet of the World, a sort of parallel metaphor. She thought of Rilke, too, and the line from his poem that kept playing in her head, "Time is a canvass, stretched by my pain." She felt herself filled from head to toe with gratitude—pure, intense gratitude—as if a bouquet of metaphors were being handed her.

"It's an intriguing image, I know," said Eve, interrupting Madeline's deepening thoughts. "And I remember, too, something in a phrase . . . something in one of those letters to his brother." She closed her eyes as if that would bring the words into view.

Madeline waited.

"I've got it now. He said, 'The best way to know God is to love many things.' That's what he said, 'to love many things.'"

"To know God is to love many things," Madeline repeated aloud, savoring it.

"Yes. That's what our Vincent said." Eve gestured with her cup toward the door. "But we'll have to leave those lofty thoughts for later. I see Matthew and his yellow legal pad are anxious to get in."

*　*　*

Madeline thought it strange that Alex Moore could not wait one more day—Sunday being his usual day at Van Gelder's—to see the new book Sam had donated to the shop for the California Writer's section. But there he was, on a Saturday, sitting comfortably at the Oscar Wilde table, turning the colorful pages of Henry Miller's new book on art, Sam at his side. Had he actually come in on Saturday . . . to see her? She chided herself at the thought. Ridiculous.

Eve came in to stand over the two men, and the three fell into conversation over Miller's artwork. They had a small argument over whether he was a better artist or writer. Madeline felt a little left out as she cleared the Jane Austen table. She would have loved to sit down next to Alex and peruse the book herself. She had opinions, too, but he didn't even look her way, enthralled as he was with the book.

It was just as well. She didn't want to get too chummy with Alex. After all, she had a date with Ben—or at least a quasi-date —on primary night. There would be scads of other people with them, but still, it was an event that the two of them were anticipating together, and they would be dressed to the nines. Who knows? The occasion might even present the opportunity to revisit the awkward kiss mishap.

Did she want to revisit it?

Ben was in Berkeley this weekend for a conference with some bigwig psychiatrist, Fritz Perls, on something called Gestalt Therapy. This would give her some much-needed time to sort out her feelings for him. But it also created a problem. He wouldn't be able to go with her to see Bobby's motorcade wind through L.A., the last big push before Tuesday. Madeline did not want to miss seeing Bobby, but the place where she wanted to see him was a place she couldn't go alone.

A reckless idea formed in her head, and before good sense could stop her, she blurted out, "Alex!" He looked up with questioning eyes, and she retreated quickly, scrambling for words. "When you get a chance, could you have a look at the broken teapot in the kitchen?"

"Right. Be there in a sec," he said, returning to his book.

In the kitchen she studied the crippled teapot that had been tucked away in a cabinet for mending, when she got around to it. She fiddled with the broken handle against the rough white bare spot where it had been attached, thinking what a lame idea this was. *Was she now stooping to the level of helpless female? God!*

"Ah, the case of the broken teapot," said Alex, breezing into the kitchen in his carefree style.

"Yeah, my fault. I knocked it off the counter when I was drying the dishes, and the problem is, it's one of Eve's favorites."

Alex took the pot in hand and then looked up at her. He

smiled in a way that made her heart leap and her knees weaken. Perhaps he had already seen through her, since a monkey could have fixed the damned teapot blindfolded.

"I've been following the campaign," he said cheerily as he retrieved the cement tube from one of the drawers.

"Really?" Madeline was surprised, but also felt her courage rise.

"Sure. I've been reading up on your Bobby Kennedy—some of his speeches of late. He likes to quote George Bernard Shaw, so he must be a good man." He chuckled. "And I think he is. A good man, that is."

"Those are pretty words coming from a cynic like you," she said, feeling more at ease, ready for banter.

"Hmph," Alex said, but then smiled.

"He's going to be making his last push in L.A. before the primary," she said, emboldened. "Tomorrow, actually. I really want to see him. Get a glimpse. Maybe even shake his hand. Who knows?"

"Shake his hand? Why not grab a cufflink? A shoe? That's what they're doing, you know. You better be careful in a crowd like that."

"Well, as a matter of fact, that's why I brought you back here. I really don't need help fixing a teapot." She chuckled like an idiot.

"I didn't think you did," he said, wiping the cement from the freshly mended handle. "Now, hold this firmly."

Madeline held the handle in place while Alex moved to the sink to remove the sticky cement from his fingers.

"So," she said, and cleared her throat, "would you like to go?" She held onto the teapot handle for dear life.

He turned to her, thoughtfully, not smiling as she would have liked, as she would have preferred. *As she would have hoped.* She felt excessively attracted to Alex, even more so since her asthma attack, which she realized with deepening reflection had been a close brush with death. Ben would probably say (but would never say, because she would never spill the beans about her feelings for Alex): *Ah, the Eros and Thanatos effect.* She could see Ben now, one hand tugging at his hairless chin, lecturing her on how death and sex were bound up with each other, some Freudian mumbo-jumbo. All she knew was that her knees were perilously close to collapsing under Alex's gaze, and she no longer seemed to mind. Was she high on the thrill of being alive? Was that why she felt so reckless, so sexually alive? Was she crazy or what? Just a moment ago she was thinking about Ben, for God's sake.

Alex stood there wiping his hands on the tea towel, while her heart seemed to pound as loud as a Ringo Starr drum solo.

She wished she could take back the invitation.

"But aren't you going with that bloke . . . what's his name— Ben?" he finally said, brows knitted.

"No. No. He's at Berkeley this weekend for some shrink fest. But I'll see him on Tuesday night. We're going to the Ambassador Hotel . . . I mean, we're going to the *party* at the Ambassador. With a lot of other people. You know, primary night and everything . . ." She trailed off, fearing her cheeks to be mottled with hot red embarrassment.

Alex now looked to be holding back a smile.

"But even if he *were* here," she said quickly, "I'd like you to go. I think it would do a cynic good to see Bobby Kennedy up close and personal. You would only be gone a few hours. I could meet you here in the morning, and we'd be back before it gets busy around here."

Alex, having dried his hands, put down the tea towel. "Hang on a minute. Be right back. And don't let off that handle."

He left the kitchen, leaving her to hold onto the restored teapot. She realized, too, that her thumb and forefinger were stuck to the pot, the cement having oozed out. *Damn!* She shut her eyes in defeat. Of course this was an insane idea, really stupid. And she was stuck to a teapot to boot.

Alex reappeared wearing a broad smile. "Mum agreed to do without me tomorrow. She'll get Simone to help. Seems our resident hippie has a tab to work off. So, looks like I'm free." He stared down at her stuck fingers. "And now, to free you."

* * *

"Bloody Hell!" Alex said under his breath, as they approached the intersection blocked off with police barricades. (She had never heard Alex curse, and it made her smile.) Policemen sat on motorcycles and a sea of black faces undulated in front of them. This neighborhood was old hat for Madeline Prescott, canvasser and political activist. But for Alex, Watts was new territory. And she had to admit, it was a mob for all practical purposes: hundreds of people filling the sidewalks and spilling onto the street. But it was a smiling mob, edgy and anxious and eager, as if waiting for the kickoff at a football game.

The walk from the USC parking lot to the street where the motorcade was to pass was like a walk through Alice's looking glass. A different world. She certainly stood out, she thought, given the color of her skin and hair, but she wasn't afraid. This was not the Watts Riot of '65—a riot of despair. This, she thought, was a riot of hope.

Alex guided her through the crowd with the palm of his hand on her low back, a gesture that made her feel respected (unlike Mike Riley, who always walked ahead of her in a crowd, expecting her to follow).

Soon the crowd's murmurings rose like the roar of the sea during a storm, waves of shouts and applause even before Madeline could see the entourage carrying the longed-for candidate.

Signs were thrust high into the air and people began to cheer. She looked at Alex and smiled. He stood beside two plump teenage girls—all proud and giggly—holding a sign that read, "Sock it to 'em Bobby!" He ducked just in time as the girls, careless in their excitement, almost brained him as they waved the sign in the air.

"We love you, Bobby!" the girls with the sign cried out, as the crowd grew more ecstatic. Madeline was not tall enough to see over the people in front of her, but Alex was.

"I can see him now, standing up in a convertible," Alex said. "He's in a light gray suit . . . I can see his hair."

Madeline finally caught a glimpse through a hole in the crowd and edged forward to get a better view. The motorcade inched forward, and a little black girl with long, thick, shiny braids caught her eye. The girl was running just ahead of the convertible as if she were part of the entourage. It seemed to tickle the people in the car—the sight of this little braided mascot. And then the car stopped briefly. The little girl reached up. A hand reached back to meet hers. It was Bobby—Robert F. Kennedy, himself—she could see him now. The little girl grabbed his hand, shook it rather shyly, and then went on running beside the car as if she were in it for the duration.

He was in full view now, standing up and looking out to the crowd, flashing his smile like the flash of chrome on the car, a huge smile that she had seen over and over on flyers and buttons and television. And now . . . now: *here he was—him! Bobby! President Kennedy's baby brother.*

He was much smaller than she had imagined. And so thin! And there was something around his waist, like a black belt, and it seemed to keep him upright and safe from capture by the crowd. She then realized that the black belt around his waist was actually an arm: a black man, large and muscular, was crouching down behind Bobby, holding onto him with his arm while people reached for him. He could be carried away by the crowd so easily, she thought.

So easily, he could just be carried off . . .

The crouching black man held on to him for dear life, as if holding on to hope itself.

The electricity was palpable, bursting out in the roar of the crowd. And on the little girl's face—the one with the braids swinging about like little wings—was a look of pure ecstasy.

In that instant Madeline knew she could not be just an on-looker, a rational observer of history, holding back in the crowd. "I've got to get closer," she said, turning to Alex.

"Sorry?" Alex said with a confused look. The roar now made any communication near impossible.

"I said, I've got to get closer!" she yelled and grabbed his arm. They weaved through the sea of color and joy like two salmons swimming upstream.

Finally, they reached the front of the crowd.

Bobby Kennedy now stood, more or less, in the slow moving convertible only a couple of feet away. And her heart leaped. She reached and stretched out her arm, like the little girl with braids had done. But she was no match for the taller men and women who were crowding in front of her, all reaching out to grasp Bobby's hand.

Suddenly, she felt herself being grabbed tightly around the waist. Her head flew around to see, with relief, that it was Alex. With a firm grasp he lifted her off the ground. The car was now moving at a snail's pace. *She reached out.* She reached for Bobby Kennedy's hand and he grasped hers—a mere moment, a mere touch. A connection.

Alex set her down (and she had no time to blush or be embarrassed by his gallant act). Others crowded in. The senator bent over even further to meet the need, and would have toppled over the side except for the strong black arm around his waist. The car slowed almost to a stop again to meet the great throng of those who loved him: Large bosomy women, some with missing teeth. Young burly men bearing the scars of street battle. Old men with eye glasses and feathered fedoras.

Children with bright white smiles and soft black skin. All of them, crowding around a little white man with unruly golden hair; it seemed impossible in these times. Utterly implausible.

But there it was.

She studied his face—she studied Robert Francis Kennedy's face as he bent down to the crowd. Prematurely wrinkled and slightly sunburned, yes, but it was his expression, the flash of his eyes, the immediacy of him that grasped her. For her, the moment was like standing before a great painting at a crowded museum, an intense, full-bodied moment where the self—the inner will—tells time to pause. And in that moment she was able to study him and his connection to the people: He was not put-on, not practiced or tightly controlled like politicians she had seen on television. Not polished like his older brother had been. Here, she thought, was just a little man all raw with feeling, sweating buckets in the sun.

Now he was moving away—or trying to, but hands kept popping up, holding him back. He strained to reach back, to touch every last hand, as if being torn away from a family he loved and whisked off to a duty beyond. She watched as he paused to push back the front lock of his hair, a familiar gesture she had seen countless times on TV. From this angle, she caught a glimpse of his hands, all scraped and scratched and reddened from the rings and wrist watches of the crowd.

But he didn't seem to mind. The little golden-haired man seemed infused with a power of inner expansion. It oozed out of him, this bigness, this fatness of spirit—his ability to feel, to bleed, to struggle. It poured out of him through his pores like some silent, visible breath: Poetry without words.

Empathy. The word came to her, a word she constantly dissected in neat philosophical banter, as if she knew what it was. As if she knew *anything*. Now, she realized, she knew nothing until this moment. But here it was. In the flesh. A picture of *what mattered.*

She had a sense now of being in the presence of a great power, an energy that transcended Bobby Kennedy. Not a top down sort of power that squelches, but an infusing energy that unleashes something bright and noble within. It has no gender, this power. No race. No exclusionary clauses. Just a sense of shared suffering, shared humanity. Shared hope.

He was, she thought, like a solider tossing out grenades of hope—bombs that exploded upon impact into smiles the likes of which she had never seen. Like the Anti-Napalm, the Anti-Rocket Propelled Grenade, the Anti-H-Bomb. Everything seemed turned on its head. Everything seemed *possible*.

And, too, she felt a kinship. *Brothers lost*. This man—assaulted by grief of his own—knew all about the garish sun. But here he was, taking on that sun, drenched in it, sweat rolling down his face. The heat of his grief had not destroyed him. But it could have. It could have burned up everything. He could have closed himself off so easily, retreating into a rich man's cloister. But instead, he reached beyond his grief- or through it?—to take on their grief, their slums, their homes filled with languishing despair.

And that is why these people loved him, she thought—why their faces lit up like moonbeams and their arms stretched and reached to the breaking point.

She watched the convertible bearing Bobby Kennedy move farther away, the little braided black girl still running alongside, like a tiny blackbird, flying.

Chapter Twenty-Five

On the fourth of June, Madeline Prescott drove north on the 5 freeway, feeling strange in her new form-fitting green dress with delicate oriental flowers, a design the clerk from Chelsea's boutique in downtown Laguna assured would compliment her hair color. She was not used to dressing up and wearing high heels. Or make-up. Her inordinate time in front of the mirror today made her feel nervous and excited, like someone else— someone more glamorous than she would ever want to be on a regular basis. But all this self-conscious primping and lip smacking and eyeliner re-dos felt good for a night like this, a night she would surely hold in memory.

Madeline spotted Ben coming toward her almost immediately after she entered the lobby of the Ambassador. He wore a navy blue jacket and a wide grin. "Bobby is definitely in the lead," he said, nearly bursting. "Cronkite is predicting an eight-point win over McCarthy—but it's still early, and you look stunning, by the way." He took her arm as they walked toward the elevator that would take them to the second floor ballroom.

"Hello to you, too." She smiled and scanned the crowd. The women were dressed to the hilt and showing off high, elaborate hairdos that must have taken hours to put together (unlike her rebellious head of massive waves that could only be tamed at best. Yet, she consoled herself by how much money she saved by not going to the hairdresser.)

"Looks like it won't be easy to get to the second floor ballroom," Ben said, pulling her back from the crush of the packed elevator. "Let's take the stairs . . . and our time. Look around, Madeline. They filmed parts of *The Graduate* here in the lobby. It seems that every major movie star has stayed here at one time or other—Harlow, Fairbanks, Valentino. And they say," Ben said, pointing up, "that the reclusive Howard Hughes keeps an entire suite up there somewhere."

Hughes, as in Hughes Aircraft, thought Madeline. This made her think of Alex. *Damn!* She felt guilty thinking of Alex with Ben beside her, sparks of hope in his eyes. Not just hope in Bobby's victory but, most likely, hope of another attempt at her lips before the evening was out.

But she had no reason to feel guilty about Alex. Did she? But they had shared something significant together—as friends only, of course. After a banner day of cheering on her candidate and listening to his impassioned stump speech, she and Alex had ended up having tea with Simone and Eve, recounting every detail. They entertained the others with tales of traffic, car splitting screams, and Bobby's Bostonian accent, which Alex comically tried to mimic. She smiled at the collage-like memory of the day: Alex lifting her up out of the crowd, the little black girl with flying braids, crowds of smiles, hope bouncing and shimmering in the sunlight. Alex was now all bound up inextricably with that day. Of course—not being made of stone—she could not help but wonder if Alex could ever be romantically interested in a woman whose nails had not seen polish since 1963. And she had no idea if her own feelings for Alex were the kind she could trust. But she had them. Oh, she had them, all right, however ridiculous they might be.

And here was Ben, another whole reality: loving, wise, a man who was so . . . so *fully-actualized* (in shrink lingo). She could hardly let Ben get away without serious consideration, could she? But tonight was not a night for such quandaries of the heart. Something massively important was about to happen.

Having taken the stairs to the second floor, she now surveyed the ballroom: an ocean of energy and color and life. White RFK campaign hats, like buoys in the harbor, bobbed up and down. A young man in a bright orange shirt played guitar while a black man waved his arms as if leading a church choir.

This land is your land, this land is my land,
from California to the New York Island . . .

"Someone said César Chávez is here," Ben said loudly, trying to make himself heard over the boisterous crowd.

Madeline nodded and felt her spine tingle at the whole scene. She looked up at the grand wood ceiling, slightly arched like a boat, as if they were on Noah's Ark, safe and sure in the stormy sea of 1968.

* * *

Eve sat in front of her console color television and studied the blue election scoreboard behind Walter Cronkite's head. The blue seemed too bright for her eyes, and Mr. Cronkite's face a bit too red. With Earl Grey snuggled on her lap, she didn't feel like fiddling with the color knobs just now. But she forgot the color problems altogether when Mr. Cronkite, with his steady deep voice, projected the Senator from New York, Senator Robert F. Kennedy, as the winner of the California primary. She vowed to stay up to hear the Senator's speech; but, on the other hand, she needed to get up extra early to bake and prepare the shop for "Poetry Night."

Eve scratched Earl Grey behind his ears and asked him his opinion. Would they get a glimpse of Madeline's red hair on the telly? She decided to stay up as long as she could keep her eyes open, just for the hope of it.

* * *

"Cronkite now says Bobby will beat McCarthy by fourteen points," said one of the staffers into the microphone at the Ambassador Ballroom. "He's won!" a woman cried out, and others followed. The crowd cheered as if the war were already over. As if the soldiers were coming home. As if there were a cure for the disease of poverty. As if the world had suddenly come to its senses.

Madeline moved toward the front of the crowd, having lost sight of Ben. She looked around and finally saw him weaving toward her, exuberant. Everyone was clamoring for Bobby to make his acceptance speech. Close to midnight the crowd was growing restless, a chorus of insistent voices rising in a jubilant crescendo, waiting, waiting, waiting . . . Where was Bobby?

Signs bobbed. People chanted.

Bob-by! Bob-by! R-F-K! R-F-K!

Minutes passed. Still, no Bobby.

Bobby Power! Bobby Power! Kennedy Power! Kennedy Power!

Madeline shot a look at Ben. He shrugged his shoulders. Where was he? It was now just past midnight.

Then she caught sight of flashing diamonds. Ethel Kennedy, with her glittering earrings, entered the ballroom, her peach and white sundress highlighting her bronzed skin. Her smile, so white and huge, could have no match, save for her husband's own famous grin. Madeline was close enough to see every detail of Mrs. Kennedy's stylish dress, but she would not have time to examine it, for just then, the man of the hour emerged.

He appeared out of a barrage of camera flashes and TV lights, surrounded by reporters with microphones and notepads —and smiles. Even the reporters seemed caught up, dazzled by JFK's little brother, who had finally come into his own.

Bobby Kennedy pushed back a lock of hair and flashed a V-for-Victory sign. The crowd roared.

* * *

Eve bolted upright, her heart racing. Surely she was just dreaming. She was, after all, very tired, having given out before Kennedy's appearance. Feeling a bit frustrated with herself, she had gone off to bed, Earl Grey in tow, with the radio tuned to a news station in hopes of catching the speech before she drifted off.

But she had drifted off. Now she was disoriented, but too much awake as the voice of the reporter grew louder and more urgent.

"Senator Kennedy has been shot," the reporter said, his voice rising, "and another man, a Kennedy campaign manager—and possibly shot in the head. Rafer Johnson has a hold of the man who apparently has fired the shot."

Eve let out a scream. Her hands flew to her mouth. Earl Grey jumped from the bed, but she grabbed him before he got away from her, as if he, too, were in some kind of peril—as if the whole world were collapsing.

She sat trembling, holding on to the squirming Earl Grey, listening to the desperate voice of the reporter.

"He still has the gun," the announcer said with his voice suddenly lowered. "The gun is pointed at me right at this moment. I hope they can get the gun out of his hand. Be very careful, get that gun get that gun GET THAT GUN!" he yelled. "Stay away from the gun; stay away from the gun. His hand is frozen. Take a hold of his thumb and break it if you have to. Get his thumb!"

Eve froze, her heart barely beating. Earl Grey finally wiggled free and leaped from her arms.

"All right, that's it," the man said breathlessly. "Hold him, hold him. We don't want another Oswald."

Eve took a breath, gathered her wits, and hurried for the phone in the living room. She dialed Sam's number.

"Sam, it's me . . . " She faltered, her voice cracking.

"Eve? Are you all right?"

"Senator Kennedy has been shot," she managed to say in a breath. "And some other people, too—at least one, maybe more, I don't know."

"Oh my God."

"Madeline is there."

"Madeline? Are you sure?"

"Of course I'm sure," she said, half annoyed. "I thought you knew. I need to ring Alex now. And her mother . . . yes, I should ring her mother." She paused. "But I wanted—I needed —to ring you first."

"I'm coming over," he said.

Eve hung up and dialed her son. At times like this she wished for a modern Touch Tone. The rotary dial was too slow, and on the third number, she misdialed.

"Bloody hell!"

She dialed again, and he picked up on the second ring.

"Alex Moore, here."

"Have you heard?" Her voice was high and frantic.

"Yes," he said curtly. "I watched the whole thing . . . on the telly. Have you heard from Madeline? Or her family?" He didn't wait for her to answer. "Give her mum a ring. See if she's heard anything. I'm coming over."

"But Sam is—"

"Look, you ring her mum's house. You've got the number, right? I'll be there in fifteen minutes."

"Right." She hung up and fumbled around in the kitchen drawer for her notebook from the job interview that contained Madeline's Anaheim number. She pulled out the drawer, finally spilling the entire contents onto the linoleum. There it was, finally. She grabbed the little notebook, madly turning pages until she found where she had written, "Redhead—home #." She misdialed, cursed, and dialed again.

* * *

"Did you get hold of anyone?" asked Alex without prelude, as he and Sam, arriving at the same time, followed Eve up the stairs to the flat.

"Yes, she's frantic, the poor woman. She hasn't heard from Madeline and she can't get hold of her husband. Their estranged, you know, so—"

"And?" pressed Alex.

"And," said Eve, as they entered the flat, "I offered to go look for her—the three of us—since the poor woman doesn't drive in the city."

"Good work, Mum."

"We can take my car," said Sam.

"No," said Eve. "Let's take the Jag. Alex is familiar with it, and he's driven in L.A. far more than either of us. Let me just get my keys and a wrap."

Minutes later, the three sat in uneasy silence as the Jaguar sped through the shadowy, moon-lit stretch of Laguna Canyon. It was nearly 1:00 a.m.

"We should make good time," Alex said, merging onto the 5 freeway. "No traffic to contend with at this hour." He glanced at his mother in the passenger seat. "Can't you find another station? That one keeps reporting the same thing." He glanced at Sam in the rearview mirror. "Sam, are you any good with maps?"

"Not really. Didn't need them in New York. I relied on taxis."

"Welcome to California. There's a *Thomas Guide* on the seat beside you." He switched on the dome light. "Look for Good Samaritan Hospital. That's where they took him, according to the bloke on the radio."

"Do you really think she'd go there?" Sam asked leaning forward to be heard over the radio. "Wouldn't it make more sense for her to just go home and wait for news?"

Eve and Alex exchanged a knowing look.

"I forgot," Sam said dryly. "We're talking about Madeline." He settled back in his seat with the map. "I'm on it." Sam rifled through the pages of the *Thomas Guide*. "Okay, it's simple. Take the 110 to Wilshire and exit to the left."

"Five people!" Eve said breathlessly into the lonely headlight beams of oncoming cars.

"What are you talking about?" Alex glanced at his mother.

"You didn't just hear? The man said that five others, beside the Senator, were shot. What do they mean, I wonder? Five people in the crowd?"

"Don't worry, Mum. It's highly unlikely that Madeline was anywhere near the gunshots. The pantry, that's where it happened. I got that much from the telly."

Eve shivered, only half-listening to her son, for her imagination had taken hold of her. She envisioned Madeline sprawled on the floor, blood flowing through her beautiful red hair. She shook off the image. Ridiculous to worry. Alex was right, but the nagging uncertainty felt like a stone in the pit of her stomach.

"See that?" Alex said suddenly, pointing to the instrument panel. "The temperature gauge. It's too high! Didn't you have this blasted car serviced recently?" He shot an accusing look at Eve.

"Yes, of course. It *can't* be the water pump, not again."

"Well, it bloody well looks like it."

Sam sighed from the backseat. "This is no place to break down," he said, looking down at his map. "Not the best neighborhood."

Eve stared at the gauge. She imagined being stranded on the freeway in the wee hours. "Alex, take one of these exits. Any exit, it doesn't matter. We've got to get off the freeway."

"Bloody hell! We'll lose so much time."

Alex exited on Olympic Boulevard toward a brightly lit sign above a service station. He pulled in. "With any luck, they might have a mechanic on duty."

Sam and Eve climbed out of the car while Alex spoke to the attendant, a young Latino who seemed ready enough to get under the bonnet of the Jag.

Eve looked around frantically. "Sam, exactly how far are we from the hospital?"

"Not far, but even when we get there I expect we won't get too close with all the police and news vans and such. I wonder if it would be better for Alex to hail a cab while we wait here with the car."

"Hail a cab? Sam, this isn't New York. You don't hail cabs here. You have to ring for them."

They stared at Alex, dressed in jeans and a jacket, shirttail sticking out the back, talking to the attendant.

"Busted water hose," Alex said, walking toward them, shaking his head in disbelief. "Look," he continued as the three huddled in the pool of bright, artificial light, "the attendant has offered to loan me his own car while you two stay here with the Jag. They have coffee and snacks and a pay phone inside. Keep checking with Madeline's mum while I try to track her down."

Eve and Sam barely had time to look at one another, and no time to respond. Alex's back was already to them as he headed for an old rattletrap of a car.

* * *

How did she get here? How did she get to this place? *All these people. Cold. Lights. Silent sobs.* Madeline hugged herself and shivered in the cool night air.

Why was she so cold? She looked around her. So many faces, faces masked with worry lines and tears and vacant stares. Ben was beside her, his arm around her shoulders, but in a sorrowful way—drooping. He was sniffling, crying. *Ben was crying.*

Her heart was beating too fast, as if she had just used her inhaler. She looked down and saw the inhaler glued to her right hand, knuckles white around it, as if holding on to life itself. How many puffs had she taken? When had she had the presence of mind to get it out of her purse?

Everything was a blur.

She remembered dizzying cheers . . . then sounds of something popping—balloons? Then everything happened in slow motion: A black woman in a boater hat with hands covering her mouth, falling forward in a gesture of horror . . . Someone yelling, *Oh, God! It's happened again!* . . . A black man pounding the wall with his fist . . . A man in a suit at the microphone, calling for a doctor . . . *Is there a doctor? We need a doctor* . . . Climbing into Ben's car . . . The hospital lawn.

It was all so confusing. A Kafkaesque nightmare.

And now she was standing here with hundreds of people. She returned to hugging herself for warmth and gazed at the intensity of the eyes all about—wide eyes, closed eyes, eyes glistening with tears, liquid eyes lit by candles in the darkness. But there were other lights, too. Garish lights. TV cameras. No one spoke intelligibly. There were only sounds of waiting: a sigh, a moan, spontaneous prayers, an aching whisper behind her, "God help us all!" The crowd seemed united in a way, staring as one at the white façade of a hospital. She understood little, only that all hope lay on an operating table on the ninth floor, high above the sobs, silent and out of reach.

And then—she must be hallucinating—there in the crowd was a familiar face. *Alex?*

He wasn't supposed to be here. It must be a mirage, another one of her delusions. An LSD flashback? She couldn't trust herself. She closed her eyes and rocked back and forth in the cold air. Strong hands clamped onto her shivering arms.

"Madeline!"

She heard her name spoken, as if someone was angry. But she couldn't answer. *Why couldn't she answer?*

"Madeline! Are you all right?"

She opened her eyes and stared at Alex Moore. Then at Ben. Confusion mounted.

"Madeline," Ben said, now fully engaged, as if he were himself again, instead of one of the walking wounded. "Madeline, can you respond to me? I think she's in shock," he said, turning to Alex. "I think we all are."

Alex took off his jacket and put it around Madeline's shoulders. "Madeline," he said gently, "you're shivering. You're in shock. Let me take you home."

Chapter Twenty-Six

The morning of the sixth was unusually warm and sunny for the month of June. Sitting barefoot on the sandy steps leading from the cottage to the shore, Madeline tapped her cigarette ashes and brushed them onto the sand. Having thrown on a pair of ancient, tattered shorts and a stained tee shirt, she watched the waves batter her chocolate rocks with fury.

On these very steps in fresh mornings past, she had listened to Grandma Daisy rattling about in the kitchen, preparing breakfast. The clink of dishes and the smells of sausage would rush out to her. Sean would be roaming the beach, searching for sand crabs and indigo shells. She could see him with baggy shorts and dirty shirt, jumping around the tide pools with solitary joy.

She pulled her thick, curly pony tail through the back of the cap, Grandpa Abel's old Irvine Ranch cap that he kept on a hook by the door. It felt right, this worn-out cap. Protective, too, with memories attached. Such little anchorings tied her to a world she once had faith in.

The heavy breath-like regularity of the waves was both comforting in its familiarity, and disturbing, too. The breakers rolled onto the shore with perfect indifference and then receded, as if nothing had happened, as if Bobby had not been shot by some angry young man—as if this murderous spring of 1968 had only been a nightmare. Her eyes flooded and salty tears dropped, making dark spots in the dry sand.

Now that the shock of it was over, reason set in, settling right next to her tears. Why hadn't RFK—the brother of a slain president, for God's sake—been better protected? Her thoughts contorted into endless whys and what ifs. What if he had gone out another way, instead of through the kitchen pantry? Was it our fault, she wondered, all of us screaming like teeny boppers at a rock concert, a solid wall of people that forced him go out that particular way? But how did the murderer know that he would go that direction? Why couldn't someone, anyone, save him from that maniac? *For God's sake, why was it so damned easy to shoot someone in this country?*

The ocean seemed apathetic to all these questions and remonstrations. It roared on indifferently, but perhaps this was exactly what she needed, something regular and dependable and soothing, like a giant breath, bringing her back to herself. The roar of it at least drowned out the horrible echoes in her head: the wailing in the ballroom—a contagion—voicing the unspeakable, the utterly unthinkable. The man pounding the wall. The shrieks. These, she thought, were the sounds of hope dying.

An hour passed. Or was it two? Time had stopped since the early morning radio news had pronounced Senator Robert F. Kennedy dead.

She reached for another cigarette. *What the hell?*

Another thirty minutes vanished. Her legs, so pale, so vulnerable to the sun, had turned a light shade of pink, but she didn't care. So what? Let the garish sun do her in, turn her into a lobster. It had won after all, had it not?

She didn't want to move, even if it meant Biddy Gelson might come by to check on her. Biddy had been so good to her when she arrived home yesterday after spending the night at Eve's apartment. Much to her surprise, Biddy brought along not only a German chocolate cake, but grass. The two of them commiserated on the sorry state of the world, smoking the pot under the palm tree until the stars began to dance.

But no Biddy this morning. She must be sleeping off the pot, or the chocolate cake they ate in its entirety. Even the twins were strangely absent from their usual morning frolic on the beach, and she was glad of it. All she wanted was to be alone with the sea and its rhythm.

Rhythm. The thought struck her: Bobby had been there to offer poetry when Martin Luther King had been shot. Who would offer poetry now? Who would do that for Bobby? Who would speak the words to soothe a sorrowful nation now? All the poetry was used up; all the poets were dead.

The sound of the ringing phone pulled her out of her ruminations. Her heart raced at the sound of it—abrupt, alarming, as if an urgent message awaited her. Who was dead now? What new disasters awaited?

Madeline heaved herself up, brushed off the sand, and went inside, feeling older and more incapacitated than Grandpa Abel.

Eve was on the line. She had called to say that Poetry Night had been changed to Saturday, June 22, "given the circumstances," and to inform her that Alex was coming to see about her, "like it or not." Eve could be persistent, quite motherly at times. Madeline started to protest—red-eyed, disheveled, the whole mess that she was—but didn't have the will to say anything. Strange though it was, she was not completely at odds with the idea.

She changed into another old tee (unstained, at least) and jeans. Even that was an effort. She couldn't bear anything more presentable at the moment. Anything nice would amplify the puffy state of her face and the redness of her eyes. At least she looked uniformly a disaster.

Of course, she winced inwardly, Alex had already seen her at her worst. She must have looked pretty awful when he found her with mascara-smudged cheeks, staring up at the window of Good Samaritan Hospital. He had been so kind, and she had gone with him, following him in a daze—shock, he had said—and they had gotten into some strange, jacked-up old Chevy.

Her memory of what followed was surreal and confusing: Eve and Sam waiting for them at a gas station along the way; Eve hunched over the steering wheel of the Jaguar as Madeline blubbered on Alex's shoulder; Sam trying to force M&Ms and coffee down her; waking up in the morning in Eve's apartment, staring into the eyes of Earl Grey.

Eve had insisted that Madeline stay over for what was left of the night. She had made up the sofa bed, and had tea and toast ready for her in the morning. She had said, "Stay here and listen for updates on the Senator's condition. Just rest, dear," she kept saying, "just rest. I've already called your mother and told her you're safe and sound, but you may want to call her soon. A mother needs to hear her child's voice, you know."

All of this kindness had touched her, but embarrassed her, too, because of the state she was in. She was a little reluctant to see Alex now. But he was coming, "like it or not."

She planted herself again on the steps in front of the cottage and waited with a couple of perspiring Cokes at her side—the only hospitality she could muster.

Finally, she heard his footfall on the boardwalk.

"Brought you some provisions," he said, his warm, deep voice floating over the top of her head. "Or I should say, Mum packed some scones for you." He smiled, and her heart leapt, a reflex she was getting used to.

He sat down on the step beside her and opened the sack of "provisions."

"Thanks," she said, accepting a Tupperware container. She set it behind her on a step, out of sight. The thought of food gave her stomach a tumble, given that a German chocolate cake was still churning somewhere in the deep recesses of her stomach. But it was such a kind gesture. It moved her, as everything did at the moment. "All I've got left in my cupboard are a couple of Pop Tarts of unknown age and origin. But I did manage these," she said, handing Alex a bottle of Coke.

He took the bottle with thanks. "I also have something here from Henry Graham."

"Henry?"

"A really nice chap—or chaplain, I should say. I remember him from the book club. He stopped by to see how you were, and I told him the situation. He left with an armload of biscuits, and later returned with this." Alex reached inside the sack and pulled out a book.

She sighed with pleasure at the sight of it: Rilke's *Duino Elegies*. "He knows how much I like Rilke." Madeline saw a note sticking out of it, like a book mark. She would save it for later.

"I never actually thanked you," she said, setting the book on top of the Tupperware behind them. "You and Eve and Sam, you were all so great. And about my car . . . thanks for going to get it, you and Sam. I don't think I could have faced going back to the Ambassador."

"It's all right. I rather like your little Bug, but the blasted tape deck doesn't work, did you know that?"

Madeline nodded. "Yeah, it's something I need to talk to my dad about." *Among other things*, she thought.

There was so much she wanted to say to Alex, but where to start? She sipped her Coke while it was still cold.

"You were right," she said at last.

"Right about what?" asked Alex, his lashes golden brown in the sunlight. He looked too good in his chinos and golf shirt, especially next to her Skid Row attire.

"About Bobby," she said. "You were right all along. He should never have run for President."

Alex frowned. "Madeline—"

"It's just that I can't get his face out of my mind," she went on, her emotions taking over. "His last words, 'It's on to

Chicago and let's win there!' and that huge grin of his . . . it all seems like a nightmare."

"I know." Alex nodded.

"Sean had stopped believing in the war," she said tonelessly. "He hated it. He said so in his letter. But it's no use. No matter how hard anybody tries to stop the madness, the bullet always wins. Or the Napalm, as the case may be." She exhaled slowly and looked sideways at Alex. His was an easy presence, a listening presence just now. "Alex, I shouldn't be rattling on like this. You're supposed to be at work, aren't you? I hope you don't mind—"

"Look, I know you need to talk about it, about what happened. I took a sick day at work to be available—not just to Mum, but to you. Thought you might need a friend."

She smiled. "Yeah, I guess I do. I mean, I feel like I'm trying to climb out of a well . . . with slippery shoes." She leaned her head back and rested on her elbows, taking the full force of the sun. She was fully aware of her irrational, disjointed thoughts, moving from sadness to anger and back again, with no steadiness at all, as if she were a bunch of disparate clumps of feeling.

"You know, Alex," she said, pulling her cap down to shade her eyes, "I finally understand about fiery hells and vengeful gods and all that."

Alex's eyebrows shot up. "You don't believe any of that stuff. Do you?" He took a drink of Coke and leaned forward with elbows perched on his knees.

"No," she said, "I don't *believe* any of it. I said I *understand* it—how people came up with all those images of screaming, tormented bodies writhing in pain in some eternal pit of fire. You know, like those medieval paintings. It's because we need a place to put our rage—that's what it is. Miserable, powerless people just wanting a place to put their rage. I feel that way right now, every time I think of the guy who shot Bobby. What's his name? They said on the radio this morning—"

"Sirhan Sirhan. Nobody knows yet why he did it. Maybe we never will."

"Does it matter *why* he did it? He *did* it. That . . . *monster* did it! I would love to take him out in a boat," she said, pointing to a sailboat in the distance, "and toss him overboard. Let the sharks have him." She turned to Alex. "Did you see the picture in the paper—Bobby lying on the floor? Did you see it, Alex?"

"It was the first thing I saw when I opened the paper yesterday morning. It must have been especially hard for you to see."

"Biddy, my neighbor down the beach, showed it to me." Madeline thought of Biddy unfolding the *L.A. Times* on the table in the cottage. "I almost fainted; it was too painful. Too awful. They shouldn't show something like that. His face, his eyes . . . it was too terrible!" She felt her lip quiver.

"It was that," he said. "But he was still alive then. Barely."

She shook her head slowly. "And I was there, Alex. *I was there.* Only a few feet away. It doesn't seem real. Not real at all." She looked up and saw a formation of pelicans overhead. "It's like hope itself was shot out of the sky. Maybe that's why they always call us anti-war people 'doves,' because it's so damned easy to shoot us. Easy prey. Dr. King. Bobby. Even Gandhi was shot, come to think of it."

Alex shook his head. "You're exhausted, Madeline. You were in shock when I found you. I think you're still in a bit of shock, even now."

"No. I'm not. It's just that I feel . . . bereft, I guess that's the word. I feel like part of me died. *Again.* How can I—I mean 'we'—any of us—ever hope again? The killing just won't stop, Alex. It just won't stop!"

She felt her anger rise and beat against the wall of her despair, like the man pounding the wall of the Ambassador ballroom. She wondered if all her ranting was partly for Bobby and partly for Sean, as one grief swallowed another. Where did one start and the other end?

Alex moved closer. He put his arm around her shoulders. They sat in silence and watched the surf. She was too upset (and too overcome with Alex's nearness) to cry now. Her tears were all dried up anyway. She watched the sailboat in the distance. She wondered if the occupants were laughing and having a good time.

"It's not true," he said, suddenly, and removed his arm. He picked up his Coke from the sandy step and took a drink.

"What's not true?"

"My being right. I wasn't, you know. Not about Bobby. He *was* right to run for President. I was wrong about that, wrong as I could be. I've been wanting to tell you that for awhile now."

"But—"

"Let me finish. I've done a lot of thinking about it. Bobby Kennedy couldn't have done anything less and lived with himself. You can't just stand by and go along your merry way, not if you have the ability and clout to change things. He was a courageous man, I see that now. A moral man in an immoral world."

"But what good is all that moral courage now? He's dead, just like his brother. Just like *my* brother. Just like King. Damn it, Alex! It only takes one bullet to ruin everything. *Everything!* And one bullet leads to another bullet until . . . all hell breaks loose."

"Let's hope this is the end of it."

"Don't count on it," she said. "It's almost as if, instead of evolving, we're regressing, going backwards. And now, with Dr. King and Bobby both gone, there's no one left to hold it together."

"Do you think it's as bad as that?"

"I don't know, but I already see the student movement collapsing. In fact, the SDS—that's Students for a Democratic Society—"

"I know what it is," he said with mock irritation.

"Well, they're all in disarray. One faction's losing patience with non-violence. Especially with Dr. King gone. And I can only imagine what Bobby's death will do, not to mention the wider political ramifications. It's like the snowball effect. JFK. Malcolm X. Dr. King. Bobby. It's enough to make you want to give up, throw in the towel. Violence is just too damned contagious—"

"But so is hope," Alex said quickly. "Hope is contagious, too, isn't it? At least that's what I saw that day in Watts."

She looked at him, stunned. "Go on," she said.

"The way I see it is this: If people like you—clever and caring—lose hope, then we *are* lost. You, of all people, Madeline, can't just chuck all your ideals, even if everyone else wants to revert back to the Planet of the Apes."

"But, Alex, you made fun of my ideals. 'Oh, Madeline, you're such an idealist,' you said."

He looked down and twisted the pop bottle into a pile of sand beside the steps. "I was wrong on that, too. I think it would be daft to give up hope in the face of this tragedy. You'd be saying that Bobby's death means the death of everything he believed in. Do you think he'd want that? Bloody hell, Madeline, you might as well say his life meant nothing if you think his ideals died with him." He looked away from her toward the sea.

An enormous wave burst on the rocks, the sound of it almost deafening.

She looked at him. Was this coming from the same guy she first pegged as the shallow Ken Doll type? Now, in the full brunt of sunlight, the irregular bump in the bridge of his nose—the only physical imperfection she could find—looked a bit more crooked than before. She may have been initially guilty of stereotyping him, but you couldn't help but see it now—see the soul in him rising up like a wave, cresting, wanting to break onto something firm. To be seen and heard and felt. She needed to be that rock for him, even if he came here to be hers.

She cringed at her own misjudgments, her own smallness in light of his expanding presence. She felt not only humbled, but a little ashamed for her theatrical fall into despair. Here he was, sitting next to her on a warm and sunny June morning, saying everything she knew to be true, everything she believed so passionately. Yet she could not seem to summon her idealism. It was as if she had left her dreams, her ideals—her own soul—back at the Ambassador Hotel.

"Keep talking," she said, putting a cigarette between her lips and flipping open her Zippo lighter. "I'm listening."

"I thought you quit that bloody awful habit—after that asthma attack of yours."

"I did. I keep the odd cigarette for times like these." She lit up and took a puff. "I'm still in shock, you said it yourself."

He looked at her with reproof.

"Oh, all right." She stubbed out her cigarette in the sand.

He waited, watching her, and then said, "What I'm trying to say is that if Bobby's ideals die with him—well, that would be the unforgivable thing, the greater tragedy. Am I not right?"

"You are. You are right, Alex, but my question is this: Why are you, Alex Moore—a. k. a. Mr. Realist—all of the sudden Mr. Idealist? You're the cynic, not me, so what's all this song and dance about saving ideals and rescuing hope? I don't get it."

"Truth is, I've been . . . converted."

She looked up in surprise and mock horror. "Oh?" she laughed. "Converted to what, exactly? The Hare Krishas? The Jesus Freaks? Who got to you, Alex?"

"You got to me," he said. "Bobby got to me. I don't know how to explain it, except that I woke up one day and found myself different, swept up in," he paused to form his words, "well, in the possibility of things, I guess. Talk about contagious. You, Madeline Prescott, are contagious. Did you know that? Did you know you have that effect on people? Or are you too busy ranting and raving and being clever to notice?"

She looked at him, speechless.

"And furthermore, you know what they say about new converts. They suffer from over-enthusiasm. You can't just leave me hanging, flapping in the breeze."

She smiled. "What are you talking about?"

"I'm talking about hope. About changing things for the better. I never really thought in those terms before I met you. And then, seeing Bobby that day in Watts"—he turned his body toward her—"I mean, did you see the faces of those people in the crowd, how he affected them?"

She nodded, studying his face. "But why were you so cynical in the first place, Alex? I don't get it."

He shrugged. "I suppose I always thought that hope was for choir boys and mums, that it was somehow naïve to believe in anything but the worst of humanity. But I can't call RFK naïve. He is—was—brutally well-informed. He knew the risks. And yet, he still believed in the possibility of change. That's what did it for me. That's what really 'blows my mind' as you Americans are fond of saying. I mean, we have to believe in goodness and beauty and love, don't we, Madeline? Otherwise, why go on? What's the point of anything, really?"

Madeline could see tiny beads of sweat forming on his forehead. He was searching for more words. She held silent, waiting.

"I guess what I'm trying to say, rather badly, is that moral courage is just that. There are no guarantees. The courage is in the trying, don't you see?" He paused, his face frozen in an expression of utter seriousness. "And someone has to bloody well try."

She nodded, deeply moved, holding back the threat of tears —for Bobby and Sean and Dr. King. And for herself, too. For that little girl who once sat on these steps and had faith in things.

"Am I making any sense?" he asked, "or does this sound like

a sappy scene between Pa and Little Joe on *Bonanza?*" He chuckled.

She laughed out loud to keep from crying. "Little Joe aside, you surprise me—all this talk—but I have to admit, it helps me to hear it." She paused. "In fact, I think I like the new you. I really do." She looked at him.

He smiled. "And I rather like the old you."

"The *old* me? We've only known each other—"

"What I mean," he cut in, "is that I'll be really disappointed if you decide to hang it all and become some else. To give up. To lose your spark—"

"Give up? Me?" Of course, she reasoned, she had just given that impression—rather robustly. She had given the same impression to herself in her own solitude. But now she knew it was just that: an impression, like a dark bruise on delicate skin. She was hurting, that was all.

"Yeah, people do that you know," Alex continued, "become disillusioned and fade away. Or just get stoned. Permanently. You could do that, if you wanted."

Madeline looked at him with mild horror. Did he know by some mental telepathy that she and Biddy and been smoking pot under the palm tree? Did Simone open her big mouth about the Mystic Arts fiasco?

"Not me," she said. "I don't plan on tripping my way into the future." She gave a nervous laugh.

Alex did not laugh. "But you could just hang it all. You could go off with Leary's bunch and stay high all the time because you can't face the world as we know it."

Why hadn't she thought to swear Simone to secrecy? But for some strange reason, the thought of him knowing her flaws, her impetuous and ridiculous side, no longer mortified her. Perhaps she was just too emotionally drained to care. After blubbering on his shoulder that awful night, she was now beyond mortification.

"Well, don't worry about me," she said. "I'm not much for communes, long dresses, or patchouli oil. Or psychedelic colors. They go so badly with my hair."

Alex laughed and his brown eyes gleamed with that familiar lightness. She, too, felt lighter, unburdened—in an exhausted sort of way.

Suddenly, she thought of Ben, and the way he laughed at her jokes. She thought of leaving him in tears at Good Samaritan Hospital. She felt a little guilty about Ben. He had called her as he was preparing to fly to New York to attend Bobby's funeral.

Without thinking, she blurted out, "Ben asked me to go with him to Bobby's funeral. He has friends we could stay with in New York."

Alex gave a familiar, "Hmph."

She knew she'd spoiled the moment. *Damn!*

"Are you going, then?"

"No, of course not. It's Saturday. Saturday morning. I told Eve that I'd be at her apartment to watch the funeral on television." She paused. "And I'd like you to be there, too. If you want."

He put his arm around her again, as if for solidarity against all the pain in the world. They sat in a languid silence and watched the hypnotic waves.

"Alex, do you think history will remember him? Bobby, I mean. Will he be remembered, say, fifty years from now—that is, if we haven't blown ourselves up in a nuclear holocaust?"

"I think he will be remembered, yes. But what he stood for —well, we'll have to wait and see on that one, won't we?"

She suddenly thought of Alex's hands around her waist, hoisting her up to reach Bobby's hand. Emotion welled. She turned into him, away from the sun, and wept into the soft fabric of his shirt.

Alex squeezed her gently, with a tenderness that made her weep all the more. "Hey, now. It's all right. Oh, I almost forgot.

I have a confession to make."

"What?" She sat up to look at him. The salty breeze cooled her tears.

"I read the note, the one Henry Graham stuck inside the poetry book. I think you should it read it."

"Now?"

"Now." He turned to get the book, pulled out the slip of paper, and handed it to her.

> *Madeline,*
>
> *Rilke is good consolation in times of tragedy. Don't give up hope, my dear. Augustine said, "Hope has two daughters, one is called Anger and one is called Courage: anger at the way things are, and courage to change things." Looking forward to seeing you—and hearing you?—on Poetry Night at Van Gelder's.*
>
> *Henry*
>
> *P.S. We Scots must stick together!*

Chapter Twenty-Seven

Clad in jeans and a short-sleeved tee, Madeline sat cross-legged on the floor, staring at the console television with a mug of tea and a box of Kleenex nearby—a box well-used after Leonard Bernstein finished conducting Mahler.

"*My brother need not be idealized,*" she heard Edward Kennedy say, "*or enlarged in death beyond what he was in life; to be remembered simply as a good and decent man, who saw wrong and tried to right it, saw suffering and tried to heal it, saw war and tried to stop it. . . .*"

She blew her nose and glanced at Alex, who occupied Eve's easy chair, Earl Grey curled on his lap. Alex looked at her and nodded, as if to say, *Poignant, those words. Heartbreaking, really.* He stroked Earl under the chin, seeming to forget his indifference to cats.

Now she readied herself for the final stretch of the memorial —the funeral train to Arlington Cemetery, where Bobby would be buried near his brother's eternal flame. One of the news reporters, a young man with a sympathetic voice, had said before the memorial at St. Patrick's Cathedral, "The train that will carry the Senator's remains from New York to Washington is the second such funeral train in U.S. history to make this trip. The first was the train carrying the body of Abraham Lincoln."

"Madeline," a breathless Eve said, having come up to the apartment from the shop, "your friend, that marine from the mission, is here to see you." Eve had been running up and down the stairs all morning with her preparations for opening, while catching as much as she could of the RFK funeral mass on television. She had insisted that Madeline take the day off and spend all day in front of the television, if she wished.

"Joey Lobo? He's here? Now?"

Eve stood in the doorway, still catching her breath. On the wall next to her hung the very painting that she had turned down the day of the picnic—Sam's beach painting. Madeline had been so preoccupied with her grief that she hadn't noticed it until now.

Eve shrugged. "I told Mr. Lobo—Corporal Lobo, I believe it is—that you were occupied, but he seemed rather insistent on seeing you. I was just getting out the scones for defrosting when I heard him knock."

"It's okay, Eve. Thanks."

Joey Lobo. For God's sake, she'd given up on Joey Lobo. A wave of dread, followed swiftly by anger, swept over her, for his not coming sooner, for being so mysterious, and now, for coming when she was already emotionally drained.

"Do you want me to come with you?" Alex asked.

"No. I need to talk to him alone, thanks. I'll be back to watch the coverage of the funeral train. *That* I can't miss." Something about a journey—even a journey in death—seemed to rivet her more than any staid church service. She started toward the door and then returned to grab a couple of tissues and stuff them into the pockets of her jeans.

* * *

Joey looked just as she remembered, dressed in his familiar fatigues and boots, cap under arm. She could see something sticking out of his back pocket. He was standing at a bookshelf, a hardback book opened in his hand. When he saw her, he closed it quickly, as if he had been caught stealing candy, and returned it to the bookshelf.

"Joey, you came."

When he turned toward her, she noticed there was something different about his appearance. He wore something around his neck that wasn't there before. As she approached him, her eyes riveted on the heavy metal pendant hanging where one would normally see dog tags—hanging like a giant tear drop of rough, thick, silver metal: a peace sign.

"Maddy," Joey said as a greeting, his discomfort palpable.

"Do you want some tea or something to eat?"

"No thanks. If ya don't mind." He gestured for her to sit, as if wanting to get down to business with no preliminaries. There was a secretive intensity about Joey Lobo, but she sensed it was not so much a part of his original personality as it was a self-constructed inner chamber, built by war—a survival mechanism.

She sat across from him at the Thoreau table where Matthew, the writer, liked to sit. She had imagined this day, but not quite like this, not revisiting her first grief on the very day of nursing a fresh grief.

"Are you . . . okay?" he said awkwardly. "Your eyes, they're so red."

"I was watching the funeral mass on television . . . you know, Bobby Kennedy."

Joey nodded. "I guess that's why I had to come today. Not wait any longer to do what I have to do. Kennedy's death made me realize"—he sighed deeply—"oh, I dunno, the urgency of things, I guess."

"But where have you been all this time?"

"Spending time at Camp Pendleton—a coffee house there, you know, for G.I.'s." He paused as if this might have meaning for her. "Lots of Janis Joplin and Jimmy Hendrix on the juke box."

"A coffeehouse? Janis Joplin?" she said, trying to keep the irritation from her voice, but then it gave way: "You've just been hanging out and rapping with your buddies? Forgetting me? My family? What we're going through?"

He held up a hand. "I don't think ya understand what I mean by the G.I. coffeehouse."

"I've worked in coffeehouses. I know what they are."

"Not this one, ya don't. Sean told me about all your goings-on up at Berkeley, so I thought ya might get it."

"Well, I've been away from Berkeley, obviously."

"Okay then," Joey Lobo said, pulling out a tattered news-paper from his back pocket. He plopped it on the table, turning it so she could read.

"What's this?" She read the name on the front of the newspaper. "*Vietnam G.I.*" She opened the crackling pages and glanced at random, forgetting her irritation in favor of curiosity. "Some kind of newsletter for G.I.s? I don't get it. What am I supposed to be looking for here?" Her eyes were drawn to the letters that appeared on each page: FTA, in bold black. "What's FTA?"

"Fun, Travel, and Adventure," he said, but with an edge to his voice.

"My . . . God," she said as it dawned on her. "This is an underground paper. The G.I.s have an underground paper! And this FTA—or Fun, Travel, and Adventure—it's code, isn't it? What does it mean?"

Joey Lobo looked uncomfortable. He clenched his fist in the air, in the place of a word. " . . . the Army."

"'*Fuck* the Army'? That's it, isn't it? That's the code."

"Well . . . yeah." He looked around as if there was some-thing sacrilegious about saying the "F" word in a nice little shop where they served tea and scones.

"Joey," she said, turning the pages of the paper, "I had no idea there was any kind of resistance in the military itself. This blows my mind."

Joey shrugged. "There's nobody better to protest a bad war than those who are fightin' it, wouldn't ya say?"

"Well, sure. You're the ones bearing it all. It makes sense, but still, it just isn't what I expected." She smiled, sorry for her initial impatience. Protest was her language, and she felt at home in the conversation. "How large is this movement?"

"Small, but growing, really gettin' some teeth into it now — ya know, since Tet. Expanding all over the country. That's where the coffeehouses come in. It's where guys go to blow off steam and rap about all this stuff. It's where we warn guys on their way to Nam and where guys comin' home can decompress. Ya know, a place to organize."

"I've been away from Berkeley too long," she said. Then it occurred to her, Sean's words about his friend, Joey, how they thought alike. She hadn't understood how two so very different souls could have anything in common, until now. "Sean was involved with this movement, wasn't he?"

Joey nodded. "He was. Not that there is any, what you'd call a real movement over there. Not yet. But there's this underground rag. Passin' it around is at least a start. If we get caught readin' it," —he flicked his hand in the air—"it's to the stockade. Solitary confinement. But it tells the truth, the kinda news ya ain't gonna find on T.V."

"Like what?" She rifled through the paper, as if looking for clues.

He pointed to a headline, "Look here. '50 Women and Children Killed.' Ya don't see that in *The Register*, now do ya? That's 'cause they're not American women and children."

Madeline felt a shiver of disgust.

"This paper may shock ya, but it gives guys like me and Sean hope. And a reason to keep alive, just by knowin' that we're not alone. That we're not crazy-in-the-head. Not cowards. Guys like us need to know that it's the war that's crazy, not us." He paused. "Anyway, I think ya'd have been real proud of your brother."

"Would have been? I *am* proud, you better believe it. But I'm not all that surprised, not after reading Sean's letter. This is exactly what Sean would do, because he was a moral human being and smart enough to think for himself." (So was Joey, evidently. Her regard for him was rising exponentially.) "But how did you even get these papers without your commanding officers knowing about them? You surely didn't take out a subscription, like you would to *Time* magazine."

"Oh, that's easy. They come from the Midwest in brown bundles, with return addresses from churches. Look, Maddy, I want ya to have this copy. Keep it. It was the last issue he read before . . ." He lowered his head.

She blew out a sigh, still thinking of the ramifications of a G.I. movement. "What you're doing, Joey, makes what I was doing for the movement look like kindergarten stuff. I mean, it doesn't cost me much to hold up a sign or go to a sit-in. It costs you so much. I really had no idea—"

"Well, now ya know. But I've got more to say and not much time to say it."

"Not much time? We have a few minutes before we have to open—"

"I mean, I don't have much time left."

"You mean, until your second tour? But I didn't think you were leaving until the fall?"

"I'm not going back."

"Not going back?"

He looked serious, almost defiant.

"But how can you just quit the war? Won't you go to jail or something?"

"Court martial and twenty years to life, most likely."

Madeline took in a quick breath. "But why, Joey? Why not Canada? Sweden? Anywhere—for God's sake. Joey, this is your life we're talking about!"

Joey leaned back, stretching out his arm over the back of his chair. "I know it's my life; it's my decision, too. The hardest one I've ever made. Believe me. It's not that I put down any of my buddies who went up to Canada or disappeared in Saigon. I'm tempted everyday to disappear with 'em."

He paused and looked down, as if trying to find the words. "I'm a Catholic, ya know; 'lapsed' as they say, but still, I have a namesake."

"A namesake?"

"St. Joseph. I told you at the Mission. I was named for St. Joseph and the damned saint follows me around like a shadow. Not always comfortable," he said with a melancholy smile. "But he reminds me that I have to think about more than myself. I was raised that way, but haven't exactly lived up to it," he said with a laugh. "Ya could say I'm a man in need of redemption." He plopped his arms on the table—the muscles huge and well-defined—and looked at her with resolve. "Look, I can't skip the country. I'd be leavin' behind the truth, and that would make me a man without a soul, now, wouldn't it?"

"The truth?"

"Yeah, the truth that's gnawin' it's way from my insides out to my skin. I'm tired of tryin'—"

Madeline grasped hold of his arm. "Just say it. Truth about what?"

He began to rub the scar on his face, like a nervous habit.

"Truth about *what*?" she pressed.

"The truth about your brother's death."

She felt her heart in her throat.

He looked at her with those intense, dark, muddy eyes and sighed heavily, still rubbing the scar. "I've been goin' through my own personal hell tryin' to make sense of what my next move should be, and it's taken this long—it just has—and I'm sorry. But Bobby Kennedy's murder jolted me to make a decision. I mean, that guy risked his life to stop the war. So, here I am."

"Tell me, then, Joey," she said gently, as the world stood on his next words. She tried to lock onto his eyes, but he kept looking away, then down, hiding. Hiding something awful, she thought, with a sudden lurch of her stomach.

Something awful.

Chapter Twenty-Eight

She looked at the starburst clock over the shop door and realized that it was now or never. They were alone, but people would be coming within half an hour. Eve would be coming down to open. She finally caught his eyes and held them with her own, willing Joey Lobo to get it all out on the table. It was as if everything else—Bobby's death, the funeral, her father's affair—was receding with the tide, taking everything with it, leaving only Joey's words naked on the shore: "the truth about your brother's death." She sat back, crossed her arms, and waited.

Joey laced his fingers behind his head and closed his eyes, as if going back to Vietnam in his mind.

"Me and Sean, we were sent out on patrol to a village near Khe Sanh. We heard this village was a safe house for V.C. It was our mission to check it out—a reconnaissance. When we got close to the village we saw smoke comin' outta the treetops. Then flames. Another platoon had been there, ya see. They'd set the fire, that was clear enough."

"They set fire to a village? With people in it?"

Joey opened his eyes. "Yeah, with people in it. Little kids, too. And mothers runnin' and screamin' like nothin' you've ever heard. The sound of those screams—damn! I can't get it outta my head. Wakes me up at night."

"But why?" Madeline hugged herself in a protective gesture. "Why burn a village?"

"We were told to punish villages that hid V.C. All these women and children, just takin' care of their own. Providin' water and food, places to hide. For that, they gotta be punished and burned out. Like animals."

Madeline shuddered but kept silent, closing her eyes, trying to form a picture of the horror. She'd heard stories of children and napalm and tried to keep the images vague in her head because she couldn't stand the details. But this—this was a new horror, setting an entire village on fire.

"Some of the guys liked that kinda thing," he said, "liked killin' Gooks for sport, I mean. Not me. I never went 'round the bend like that. But war does things to people, Maddy—twists the mind. These are mostly good guys, or they started out that way. But in a war like this, ya just lose yourself in the madness. Ya just snap. It gets so . . . confusing."

"Confusing? How is it confusing that it's wrong to kill civilians?"

"It gets all mixed up, ya see. Not like any war I've ever heard of. Civilians get caught in the cracks. The grandma doin' the platoon's laundry one week might toss a grenade at ya the next. Jesus! Grandmas! Who said we're supposed to kill grandmas?" Joey shook his head. "So, you start thinkin' that it's all fair game—even civilians—animals to be shot for sport. All of them are Gooks—little kids, pregnant women. All Gooks. They aren't really human. That's how ya have to think, Maddy." He looked at her hard, almost pleading. "Or at least, that's how it ends up." He paused, as if unsure about going on.

Madeline reached out to touch his arm again and felt the tight muscles relax a bit. "Go on, Joey. Please."

"Anyway, I lost it when I saw the fire and realized what was goin' on. Honest to God, I just froze like a deer in the head-lights. Couldn't move. Me and Sean, we'd heard about this kinda stuff, oh yeah, we'd read about it in the underground paper. They call 'em Zippo Raids. But still, we—"

"Zippo Raids?"

"That's when they torch the huts with Zippo lighters. Ya know, one flick against the thatched roof and the whole damned hut goes up. Pretty soon the whole village. Me and Sean, we tried to get our wits about us, but what could we do? Nothin' but burnin' huts and screamin' women and children everywhere. We looked at each other like this-ain't-happenin'-man. There was so much chaos and screamin' that I can't quite make out in my head how we decided on this, but we separated to try and see what we could do. See if we could stop it, or save someone, or . . . I dunno what in the hell we thought we could do. So I started on the north side and Sean on the south end. There were just burnin' huts on my side. All the people had run in the other direction, so I headed in Sean's direction. And then—" He stopped.

"What?" Madeline burst out, her heart beating wildly.

"I saw Sean's M16—it was on the ground. I knew somethin' was wrong. Ya just don't leave your weapon layin' on the ground. Ever. I looked around but I couldn't find him. Then I spotted the marines who torched the village—least I assumed they were the same guys. Anyway, they started to raise their M16s, and I knew what was comin'." He paused to shake his head.

"What was coming?"

He sighed as if gathering courage to go on. "I grabbed Sean's M16 and started yellin' for him 'cause I knew damn well they didn't know we were there. I tried wavin' my arms at the marines, but they didn't see me. They were intent on their targets. They weren't lookin' for soldiers. They didn't know we were there." He stopped to catch his breath.

"What did they do—these marines?" she pressed.

"They started shootin' everyone. Women, children, old men, all of 'em runnin'outta their huts—clothes on fire. They just shot everyone."

"They . . . they *what?*"

Joey went on quickly, as if the horror of it had to all come out in one lump or not at all. "I suppose they thought, in a twisted sort of way, they were doin' the humane thing, puttin' people outta their misery and all. I mean, if they're gonna set 'em on fire, the least they could do was shoot 'em. Like sufferin' animals."

Madeline felt herself about to be sick, but didn't move. Didn't breathe.

"Ya look pale, Maddy," he said, looking grave. "Gonna be sick? Want me to stop?"

"Go on," she said in a near whisper, willing herself to get through it.

He raised his eyebrows, as if to say, *you asked for it.* "Well, finally I saw Sean. He was runnin' out of a hut. He had a little kid slung over his shoulder like a rag doll, a kid about five years old or so. He kept runnin' till he got to a grassy area by some trees and put the kid down. I saw some woman come outta the trees and grab the kid and run away.

"And then—Jesus!—he started back in. I yelled at him. I screamed at him to get the hell away! He couldn't hear me, or he wouldn't listen. The hut was goin' down—burnin' up—and he musta heard the rounds goin' off, but he went back in anyway. *He went back in!*" He said this as if Madeline would somehow doubt him, as if he could hardly believe it himself. "He musta seen more kids in there, 'cause I yelled for him but he kept on. He was just so driven, so set on goin' in. He just went back in."

He looked straight at Madeline, his eyebrows crushed together in sad incomprehension.

Madeline rocked back and forth, hugging herself. "But the marines—didn't they see Sean? They must have—"

"They didn't know he was in there," Joey said, shaking his head. "They kept firin' without seeing what in the hell they were hittin'. But I could see. I could see Sean real clear from where I was. He was half-way into the hut. I heard gunfire and saw him pitch forward."

She let out an involuntary scream and felt herself pitch forward, toward the table. Joey grabbed her wrists.

"I don't know how else to tell ya this, Maddy" he said, shaking his head. "I just don't know how else to tell ya."

When she closed her eyes, she saw Sean. She saw the flames. "Was he . . . did he—?"

"Dead before he hit the ground," said Joey, seeming to know her thoughts. "He was already dead . . . before the flames. I'm sure of it. He died a real quick death with all those rounds hittin' him at once. *Real quick*, Maddy. Ya have to believe me. I saw it with my own eyes."

She nodded, her eyes squeezed shut as globs of tears rolled onto her cheeks. He released her wrists, and she settled into the horror of it with resignation. She opened her eyes. "Don't stop."

"At that point I ran yellin' like a wild man with my arms in the air. I knew Sean was dead—'course, I knew it—but I couldn't just leave him there. I couldn't figure out why in the hell they wouldn't stop firin' even though there was nobody left to shoot. They were like crazy men. When they finally saw me, they stopped and stood there in a daze. I ran to Sean and pulled him out by his boots and rolled him on the ground to put out the flames. Those marines—they were outta their heads when they saw what they'd done. They came runnin' towards me cussin' and screamin' to high heaven. One guy threw his gun on the ground and retched his guts out. I mean, they had no idea they'd mowed down a fellow marine. No idea."

"Which one killed Sean?" she asked quietly. "Which marine killed my brother?"

"There's no way to tell. They all fired at once. There were four of 'em in all—so there's no way to tell."

"But what happened to you, Joey? Afterwards, I mean. Why didn't you go to your commanding officer and tell your story?"

"I did," Joey said firmly. "He looked all white and shocked and upset. He said he'd report it, and that I'd need to give a statement. But later, he called me in and told me that 'officially' Lance Corporal Sean Prescott had been killed by enemy fire, and that if I said anything different to anyone, it would hurt the Corps—'tarnish the Corps'—that's what he said. He said I'd get my day to tell my story, but not now. I was to keep quiet for the good of the country. It was my duty."

"You're *duty*? For God's sake!"

"I was all mangled up inside my head, sorta paralyzed. So I kept quiet. But after awhile, I realized that I'd be waitin' forever if I waited for military justice. I was at the end of my tour anyway, so I endured two more weeks. And when I got home I began really thinkin' about it all. Tryin' to make sense of it, ya know." He looked at Madeline, as if for understanding, assurance. "Then I met some other guys at the coffeehouse, who had their own stories of Zippo Raids. A lotta messed up guys—lost guys—probably'll blow their brains out before it's all over." Joey shook his head and tapped the underground paper that lay spread between them. "But not all of 'em. Some of 'em are organizin'. Tryin' to stop the war from the inside. But somebody has to talk, or nothin' will ever come of it."

"And that somebody would be you?" She looked directly at Joey. Tears floated in his dark, pained eyes, eyes which had seen Dante's inferno. So it was real after all, she thought, this hell that she had always heard about, but it wasn't in some murky underworld where heathen writhed in pain for sins past. No. It was right here. It was Vietnam. She looked straight into his brown eyes. "It's a brave act, Joey, what you're about to do."

He shook his head. "No, what Sean did was brave. He was the one—" He paused, took his cap in hand, and fiddled with it, as if it would help to keep his composure. "He was braver than anyone I knew in Nam. He saved a little kid while I just looked

on, yellin' like a wild man, tryin' to stop him. Jesus! Your brother was brave, not me. *Not me.* He would've saved the whole
damned village if he could've."

"Was . . . the child," she said slowly, "a boy or a girl?"

"I think it was a girl. Yeah, I'm pretty sure it was a little
girl."

She nodded, still shaking. She tried to imagine the little girl,
how she would think of Americans when she grew up. Would
she hate them all? Or would she remember that one good
American?

"And so you'll give your statement to . . . who? The press?"

"Yeah, I'll start with the *L.A. Times*, but ya think they're
gonna believe me—over the brass?" He gave a cynical laugh.
"The only American witness? A dark skinned one at that. The
shooters, at least one of 'em, will have to come clean. Or maybe
the woman in the trees who grabbed the kid. But what are the
chances of that?" He shook his head. "But, I have to try, don't
I?"

"Yes, I suppose you do, Joey."

"Well," he sighed, looking exhausted from telling his tale, "I
have to be leavin'. I've said what I came to say."

Madeline looked at Joey Lobo, cap in hand. She bit her lip,
knowing that whatever she could say would be inadequate.

"Thank you, Joey. Thank you for telling me the truth."

"What about your family?"

"I'll take care of them, don't worry." *But would she?* Would
she tell her family this horror story? Or would she hold onto the
secret, as she did Sean's letter? How many secrets could one
heart hold, anyway?

* * *

The Holiday Inn receptionist connected Madeline to the
room of her wayward father.

"Dad, we need to talk." Madeline spoke into the heavy,
black telephone receiver in the tone of one reeling in a delin-

quent child.

"If this is about your mother and me—"

"It's not about you and Mom. That's . . . none of my business." She sighed into the phone as if not sure how to go about this, even after a week of practicing different conversations in her head. But she knew she had to go through with it now, or she would lose her nerve altogether. She tried to sound casual. "Look, Dad, it's Sunday morning. We haven't talked in so long. It would be good to talk, to catch up, and I need you to look at my tape deck in the car. It's all messed up."

"This can't be just about your tape deck. I get the feeling you've got something on your mind."

She took a breath. "It's about Sean. You need to know something about Sean."

There was a pause.

"I'll be there in an hour," he said. "Make some coffee. Black."

Madeline hung up the receiver and sat on the twisted blankets and sheets of her unmade bed. My God, she thought, what have I done?

* * *

John Prescott sat with his daughter at the tiny kitchen table inside the beach cottage. "Sorry about what happened to Kennedy," he said, looking up at her as she poured steaming black coffee into his mug. "I didn't hear about it until the next morning, and that's when I called your mother to try to find out how you were. I don't know what's become of this country—"

Madeline waved off the whole discussion. "Let's not talk about it now, Dad."

They sipped coffee in an awkward silence.

"Well, are you going to tell me or not?" her father said with familiar irritability. It somehow made her smile. At least there were parts of him that didn't change.

She looked up at him. "I had a visit from one of Sean's

marine buddies. I think you need to know what he told me."

Madeline began to retell the story of Sean and the village near Khe Sanh, leaving out the part about the underground paper. No need to be reckless with a truth that could destroy. That was the deal she had made with herself after days of hair-pulling inner debate.

When she finished the story, she watched her dad's eyes brimming with tears, as if he would collapse with emotion. She was terrified and wondered what in the hell she would do now. Suddenly—and reassuringly—his fist hit the table.

"God damn it!" John Prescott began a fifteen minute rant, wanting to "string up" the officer who set in motion the cover-up, and to take the marines in the raid and "hang them by their thumbs." Madeline watched her father's rage pour out of him like a volcanic eruption—hot molten rocks spewing to the ends of his verbal ability, which was, to Madeline's surprise, quite amazing both in shock value and variety. When he finally ran out of expletives, he sank into his hands and wept.

Madeline could handle the rage. *But this weeping!* She ran for the tissue box and returned to find a more collected man.

He took a Kleenex and blew his nose. "Sit down, you're making me nervous."

Madeline, having made it a personal policy never to follow her father's orders, did not sit down but tried to hug him, to show some affection. To comfort. But he would have none of it, apparently embarrassed with this show of emotion.

"I'll be all right." He brushed her away, his anger re-surfacing. "I suppose Lobo will catch hell for going to the press. I'd better call a lawyer—"

"Dad," she said, "there will be time for all that later. Lots of time. The press won't take him seriously without other wit-nesses, and that could take months. You need to calm down." And then more gently, "Let's get some fresh air, out on the deck. I'll refresh our mugs."

They sat at the weathered picnic table, looking out at the ocean. The sea air calmed her father, or perhaps he was just emotionally exhausted. There seemed to be a silent understanding that they would set aside Vietnam for the moment.

He looked at his daughter across the table. "I've kept something from you, Maddy."

She looked at him with widening eyes. (How many more surprises could she take, for God's sake?) She steeled herself. "What is it, Dad?"

"I never told you that I . . . that I always hated Pastor Bob's sermons." He smiled weakly.

"No way!" she said and laughed aloud.

He nodded—and even chuckled. "I despised them, every one of them, week after week. Torture."

"But why—"

"Oh, I figured you kids needed some kind of religious upbringing, and the New Hope Baptist Church was your mother's choice. I deferred to her on those matters."

"Well, I'm glad to know that we actually agree. On something."

They sipped their coffee in a companionable silence, as though cleansed by the levity.

"Are you a believer, Maddy?" her father said out of the silence. "Do you believe in God?" He spoke as if asking her how her car was driving.

It was the question she always dreaded. A loaded question. A pushy question, one might argue, and she wasn't quite ready for it.

"Look, Dad, I'm not crazy about the word 'believer.' I mean, it carries the idea of a rigid certainty, an absolute truth—too closed off a word for me at the moment, too dead-end of a word . . . yeah, that's it," she said thinking aloud, "like you've got God all sewed up in your pocket. Like all that's left is giving your pocket a pat whenever you're tempted to think or question. No,

I feel like . . . I feel like I'm moving toward God—and the moving feels right to me." She looked out at the sun glistening on the sea. "I'm sort of swimming toward God, maybe. Or swimming inside God. Like a giant womb." The words jumped out of her, as words often did, before really thinking them through. But she had to admit she liked this metaphor-from-nowhere. *Womb of God.* Subversive—wildly, beautifully subversive. (Henry, she thought, would love it.) She glanced at her dad, who was wincing visibly.

"Sorry I asked," he said. He took another sip of coffee and said, "I know Sean believed."

"I know," she said. "More than any of us." Then something inside her gained momentum. "But Dad, there's something even more important to remember about Sean, at least I think so."

"What's that?"

"Sean's life, or I should say . . . his death, has shown me what really matters. I mean, it's not how long we live, but *how* we live. Not the length of our time, but well, the width of our souls—"

"The *what?*"

"Sean had a huge soul, Dad, an enormous soul, as big as the ocean out there." She flung an arm toward the sea. "And I think that matters somehow—it really matters. To God, it matters. To the world, it matters. For all eternity, it matters."

John Prescott bit his lip, hard, and his eyes shone with tears.

Madeline got up and, as if a little girl again, she went behind him and threw her arms around his neck. He grabbed her hands and held them, as if holding on for dear life. She clung to him, willing for this moment to stand still, taking in the freshly shampooed smell of his curly, coppery, conservative head of hair.

Chapter Twenty-Nine

The cool, gray June gloom, so characteristic of this time of year in Southern California, had finally burned off by noon, reviving lagging spirits of vacationers who had draped beach towels over their shoulders and legs for warmth (not something one wanted to remember about a beach vacation in California). The longed for sunshine now graced relieved beachgoers with a bright joyfulness.

Madeline Prescott and Alex Moore walked along Main Beach's boardwalk, dodging dogs on leashes, and listening to the yells of overly-tanned teens as they spiked the volleyball over the net.

They passed a guitar player with bushy sideburns, long hair, and John Lennon glasses. But there was no mistaking this young man for John Lennon. He was trying for "Eleanor Rigby," but was hideously off key. One stocky man, ripe and red from the sun, walked up to the young man whose guitar case was begging for coins, and asked the musician how much money it would take for him to stop singing. Alex and Madeline looked at each other and laughed.

Farther down the boardwalk, a tall man with a booming voice quoted something from the Bible, holding his leather-bound copy dramatically aloft as if he were a prophet of doom in the midst of a sea of sinners.

"Only in California," said Alex, shaking his head.

"Yeah, full of fruits and nuts, they say. But it's home."

He looked at her. "You know, Madeline, you need to get away from California, just for awhile. Change would do you good. After all you've been through, I mean. You need to come to London, meet Christopher Wren."

"Christopher who?"

"Well, I've done it," he said with a satisfied grin. "Finally. A piece of history you don't know. Christopher Wren, the great English architect. Designed St. Paul's Cathedral, and so many of the grand buildings in London, way back when. Seventeenth Century, to be precise."

She looked at him thoughtfully—and lustfully—his hair a bit longish now, falling around his collar, pronouncing even more his perfect jaw bone. He was a beautiful man, there was no denying it.

"I can see you're finally homesick," she said. "I wondered when the novelty of California would wear off."

"Now *there* you're mistaken. I'll never be tired of my new home. But I've got a foot in both worlds, you see. You can do that. I mean, we do have two feet, after all."

She laughed. It felt good to get her own two feet back on solid ground with quiet, silly humor and soft summer breezes. "Yeah, I'd like to see all those 'grand' buildings someday. See the history I've studied." She nodded. "It would be nice."

"I hear that the musical *Hair* will be in London by September, after it leaves New York. We can see it there—in London. Wouldn't that be brilliant?"

Madeline felt her heart skip a beat. She wondered if the sun and the off-key music might be getting to Alex. But perhaps behind his façade of light-hearted nonchalance was something significant. An invitation. A serious one, thought out ahead of time and packaged in this breezy, casual way. But they hadn't even gone to dinner yet. *And he was inviting her to skip the country with him?*

Just as she opened her mouth, they were interrupted by two

boys barreling past them, almost knocking her down. "Hey!" Madeline said in a scolding tone. She watched them stop cold in their tracks and turn around.

"Sorry," said one of the Gelson twins, looking sheepish.

"Oh, it's you," said the other freckle-faced twin with squinty eyes. "I know you because of your hair. It looks like it's on fire."

Alex laughed, looking at Madeline and then back at the twins. "And you are—?"

"I'm Tommy," said one shyly.

"I'm Terry," said the other more boldly. "We're staying at Crystal Cove, down the beach from her," he said, pointing to Madeline.

"Alex," Madeline said, "meet the Gelson twins."

The boys went on, babbling about seeing jellyfish on the shore, describing them as "Jell-O" that you can't touch.

About that time, Biddy Gelson caught up with her double-trouble offspring. She stared at Alex as if she were looking at a painting. "Nice meetin' ya," she said after being introduced, her eyes lingering wistfully on Alex.

Madeline was only slightly irritated at what she knew would be something she'd have to put up with if this relationship went where she hoped it would.

"Would ya'all like to join us for ice cream?"

"No thanks, Biddy," said Alex, "maybe another time. We've got Poetry Night ahead of us." He explained the event and invited Biddy to drop by.

Biddy declined, but expressed her undying admiration for the poet, Rod McKuen, a name that made Madeline cringe. But she tried hard not to show it. Biddy's two little darlings were by this time jumping off the boardwalk and returning via the wooden stairs and repeating *ad nauseum*, "Ice cream, ice cream, we all scream for ice cream!"

Biddy Gelson glanced over at her boys, rolled her eyes in a

whatcha-gonna-do gesture. Mother and sons finally waved goodbye as they flew down the boardwalk toward the ice cream store.

Madeline smiled now at the sight of the woman who had kindly offered her the what-the-hell-let's-get-high-and-eat-cake kind of commiseration. And Biddy, plump as she was, looked happy, unsaddled with the ardent societal pressures to be stick thin—a rather depressing trend since the advent of the British model, Twiggy. She worried about Twiggy's undue influence on Jilli. Of course, she, herself, was on the thin side, but that was because she smoked. Or used to.

The Zippo lighter was no more, buried somewhere in the lower realms of a garbage dump, which is where it deserved to be. She had sworn off of cigarettes in general, and Zippo lighters in particular.

Alex interrupted her widening thoughts as they watched Biddy and the boys move on. "Madeline, are you ready for tonight? Your poetry, I mean."

Her unfettered red locks blew gently into her face as the sea breeze whipped up. She swept back her hair and held it briefly in a knot at the base of her neck, enjoying the salty air on her skin.

"Are you kidding? I wouldn't dare show my face tonight without a poem in hand, given your mother's insistence. And constant reminders. I just hope I'm not the only one reading original poetry. I'd feel silly reading my own amateur attempts when everyone else is reading really good stuff. What are you going to read, by the way?"

"Me?"

"Of course, you. What makes you think you can escape this?"

"But I do *so* want to escape this. I planned to just to cheer you on from the sidelines, but if you want me to read something, I will."

"Good. What will you read, then?"

"Maybe something by, oh, I don't know, say, Rod McKuen?"

She pulled down her sunglasses and looked over the tops of the frame. "And how do you know that I have an aversion to McKuen? Do you read minds as well as spy on people?"

He smiled. "It was easy. Standing to the side of you, I could see the slightest wince behind your sun shades when your friend mentioned Rod McKuen. See, right here." He touched her face. "A subtle wince, but a dead give-away."

"That's scary," she said, pulling away. "Maybe you *should* go to spy school. You've got a real talent there."

"I like spying on you when you're not looking. You're a fascinating subject, all around."

"I'd say you have a lot more interesting material in Newport Beach, some of the jet setters over there." Now she watched him wince, and it pleased her to no end.

She gestured towards a bench near the old stucco lifeguard tower, and they sat down.

"You know, Madeline," he said, leaning back, one arm stretched along the back of the bench, "I always heard about California girls. You know the song—"

"Please don't sing or I'll have to pay you to stop." She watched him laugh; his eyes lit up. "Sorry, what were you saying about us 'California girls'?"

"I was dazzled at first," he said, "but after awhile I became, well, a bit disillusioned. Maybe it was just that the girls—or I should say 'women'—seem to . . . " He paused, as if trying to find the right words.

"Flock to you like seagulls going for a bag of Fritos?" she supplied.

He smiled and looked away, as if embarrassed. Finally, he looked at her straight in the eyes. "Well, since you brought it up—birds, I mean. I'd say you, Madeline Prescott, are a rare one. I notice it especially when I hear you speak."

"What's so rare about the way I speak? I talk like everyone else here in California. You're the one with the fancy British accent."

"No, I mean, it's *what* you say. You make me laugh. But more than that, you have a brain underneath all that gorgeous hair." He looked down at her hands, which were fidgeting at the moment. He took one in his, and she scrunched up her fingers to avoid him noticing her rough nails.

"My nails are a disaster."

"Polished nails are a bit overrated, don't you think?" He smiled, but kept her hand in his. She noted a particular look in his eyes, one that she had secretly—and against her better judgment—yearned for. He let go of her hand and reached to remove her sunglasses, laying them on the bench beside him.

"Ah, there," he said, looking into her eyes. "There you are. Out of hiding." He gently pushed back the wind-blown curls from her face, leaned in, and kissed her. And all she could do was thank her lucky stars that she wasn't standing up. Her knees would not have held.

* * *

The group of poetry lovers at Van Gelder's Tea and Books was small to begin with, but growing by the minute. Jilli had again created another Flower Power poster for the window. Eve had put a change-of-date notice in the *Laguna Post-News* and had sent hand-written invitations to a select few. According to Alex, Eve was expecting a fairly good turn-out, so extra chairs were brought in from Sam's gallery.

New faces appeared at the door, causing Madeline some alarm; she was hoping for a small group of friends. She had never read her own poetry at a reading, even if the coffee house poets in Berkeley had given her hope of doing so one day. Now that the day had come, she was a basket case. Even her palms felt sweaty. She checked her macramé purse for the inhaler, just in case.

The chairs at each table were turned toward the counter, so that the audience could avoid the distractions of the windows and enjoy the vase filled with fresh June roses—pink, red, and white—which the Greeter had brought.

She was glad Jilli and Kate had come, especially her mother who had never been inside the shop. Madeline had deposited the two of them at the Henry James table near the door before she seated herself close to the front. Her mother needed to get out of the house—at least Madeline thought she did—and so the three of them had planned to go out for ice cream afterwards.

Since John Prescott had settled into his bachelor pad, still "carrying on" with his secretary, as the story went, there had evidently been a huge uproar at the Baptist church. A scandal of biblical proportions, Madeline imagined. Even Kate confessed the need to get away from the cloying church gossip. But seeing her mother sitting at the Henry James table felt odd to Madeline, like worlds colliding. This little shop had served all these months as her personal island for self-discovery, like a teen's bedroom door bearing the sign, "Private. Keep Out." Despite this tinge of guilt, she was happy that all the lines and borders between the worlds were fast fading. Perhaps it was time.

Jilli and Kate were ensconced in conversation with Eve, whose new hair style, worn down, made her look years younger. Her thick hair, resting lightly on her shoulders, was held in check by a striking yellow scarf band tied at the base of her neck and flowing down one side. Her matching summer silk dress must have cost a pretty penny. But she looked radiant—much more hip, one might say—although Madeline would never use those particular words to describe Eve van Gelder, the very definition of classic elegance.

Alex sat down next to Madeline and looked at her, knowingly. Only hours before they had shared that longed for kiss. They were still in the euphoria of it, and only their eyes could communicate the hope of a widening expanse of possibilities.

And passion. But for now they settled for a conspiratorial glance of significance, laced with promise.

Her world was changing rapidly—a universe expanding and spinning all at once. And now, she sat nervously clutching a sheet of notebook paper filled with words, words that seemed to flow only after all the tears had dried.

Alex suddenly leaned into her and said, "Don't look now, Love, but we've an interesting visitor."

She turned around and looked. *Good Lord! It can't be.*

There he stood in his Neru shirt, chinos, and Birkenstocks: Dr. Timothy Leary, flanked by an entourage of devoted followers. Engaged in conversation with Eve, he emanated an aura of intensity and . . . what else? Self-importance? The two jean-clad hippies—a girl with dark hair that covered her face like Yoko Ono, and a guy whose sideburns stood out like two beards—didn't look around or talk to anyone. They just hung close to Leary, like secret service agents around the President.

She wondered what Eve thought about Leary crashing Poetry Night. Given Eve's gracious European manners, she doubted there would be a problem, even if the ubiquitous feeling among most adults was that Leary should "go back to the East Coast and take his dope with him."

Eve offered Leary a seat near Kate Prescott, the only seat available. His entourage sat on the floor—aptly, at his feet. The Yoko Ono look-alike wore beads that sounded like salt shaking when she moved. The young man with out-of-control side-burns wore tiny round sunglasses and an air of defiance, as if anyone should dare ask to look at his pupil size. These must be some of Leary's mind-expanding minions, she thought with mild amusement. The sight of them sitting next to her mother was . . . mind-blowing, to say the least. (It was, she mused, like a picture in a dictionary next to the word, "incongruous.")

Suddenly Leary's eyes locked onto hers and it was too late to look away. *Damn!* His eyes registered familiarity and he lifted a hand in her direction. She waved back quickly, hoping no one noticed, then turned away—mortified.

She caught a glance at her mother's judgmental expression in the presence of these "beatnik-types"—as she would surely call them—and turned to Alex, holding back a laugh. "My mother has no idea that she's sitting next to the infamous LSD guru."

"Should I tell her, then?" Alex asked with his teasing smile.

Madeline must have looked nervous, for Alex squeezed her hand and offered her a look of confidence before he got up to help his mother with some chairs. More guests entered the shop; her anxiety rose.

She gazed down at her dress and felt a moment of calm, just knowing that, in spite of everything, she looked nice. She was grateful that her mother had given her $30.00 for a new dress and matching sandals. She had found herself once again perusing the racks of dresses at Chelsea's Boutique where she had purchased the dress for the Ambassador (a dress she never wished to wear again). After a seemingly futile search through psychedelic colors for something that would not make her look like a peacock, Madeline had finally unearthed from the sale rack a simple dress of sea blue, fitted in the bodice with a skirt that flowed around her knees like water lapping at the shore. It was not glamorous or Mod or psychedelic, but there was something poetic about it—airy and light and a bit wistful.

Stealing glances around the room, she was thankful for this new dress to boost her confidence because, given the crowd, this night was taking on countercultural proportions. Simone was here with Kevin from Mystic Arts. Kevin looked slightly spaced-out, and, on second glance, so did Simone. Matthew sat with his male friend in the back with yellow pad in hand, as if inspiration might suddenly strike.

She glanced at Jilli, who was beet red with embarrassment (was this a family trait?) as her mother fumbled with her bangs.

She could almost hear her mother say, *Get your hair out of your face, young lady.*

Sam looked at his watch, then stood to open Poetry Night with a smile and a lets-get-started clap of his hands. His choice of a smart black turtleneck bespoke his own developing identity as an artist.

"Welcome poets, artists, friends," Sam said. "We'll begin tonight with some of our Van Gelder's regulars, who have offered to read or recite their favorite poems. A bit later, we will enjoy readings of original poems by local poets." He looked at Madeline, and she began a slow sinking into her seat.

"Before we close, around eight-thirty, we'll open the floor to anyone who would like to read. Afterwards we invite you to stay for a more informal discussion about poetry, with a cup of tea and a batch of fresh brownies from librarian, May-ling Wu." Madeline looked back to see a smiling May-ling as Sam gestured toward her. May-ling's magic brownies were becoming quite the book club companion.

Sam paused and looked at Eve, eyes lighting up. "Also, I want to introduce a very special woman who has made this night possible: Eve van Gelder, proprietor of this fine shop. Eve—" He looked at her and she offered a deprecating wave. The crowd, numbering around 30—feeling more like 130 to Madeline—clapped appreciatively.

Eve wore more than a new dress and a new hair style: she wore luminosity. She wore it like some women wore gold. She wore wisdom and kindness and curiosity, too. And visible to all, she wore a smile that drew you in, both into her establishment and into her warmth—no matter who you were, no matter what you looked like, no matter how much change in your pocket.

Madeline felt a lump rising in her throat when she thought of what Eve had meant to her these last months, but shook it off, for she knew what she had to do tonight. She must keep her emotions in check, at least until she got through her reading.

The sounds of poetry began to fill the air. Sam read a recently published poem by Robert Lowell. Eve read a poem by Emily Dickinson, and then one by Rilke. Two artists from Sam's gallery also stood to offer poems, one by Gary Snyder and the other by Ginsberg.

Where was Henry Graham? she wondered. He was supposed to be here. *He promised to be here.* Madeline sighed and listened as Eiler Larsen, a pink rosebud in his buttonhole, recited a love poem Robinson Jeffers wrote for his wife, ending with the words:

> *While the stars go over the sleepless ocean,*
> *And sometime after midnight I'll pluck you a wreath*
> *Of chosen ones; we'll talk about love and death,*
> *Rock-solid themes, old and deep as the sea,*
> *Admit nothing more timely, nothing less real*
> *While the stars go over the timeless ocean,*
> *And when they vanish we'll have spent the night well.*

Madeline dared not look at Alex, or he might see her blush, for the great California poet had stirred something crazily romantic within her. But that didn't explain the lump in her throat. No. The lump forming in her throat went deeper and wider than any romantic imaginings. It was as if she was in love the whole world.

She looked at the tall, frail figure before her. She was proud that Eiler Larsen was a part of her life. To Madeline, he was the incarnation of poetry itself: a kind of walking poem.

Finally, it was time for those with original poems. Madeline wondered who, besides herself, would be reading. The only writer she knew was Matthew, and he was far too shy for anything like this. Who, then?

Sam then called upon Dr. Timothy Leary.

Madeline shot a look at Alex. "And I'm supposed to follow *him*?" she whispered.

Leary, whose poem was entitled "Fragile," began speaking

so softly that Madeline could hardly hear, but his voice rose with his words in a staccato rhythm reminiscent of the Beat poets. (All that was missing were the bongo drums.) His voice rose in a gradual crescendo, working its way towards a climax—still keeping a clipped rhythm that was, in fact, rather jarring. By the time he finally arrived at the climax of the poem—a poem that made no sense beyond something fragile being broken—his voice became so loud and discordant that Madeline stole a sidelong glance at Eve. Eve, wide-eyed, looked mildly alarmed. The words seem to tumble out in strange couplings of nonsense. Mercifully, it ended with soft, even tones. He then offered an Eastern bow, hands pressed together in a prayerful pose.

Was this poetry? she wondered in despair. If so, she might as well turn around and leave right now. She had no idea what he had just said. Or why. It was Salvador Dali in words, for God's sake. She couldn't compete with that.

There was polite applause, most loudly from his entourage. He bowed again, as if called back to the curtain. Then, in the style of a politician, he began to make his way to the door, shaking a few hands along the way. Madeline looked back at her mother and sister. Jilli shook her head at Madeline and smiled, gesturing toward their mother. Kate Prescott's mouth was hanging open, her face blank, as if in a stupor of deep, existential confusion.

"Thank you, Dr. Leary. I understand that you have another engagement this evening." (Did she hear relief in Sam's voice?)

After Leary and his entourage departed, Sam smiled at Madeline and introduced her as "our own Madeline Prescott." She made her way to the spot Leary had occupied a moment earlier. She silently prayed to the Poet God, Henry's God, for an ounce of Leary's confidence—sans the theatrics.

"The first poem," she started, and then cleared her throat, "is entitled, 'For Robert Francis Kennedy: A Last Good-Bye.'" She cleared her throat again. The room fell quiet.

Just as she was to begin, the door jangled. There, coming through the door, was Henry Graham. Gesturing his apologies, he slipped without fanfare into the seat vacated by Leary. Madeline flashed a quick smile at her friend. Henry nodded with a generous grin as if to say: *We Scots must stick together!*

Madeline began:

> *Tufts of golden hair, lost and*
> *matted with blackish red,*
> *drift like feathers of a wounded bird*
> *into the valley of shadowy dread —*
>
> *now caught up in quivering air*
> *by rosined bows on somber strings.*
> *Strands of hope go dark, into a Deep Widening*
> *from Mahler's heartbeat to the entirety of things.*
>
> *Rolling through fields of sorrow and salutes,*
> *the funeral train (that endless cortege of pain)*
> *halts in a humble patch of summer green —*
> *an aside to another's flame.*
>
> *Soft consolations drift and fall like snow*
> *upon hard, inconsolable earth —*
> *in a last good-bye to Aeschelus' son, who*
> *himself, lingered within the comforting girth*
>
> *of old words, alluring voices of Eternity:*
> *offerings to posterity,*
> *one for John, one for Martin —*
> *words, riding a tragic trajectory . . .*
>
> *If not for Beauty to soak up the pain,*
> *the heart would bleed an endless rain.*

When she finished, she looked up. There was a moment of stillness in the room. Then a few sniffles. Then there was applause, not polite applause, but exuberant clapping. Eve looked as though she were wiping away tears. Alex beamed. Jilli and her mother simply looked proud.

She now had the confidence needed for her second reading. Why had she dared to read two poems? Was she afraid one of them might bomb? No, she thought, as the clapping stopped. She simply had two poems inside her.

"My second poem is offered in loving memory of my brother, Sean Prescott. It's a kind of prayer poem in the tradition of Rilke's *Book of Hours*. It's called, 'Poet of the Deep.'" She avoided looking at her mother or Jilli, for fear of too much emotion, but she shot a quick glance at Henry, a silent communication of his own part in the poem, his inspiration. She felt like a child, standing up in front of the class. She took a deep breath and began to speak.

> *Poet of the deep,*
> *re-framer of lost meanings*
> *and brave young words*
> *shipwrecked in the blustery gale—*
> *we move willingly into the depth of you,*
> *like hungry dolphins diving into the silence.*
>
> *Lest we slide down on slippery words*
> *onto heaps of old wreckage,*
> *let us dive deep into the pain of you,*
> *like treasure hunters swimming about*
> *in the immensity of your tears,*
> *searching for you.*
>
> *We catch glimpses of you working,*
> *moving about with pen in hand—*

a luminous center of graceful gesturing,
luring us with soft, regal gowns billowing out
like a million manta rays sweeping
through warm light.

Re-write our tragedies into the larger
sea of innumerable imaginings.
Feed our follies to creatures without violence,
by the persuasion of your pen: new words
strung together into rare pink pearls
awaiting discovery by divers who love the sea.

She closed her eyes tightly when she finished, and as she opened them the applause began, her first sight being that of Henry Graham. His beaming enthusiasm, as he rose from his seat to applaud, was only the beginning. The Greeter was on his feet soon after Henry. In a second everyone was standing. She blushed—she could feel the heat of it—and could only imagine the blotchy disaster, which was her face.

Jilli was absent from her seat, and Madeline looked for her. From the kitchen area she appeared weaving through the chairs with a bouquet in her arms. With the face of polished innocence, she handed her big sister the crinkly wrapping filled with fresh yellow daisies.

"These are from Mom and me," Jilli said proudly. "I picked them out myself—daises—because I thought Grandma Daisy would like the idea of you being a poet."

Madeline felt a well of emotion overtake her now. She made a move to sit down, to get out of the limelight, but it was for naught. Eiler Larsen lifted his cane with a theatrical, *"Hail to the poet!"* issuing another flush-inducing round of clapping. Madeline looked up to see Alex's eyes, a gaze as insistent and loving as it had been that afternoon. She looked at Eve, Mr. Larsen, May-ling, Simone, Matthew, Henry, and finally her mother, who had tears rolling down her overly-rouged cheeks. There was nothing to do but smile and weep into the daisies. These were her friends, she thought, a hodge-podge of a family: her world of belonging.

Chapter Thirty

Madeline stood on the cottage porch, mug of tea in hand, surveying a fresh flock of shore birds with marbled wings and long beaks. She felt the bite of the marine-layered morning and went inside to fetch a sweater. She grabbed a spiral note-book and pen. A minute later she settled into the droopy deck chair, clicked the ballpoint pen, and began to write:

Dear Sean,

The beach is especially quiet this morning. I'm glad to be here alone with the sounds of the gulls, the pungent smell of seaweed, and the massive chocolate rocks; they take every hit of the unpredictable surf with astonishing dignity. All of it—this huge, almost painful beauty—takes me back to the days of our childhood summers.

I'm still thinking of my first poetry reading, too, my mind still replaying the sounds and feelings of the words as I flung them into the air for the first time. It's different from writing them, you know. The sound of them changes their whole shape, gives them roundness and ripeness (interesting, these funny revelations!).

Someone once said that poetry is a window into another world, and for me, this new window is healing, even—dare I say—spiritual. And perhaps it is not just a different world but a larger one, a world as vast as the sea, that can absorb the pain of this one, and offer Something More. It is as if the fledgling poet within me is part of the Great Poet—the Poet of the World — part of some vast beauty that transcends all this madness. But, more of this metaphysical talk later —

After the poetry reading, there were the daisies (yes, Grandma Daisy was, in a sense, present, just as you were). I was surrounded by family, my newly-chosen family, as well as my blood family — sans Dad, of course, who would never be caught dead (sorry) at a poetry reading. But he's all right. Or, he will be.

Mom will be all right, too. And even if they don't get back together, which doesn't look likely, I believe Mom's going to blossom on her own (that is, if we can do something about that tootsie roll of a hairdo).

As for Jilli, she's a bright light of possibility, all Mod clothes and go-go boots. I'll not let her out of my sight for too long, I promise. She desperately needs a big sister.

And now to you, my little brother who grew up to be a soldier. This is what I want to say to you:

You wrote me that you could not "adjust," as you put it, to the inhumanity your eyes were witnessing. That reminds me of when I heard Dr. King speak at Chapman College, back in my junior year of high school. He said something that day about never intending to "adjust" himself to the evils of segregation or to the self-defeating effects of physical violence. And then he said something like, "the salvation of our world lies in the hands of the maladjusted." So, the way I see it, all that "maladjustment" inside you was really your soul hurling itself into that burning hut, then retreating to the stars to brighten the sky for the rest of us. Like Dr. King and Bobby. (How can I think of one of you without the others? How will I ever relive this murderous spring of 1968 without tears and fury and glimpses of amazing courage all at once?)

Dad and I talked about God the other day. We agreed (a miracle!) that Pastor Bob is not our cup of tea. But that doesn't mean I'm giving up on God. All I know is that your *courageous act in that village gives me reason to believe in a vast goodness beyond this aching world, and in a divine Heart that is huge and suffering and healing.*

I have learned in my stumbling through grief that the best way to this mysterious Heart is through the door of empathy: it's the beginning of everything that matters. The beginning of hope, really. It moves the world forward in a kind of evolution of the human spirit—breaking down barriers of fear and ignorance and intolerance. I wonder what would happen if we fought our enemies with the raw power of empathy? And what if this led to (God forbid) bombing people with food and clothes and education and a million Dr. Schweitzers? Infiltrating villages with troops who carry lined, yellow legal pads and take copious notes: "Where did you come from? What is your history? What do you want? What do you believe? May I drink your tea?" Would this topple any great religion or government? Or would such permeability into other worlds make one's own world larger? Bigger? Fatter?

This "fear of fatness" seems to permeate our Twiggy-mad culture (sorry, Jilli!). We are as much afraid to expand our souls as we are our waistlines, as if such soul-fatness would destroy all control we have over the world. And isn't the need for absolute control the hidden disease of our society? Isn't that fear's hideout?

Letting go of fear and letting in the whole beautiful, suffering, tragic world seems risky all right, but it's the only way to fatten our shriveled up souls, the only way to "love many things," as Van Gogh wrote to his brother. But who can do it and survive? Who can take in not only the beauty and the heartbreak, but the sheer awfulness of it all? Without other fat souls, we're lost. A whole society of fat souls could do it, though—not just living, breathing souls, but souls that embrace us from the grave, from history.

I don't have all the answers, and oddly enough, I hope I

never will. How dull and flat and bleak the world would be if the adventure of the spirit suddenly ended in easy certainties. It would be the end of metaphors! The death of mystery! The dissolution of poetry! Maybe I'm too much in love with Socrates, but I'm glad for the complexities, the questions, the interminable angles to things—the murky deepness of it all. Otherwise, we would have nothing to talk about over tea— nothing that matters, anyway.

Perhaps building a worldview for oneself is like the building of Grandpa's cottage. The great ideas—the "Aha! This is it!" insights—are themselves like pieces of wood that have washed up on shore after being batted about against the rocks and smoothed down by a tumultuous journey. One begins by building a frame for a simple hut. And, as new wood washes up from a thousand other shores and ship wrecks, the hut grows into a cottage. And when it's finished, even then, it can always be revamped, added on to (like the silly add-on bathroom in Grandpa's cottage!). It's as if you, dear brother, send me these pieces to work with from some eternal place where broken things are mended and given back to the world, out of some deep need for another chance at creation.

At least I have a little hut inside my soul now, not exactly a full-blown cottage, but solid enough to make a good start—a "fixer-upper" of sorts—a place to dwell peacefully, to dream, to scheme, and to pen my fledgling poems.

And that is enough for now. My eyes are on the horizon, and I see you smiling.

Forever,

Maddy

Madeline looked up from the page filled with words. While she had been writing, the marine layer had lifted and the gray water had morphed into vivid hues of indigo and turquoise. She put down the notebook and pen and found herself at the water's edge, bare feet wedged into the wet sand. She braced for the next chilly wave. As the surf rolled in—splashing up to her knees with a lavish, invigorating rush—she threw back her head, closed her eyes, and smiled into the sun.

THE END

Author's Note

When a novel is intertwined with historical events, readers are curious to separate fact from fiction. I have tried on every point of history to portray events accurately. Most of the novel's characters are my own creation. However, two real inhabitants of Laguna Beach have been fictionalized, using historical records and interviews to capture their personalities as closely as possible.

The beloved Greeter of Laguna, Eiler Larsen, died in 1975 at the age of 84. The Hotel Laguna provided him free lodging during his last years of illness. Today, on Greeter's Corner in Laguna, stands a towering bronze statue of Mr. Larsen, one of two sculptures in his honor. Delightful character photos of the Greeter line the entry way to The Cottage Restaurant, where Mr. Larsen enjoyed many complimentary meals. More can learned about the Greeter in the documentary, *The Greeters of Laguna* (Bapudi Films, 2003).

Dr. Timothy Leary, owner of Mystic Arts World, was arrested—not for the first time—on December 26, 1968 in Laguna Beach for possession of two roaches of marijuana, which Leary claimed were planted by the arresting officer. He was later convicted of the offense. Mystic Arts World mysteriously burned to the ground in 1970.

The speech by the Rev. Dr. Martin Luther King, Jr., that shaped the life of the character Madeline Prescott is entitled "Racial Justice and Nonviolent Resistance," delivered Dec. 10,

1961 at Chapman College in Orange, California. Audio recording and transcript are available from the Frank Mt. Pleasant Library of Special Collections and Archives at Chapman University's Leatherby Libraries.

The events surrounding the assassination of Robert Kennedy are true to historical records, e.g., the live radio account and the reactions in the hotel ballroom. The little girl with flying pigtails is also real. Many such details found in *The Metaphor Maker* can be seen in the PBS documentary, *RFK: An American Experience* (2004). The Ambassador Hotel, after a long battle for preservation, was demolished in 2005-2006. A public school will stand on the site, a fitting memorial to Robert F. Kennedy.

The cottages of Crystal Cove have been placed on the National Register of Historic Places as "the last intact example of California beach vernacular architecture." The cottages have been renovated and are open to the public for overnight stays. For more information on Crystal Cove, see *Crystal Cove Cottages: Islands in Time on the California Coast* by Karen E. Steen, Laura Davick, and Meriam Braselle.

Many thanks to Paul and Paula Apodaca for their vivid personal accounts of Laguna Beach and Orange County in 1968. In their colorful recollections of Eiler Larsen, César Chávez, Bobby Kennedy, The John Birch Society, Timothy Leary, and Mystic Arts World, I found a treasure trove of material.

Thanks, too, to Jim, a Vietnam Vet who not only lived in the communes of Laguna Canyon, but also dared to open his heart about the war. For an in-depth visual history of the Vietnam War, including events similar to those fictionalized in this book, see *Vietnam War with Walter Cronkite* (CBS News, 2003).

The
Metaphor Maker

*Reading Group Guide
and
Journaling Guide*

Available at
www.PatriciaAdamsFarmer.com

About the Author

Patricia Adams Farmer is the author of *Embracing a Beautiful God* and a contributing editor for *Creative Transformation* magazine. She lives in Southern California with her author/professor husband, Ronald L. Farmer. A former minister, she now divides her time between teaching, writing, and waiting hand-and-foot on four cats. *The Metaphor Maker* is her first novel.

www.Patricia AdamsFarmer.com

Praise for *Embracing a Beautiful God*

"Patricia Farmer offers us her luminescent meditations like a beautiful string of pearls. When we've absorbed them, we see the world differently."

> —Rabbi Harold Kushner, author of
> *When Bad Things Happen to Good People*

"Once upon a time there was a woman who could tell stories. When people read her stories, they heard a wisdom they had been seeking for a long time. They found themselves wanting to be kinder to others and gentler to themselves. They found themselves noticing the beautiful things in life: the music, the animals, the friends. Even, in some ways, the pain. They remembered what they already knew—that through sensitivity to beauty, God is. That woman is Patricia Adams Farmer. *Embracing a Beautiful God* tells the stories. It has the earmarks of a spiritual classic."

> —Jay McDaniel, Hendrix College, author of
> *Living from the Center*

"This is one of those rare books that *is* what it is *about*: Beauty. In poetic images, Patricia Farmer invites us into her own reveries about God and the world. Her theme is a theology of beauty, of finding inspiration—and consternation!—in the small, ordinary things of daily life. So take a 'Beauty break,' as Patricia Farmer puts it, and wander into these words that wait for you. You will go beneath the surface of things, and come up with new wisdom in your own daily participation in beauty."

> —Marjorie Hewitt Suchocki, Professor Emeritus
> Claremont School of Theology, author of
> *God, Christ, Church: A Practical Guide to
> Process Theology*

Made in the USA